I0638795

SEASONS OF THUNDER

DonnaInk Publications, L.L.C.

U.S.A.

SEASONS OF THUNDER

A Thee-Part Novel – Volume I

by

TEEDZANI THAPELO

DonnaInk Publications, L.L.C.
17611 Aquasco Road, Annapolis, MD 20613

Editorial Team: DonnaInk Publications, L.L.C.
Mr. Philip Bartholomew, Mr. Quante Bryan, Ms. Shelby Catalano
Cover:, Layout and Design, ZenCon Art of Zen Consultancy, Ms. Dana Queen.
First Paperback Edition: December 2014. First Electronic Edition: January 2015.

Library of Congress Cataloging in Publication Data:
Teedzani Thapelo, 2014 -
   Seasons of Thunder: A Three Part Novel – Volume I / Thapelo, Teedzani. - 1st ed.
     ISBN: 978-1-939425-63-8 (print aka)
     250 p.cm.

Summary: "Batjibilibili, a well-known writer and newspaper columnist in Gaborone, loves her husband, Ntungamili, a recluse poet consumed with contemplative inertia and angst. She spends most of her time with Satjilombe, a Member of Parliament and senior minister in the Office of the President. She does not love the politician. He is a complete clod, a goat-herd god that loves pretty women just for fun. She feels dirty and disgusted after making love to him. The story of her life is unraveled against the bedrock of four successive political rulers." ~ Summary provided by the author.

[1. Literature - Fiction, 2. Drama - Fiction, 3. Adult Relationships - Fiction, 4. Family History - Fiction, 5. Women's - Fiction, 6. Social Issues – Fiction, 7. Africa – Fiction, 8. Botswana – Fiction, 9. Zimbabwe – Fictions, 10. United States – Fiction.]
I. Title. II. Title: Seasons of Thunder: A Three Part Novel – Volume I
Dewey Classification: 813
10 9 8 7 6 5 4 3 2 1

2013957252

Table of Contents

Other Titles
by Teedzani Thapelo

Love and the Degenerate Politician

Seasons of Thunder, Volume II

Seasons of Thunder, Volume III

Tales of Woe and Wonder in Kalahari Country

Dedication

The novel is dedicated my sons; Alexander, Davis and Rabasi with great love.

Prologue

Christmas Day

1970

I̵t was a quiet morning in Somerset. Francistown was still sleeping. It was so silent that one could be forgiven for thinking even the day of God's only son, Jesus Christ of Nazareth, was something yet to come or simply unknown. Batjibilibili lay in bed, listening to nothing but her throbbing heart and frightfully intrigued by the noiseless-ness. The house stunk of Christmas. What was happening outside, she asked herself silently. In her mind's eye she could picture the world outside. Christmas was always a great day. She just loved it. It irked her she had not been allowed to spend the night with her mother. Why should Mama sleep with Dad, and not me, she wondered idly. He smells funny. Aunt Chandiwana smells alright. Mama smells divine. She knew her aunt had left the bed early to make breakfast. But, she did not feel hungry right now. She wanted to see her mother, to be with her mother, to enjoy her mother's deliciously celestial smell. She threw the blankets away, yawned languidly, stretched herself like a lioness enjoying the morning sun, rubbed her eyes and sighed. Slowly she got out of bed, opened the bedroom with a most discreet unobtrusiveness and soundlessly tiptoed to her parents' bedroom directly opposite. Giggling quietly, she reached the door and knocked softly, timidly. There was no answer. Soon something reached her straining ears, fleeting sounds that only started making sense when she put her ears to the keyhole. Her parents were talking, not in a very friendly way.

"John, you aren't listening to me. I say I'm through with changing nappies, bathing kids and putting them to bed?"

"But you don't have to do that all the time. We can always help you. We've always helped you."

"I'm tired of the whole business. I've given you three children."

"Two."

"Three children, John. A dead child is as good as a living one, John. Every mother knows that."

"Okay, three then."

"So what more do you want from me? I'm your wife damn it, not a factory for manufacturing children."

"All I'm saying . . ."

"All you're saying is that I should not have a life of my own. Adam is old enough to look after himself. Batjibilibili will soon go to school. Now you want another child just so you can tether me to the house. I'm not having any of that nonsense. Marry another wife if you want to have more children. Your culture allows that sort of thing. But mind she brings her own money into the marriage. I slaved all my life for everything we have in this house. No harridan is coming here to make my life miserable. She can stay with your mother in the village at home."

"That's not what I want, and you know it, Chandapiwa."

"Well, I'm not having sex with you then, ever."

"But that's not what I'm talking about!"

"What are you talking about, John."

"All I'm saying is that we really are no longer a family."

"I explained to you why I moved to Gaborone. I wanted to . . . I need to live close to my own people in Mogoditshane. I'm sick and tired of being an orphan of the world."

"But, you're a married woman, Chandapiwa."

"Don't married women have lives to live?"

"There're certain choices that . . ."

"It's funny you say that. You're beginning to sound like Marie van Nierkirk. I'm way past that way of looking at life."

"Why did you marry me then?"

"Because I love you, that's why. I don't see any reason why we should live here. You can't even get a decent job in Francistown. Gaborone is so much a better place."

"It's not a nice place to bring up children."

"You mean living with my people is not a nice thing; is that it?"

"I didn't say that; I never said anything of the sort. Only the way you live . . ."

"How do I live, John? What do you know about my life?"

"Well, I've heard things."

"What things? What have you seen?"

"I really don't think a woman who behaves like you should talk to her husband this way."

"What way, John? I'm just answering your questions."

"No, you're being rude and arrogant."

"Good God, why are we having this conversation, really?"

"You have never been the same since she died. It's as if she was your only child. A married woman, a mother has no right to behave this way."

"I'm not just a married mother and a woman, John. I'm a human being. There are things you'll never know or understand about me. Just live and let live. That's the way I see it. I tried to explain things to you, but you never listen."

"I can't waste my time listening to excuses. I know the difference between an explanation and an excuse."

"Are there rats in this house?"

"Are you calling me a rat?"

"No, John, of course not. But there's a slight scratching at the door that's been reaching my ears for some time."

"Oh, my God! Batjibilibili. Look now what you've done, Chanda-piwa! I've never seen such a stubborn woman in my life. And your daughter takes after you in every way imaginable. What kind of a family is this?"

"We're quite a normal family actually."

"Help me, God!"

That was a Christmas to remember.

Batjibilibili was four years old.

SEASONS OF THUNDER

Chapter 1

Fatal Attraction

1943

Segomotso listened to the commotion in the kitchen. Of course her mother would be up, to make breakfast. She had spied her father talking to the handsome Afrikaner troublemaker, van Nierkirk, down the street just a minute ago. It thrilled her to bits to see such a visitor in their neighbourhood in a beautiful morning like this. The birds were still singing their silly morning songs, welcoming the new day and celebrating the little fortunes of the past ones. It was really as things should be. Every earthly creature should have its own gods to propitiate, and thanksgivings of all sorts were probably an all-round ritual in the entire animal kingdom. Every morning signalled the arrival of new things and new experiences for all God's creation. Today was indeed a good morning. Even the small thrush nesting above her bedroom window had hatched its eggs over the night, a good signal of happy things to come.

She hoped Mr. van Nierkirk would take his meal here with them and share in the little magical spells and rituals that marked the beginning of every day in her home. She would sit next to him, perhaps. She'd not be able to digest a mouthful. What would Mary think? I hope the Reverend does not go on and on about God before we eat, she said to herself. Grace is such a silly thing. It's the sort of thing that is bound to put the spark off the romantic encounter she had in mind. And Mr. van Nierkirk, did he suspect anything? If he did, what did he feel? So this was folly undoubtedly, to trail, spy on, tail, and dog such a dangerous man and desirously determine to gain fulfilment whatever the cost, it was no doubt the stupidest, the most senseless and imprudent folly—but to return to bed now would amuse her little niece, Sarah, for months, to renege at this moment, to go back, to back out, to change her mind, would be madness. Anyway, silliness of that sort never accomplished anything. She held her breath and tiptoed down the stairs and across the passage. The shop door was open, and a moment later she stood on the street, cold and shivering from head to her bare little feet. The two men had vanished, and it was too early for anyone to be about legitimate business. In the windswept chilly dawn, Tati Town huddled at the edge of wine-dark Tati river, half a dozen dusty streets containing less than a thousand shabby and dirty wooden houses, a few iron-corrugated ramshackle buildings, dominated by the Tati Company Director's mansion perched delicately on the rugged and craggy shoulders of Nyangabgwe Hill, and beyond, to the west, stretched the forest, green and brown, silent and empty, carpeting low mountains and damp steaming valleys, the refuge of things and terrors strange and unknowable, a land traversed by bridle paths which led sometimes to a farm of decaying mill and dwindling acreage, and many times to nowhere but a huge emptiness rolling on and on to infinite and immeasurable dimensions and horizons, a stupendously vast and inestimably unbounded world. The town had declined with the settlers; enough houses, even in these few streets, stood empty to tell of whole families who could stand no more rising prices and dwindling prospects. The recruitment of young men for the war effort and the imposition of heavy taxes were destroying whole families and communities.

And now there was talk, mostly among indigent Afrikaner families, of moving on to the Kalahari wilderness where the colonial government was carving out farms to farmers with such reckless prodigality that even the most dreadfully impecunious trekkers were said to own large tracts of land suitable for raising cattle and getting rich. Her father, the Reverend Shangoyapalala, and Mr. van Nierkirk had said so much during their long conversation with the visiting Resident Commissioner yesterday afternoon in the shop. There was also talk of the possibility Mr. Black-beard, a friend of the family recently relocated to Gantsi, might come across her wandering people, the Lefatshe band of Basarwa, among whom it was thought may be found her mother, Segofatso. In Segopotso's lifetime, only few settlers had sought either refuge or commercial opportunity in these treacherous parts. Empty stores and deserted houses were commonplace to Segopotso. Born Segopotso Lefatshe months after the world was hit by the depression and growing up behind the counter in the big room down stairs—which boasted the exaggerated title of John Blackbeard's Trading Company—she accepted the Boer farmers as unfortunate men who found money hard to come by and ruin almost as inevitable as death itself. Blackbeard's father had raised cattle in these parts, before the previous war which had forced him, and many others, to choose between king and common sense. He had chosen king and common sense. He had chosen king, and been forced to flee to Southern Rhodesia, there to rebuild his life, if not his fortune. He had avoided bankruptcy at least by accepting the inevitable and descending a class in the political order of things. And with his departure, had gone, too, his small Wesleyan church. There just was no one to minister to his parishioners.

Many of them joined the London Missionary Society congregation run by the charismatic Reverend Paul Shangoyapalala, but her own family, independent, self-sufficient Basarwa who greatly worried about enslavement by desperate Tati officials, cattle speculators and private white ranchers in the expansive Tati region, retreated into the silent Kalahari Desert, thousands of miles away to preserve their freedom, leaving her behind because she was a sickly child, and Mary Shango-yapalala, then a childless youthful bride who admired their courage and free will, clung to the infant, adopting it as her own child. Paul Shango-yapalala was happy to stay behind and run the abandoned Blackbeard business as best he could. In any case he got it for a song. Where there is war, there is money, and the priest was a fervent believer in the marriage between commerce and Christianity. He was determined to do the best he could to set himself up.

Growing up, Segopotso did not resent this arrangement; she had never known her own people. In many ways, she thought herself a child of this loving Christian black family, and Mary certainly did nothing to disabuse her of this idea. She was also very useful in the shop and got on very well with all sorts of customers. She was also a very sensible girl, in her own way. Mary had wanted her to further her studies in South Africa where the other children, Chandiwana and John, went after all the children had done primary education at Dombodema in Southern Rhodesia, but the Reverend's stipend was too small to cover all the costs. And she could dream. The two tapestries that hung in her mother's bedroom, the carved chair in which her father sat to smoke his after-dinner pipe—there were houses with things like that. The man she now followed, Erasmus van Nierkirk, rake, voluptuary, drunkard, libertine, but wearing soft new boots and careless at once of law and opinion—he would live in such a house. His very presence excited her, and she saw him often, for he was her father's best customer. The van Nierkirks had lived in these parts before there had been a community or commercial company. They had been the true Boer Trekkers, true pioneers into the interior, way back in the early nineteenth century; one of their ancestors had fought the British at Majuba and then trekked into the Kalahari where he married a Mosarwa woman and became a famous game hunter. Even after the defeat of the Boers in the ugly AngloBoer war, these people had continued to defy both law and custom, refused to surrender to British jurisdiction, and had all but

3

destroyed themselves and their farms in their defiance. Now, of all the family, only van Nierkirk and his aged mother remained, but to Segopotso they represented everything that was desirable in life, however the means of achievement. As a good Wesleyan, she recoiled from their Calvinist teachings, but they too now really had no church of their own. It was even hard to think of van Nierkirk living by any religious precept. Maybe Mrs. van Nierkirk, but . . . that too was inconceivable. Five minutes of brisk walking brought her to where the street dwindled into the wagon track, bordered on her right by the trees of the forest, and on her left by the thick bushes skirting the Tati river bank.

Here she paused, listening while the chill breeze wrapped her skirt about her ankles. Discovering would mean a whipping and tremendous embarrassment, and she was known to every white person and most of the Africans in Tati Town, but there was no sound. It was nearly light. The eastern sky was already a glorious flaming pink, dissolving in streaks of brilliant yellow that stretched upwards and outwards from the horizon. There was no cloud, for the rain season was over. The day that was coming would be warm and still, relaxing and utterly tedious, except for the combatants who were about to fight and the girl who watched them. Cautiously she parted the thick bushes, kneeling, forcing her way through the tall grass and checking with an exclamation of alarm as she accident-tally and unexpectedly stumbled into the open. The group of men was not thirty yards away, hardly troubling to conceal their activities—they looked at her with utter amazement and incredulity. Mr. van Nierkirk faced her, and he was startlingly conspicuous in the bright dawn of light. His face was composed, almost relaxed. It always surprised her; van Nierkirk, for all his size and reputation, had small, delicate features, and curly yellow hair, and the eyes that stared at her were a clear light blue. To his right stood her father; his face taut with anger, his contempt and disbelief evident. Segopotso clasped both hands to her mouth. She took a step backward, gaping, stumbled and fell. The breeze seemed to die, and she was enveloped in a fierce heat.

"My God! The thought of it, the very thought of it. Just how did such a stupid idea find its way into her head? To imagine . . ." exclaimed Paul Shangoyapalala, lost for words.

He stopped at the door and turned towards the bed.

"So you think yourself a lady, Segopotso. I'll tell you what you are now considered. A serving wench without the sense to . . ."

"Now, Paul, please . . ."

Mary sat at the table by the window; she was a big woman, considerably larger than her husband and correspondingly more placid.

"Goddamn Mr. van Nierkirk! His coming here has brought this disgrace on us. Now I'm condemned as a supporter of his cattle rustling

4

escapades, and I am regarded as having a daughter with whom he has made easy."

"Such talk is not suitable to the ears of the young girl."

"Now look here woman . . ." Paul advanced to the bedside.

"Either this . . . this shameless hussy is a woman, as you claim her to be, in which case she had best understand what I am saying and what others are saying or she is a girl in which case I intend to lay this belt across her back."

"She is a woman, Paul. Four months will see her fourteen. And, we at least know of her innocence . . ."

"Innocence!" shouted Paul, "Only last year there was that business with young Gaseitsiwe . . . her people mature early as far as these things are concerned . . ."

"Paul!" screamed Mary, scandalized and beyond herself with indignation.

"She swore to me . . . and she is our daughter!"

"And what does she know of oaths?"

"At least we can be sure of her innocence here," Mrs. Shangoyapalala declared.

"Why, surely she has never spoken to Mr. van Nierkirk except across the counter."

"What proof is there of that? I have seen him looking at her, and there can be no question that whatever he says the real thing revolves around his disgusting amours. He's a disgusting, lecherous son of a devil. You should have seen those men, my customers thinking of their own wives and daughters, and *her* crawling through the grass on her hands and knees . . . her lover at work."

"Paul!" Mrs Blackbeard was shocked.

"Now you are being absurd. We'll go downstairs to discuss this, if you please. Segopotso has behaved badly, but she has sworn her innocence, and I prefer to believe her no worse than a young girl in search of sensation. As such she will be punished, end of the matter. You are listening, girl? You'll stay in your bed for the rest of the day. And you'll fast."

The very moment they left, the door opened again immediately.

"You're the lucky one," Sarah said jealously.

"Had it been me . . ."

"You lack the stomach."

Segopotso rubbed her cheeks, but the tears had been more from fear than remorse. She threw back the covers.

"Mama said . . ."

"Why don't you run downstairs and tell her I'm up?"

5

"I warned you they'd be angry. Now look what you've done. We'll have people staring at us . . ."

Segopotso went to the window and looked down at the street. It was midmorning now and there were people about, mostly Africans, shopping and talking excitedly in small groups. Many, almost all of them, were independent farmers, here to buy domestic groceries before heading to their cattle posts in the far away cattle posts. It was warm, and there was little wind. The dust settled on feet and clothes and faces and a bubble of conversations hung on the air. They would be discussing the duelling: an illegal act conducted by white men wild enough to break their own laws for trifles, and her. She drew the curtain to shut out the glare and sighed.

"Where is Mr. van Nierkirk?"

"In Mama's bed. It's a wonder he's not dead. You should have seen the blood! Papa has sent for Mrs. van Nierkirk, but I doubt she will come in time."

"Oh shut up! And get out."

Sarah sniggered.

"No noise, Mama said. You'll disturb him," said Sarah insolently.

"Oh, you little . . ."

Segopotso snatched a hair brush from the dressing table, and Sarah squealed and hurried from the room. Segopotso sat on the bed and chewed her lip. Of all the stupid things . . . but she had never seen blood in quantities like that, and pouring from . . . she massaged her ribs. Not the heart perhaps, but surely Sarah was right, and nobody could survive a wound like that. And what an incredibly silly way to die! Oh, men . . . impatiently she stalked up and down the room, throwing her long legs in front of her for the sheer sensational pleasure of movement. But her body, excited though it was, needed comfort less than her mind. Never had she been so ashamed and so angry, and she had truly never exchanged more than a hasty smile and untidy curtsey with van Nierkirk. Why were people so anxious to create substance out of nothing? So she had been curious and then soft-stomached at an unfortunate moment—only the substance was there. She had been curious and she had been overbold, entirely for the satisfaction of watching her hero at his best, destroying another man. But, she had anticipated nothing as unfortunate as that. Yet Mama and Papa and everyone else must immediately suppose she had a relationship with van Nierkirk. What a curious, strange and muddled world. Implying that he had returned her smile? He had touched her hand, discreetly? He had kissed her hand, or more, her cheek? Her lips? She stared at herself in the mirror and found herself flushed and overheated. For, van Nierkirk in his relationships would have done nothing of these things. The spectacle of van Nierkirk making a leg and kissing a lady's hand was beyond her. A relationship with him would imply being alone with him .

.. in the most breath-taking sense, not like that startling three minutes in the warehouse with Gaseitsiwe last year, three minutes of terrible urgency and frustration which had ended in a whipping. But to be alone with van Nierkirk would mean being beyond the reach of interruptions and anxious parents for hours, perhaps for a night. She hurried to the dressing table and began to brush her hair furiously. Imagination could take her no further. The word 'night' pulled a curtain across her mind and left her breathless. Distracted, she dropped the brush. However, would she face her own parents, now she knew what they thought? And yet she wanted to face them, knowing what they were thinking. In a strange way this morning's misadventure had ended her childhood, utterly and forever. The possibility that she could have experienced some such adventure made her the equal of Mama in knowledge—perhaps even the superior. Unseemly thoughts, dangerous thoughts, flip-flopped unchecked in her mind for a long time. She left the dressing-table and moved to the door, determined to turn into some sort of action these rebellious thoughts. She was condemned as his plaything, and he had never touched her hand. And now he might be dying. She closed the bedroom door behind her and stood at the head of the stairs holding her breath. Conversation, cooking smells, safety. The other door faced her across the landing . . . but that was indeed madness. She tiptoed to the end of the landing and to the veranda. Segopotso moved slowly, holding the rail as if enjoying the breeze and warmth of the morning until she was abreast of her mother's bedroom. There she paused, fingers curling round the upright. But they had called her a woman, and fear was for girls.

Mrs. Marie van Nierkirk arrived the next evening. Mr. Shanyoyapalala, waiting for her arrival, was acutely embarrassed. It was difficult to associate Mr. van Nierkirk with firm convictions in any direction. As for what Mrs. van Nierkirk would say . . . this was the most urgent question of all. It communicated itself to Mary what would Marie say about the room in which her son slept and the sheets on the bed and the cleanliness of the house and the manners and breeding of the Shangoyapalalas? She had dressed herself and her daughters in their very best clothes. The girls' hair had been brushed and combed and little Sarah's left perfectly straight while her own was center-parted. She made sure Segopotso looked presentable but as plain and simple as possible. The girl was developing terrible ideas about her womanhood, a thing that had to be nipped in the bud. Just what would Mrs. van Nierkirk think? What would she say? They waited in the small sitting room behind the

7

shop and sweated profusely. Segopotso indeed was quite in a state. Mary sympathised with the poor thing, but deep inside she could not help but smile at her discomfiture. This was hopefully a lesson the girl would never repeat. There could be no worse experience for any child than engaging in the sort of behaviour that could summon the grand Afrikaner matron from her splendid farm to the dirty streets she was famously known to hate with such a terrible passion. Mary had only seen Mrs. van Nierkirk once before in her life—the old lady seldom came to Tati Town—but she remembered the utter contempt with which the Afrikaner matriarch had treated everything and everyone the first time she set her eyes on her. And now she was coming to her home. The whole thing was too ghastly to contemplate. Segopotso too sat transported in her own train of thoughts. The past twenty-four hours had seemed like a dream, induced perhaps by lack of food, for she had eaten very little. She had visited him again this morning and sat by his side to dry his brow when he required her, and then he had smoothed her skirt against her thigh and pinched the flesh beneath. She had left immediately and not returned. Men! They thought only to excite and to embarrass. Certainly he had excited and embarrassed her. But then for that to happen she must in the first place have excited him. Segopotso, exciting such a man as van Nierkirk? There again imagination could take her no further. But she could hardly allow herself to be the same towards him again; yet to know he lay across the landing where she could hear him cough and speak—that was certainly a dream. But, now his mother was coming, a woman he obviously held in as much awe as did everyone else. What would she make of the whole situation?

"She's here," Mary hissed, almost breathlessly.

"Segopotso, go to the door. Quickly, girl, and remember to be in your best manners."

Segopotso forced herself forward and opened the street door. She glimpsed the road and the crowd for most of the neighbours, and the town layabouts who infested the streets had followed the carriage along with her father, bareheaded and damp browned, and the woman who stood in the doorway, she said, "Good afternoon, Mrs. van Nierkirk," and her knees gave way and stuck the wooden floor very hard; she stayed there kneeling, the entire body in a tight clutch of paralysis, her mouth open. She had at least achieved a measure of surprise. That should help ease the tension in the house thought blithely. The humiliation had not yet sunk in. Marie stared back. She was a small woman, scarcely more than five feet tall, and her age was apparent in the mass of wrinkles which streaked away from her eyes and mouth. But the van Nierkirk features—small, delicate, and quite unnaturally beautiful—remained firm and flawless, and there were still streaks of gold in the white hair which was confined in a tight chignon on the back of her head. Despite the heat, she wore a

8

deep blue velvet coat over her white lawn gown, and her hat was also blue velvet and decorated with ostrich plumes. In every way she was a reincarnation from another generation, but she stood very straight and walked without a stick, and almost girlishly she allowed her handbag to swing from the forefingers of her hand. Her eyes were a choir of colours under heavy dark eyebrows, the eyes of a true wanderer, and cold, for a long second, then they softened, and the tight lips relaxed. The matriarch was in a jovial mood.

"A royal welcome, child. Come, get to your feet."

She inclined her head toward her mother.

"Mrs. Shangoyapalala? You'll take me to my son, please."

"Oh, yes, madam," Mary gasped and hurried out of the room.

Paul stood above his eldest daughter.

"You go to your room, girl," he hissed, "And wait there."

He followed the woman. Segopotso pulled herself to her feet, and Sarah snorted.

"You're a donkey," said Segopotso venomously.

"And you . . ."

Segopotso lunged forward and swung her hand, but Sarah easily evaded the blow.

"I'll tell Papa."

"Ooooo . . ."

Segopotso tramped up the stairs but had the good sense not to slam the door. She pressed her ear against the wall but heard nothing. Of course there was the landing between. If she was really as bold a hussy as she imagined herself, she'd risk the veranda. But that would not do. She was sufficiently unpopular with her father right now. She lay on the bed. Again she was resentful. It seemed she had come out worst in this business, and she was entirely blameless. Why, Mama had not even let her go out since the incident because she had said of the talk of the town. People always talked in Tati Town. It was all they had to do. But that had been bearable while van Nierkirk was here alone, and the whole affair had the quality of romance. Now his mother would take him away back to their farm, and he will forget all of this except perhaps her father's utter consternation and conduct. She did not think he would forget Papa for a while. But she, she would be left here with the gossip and the disgrace. Papa was even angry with her for overbalancing. That was intolerable. Why, it would have been far more sensible had she done something to be guilty of, had she for instance not scuttled from his room like a frightened mouse when he had squeezed her bottom. Then she could have faced them and sneered. Then she . . . the door opened and she set up. It was dark. She had lain here for over an hour, left here, without supper . . .

"Get up, Segopotso."

9

Mary placed the candle on the dressing table.

"Sit here."

Segopotso threw herself out of bed and smoothed her skirt. Marie sat at the table.

"Kneel in front of me, girlie," said the matriarch.

Segopotso glanced at her mother who had remained standing by the dressing table. But there was no explanation there. She hitched up her skirt and knelt on the floor next to the table. Marie cupped a thin hand beneath the girl's chin and tilted and turned the face to catch the flickering candlelight.

"She has fine features," she said softly and smiled.

"Now stand, girlie."

Segopotso scrambled to her feet.

"Stand still," said Marie.

"Yes. A good carriage, and that's important. The rest of you may change, will, indeed, but your carriage will maintain your dignity at all times. They say you are infatuated with my son."

"Madam? I . . ."

"Your mother tells me she has suspected it for some time. He has turned your head. Is that true?"

Segopotso twisted her fingers together.

"Answer Mrs. van Nierkirk, Segopotso."

"I . . . he . . . he is a fine figure of a man."

"Do you imagine yourself in love with him?"

"I know nothing of love."

Segopotso muttered.

"She dissembles well."

Marie seemed pleased.

"Your mother has also assured me of your innocence despite the talk."

"Madam, I . . ."

Marie turned to Mary.

"I find her charming. I must congratulate my son upon his choice. The age alone bothers me. Van Nierkirk is thirty-nine. You did not know that? He could be her father. But perhaps that is to the good. And his body and mind are both young."

Segopotso sat on the bed; she no longer trusted her knees. The low voice seemed to play around her head like a shallow, sun-warmed sea, mesmerizing her. Her mother was in a state.

"Mrs. van Nierkirk? Do I understand you to . . .?"

"I am acting for my son in this matter, Mrs. Shangoyapalala, and asking for your daughter's hand. It would be best in view of what has happened."

"But . . ."

10

Mary bit her lip. Surely this could be no more than Marie's idea of a jest.

"I understand your concern, Mrs. Shangoyapalala. Alas, my son's reputation is scarcely one of which I am proud. For far too long he has considered marriage a weakness rather than strength. But now he is no longer in the first flush of youth, and he understands it is high time he provided himself with an heir. At least you may rest assured that I have your daughter's best interest at heart."

Mary glanced at Segopotso sitting open-mouthed and shell-shocked on the bed.

"I . . . I will have to discuss it with my husband."

"Then do so immediately. I must return to the farm in the morning and van Nierkirk with me."

"She is only fourteen," said Mary with a broken heart.

"Fifteen in March, you say. That will be time enough. April is a good time for a weeding. Think nothing of the expense. It will lie at my door."

"I should like to be alone with my daughter."

The room was dark. A heavy curtain was drawn over the window, which allowed only a faint light from the veranda. The air was already stale and heavy with the jasmine added by Mary adding to the stench. Segopotso closed the door and leaned against it, wrinkling her nostrils and listening. Close to her, van Nierkirk breathed heavily and unevenly. She moved against the bed and looked down at him. He lay on his back, motionless, the small features composed—strange how small his nose was and his mouth. Mama always said a small mouth meant meanness, but surely there was nothing mean about him. Certainly not his face. Arrogant, yes, too confident by far. She'd like to take some of the confidence from it, to see it just a little bit uncertain, unsure; she smiled, and sucked her lower lip in beneath her teeth—her favourite dream. The man on the bed stirred, and she stepped back. Now that would be a disaster and she had known enough disaster for one morning. She tiptoed to the door.

"Girl," he said.

His voice was no more than a whisper, uncannily changed from the confident boom of fire hours earlier. She hesitated, afraid to turn. "Open the door," he said.

"This room could be a tomb. Not for a van Nierkirk for sure but a tomb nonetheless. The devil's handmaiden, by God."

She stood above him.

"You are not dead, Mr. van Nierkirk," she said foolishly. "You are resting on Mama's bed."

"Aye. A good woman, your mother, Segopotso. That's your name, eh? Sarah would be the ugly one."

Segopotso smiled.

"The ugly one."

She must remember to tell Sarah.

"Aye, you're that tall and skinny," he said. "You shoot upwards like a palm tree."

His hand brushed against her skirt, and she jumped backwards.

"And frightened like a kitten."

"I'll leave you to rest," she said angrily.

"Stop there, girl. I'm thirsty."

She filled his cup from the water jug by the bed.

"You'll have to help me," he said.

She sat on the edge of the bed and thrust one arm under his head to raise him. Her fingers trembled, and water spilt on his chin, but he drunk greedily.

"Now that tasted like nectar. What happened to me, Segopotso?"

"You were hit, sir."

"Aye. By that wind giving bastard de Kock. And you're sure I'm not dead?"

"You're badly wounded, Mr. van Nierkirk. The bullet took you in the chest. You must rest."

She placed the cup on the table.

"I came in to see how you were sleeping."

"And instead you woke me. You are a poor nursemaid, Miss Shangoyapalala. Come, child, stop trying to run away. And stop the frowning. You'll wrinkle your face, and until your breasts swell, it's your prettiest feature."

He kissed the bodice of her gown.

"Sir . . ." she jerked away from him.

"Easy, child. I'm in pain. I am wounded close to death, and they have me strapped up like a madman. I cannot move, even to dry the sweat on my brow. Assist me."

"I have no handkerchief."

"And you a lady? Use the sheet."

She lifted his head on the pillow, knelt beside him, and brushed the sheet across his cheeks and forehead.

"Good girl," he whispered and caught her wrist with surprising strength.

"Dying, but not dead."

"You must not excite yourself," she panted.

"Therefore, you must not excite me, Segopotso. Disobedience excites me. Now just kneel there and tell me: how long have I lain here?"

"Since dawn, sir. Five hours."

"Great God above! Shot down and left helpless by that brute de Kock. And I am still alive? What does your father seek from this?"

"Sir?"

"Aye, you're a simple child with never a thought but where your next food will come from." He threw her wrist from him, and she scrambled to her feet.

"Fetch me your father."

"Yes, sir. I will say you shouted."

He turned his head.

"Eh?"

She smoothed her gown.

"I should not be here, sir."

His lips twitched. Smiling was evidently painful.

"Even with me half dead? By God, girl, it must be a dreadful thing to be timid."

She flushed.

"I am not afraid of you, Mr. van Nierkirk. But this business has brought me enough trouble and . . ."

"Trouble? Can you explain what you really mean?"

She chewed her lower lip. But she did wish him to know.

"I saw the whole thing."

"You did what?"

"I . . . I followed you and father and hid in the bush and saw . . . and then I fainted. So you will understand . . ."

Again the beginnings of a smile.

"There is more to you than a pretty face. Now tell me. Why did you do that?"

She stood next to the bed.

"I had never seen a gun fight"

"That is your reason? You must be a bloodthirsty child."

"But . . . my father supposes I had an interest, and he is very angry."

Mr. van Nierkirk's mouth widened and his eyes sparkled.

"Now there is a confession. Very well, Segopotso. I'll not land you in more trouble. I'll wait for someone to visit me. But tell me this: have they sent for my mother?

"Yes, sir."

He closed his eyes.

"Your caring father, I suppose. He would do that. The fool. Oh, be off with you."

"Yes, sir."

13

She moved to the door.

"Forgive my irritation Segopotso," he said softly. "You do not know my mother, and in that you are fortunate. You'll visit me again?"

"I cannot, Mr. van Nierkirk. I dare not. If anyone was to find out . . ."

"At this hour, Segopotso? With your father busy in the shop and your mother in the kitchen? They can discover only if I tell them."

"You would not do that, Mr. van Nierkirk?"

"I would not dream of it, Segopotso. You come back to me tomorrow and let me hold your hand. A sick man needs comforting."

The candle flickered, whipping shadows up and down the wall. The woman in the chair became intense and then dwindled to her proper size. But, what was her proper size? Surely she had fallen asleep in the bed Segopotso thought.

"Have you nothing to say, child?"

"Madam, I . . . I . . ."

Her throat was dry. Words defied speech.

"Now there is to be an end to this stuttering. I am not an ogre. I am a woman. Seventy-one years old, Segopotso. Now sit here beside me. I want to touch your hair."

Segopotso sat on the floor by the table. She was no longer capable of resisting any suggestion from this woman, even of coherent thought. She kept her attention fixed on the faltering flame while the hand of the older woman settled gently on her head like a cap, except that the fingers pressed into her scalp.

"I wish you to know I care nothing for the damage done to your reputation by this affair. We the van Nierkirks make our own reputations. Besides, your innocence is apparent to me. I know my son. I doubt he understands or cares to understand any of the issues involved. He owns nothing. The cattle, sheep and horses in the farm are mine as the farm itself is mine. I doubt you knew that. Do not shake your head. He is a fine figure of a man but full of captious and unstable emotions inherited from his father. You'll be aware that I never enjoyed the benefits of marriage. His father died fighting the Africans many years ago. Now the fool has all but got himself killed. What a silly thing to do. Not that he will die or even suffer long; we the van Nierkirks are not that easily disposed of. My great-grandmother lived to past eighty and then died with a pistol in her hand. You've heard of her? Maria of Bengal. She first came to Cape Town as a slave from India. They called her a harlot. Well, she was. She found it necessary for her survival in those troubled times. They say I have always

14

resembled her. I am proud of that. You understand, girlie? She made us what we are, and we are something now. You must borrow your strength until it becomes your own. Your name is being bandied on the street without regard to propriety as of now. Erasmus tells me you have been sneaking into his room. Is that true? Now that's another silly thing to do. I think you're a sensible girl. But never allow feelings for anyone to overshadow the realm of reason. That way lies certain ruin. This is your father's house. Such things are just not done."

Segopotso had recovered some of her composure. Indeed she was almost angry at the manner in which her future had been so suddenly decided. Besides, she suspected she could now follow the gist of this inquisition.

"I sought nothing from Mr. van Nierkirk."

Marie chuckled. A low brittle sound.

"But you visited him because of your infatuation. Do not deny it. Then, like a true seductress, you ran from the room when he touched your body."

Segopotso turned on her knees, freeing herself from the old woman's grasp.

"Should I have stayed, Mrs van Nierkirk, as he is your son?"

"La-de-da," Marie said carelessly.

"Whatever your instincts, girlie, you can take umbrage like a lady." Segopotso scrambled to her feet, skirts flying.

"I sought to uncover your spirit. I could see it there in your eyes. I recognize you, Segopotso. Your grandfather, Thula Shangoyapalala, was a cattleman, as I am a rancher. You are fallen upon hard times through no fault of your own. But there is no blood connection there. Erasmus may have chosen better than I hoped. Your real grandfather, Lefatshe Kaboyamodimo, was a fine artist, a great hunter, and he loved his women well. I should know . . . but that's all in the past. They treated him like dirt because he was a Mosarwa. You could be a van Nierkirk, girl. You stand like a van Nierkirk. You have the height. That is the only characteristic I lack. You have some spirit and will doubtless develop more. Only the will remains an uncertain factor. Have you sufficient will to be a van Nierkirk?"

"I don't know. Why do you ask?"

"There is no doubt that you think will to be unseemly in a woman. You would be a pale shadow of your husband, content to yield him your body and your mind. That is for common people, Segopotso, and we the van Nierkirks are not common people. I wish a will in you. You will be wedded to my son, but he must prove himself worthy of your bed. Basarwa women are known to be tough, strong-willed and good mothers. I knew your people well enough."

Segopotso rubbed her cheek.

"If . . . if . . . I don't understand these things. I serve behind my father's counter. I have never left this town."

Marie chuckled.

"It is a bad beginning to a marriage to presume yourself the inferior partner. Have you not considered that may be part of van Nierkirk's motive in asking for your hand?"

"Then I hardly feel . . ."

"Tish, girl. Of course he is attracted to you. But he is nearly three times your age. Naturally, he wishes for a wife he can dominate. But, he will value you the more as time goes for a mind of your own. I will help you. You will provide me with grandchildren I can love, and in return the van Nierkirk Farm will be yours. Do not forget the prize. Now you will wait here for half an hour and prepare yourself, and then you will go in and sit with van Nierkirk. I doubt you will see him again before next spring."

"But Papa has yet to consent."

"Do not trouble with trifles. Your mother is overjoyed."

Marie stood up.

"You are my protégée, my sweet Segopotso. You will need me, for your own mother will be twenty miles away from you. You must trust me, and together we must work for the happiness of van Nierkirk and your children."

She paused at the door.

"As of this moment you are a van Nierkirk, Segopotso. You'll remember that if you please. It's an honour."

A gust of wind doused the candle, and the room was dark. The night was quiet. The breeze was brisk. But Segopotso would hardly have heard a gunshot. She sat on the bed and stared into the darkness. She could imagine no more pleasant fate than marriage to van Nierkirk, but the reality of it, the thought that she was to go in to him only a few minutes, as his betrothed, without their having exchanged a word of love or even of regard, was unnatural. But, his mother had explained. No, Mrs. van Nierkirk had explained nothing. That was the worst of it. There was no explanation. The man was thirty-nine. For twenty years and more, he had been happy to live his own life. Now, suddenly, he had decided to marry and had chosen a wife, without a thought that she could object. But somehow objection from anyone seemed impossible. People like the van Nirkirks ruled the world. Their word was sufficient explanation, their wish the ambition of everyone. If your word is the law, explanations do not matter.

Marie wore a flowered house robe and a white mobcap. She looked domestic, almost soft, and pleased to see her daughter-in-law.

"Now, welcome to the van Nierkirk Farm!" she cried.

"For shame, van Nierkirk. You will not permit your bride to walk across her own threshold."

Segopotso turned, her mouth open, a frightened look mounting into her cheeks. Erasmus smiled at her and stooped to gather her legs and sweep her from her feet. He carried her easily and mounted the stairs without an effort. Then, he released her and she stepped away from him to smooth her gown. Marie grasped her hand and kissed her cheeks.

"You are the first bride ever to enter this house. Did you know that? My brother Pik never married. God rest his soul. But you will not be the last. I am sure of that, eh, van Nierkirk!"

"I doubt it, mother."

His face was expressionless, his eyes relaxed. Segopotso glanced from one to the other. Still Marie beamed. There was no tension here, or at least it was well concealed.

"Mrs. van Nierkirk . . ." she said.

"I know, my dear. You want a bath, and then a rest. But come. You must see your house and meet your servants first. Erasmus?"

"I'm sure you ladies have a lot to say to each other. I'll see you later."

He bowed to Segopotso.

"I will say this for my son," Marie remarked, "He works, when it is something that holds his interest, such as cattle. Now come. Here, you are mistress. You must behave as one. The blacks expect it."

From the veranda, the black servants looked down the rolling grass plains and the green valley beyond. The servants were loading her luggage, piling boxes and bales upon the ground, but each man, at every second paused in his labour and stared up at the house. Van Nierkirk had married at last, to a Mosarwa woman. And, they were to be her servants. What was the world coming to? Segopotso felt like a bird in a cage, and the feeling was not lessened by the wide verandas and enormous curtained windows. Marie led her through a glass door into the drawing room. Here were rugs upon the floor, upholstered chairs and a settee, mahogany tables covered with china figurines, a polished brass spittoon—expense she thought without luxury. She was disappointed and disconcerted. There

17

were no pictures, only mirrors, one to each wall so that, wherever she turned, she looked at herself and Marie.

"Beauty should behold beauty," said the old woman enigmatically. "These mirrors have beheld much beauty."

Marie bit her lip. She discovered she looked positively dishevelled. Marie walked across the room and laid her hand on the piano.

"Are you accomplished? Erasmus plays quite well. Perhaps he could teach you."

An arched doorway on the right led to the dining room. The table was heavy mahogany with six ornately carved chairs and an enormous sideboard laden with silver, and it was surmounted by two crystal decanters. "To the pantry."

Marie clapped her hands, and two servants came up the steps.

"These are your servants. Rose is cook, and Sarah is our housemaid." Segopotso was embarrassed. They never had servants at home. She also found Mrs. van Nierkirk's attitude to the two girls condescending. But, she reminded herself the van Nierkirks were pioneer Boer farmers. Their attitudes to black people and black labour were different. This was one of the reasons they had abandoned Cape Town: to do as they wished without regard to English rule and sentiment. She was pleasantly struck by the coincidence that a *Sarah* was the housemaid here. Segopotso couldn't wait till her niece got wind of this little morsel.

"It is a pleasure to kiss your hand, mistress," Sarah beamed, and did so. The housemaid was extremely stout and possessed a flashing smile. She wore a white apron and bodice over her blue and white calico gown, and her hair was concealed beneath a crisp, white cap. Segopotso followed her mother-in-law back into the drawing room.

"They look like very nice people."

"Yes, but they are not to be trusted. They are no more than animals. They work, eat, sleep and fornicate . . ."

"Now, Mrs. van Nierkirk . . ."

"In a moment, child."

Marie led her across the room and through another pair of doors.

"This is the library and van Nierkirk's office."

The walls were lined with books, and there were three easy chairs. The desk stood under the further window. The room suggested comfort, and the leather-bound books absorbed the glare. Segopotso could feel her eyes widening in relief.

"You do read?" Marie asked.

"Yes ma'am. I love books. But I have lacked the material."

"Then this room will interest you. Ah, the world of books. In truth, there is not much to do on the farm. Erasmus reads a great deal. He has his bedroom opposite."

She opened a single door set between two of the bookcases leading this time to the rear of the house, and Segopotso followed her into a lofty passage that ran the entire width of the building, neatly separating the three front rooms from the bedrooms at the back. The first bedroom was sparsely furnished, containing only a gigantic tented, a bureau, and a washstand. But, there was no doubt about the owner of the room. A pair of boots stood against the wardrobe.

"You'll see it opens into the next," Marie said.

"This is yours."

Here was a smaller bed and a dressing table and a wardrobe and a china washbasin with flowered design and a matching ewer and slop bucket. The furniture was all in the heavy mahogany that was the hallmark of this house, and inevitably a huge door led to the back veranda.

"You look down at the ranch and the mill. This is the house. There are two more rooms, a guest bedroom and my own bedroom. We will have a long talk sometime. This afternoon, perhaps. I will send your maid to you. I chose her myself. She is just a child, really. But you will be able to train her as you wish. Her name is Bikani. I gave her a Christian name, but she won't answer to it. Some Bakalanga girls are very difficult people to work with. I mean, what's wrong with a Christian name? What's in a name after all? But, every time I call her Grace, she corrects me. Still, I like that. It shows character."

The door closed. Segopotso threw herself on the bed. Never had she known such a soft mattress. It seemed to rise about and smother her. With a gasp, she rolled on her back and lay there, gazing at the tent of the bed and the white painted ceiling and feeling the tears start. This was the day of her life. She was lovely, young, and fresh and so innocently happy. She had married a man with whom she was in love. Her earlier doubts had disappeared. At first she had wondered how van Nierkirk could ever accept her as a wife, even desire her as a woman. But when she remembered his banter that very first morning along with his pinchings, things took a different shape altogether. And, of course when she had sat beside him as his betrothed, he had smiled at her, showing his enthusiasm. But this was to be expected in view of the difference in their ages and in their experience. Now she was Mrs. Segopotso van Nierkirk. She twisted the thin gold band beneath her glove. This morning had been the last moment of fear and indecision. In church, he had been gloomy, but Mary had assured her all men were so. She closed her eyes to enjoy the warm April breeze, pregnant with the promise of summer rain, a delicious breeze promising much to a bride of fifteen.

"Madam!" a young black girl stood in the doorway.

"I got your bath here. And the men are waiting with the trunk."

"Tell the men to bring it in."

"Yes madam. And I will bring in the bath too."

"Yes, thank you."

She pulled a pillow across her face and lay still while the men manhandled the trunk through the door. She wondered what they thought of their mistress spread-eagled across the bed. Then they were gone. But immediately there were more bumps and grunts as the bath was brought in.

"You want me to help you, madam?" said Bikani.

Bikani was indeed young, almost her own age, with a long neck and pouting somewhat resentful features.

"I would prefer to be alone."

Segopotso threw the pillow aside and set up. Bikani backed to the door.

"Wait a moment."

She could expect to be obeyed now. Bikani waited. Segopotso stood up.

"My husband . . . Mr. van Nierkirk . . . your master . . ." she chewed her lip. But, of course, she could not ask this girl anything.

"I would prefer to be alone," she said again.

Bikani left.

"So there, my pretty little Segopotso. You have achieved your fondest ambition, I'll wager."

"Do you grudge me that, sir?"

She asked softly.

"By no means. All life is a struggle to reach some ambitious peak. It remains but to consummate this business."

Segopotso bit her lip. His voice was eloquent of boredom. But she would fall in with his mood.

"I shall have to be your servant," she murmured and flushed.

"Married women don't do that."

"But I shall be willing."

"You need have no doubt about that."

Suddenly the breeze had dropped, and she was conscious of heat and sweat and of a vast loneliness. There had been no affection in his tone. Almost he sounded angry. He had been gone the whole day, the day they got married.

"I . . . I had no wish to offend, sir," she said timidly.

"I have no conversation. You will have to teach me that also."

He glanced at her then rubbed his chin and turned away. It began to rain.

"It's a nasty evening in truth," he muttered.

The air retained the heat of the day despite the raindrops thudding on the roof. She would not look at him. Her husband was out of humour, regretting, perhaps, that he had chosen an ill-bred chit of a girl to make his wife. But she was his wife. If he was both angry with her and bored with her nothing could be done about that.

"Mr. van Nierkirk," she said, "Please believe me. I understand nothing of what is troubling you. Your mother asked for my hand in your name as I understand it. I did not anticipate it."

"You accepted with rapture."

"Would you have had me refuse her?"

She gasped.

He stared at her almost as if he was seeing her for the first time. The effluvium of wine laden breath assaulted her senses.

"No," he said at last.

"Aye, girl, I asked for your hand. It seemed natural, lying in your mother's bed, feeling myself half dead, expecting to be dead. I had thought you might become a friend to me—but of course that old bitch has turned your head."

"Turned my head?"

She cried.

"Oh God . . ."

She bit her lip.

"I married you to be your wife, Mr. van Nierkirk. I will be your wife. I will do anything for you."

He put his hands on her cheeks and forced her head backwards until she thought her neck would break.

"And I almost believe you," he muttered.

"That woman is more devilish than I imagined."

His face hardened.

"So you will be my wife. Then let me see what you can offer me in capacity. Come on child. Did you not know what was involved in marriage?"

She pulled away and stood up. Her physical strength took him by surprise.

"I had thought of love, sir. Or at least consideration. But you seek only to humiliate me."

She had to clench her fist to keep her fingers from shaking. But even through the fear she was angry.

"You are a discerning child," he remarked.

"Aye, girl, I will humiliate you, I think, to put our relationship on an acceptable footing from the start. I know not what ideas my mother will have pumped into your head."

"You'll explain your hatred for me, sir," she whispered desperately trying to erect a barricade of words between them.

"Perhaps, when you are sufficiently humble to understand my explanation."

He sat beside her and twisted his fingers in the bodice of her gown.

"It was a pity to tear this."

She moved away from him, sliding up the bed until she touched the bulkhead. Still sitting, she gathered the garment and lifted it over her head then threw it in the furthest corner of the room. Her cheeks flushed with anger.

"Your heart is throbbing. It's almost quickening my blood. But indeed you are no more than a child. What will you do?"

"I hate you," she whispered. He stared at her in silent disbelief.

"I had thought . . ."

"Now there is the mistake of inexperience."

He reached for her, and she closed her eyes. He held her round the waist and pulled her up against him.

"You should not think about people. You should treat them with suspicion until they are known to you."

He sat her on his knee to unfasten her stays. Her breath came in great gasps.

"Now you . . . you I know, little Segopotso. You are as clear as a phantom of water in the noonday sun. You are proud of your height, and you try to carry yourself like a lady. You have ambition and just enough intelligence to give promise to your dreams. Your pride and your intelligence have brought you to this proud eminence. You little bitch!"

The caresses ended in a slap on the cheek, which jerked her eyes open and thrust her head backwards. Erasmus stood up, still holding her bundled in his arms, and threw her from him. She landed on the bed with arms and legs out flung.

"But since you are here, my sweet Poppet, I will show you what you really are."

He pulled at his collar.

"Just flesh. And there is no difference between flesh and flesh in these circumstances."

The rain had stopped, and there was little wind. It was past dawn. A faint light found its way through the window. She sat with her knees drawn up and her head resting on her arms. This was the first morning of her married life. She turned her head, but the other side of the bed was empty. She lay on her stomach and buried her face in the pillow. Perhaps, since he so obviously loathed her, he would not come back. He had done his duty. He had made her his wife, unwillingly, but with demonic efficiency, hating her every moment and making sure she knew of his mounting hatred. She brought her hands together and squeezed so tightly her knuckles cracked. She was not herself this morning. Now, there was a silly thought but true enough in more ways than the obvious. She could not recognize her own emotions. She hated him, hated him, hated him . . . but she wished he would come in and smile at her. He would never do that, of course. What would he do when he next saw her? She was still his wife, a van Nierkirk. Strange, how Marie had stressed the importance of that almost as if she had expected something like this to happen. Expected? She had known! And counted on it! She thought of those colorless eyes and rolled on her back, appalled by her helplessness. Whatever van Nierkirk wanted, Marie wanted her as a daughter-in-law. There could be no going back, no begging for release. But he must treat her like a wife, or she would be nothing to Marie or to him. Things had to change. He had enjoyed his magical ritual. Once was enough.

They lunched at one. Erasmus sat at one end of the table and Marie at the other. Segopotso was placed between them. She had bathed and rested, but she was not soothed. She had tried to find her mother-in-law during the morning, but the houses had been deserted, and she had been afraid to descend the stairs to the library and walk the verandas looking down at the rolling valleys all around and the sprawling brooding ranch. She knew her husband would be there somewhere. She had seen the horse tethered to the step. She thought it must be wonderful to be so competent, so confident and as brutal as he had been last night. Now she sat between a barrage of gossip concerning the wedding and the guests and the intimate details of the personal lives of ranchers and the wives she had always known only as 'sir' and 'mistress'. She had no means of knowing if they had discussed her at all. They both treated her as their equal in station and knowledge as she picked at her food.

"You want some more wine?" said Marie cheerfully.

She fingered her glass. She could feel the heat in her cheeks.

"In truth, Mrs. van Nierkirk, I am unused . . ."

"Well, then, my dear, you must become used."

"Wine is the balm of intelligent minds," said van Nierkirk.

"It softens the harshness of the sun and wind and allows you to face life with a sense of calmness."

"And it brings a sparkle to your eye," Marie said.

"She is a nervous child, mother."

"All the more reason for wine then."

"No. I . . . I have had enough, really."

"And she has a mind of her own, mother. I thought you knew that."

He thrust back his chair and stood up.

"I rest after lunch—until the heat leaves the sun," he smiled at his wife. "But in the library. I shall not intrude upon your privacy this afternoon, Poppet."

Segopotso flushed and glanced at Marie.

"I also rest after luncheon," the old woman said.

"You would do well to acquire the habit. But come, you have not seen my room."

She led the way across the great passage and opened the door. Segopotso stopped in surprise. Alone, of the rooms in the house, Marie's bedroom was carpeted, from wall to wall, with thick white piles.

"All the way from India and worth a fortune."

Marie stepped out of her slippers.

"You see? I like freedom for my toes and softness for them to walk upon. One of the privileges of wealth is that you are able to gratify your every whim."

Segopotso gasped at her and at the room. The bed was no less remarkable than the carpet except for a couch set against the wall, a place for repose or thought, perhaps, but hardly for deep, limb-gripping sleep. She found the difference grotesque—luxury for the feet, discomfort for the back . . . the dressing table and wardrobe seemed unnatural in their normalcy. Marie closed the veranda door, shutting out the glare.

"One must always consider ones privacy in these houses."

She sat on the couch.

"Well child? Come, sit on the carpet. You will find it very comfortable."

"I prefer to stand."

"As you wish. You feel you hardly own yourself, do you not? That is common enough . . ."

"Mrs. van Nierkirk . . ."

"I knew he would find you irresistible. You are so lovely. But I feared that perhaps . . . until this morning. You will not know my relief when I saw you. A clever woman can sometimes hide the fact that her maiden head remains inviolate, to appear worldly . . . but there was never a girl could disguise her recent conquest. It shows in the eyes and the mouth . . . the mouth most of all, I think."

"Mrs. van Nierkirk, I . . . I have been debauched."

Marie smiled.

"Sexual encounter is the one means left to us poor mortals to enable us to forget that we are cast in the image of God. Such experiences are necessary, or we grow conceited in ourselves. And a wise woman learns to enjoy them."

The smile became a gentle laugh.

"As you did, girl. Why pretend to me?"

"It was the spirit, not the deed. He took me with hatred as if disgusted with what he did, with what he had to do. Mrs. Van Nierkirk, you have been uncommonly cruel to me."

"So I have been cruel. I made you a promise. Look around you. Is not this farm worth a prize?"

"I had thought to marry a man who would at least respect me, not a farm."

"And you have done that also. But you must have patience. Sit down and listen to me. You swore to me that you loved my son. Then it is your responsibility—it will be your glory—to save him from himself. He will come to you again. He will not be able to stay away from you. He will come to you, and he will make you pregnant, and with that victory, you will bind him to you. You are a van Nierkirk. I have made you so. He is a weakness, an insertion into our stream of strength. But, he is my son and I must save him. God above, child, he lacks the strength of character to follow any path steadfastly, much less one as thorny and unreasonable as marriage. He is guilty only of a perverted taste. I blame myself, in part. He was born in this farm, and he has left it too seldom. He was raised at the breast of a black wet-nurse; in that also I failed. He prefers a black body like yours, Segopotso, or he would pretend so."

"But he asked for my hand . . ."

"Yes. That he did. In the same spirit as he . . . never mind, girlie. The bitch is dead. Dead and buried, I say. That bitch, my God. He conceived himself in love with . . . with an uncouth, most uncultured, black woman. He brought her here . . . in my house, Segopotso. Oh, the girl had presence. She was big and strong and she had spirit. She was a Kalanga—a mulish people if ever you could think of one. She was violent. She could spit like a wild cat and would, given the slightest provocation. No doubt, he discovered in her bed some strength to compensate for his own weakness. But consider me, Segopotso, living here, watching this hideous thing . . . you take this calmly."

Segopotso sat on the carpet, her shoulders slumped.

"It is not uncommon amongst free burghers to sleep with black women. It would have been strange had Mr. van Nierkirk acted differently. It would seem there is a human side to him after all."

"Indeed? Well, there is more. This perverted passion of his did not go unrewarded. There is a child, a boy who stands between you and your husband. A bastard, you hear! Kalanga people are nothing but trouble, clever by half too. They won't even work for us. He is the poisonous growth that you must destroy. Do you know Erasmus would foist that miscegenous thing upon me as my grandson? He wants to send the boy to England and bring him back with an education surpassing my own. God give me strength to hate the simpering misbegotten droppings of my own loins. I won't allow it."

"Mrs. van Nierkirk I . . . I have no knowledge of hatred. And to destroy a child whose only crime is to have been born with a black skin . . ."

"Black blood, Segopotso. Black blood. Do you know what that does to human beings? Do you have any idea? Aye, you would do nothing to harm a child. You are a good girl, Segopotso, well brought up, I should think, and educated as well. Your own people too are good people in their own way. Quite harmless, though by far the most abused people I've ever known. But you know far too little about human nature. I mean, what do you know? Are you going to bolt your bedroom door and shut Erasmus out forever?"

The tears came out without warning. Segopotso bowed her head and wept, her shoulders shaking. She felt the old woman move and stand above her. The thin fingers were thrust into her hair as they had been that first evening.

"I deceived you, Segopotso. I admit it, and I ask your forgiveness. I do not know what suddenly made him desire you. I suspect it was to do with having survived the gunshot. He is uncommonly superstitious. But whatever the reason, he saw in you, the poor humble daughter of a dignified man of God and shopkeeper, a sop at once to his demands and his conscience and at the same time a green shoot for him to bend as he chose. I had either to take advantage of his weakness or let my chance slip, perhaps forever. My decision had to be made quickly, without proper investigation or thought for all concerned. I chose to follow my instincts, and I will not believe my instincts have led me astray. You are no shop girl, Segopotso. With your beauty and love and courage and my determination we shall save this family and this farm. God above knows, others have died for that! Purity and honour! At least I have not duped you. Be a wife to my son. Learn from me and from your own experience how to make him come to you. Learn to hate those who would drag him down to the level of an animal. Be my daughter, as he would not wish to be my son, and I swear you will never regret it."

Her eyes gleamed, and the blood veins stood out of her temples.

"We must hope, Segopotso. Without hope there is no form to life. These are the very words once uttered to me by your grandfather. An intelligent man I knew as only a woman can know a man, and they almost killed us for loving each other. I'm an old woman now, rudderless and with one foot in the grave. But I still have ambition. I will die a true van Nierkirk, undefeated by life. This I owe to my ancestors, to my long life, to the roots of my tortured past as far back as Bengal in India. I'm a human being, and I will die with respect and honour. It's the only way I know. I need you, girlie, more than you can ever imagine."

Segopotso lay on her face in bed. She found that strange. She never slept on her stomach. Nor was she a restless sleeper. But now there was a pillow beneath her stomach and none beneath her head. And . . . she moved, and frowned. There was something on her back, heavy and painful, burning into her flesh. Obviously she must get up. It took her some moments to find her arms, and each movement was accompanied by the burning feeling in the middle of her back. But at last she could see her fingers. She brought them together in front of her face and pushed against the bed, but nothing happened. She found that strange too. She relaxed and lay still. She was very tired.

"Eh-eh . . . are you awake, madam?"

Bikani spoke from somewhere behind her.

"Bikani . . ." her voice was no more than a whisper.

She tried to roll over but felt hands on her shoulders holding her still. "You've got to lie so, madam," Marietta said softly and gently.

"Your back is burnt up. I am going to call Mrs. van Nierkirk. She said I must tell her when you wake up."

It took all her strength to turn her head and watch the girl through the door. Then she was alone, listening to the rain.

The clouds obscured the sun, and it was difficult to decide what time of day it was. She was in her own bed and her burn had been dressed. But how had she gotten there? She remembered the hut and van Nierkirk and Abraham, his son. His skin was light and his features were European— fine features, small and delicate. His hair, if curly and combed, was not that of an African. His brown eyes were a curious mixture of lazy softness and sudden quick flashes. He wore a threadbare shirt and faded grey trousers, and his feet were bare. He possessed a sturdy body if not a great deal of height. He was at once quiet and well-spoken and handsome and intelligent. But Biganani, his black nurse . . . she would never forget Biganani.

"Segopotso!"

Marie sat on the edge of the bed.

"How good it is to see you awake! Do you know you have lain there all night? But I suppose your system received a severe shock." Segopotso moved her tongue round her lips. She articulated slowly, uncertainly.

"My back," she whispered.

"Yes, my dear. A nasty wound. I'm afraid you will carry a scar. But . . ." Marie rose and walked to the window.

"It is a strange thing . . . are you superstitious?"

Segopotso turned her head to follow the voice but found the effort too great.

"I do not think so."

"You should be, girl. Life moves in a mysterious fashion. My great-grandmother, the matriarch of this family, had a scar on her back. The wound was inflicted on her by some drunken Dutch soldier. Oh, when she was no more than a child. It faded with time. But you could still see it. If you looked closely. She allowed me that privilege, once. It made my skin crawl. Now you will carry the scar in almost the identical position."

She came back to the bed.

"You find nothing significant in that?"

Segopotso frowned.

She could see nothing pleasing in having a scar in the middle of her back for the rest of her life. And suddenly she was bitterly, furiously, angry. She moved her head, slowly, and found the old woman.

"Your son did that to me, Mrs. van Nierkirk."

"I was hoping you might tell me what happened."

"He . . . my presence in the boy's hut seemed to anger him. He was drunk. He had a . . . a fit of madness, really. It was no less than that. He seemed to want to kill me."

"I understand your feelings, of course, child, but . . . ."

"I swear it, if he comes near me again . . . ."

"Of course, Segopotso. Of course. But I am sure he knows the wrong he has done you."

"I want a bolt on my door, ma'am. I want it there this day."

Marie sighed and sat on the bed again.

"You will have whatever you wish, Segopotso, as long as you do not let your anger cloud your judgment."

"My judgment? After he has burned the skin from my back and . . . ."

"I have said he will not touch you again unless you desire it. You can believe me. And your back will mend. It is of Biganani I wish to speak."

"I bear her no ill. She tried to protect me."

"And now she is dead."

"What?"

28

"It seems that when she tried to prevent him from striking you he struck her instead, harder than he intended, and in falling, she split her skull on the table."

"Oh my God!"

"She's dead. It is the living we must consider."

Regardless of the pain, Segopotso turned on her side and rose on her elbow. She could not remember ever being so angry in her entire miserable life.

"You're glad," she hissed.

"It is not my habit to lie. The woman was a cancer eating into our family. I do not regret her death, only the manner in which she died. Erasmus fled from the hut in terror when he discovered what he had done. In his strange way he was as fond of this Biganani as he had been of her older sister. But at least he had the sense to come straight here and tell me and no one else."

"But, Mrs. van Nierkirk . . ."

"Oh, the blacks know she is dead, of course. But they have been given to understand that it was Biganani who attacked you and that Erasmus accidentally killed her in trying to save your life. Then he returned here. You will have to make a similar statement in your deposition. There will have to be an account of this business, you see."

"And you expect me to perjure myself? To save a man who has half killed me?"

"I expect you to save your husband and the name of your family. This is your family now. Can you understand the circumstances? If Erasmus is indicted on a charge of murder, they will very likely hang him, swine that they are. The British have no sense of justice." Segopotso shook her head.

"Mrs. van Nierkirk . . ."

"Can you not see that he has suffered enough? Segopotso, would you pull us down into the dirt? You will fall with us. And this farm is yours, Segopotso. Yours. All you have ever dreamed of, girl. And Erasmus will treat you as a sister from now on. I swear it. You have only to act that part of a sister now."

Segopotso chewed her lip. Her back was burning, and she rolled on her face, pulling the pillow up to her chest and hugging it fiercely. "It was not just me alone there, Mrs. van Nierkirk," she whispered.

"I have already spoken to the boy. He will not betray his father."

"He tried to assist me. I want to thank him."

"I am sure he understands your attitude. In any event, you would have done better without him. He put salt on your burn and made sure of a scar."

"He tried hard. And that was his home that has been destroyed."

29

"Yes. He is a confounded nuisance. Perhaps, in view of everything that has happened, it would be best to fall in with Erasmus's idea and send the boy away."

"To England?" Segopotso cried.

"Good heavens, no! That would be money wasted. And God knows there is little enough to be had. I think the army would suit him fine. The whole bloody world is at war. I'll send him to the madness in Europe. That should make a man of him."

"But he is only fifteen years old."

"That is all to the best. He has time to make his way in the world."

"I would like him to stay."

Marie smiled.

"Really, Segopotso . . ."

"I am married to his father, as you keep reminding me. So he is my son. I would like to take care of him."

Marie frowned.

"You force me on to matters I had not intended to discuss, Segopotso. I find your affection for this boy inexplicable and distasteful. He is no friend of yours. He will stand between you and your children. And never fear. You will have children of your own one day. Besides, I fancy your ideas of his upbringing smack more of the sister than the mother. Mothers need to be harsh with their sons to make them men."

"Mrs. van Nierkirk . . ." her cheeks flamed.

"He is only fifteen years old."

"As you are only fifteen as well."

"Well . . . at least the dog...I would like . . . ."

"Rubbish. I'll have no filthy animals in my house. It will be destroyed. I will have no more discussion of this matter."

"Just now you asked for my help," Segopotso muttered.

Marie smiled.

"And because of that you want to assert yourself? Segopotso, you are a sweet child. But still a child. I need your help as you need mine. We work best in harness. Save your assertiveness for when I am dead and gone. It will not be long now. As for this matter you may be sure I seek your advantage as well as my own. You cannot conceive the service you have done me by your irresponsible behaviour. Do you know how long I have wished to destroy that boy?

"Mrs. van Nierkirk! I . . ."

"Now I will reward you. When this story reaches Tati Town, all the settlers will think of you as a woman of character who had no love for her husband's bastard family. To survive an attempted assassination is no disgrace. Follow my example and you will find yourself respected and feared. You can build on such a reputation, girl. Only a fool would cast it away."

Waiting, waiting, waiting. Segomotso thought that if summers were given names, the summer of 1945 would be called the Waiting Summer. There was no substance to life. There was no pleasure in watching the fields burst into bloom at the beginning of spring. It seemed to her that all life was a waiting, as she waited for Abraham's return from the theatre of operations in southern Europe, a futile waiting, a waiting without fulfilment. The fulfilment of being an adult, first and then of marriage seemed to be eluding her. All things had been reversed, and neither had been fulfilled. But then, surely, she had a right to expect the fulfilment of motherhood, now that was relegated to a dream. Marie had known. Oh, damn Marie. Oh God, damn her! But if there was no fulfilment in any of these things, where would she find it? In love? She had never loved. Her craving for van Nierkirk had been an infatuation as foolish as Abraham's adolescent passion for her. Abraham was the lucky one. He was a free agent, and had chosen wisely or done well, all things considered. But she had been given no choice, and now—now her chances were slender on the farm, with an occasional visit to Gaborone thrown in. Perhaps her fulfilment lay in death, or something more awful; the last visit to Tati Town had left her terribly aware that, to each white person in the Protectorate, there were over a thousand blacks—a hideous thought if carried to a logical conclusion. Millions of men, among them Abraham, were fighting for freedom in Europe, for freedom round the world. What would happen after the war? Would colonial empires survive the triumph of global democratic culture? It was unlikely, highly unlikely. The colonists were doomed. Even the nebulous protection of the mother countries would be denied to them. If blacks took power, what would happen to the farm? What would happen to her? No doubt, they considered her a traitor, an uppity Mosarwa who lived like a white person and loaded it over them like all colonists. Segopotso wrapped a shawl round her shoulder and went on to the veranda. The clouds were very low. There was not a star in the sky. The night was utterly dark.

"An army could creep up the hill in these conditions and we would never hear them," he said.

She had not heard him move. She pulled the shawl tighter.

"Are you afraid, Erasmus?"

"Afraid?"

She heard his breath rushing through his nostrils as he smiled.

"Now, there is a remarkable thing, Poppet. I don't know. I have never had occasion to find out. My uncle, my father, my grandfather—they defended this part of the world against the Africans and the British. But me—the last war began when I was just a little boy, and I was still young when it ended. I thought of going to war and playing my part, but there was always so much to be done here. And I thought it would find me out. Maybe now is the time. Strange, how things run along. We, the van Nierkirks, have never had to seek trouble. That old bitch in there knows what it's like to see a horde of armed men walking towards you. But me— I have to show my boldness by duelling and taking a hit from some wind-blowing bastard."

"Surely that requires certain courage."

She glanced at his shadow, immobile by the door.

"You think it unjust that one time should differ so much from ano-ther?"

"Not unjust, Poppet. Remarkable. You are still young. Whatever happens to you this night can be absorbed and put to good use, like mother. But I am old, and I have no experience of warfare or even tumult to draw on. That is hard of nature, I think."

"You encourage me immensely," she muttered.

But how strange, she thought, to hear Erasmus, tall, fair, handsome and arrogant Erasmus, speaking like this. Times were changing.

"I had not realized you were a philosopher."

"Thinking is about all a man has to do. You'd better go to bed, Sego-potso. I will keep watch."

She shook her head.

"I cannot sleep."

"Then shall I bring a chair for you?"

"I will sit on the floor."

She sat down and stretched her legs in front of her.

"But do you know what I would like, Erasmus? A glass of wine. No, not wine. Could I have a, what is it, a tot? A tot of rum."

He chuckled.

"Hardly the drink for a sixteen year old."

"But you always remind me to experience in various matters is what I need. Perhaps you will teach me."

He laughed again, and sat beside her on the floor in the darkness while the rain pattered on the roof above their heads and whispered on the grass below them.

"You pour a little . . . so . . . into a glass, and follow it with this tumbler of water. The rum will burn your throat."

"It scarcely seems to trouble yours."

She held a glass in both hands and downed the liquor in a single gulp.

"God," she gasped, and choked, tears springing to her eyes, while the alcohol seemed to scorch her very lungs.

"Drink the water," he said.

Instant relief. And now the burning ceased and immense warmth spread through her stomach.

"Now show me how the experts do it."

He drank, and sighed, and drew the back of his hand across his mouth. "The answer to uncertainty," he said.

"But to drink oneself insensible is to court disaster," she said quietly.

"Something in your mind?"

"Only one thing grieves me."

She held out her glass.

"If I was to die at this moment there would be one life utterly wasted." This time the operation was far simpler, and the burning was alleviated. But her mouth continued to taste bitter.

"Brrrrr. There is no pleasure in drinking this stuff, at any rate. I await the effect. There is an effect, Erasmus?"

He did not reply.

She could see him in the dark. A serious, deep-thinking man, van Nierkirk, lacking in imagination . . . no that was hardly correct. Not after the thoughts he had expressed. A strange man, then. A man of depths. Quite unsuspected. She attempted to stand, and turned on her knees.

"Do you drink, then, merely to lose your balance?"

She groped at his arms, and slipped, and fell against him, and suddenly his hands were pulling at the bodice of her gown; instinctively she pushed herself away, but he fell forward with her. She lay on her back on the veranda floor, and she gazed at him.

"Lie there," he muttered.

"Do not move, Segopotso. Just let me look at you, all that long crinkled hair and green muslin gown and seething breath. You are a lovely picture, Poppet. Something to cleanse a man's mind."

He pulled her gown from her shoulders.

"I imagine I have been many kinds of a fool this past year. Do you not think so, Segopotso?"

"You know your own mind, Mr. van Nierkirk," she whispered.

"But I have not been guiltless."

"God, girl do you imagine you have performed a single action of your own free will since entering your mother's bedroom to gape at a wounded man? My mother conjured you up like a spirit, and you have danced only to her bidding. It is time to put a stop to that. Only I have ever had the courage to defy her. Only I can save you from her clutches. But when you first came to me you were an uncommonly simple girl, and your figure lacked the fullness I admire in women. And then I was beside myself with grief. I suspect you knew that. I had no wish to survive my encounter with de Kock. I regarded that as but one more manifestation of the misfortunes that have dogged my footsteps since I can remember. I wished only a companion to share my misery, and your innocent happiness drove me to frenzy. And then . . . you will not believe this, Poppet, but that morning at the hut, I felt a sudden desire for you. You were not meant to be a lady, I think. When I saw you there, standing next to Biganani, bare of foot and wild of hair, then I wanted to satiate myself with you, rather than merely maul you."

He sighed.

"You will understand this is something of a confession for me, Segopotso. I am aware of the perversity of my passion."

"I am your wife, Erasmus. I swore to honour you and obey you, whatever your faults."

"By obedience? No more?"

"Ereasmus . . ." she panted as he completed the destruction of her clothing and lowered his head. His lips were cold, but her breasts were warm, and surely they could comfort each other.

"You saved my life," she said, while she wondered at her enthusiasm over him. But she had looked forward to his return for so long. She had promised herself that she would make him her friend, this time, and find in him the variety that was lacking in her life. Her days followed too invariable a pattern. In the mornings she visited the farm. In the afternoons there were books to read, and in the evenings she could either sit on the settee listening to him playing the piano—he played quite well, she thought, only the music was dreary—or roll dice with Marie. A strange vice for so dignified a matriarch, especially as they used neither money nor favours; Marie merely liked to win as many throws as possible, and as she was extraordinarily lucky, this was not difficult. As for him, she had long ceased bolting her bedroom door. They treated each other with polite circumspection; she had even grown sorry for him. He hated Biganani passionately, that was obvious, and his memory of the black woman threw him into daily fits of depression. Segopotso suspected it was this memory which drove him to the bottle. Certainly he got himself drunk every evening, without any apparent effect on his health, for in the mornings he was always first out and about. And there could be no other reason. Her only misery arose from the realization that she would never be a mother. Thus, she dotted on Abraham hungrily. This boy, tarnished by his black blood, nervous and unsure of himself, was the only van Nierkirk there would ever be, after Erasmus. An astonishing thought. But at least he had his own life to live and she could be his friend, his mentor, indeed as she was his stepmother. She desperately hoped he would survive the political madness in Europe and return home a stronger man.

She opened the door to the veranda and sat on the cane settee.

"Have you nothing to say to me?" she said.

He closed the door and leaned on the veranda rail.

"There are no women in the army, Mrs. van Nierkirk. I must apologize for my father. He lies all day like a man without purpose."

"Don't you think I am aware of his weakness?"

He turned.

"Do not say that, ma'am."

"The thought . . . I do not like to think of it," she frowned.

"Abraham, you have become surprisingly serious. Or were you always so?"

He licked his lips.

"In the army, there is no time to think."

He sat beside her.

"There are watches and lonely hours and a great deal of hard work and even more cold and wet to endure. It's a terrible experience."

He smiled.

"And a rope's end for neglect," he laughed.

"Does all this frighten you?"

He nodded assent.

"Sometimes," he glanced at her and flushed. She seized his hand.

"But reassure me. I would not have you grow up too fast. And now you are home. Do not shake your head at me. I have been a van Nierkirk long enough to assert myself. Indeed, Marie insists upon it. You shall live in the house now, and we will walk together and read together and . . ."

"No, ma'am. I will not be home for long. We are here for a few days. We leave in three days' time."

She stared at him.

"The Bulawayo Garrison, you mean?"

"Yah. Don't worry about me. This place is good. Think of it, ma'am. There are opportunities in these parts, the land, and this entire open wilderness. Who knows what fortune is hidden in it?"

"Aren't you afraid of the danger of it? Have you considered that we will need you here? The Africans are restless. If we are driven off the farm, can you imagine what that will involve? Poverty, for one thing. Even death. Complete annihilation. I tell you, we have laid in a stock of firearms, and even I am practicing daily. Your grandmother is preparing for a small war. I think she almost welcomes the prospect. To die like a van Nierkirk, pistol in hand. But we—your father and I—we will need loyal friends . . . and our son."

"You count me loyal, ma'am? To my mother or my father?"

"Your mother was a strong and loved woman, Abraham."

"After she bore me, ma'am?"

"But . . . do you mean . . . you feel an affinity for the blacks?"

"Should I not? I was raised by them, ma'am. Or have you forgotten my aunt Biganani already?"

"Ah . . . you hate me for that. I may have provoked what happened Abraham, but I meant her no harm."

"I do not blame you for that, ma'am. I know my father's guilt." Segopotso leaned forward.

"But there that day, you chose your future, Abraham. Instinctively, as you are a van Nierkirk. They tell me you attempted to save my back. You! A boy of fifteen, with death lying close at hand."

He turned his back pressed against the railing.

"A boy of fifteen. You thought me a child, ma'am?"

"I do not make that mistake; Abraham, you will soon be a man"

"As you are a woman, ma'am."

"As you will."

"And you remember nothing of that afternoon?"

"Only vague impressions . . . it has the quality of a nightmare which haunts me in the small hours. The fire . . . and the pain . . ." she raised her head.

"But I am nonetheless grateful."

He threw himself away from the rail.

"I do not need your gratitude, ma'am," he shouted.

"You do not understand. I remember that afternoon. Like you, it haunts my sleep . . . only for me it is no nightmare, except in my conscience." Impatiently he paced the veranda.

"I attempted to soothe your burn, ma'am. Now, how do you think I accomplished that? By prayer? How did I reach your flesh, ma'am? I fought my way through gown and petticoat and underpants. See, I know them all. I did not then. That afternoon was my first encounter with such things. Neither my mother nor my aunt wore more than a single garment. But you . . . I bust my way through those things in my haste to reach your back, ma'am. I . . ." the tongue flicked quickly round his lips.

"I laid you bare from neck to thigh."

She kept the smile on her lips.

"Be sure that I will never hold it against you."

"Hold it against me?" he cried.

"Can you not understand, ma'am? I dream of . . ."

He turned away.

"You are my father's wife . . ."

"Abraham! And you are still . . ."

36

"I celebrated my sixteenth birthday three days ago."

"Abraham," she said softly.

"Turn round and face me. I did not mean you could not be a man at your age. I mean at sixteen it is easy to fall in love . . . with love. Like a calf running after his mother. You choose the first woman at hand. And a season away has only intensified your longing. To stop wondering and return to the farm would be the best way to end your fantasy."

"And suppose I crawled into your bed one night, ma'am?" he demanded.

"I do not doubt your manhood. But you will not gain anything by vulgarity."

He leaned on the arm of her chair.

"I know of what I am guilty. I . . . I desire my father's wife. Perhaps if he was a man I could love and respect . . . but knowing him for what he is, a . . . a drunken lout who is also a murderer . . ."

"Abraham! You know it was an accident."

If only he could give her time to think. However ridiculously he was behaving, obviously he believed what he was saying. And now she was in danger of losing him.

"At least you may rest easy on my score. He has not touched more than my hand for a long time."

He stared at her.

"I have not been able to forgive him for your aunt's death either, you see."

"Then . . . why do you live with him?" he asked.

"I am a van Nierkirk. Whatever difference may lie between us, I am your father's wife. I am your mother, Abraham. As I shall have no children of my own, I count on you doubly valuable."

"My grandmother has turned your head."

"Now you are talking like your father."

But she smiled at the thought.

"Well, ma'am, my time in the army has taught me something about life. Whatever misfortunes my family has suffered it has surely brought on itself. And if I was to remain in the farm would I live in the same house with you? I will scarcely feel myself . . ."

She put her hand on his arm.

"I do not doubt your sincerity. I can only convince you that this will not last. Are you afraid I will tell your father? It will be our secret. And because of it, we shall be friends, Abraham." He stared at her for a moment, then wrenched himself free and ran for the stairs.

Chapter 2

Indecent Proposals...

Gaborone, 1986

A s I sit in the sunlight on the stoop of the veranda, a fighter jet plane goes by slowly, very ugly, painted green to match the spring forest, the one flaw in our life today; camouflage, the pretension that by playing dumb we can make life beautiful. I wonder how much the soldiers see of me down here, crowded in that unpleasant metal thing. Perhaps they see a figure, a remote and tiny enemy breaking rolls apart, staring up, a black face. Sin. Nothingness. Apart from this, they see the grey-greenish trees, fruit trees, and the long grass running down the slope from the house to Notwane River, maybe the Hill of Lovers to the south as well and nothing else. A Boer commando is going to boom Gaborone city to smithereens. In the meantime, I continue to break bread rolls into pieces, to eat the hard-skinned, very sweet grapes from the garden, and wish I could swim. There is death and blood in the air. I can smell it. Tears accompany the breeze from Gaborone.

A few African National Congress freedom fighters are dead, a number of few civilians as well, an excellent mathematical equation. Another nation is being born. It's all so civilized, human, a curious but acceptable way of doing things. Also I think how much better this is than the school dormitory, the heat drumming off the walls all day, and that terrible thing the authorities conveniently call classrooms; the smell, the intolerable human odour, and, worst of all, the feeling of being under someone's eye the entire time—being roasted in a white oven, in pain, and, at the same time, part of an experiment in a laboratory; unclean, watched all day by unseen and unblinking dirty eyes. Oh, how I hate life. How I hate myself. But here all this is discarded. To be home is quite something. Here I can almost feel like I just came up out from the womb each day. I feel like some unique, primeval god from the sea, coming ashore in the freshness of a new day. My mother, they tell me, is a whore in the city. Never mind. She is still my mother. The sea, I really should like to be able to swim, to drag this ugly body to the river and to forget everything altogether, at least for as long as I was in the water. The only thing I like, and there is no one to teach me.

To my father such things hardly matter. Left to himself he would do nothing. All he wants is warmth from clothes, just covering enough to avoid comment, scandal or worse still, fuss. Wounded, yes, my father was wounded. He limps about, upsets chairs with his clumsiness, and coughs with those lungs that had been filled with unmentionable earth grit in the mines in Johannesburg after demobilization. They refuse to officially call him a war veteran. The wound is from Lesoma where Ian Smith's unruly mob routed our soldiers in 1977. One battle, they say, does not constitute war. So the poor fellow is out in the cold. No pension. Nothing. I wonder what sort of soldier he was. What happened to his decorations, to his uniform? All I can remember is a bundle of rags, part of an army greatcoat which was used to polish my school shoes when I was little. Did he fight in it, bleed on it? Is it because in the end he was betrayed and vanquished by both soldiers and politicians that he takes no pride in these things? That he keeps so quiet about the house, eschewing any mention of them, humiliated by the same deeds of his life for which I would have loved him more than anything else? It's impossible to think of his being in any army, impossible, quiet impossible. A drifter, yes. Nothing, else.

I suppose he deserves my love and pity. After all, he is a good father, a good man. He is free to brood in the broth of memory for eternity for all I care. This morning, I received my long awaited admission to the University of Witwatersrand. I'm keeping my fingers crossed for another from the University of Cape Town. I so wish to be part of the sea. If I have to be a drifter like my father, I would rather do it at sea. It's amazing how very little there is in the end to hold me at home, an old rope frayed to the last fiber. It's time to quit. What, after all, have they to give me here? Life, and after that little enough. Some food, soup and some pleasant aimless conversations about nothing. Truly I can remember hardly a phrase out of all those millions of words we must have used during so many years. I've almost forgotten them all.

My mother, the good whore, writes, and my other relatives write. If they were bombed by Boer commandoes, would I weep now, such remote people? Talk about sentimental bullshit. Yes, I can be very sentimental. I could create something to cry over, out of all the horrible things happening around me, the boring school poems, the sad village songs, the childhood memories changed into something else. It makes so much more sense than crying over a war that never was, like my father. One battle and he thinks he lost a war! What madness.

My mother, the woman who hardly exists for me now, she who provided the warmth around me for all those months until I needed it no more, cast him off, possibly in the most ignorable fashion, she even despises him. Nobody likes pain and disappointment. No wonder my mother bolted to the city the moment it was all over. The scripture says be fruitful and multiply; a well understood mathematical imperative. But there is nothing there about nurturing; faeces, endless wailings, vomiting and all the foolish antics children do, milk, clothes and bathing. Isn't the greatest mystery on earth this fact that I had need of a woman at all to come into this wretched world, that I ever came from a woman, from this *woman* in particular? Better, even easier, I think, to believe that one sprung, fully grown, already a cantankerous beast, from the soil, from trees, from the sea, like the characters in mystery stories. Yes, I could be sentimental, I could create a tale. She it was, after all, whose expensive clothes, wet from a shower in the streets, introduced me to the scent of womanhood. The smell from her clothes brought me visions of the modern woman, so different from the neutral tang of soap and the sexless smell of Aunt Chandiwana, a distinction to motherhood. My mother and the other women out there tend to merge together in my consciousness into a single figure. I often wonder at that strange, indefinable, warm presence common to those women and the way it so easily transposes with the admixture of decent sentiment and the slow withdrawal of energy, of ambition; and the reconciliation, the unthinkable truce, the ransom that the world of established feminine domesticity demands of us all women. Are those women really? Once it made me dismayed that I could no longer close my eyes and remember my mother's features. Now it almost reassures me. I write letters back to her mechanically, thinking whatever I want to think, certainly not about her, repeating the ancient formulas of affections. In my mind I have already placed her long ago in the grave where she belongs. A good mother, my foot!

I'm off to Johannesburg. I am astonished that people choose to exaggerate death: it is so easy to surrender to death those whom one loves. After all God places no premium on death. Thousands of souls vamoose every day. In the village we surrender someone to such oblivion ever so often that I doubt anyone counts anymore. Today I find I have given up my whole family almost without knowing it. My best friends are more alive to me, more immediate than those who gave me life. What would I feel if a message arrived this morning announcing that my mother has been bombed? Nothing. I have already boomed her out of existence, delivered to dust that elegantly magnificent figure. I know what you think, you slimy spy! Of course, she is my mother, a matter of divine technical

41

efficiency. Nothing else. Look, perhaps this is a matter of greater regret, for wider black borders. Do we all know this? Is it everywhere acknowledged that we do these things not in a spirit of homage, but in shame? How afraid are we that this same oblivion will turn upon us, that those who should be doing all they can to keep us alive are, perhaps at this very moment, consigning us to such a death? How we fear this oblivion in all our moving through life, in all our departures, is a matter of individual choice. How pathetically, how despairingly we go on offering these colossal bribes to others to remember us—a monument, memoirs, libraries—all this is a matter of vanity. There are so many such bribes, from the smallest scale to the greatest, and the world is so cluttered with them that one can hardly move; the minds of the living are so distorted they can scarcely think. Yet, we accept this tremendous burden, we even add to it, gladly, joyfully, searching out the past, memorizing each detail of the present, researching, not living, all in the faith that we have bought some such treatment from the future; that those who come will not forget us entirely; forget what we were, as if we had never been . . . blast the myth!

I've already consigned my mother, a good whore, into the black hole. Oblivion. Farewell to memories! Why really should my own memories live? Why not let them walk to the river tonight or bury themselves among the stones of the Hill of Lovers? Why should I want to carve such thoughts upon every page, every stone, every parchment, every tablet, burn the words, the ideas, the actions like brands into living flesh so that these marks may carry from generation to generation? Why? Oh hell and damnation! Just how long have I sat here brooding? It is now a hot, sultry, grey day. And my headaches and throbs! Are we waiting for the wind or for heavy rain?

The Boer commando is now safely in their barracks, celebrating in the officer's mess as true heroes always do. The garden this morning is no garden, the green no green and there is nothing moving, except for the inane trickling of water from the backyard narrow stream. Everything suffers the same torpor. Even the few flies and white butterflies remain battering feebly at the bottom of the windowpanes without attempting higher flight, and more strenuous efforts to free themselves. I have a bus to catch. I'm visiting my friend in Gaborone, and hoping that damnable editor published my article. Wouldn't it be something to see my name in print: Batjibilibili Shangoyapalala. I love my friend Tshidi very much. I love it when we visit people in Gantsi and she and uncle Kaboyamodimo fuss so much over me teaching me Sesarwa and other things. Next Christmas she has agreed to visit my other relations in Mapoka Village where I too will have the chance to show off my knowledge of Ikalanga, and hopefully we will find time to visit Bulawayo and even go over to

Victoria Falls. I think it's a good thing to companion with the people you love. In fact, it's a good thing to love and care for anyone and everyone. But human beings are hard to understand. Far too many people seem to be waiting to be loved. They are so bent to this purpose that it is just not enough to be pleasant to them, to offer things to them and make them happy. As a little girl I gave my shoes away to a small girl in the village who had no footwear. I had met her at the village general dealer. The girl put them on. She ran up and down in front of the store, watching her feet, and I could tell she was proud of the shoes for she would stop and run her tiny figures over the shoe laces. When her mother came out of the store she followed her down the road, skipping in her shoes. I watched them and exalted in her happiness. When they got a little ways down the road, the woman stopped and looked at the little girl. She talked to her in harsh whispered tones and she pointed back towards me standing under the store veranda. To my horror and consternation, the woman went to the side of the road and cut a switch from a Mopani tree. She held the little girl by one arm and whipped her on the legs hard, and on the back. The girl cried but she did not move. The mother whipped her until the switch wore out and everybody under the store shed watched, but they did not say anything. Then she made the little girl sit down on the road and take off the shoes. She walked back, holding the shoes in her hand and my father and I watched her coming. She did not pay any attention to my father but walked right up and looked down at me, and her face was hard and her eyes shining. She poked the shoes at me, and I took them.

Then she said, "We don't take charity from nobody."

Her voice was sharp and savage. I could see she was very scared. She whirled around and walked off down the road, her ragged clothes flapping. She walked right by her, and the little girl followed her. She had stopped crying. She walked stiff with her head up, real proud and did not turn to look at anybody. You could see the big red stripes on her legs. On the way home, my father said he did not blame the poor girl. He said he thought that pride was all she had howsoever misplaced. He said the woman figured she could not let the little girl come to love pretty things they could not afford. There was also the possibility of other little kids at home. What would she give them? So she whipped them so that they should not get in the habit of liking things they could not have, and she whipped them until they learnt so that in a little while, they knew they were not to expect things beyond everyday reach.

My father said a few years back, as he walked past a shack in Old Naledi, he had seen a worn-down woman come out in her backyard where two of her little girls were looking, sitting under a shade tree, at a sparkling beautiful mail order catalogue. He said that the haggard woman took a cane and whipped them until the blood poured out of their legs. He said as he watched, she took the catalogue and went out behind the shack to a refuse dump. She burned up the catalogue, tore it all up first, like she hated that catalogue. She then sat down against the shack, where nobody could see her, and she cried. All this is very confusing to me, but still I continued to give everything that is mine with an open heart.

My father is also something of an enigma. At one time he got involved with a woman friend from the city. I tried to drive a gulf between them but failed to succeed in destroying their delight in one another. He watched the woman deliberately tear down my defences, convinced me I was ugly, stupid, lazy and incompetent. He had seen my spirit broken and personality nearly destroyed and had despised his own weakness for letting it happen. But he refused to talk about the whole affair. The strange thing is that nothing, not cruelty or weakness or misfortune, seem ever strong enough to destroy the bond between him and me. He knew that time that I felt the way he felt, that the tiny core of self, which would always sustain me, give sudden joy when I had no reason to be joyful, give me strength when I most needed it was the inner being in me under the most devious threat. Still, he refused to open his heart to me. When I returned from National Service I had grown up—well past him in so many ways—my mind was now bigger and less trammelled than his, but the bond between us was still there. Whatever I did, he could understand because if his life had been different he could have done those same things the same way.

He felt pride in my achievements, but the pride was only secondary to the fact that he had found someone in the world who thought as he did, who felt as he did, who was searching as he himself searched. He knew all these things of mine, but there was one thing he did not know. He thought that I was as he himself was. He never recognized the restlessness in me that I had inherited from my mother, a restlessness that was sometimes vivacity, sometimes discontent. He did not see this in me because it was not in himself. To me, his beloved daughter, he had imparted his sense of freedom, his belief that in this country anything could be done if one desired it strongly enough. I had studied at one of Zimbabwe's best schools and absorbed all kinds of ideas that were beyond him and the teachings of his generation. But he was proud of me because he believed I was using the chances that life in his country offered. And then one day he found that I had absorbed the idea of freedom to the exclusion of everything else. The idea of freedom had replaced God. Nurtured on freedom and the faith of personal achievement, I had discarded God. I believed in Karl Marx, in the strength of the peoples, in the dream of a utopian society where, once poverty and ignorance were abolished, human beings would become complete and perfect beings. In other words I had become like himself so many years ago, a rebel. The death of my brother, Adam, last summer, however seems to have brought us closer, that and my fight with mother.

It was the beginning of December when he came home, and for a short while he ate with the family in the kitchen. But once Christmas was over and the feeling of conviviality had passed, he ate alone in his room, plied with all the good things the family could provide, the fresh eggs and cream, poultry and butter, fruit and honey, and still, in spite of it all, losing what little flesh remained on his body. We were a practical family. We would not have survived otherwise. And all the things the doctor had told us to do were carefully observed. The house, the family, changed its pattern of life and adjusted center round the dying man. The necessity of caring for him, the extra work and money needed, were a salve, a useful therapy that helped to excise our spiritual grief. He knew he must be dying, but he fell into a euphoric condition of sleep and gentle walk out into the garden in his dressing-gown, and peaceful contemplation of the woods and fields about him, and it was hard to believe he was really going to die for he felt no pain. At first he was alone at night, just for the first couple of months, but after the first haemorrhage he had someone with him all the time. The haemorrhage came when he was on his own at night, the choking and the terrible clogging with blood of his lungs, and throat and stomach. He tried to sit up, feeling it would ease the scarlet flood, get away from him so that he could breathe again, but as he struggled and fought with the bedclothes and with his own body, it had just made everything worse. Some miracle of paternal instinct had made father to hurry to his room, lighting the candle as he came, and he had been in time to hold his son's head up so that his chest could clear off the blood swamping through it. After that father had bought a small, collapsible canvas bed to stand in the corner of the room, and someone stayed with him every night, if not father, then aunt Chandiwana, or cousin Bafi— getting up whenever the night sweats soaked over him and mopping his body dry with an old towel. Cousin Bafi was the one he needed most. In the presence of this sad sickness, she knew how to express love in terms of gently ministrations.

She was the one he would cry to in the night, saying, "Help me, Bafi. Help me!"

With his father and aunt Chandiwana, and with everyone else, he knew he must not show his fear. He must not add to their distress and he told himself that when the time came he would try to die quietly and with as little trouble a possible. But with Bafi he did not have to pretend. With her arms around him, and the sweat soaking her body as well as his, he could cry and bury his face in her shoulder and tell her he was afraid.

"Hush, my dear, hush. You won't die yet. I won't let you."

"And don't leave me, Bafi. Please don't leave me."

"I won't leave you. I'm here beside you. I'm holding you. I won't leave you!"

He wished so much that Bafi could sit with him every night, but the strain on her was too much for him to ask, even of Bafi, who gave so easily that he took without thinking. It was just that he needed her so much. One morning towards the end of his ordeal, when I came to his room he signed a power of attorney and the will of testament directing how his estate should be shared after his death.

"For you, little sister," he said.

"The money's to be used for you, to buy you things in the home and to help father with the upkeep, just as long as it lasts."

I did the paperwork and listened to the painfully whispered instructions without a word. Later I brought him a form to sign authorizing my administration. I attended to all that sort of thing. That's why he put his trust in me. He could rely on me to sort it all out. He watched the winter pass, the bare shapes of trees against a grey sky, and a fire burning in his room all the time. He watched the birds, robins and finches and shallows, and flights of big cawing crows in the sky, and then summer came, and the breeze blew through his windows smelling of light, delicate dying flowers and grass and granite dust from the Hill of Lovers to the south. He particularly loved the strong and heavy smell of the drying Notwane river, and it never ceased to amaze him that, even when submerged in this worrisome temporary seasonal amnesia, this little river never stopped to advertise its power to fight for life, struggling against the strongest forces and impulses of nature to accomplish its mission of conveying water to as far a place as the sea and fending for the lives and needs of thousands and thousands of fragile animals, plants and human beings at the same time. Bafi knew how much he needed the summer. She dug up roots and violets and planted them in an old egg crock for him, and when they died she replaced them with primroses and a few blue bells that she found in a warm sheltered patch of wood behind an old crumpling colonial building. And, Bafi understood how he wanted to see the things that were happening in the garden and the huge yard, the eggs all warm and soiled straight from the hen run, and an early adventurous bee that she trapped in her hands and fetched in to show him. And when the flowers on the strawberry plants turned into tiny, hard, green fruits, she picked a large spray and set them by his bed. It was her idea that they should buy the cane bed for him. She and Father and Aunt Chandiwana put their money together and bought it, a straw-coloured garden bed that could be

46

lifted very easily and taken into the garden. When August came and the weather was warm, Bafi and Father would wrap a blanket round him, and Father would lift his son's shrinking frame as easily as he had lifted him when a child. Gently, taking care not to bang his legs and shoulders on the narrow doorways, he would carry him up to the cane bed, and the boy would lie there on the ground he loved so much, smelling the earth and sometimes eating the dirt. Towards the end of September it became too hot, and he found after an hour or so he couldn't bear it any more.

"Take me in, Dad. Take me in," he said fretfully, and as Father started to lift him, he felt the blood come up again, felt it choking and smothering, salty and unbearably hot. He saw the blanket strain red, and the cane of the chair, and specks of blood showering all over the grass of the garden. Adam saw Father's horrified face, and over his father's shoulder, he saw Bafi begin to run towards him with her hands full of flowers. Then, he died.

I saw Bafi at the burial, of course, but I didn't have time to talk to her properly. We were so hemmed round by family and friends and visiting guests and the preachers who all wanted to ask a prayer by the graveside that private conversation was impossible. I didn't cry any tears at the burial. I had done my crying away from home, in my mother's bedroom in the city where no one could see me. The time I spent in the village helping to look after him had been too busy and concerned with physical things of illness to allow time for tears. But I had wept a lot during the weekdays in Gaborone, mostly for him but a little for myself too. I had been dreading the burial. Family burials, like weddings and birth blessings, are attended by the family in all their strength, and she I was afraid that the massed presence of all the relatives would prove the final harrowing strain on my grief.

It was with joyous surprise that I returned from Gaborone one afternoon to learn that Bafi was waiting in my room.

"Broken, she is! Just broken by your poor brother's passing-on," whispered aunt Chandiwana dramatically in the sitting room.

"She looks dreadful. I haven't ever seen her looking so bad. You don't think she's caught it, do you?"

"The doctor looked at all of us just after just after he died. He says we're all fine."

"Well," said aunt Chandiwana with relish, "your cousin certainly isn't fine. She looks as though she's going to pass on too. I'll bring you some tea as soon as I can."

She finished hastily, obviously intending to have another look at Bafi as soon as she could.

"No. That's all right. We won't want any," I told her softly, sensing that one thing Bafi would not want would be Aunt Chandiwana sitting on the bed with us for a nice harrowing re-enactment of the last few months. Bafi was terrible. She sat small and cowed, all life beaten out of her, a piece of helpless flotsam dressed in black. The papier-mâché suitcase was black as well.

"I've run away, Batjibilibili."

"Oh, Bafi!"

"I don't know what I'm going to do!"

"Bafi, honey, you'll be better. I promise you one day it will feel better. It won't hurt so much!"

I put my arms round her and hugged her. I smiled thinly to myself at my own words because, even though the grief of losing my brother, I had still not gotten over losing Ntungamili Madandume. When I had time to think about it, the hurt was still there. And Bafi's loss was so much more irrevocable, so completely and utterly final. Bafi would never see him again. She could not walk along the street and wonder if perhaps there might be a chance encounter or a message relayed from someone they both knew. He was lost to her ruthlessly and dreadfully. That's what death does to people. It steals love and honours sorrow.

"I'm going to have a baby," said Bafi timorously.

The breath left my lungs, and a sharp pain, as though I had been stuck in the stomach, lurched inside me. I heard the words, but they didn't make sense. Someone else had said them, or I had imagined them. Whatever Bafi had said it wasn't that.

"I'm going to have a baby," Bafi said again.

"I think I'm going to have it in November. I don't know. I'm not sure quite when because . . . you see . . . I'm too frightened to go to the doctor."

"But you can't be, Bafi. You can't be! You don't know what you're talking about."

Silent, uncrying tears ran down Bafi's face.

"He was so afraid, Batjibilibili. At night he was so afraid. And he needed me so much . . . so much. Even at the end...when he was too weak to move he liked me to hold him in his arms . . . just to lie and hold him while he cried."

Beneath the shock was a huge, aching admiration for Bafi, admiration and envy because Bafi had not, and could not, be persuaded from her chosen path. She had loved him to the exclusion of everything and everyone else. I tried to absorb the fact that Bafi had risked life and soul for a dying man when I had tried so hard, and failed, the previous summer to love ardent, healthy, fit and reliable Ntungamili, tried so hard and failed because a terrible reality at the moment stood between our bodies, obliterating choices, tearing asunder our hearts, turning a world of fantasy and wonderment into a labyrinthine of topsy-turvy emotions and discouragements. Bafi, unconcerned with questions of the future, or family, or even the question of catching the dread disease herself, had overwhelmingly succumbed to the needs of the man she loved.

"Oh, Bafi!" I said, believing at last.

"Only I can't stay here, in the village. I can't. I don't know how I'm going to tell them. And, I don't know what I'm going to do. You'll help me, won't you, Batjibilibili? You'll help me!"

"I'll help you. They'll have to know. You'll have to tell them, Bafi."

"What! Do you mean your mother and my mum and your dad too? I can't," and she began to sob.

"And, I can't ever stay in the village. You know what they are like, Batjibilibili. They'll never let me forget, and the child . . . Batjibilibili! You must be mad! Think about it. Just think about it. I want to keep the baby. I don't want it to be harmed or sent away. I want to keep the baby. Please, Batjibilibili, help me . . . You're the only one who knows what to do. Help me. What good is our friendship if you can't help me now? The mine disease killed a man we both loved. Let's help each other."

"We'll manage," I said, scotching hot tears streaming down my cheeks.

"We'll get a room or a small flat in Gaborone, and between the two of us we should be able to manage," I repeated myself with finality, my voice trembling.

In my heart I said, forgive me, Adam. The money you saved, the money that was meant for me, I'm going to have to use it. I don't need it as badly as Bafi does. From outside the door came the rattle of cups and Aunt Chandiwana's cheerful "Yoo-hoo!"

"For now you can stay live with us. My parents won't mind. And that will give us a chance to sort things out."

To her parents, Batjibilibili remained something of a stranger throughout much of her childhood, a strange mixture of sophistication and innocence, tall and slender, with handsome legs and a free swinging stride that attracted attention from people even before they had a chance to see her lovely face.

She had none of the psychology textbooks nervous awkwardness typical of most teenage girls. She was sure of herself. She was smooth and cool and good to look at. Her eyes were wide and dark brown and of the kind that her father, her mother and their friends had long learned to refer to as grave. Her smile was gay and artless. Her face was round and delicately plump, but under her high cheekbones, there were small, faint hollows, and when she was displeased or when she was being urged to do something she had decided not to do, her full lips would narrow down into a small, compressed knot of hard stubbornness, a circle of tiny furrows of annoyance, that came as a shock to the unprepared observer. Her fake blonde hair was so thick and long that her father urged her to have it cut, but she refused. She gave no reason.

One thing her parents learned early about their little girl was that she never gave reasons for her actions or her refusals. Her father always told his friends, with a smile, that she was a girl who, in addition to knowing her own mind, had a tremendous admiration for it. She was methodical and neat to a degree that annoyed even the meticulous housewifely instincts of her aunt Chandiwana, who nursed her from infancy, to youthful teenage-hood, after her own mother, Chandapiwa, had exasperatedly dumped her at her classroom door one fateful morning in a fit of temper and headed for the delights of city life never to return. Everything she possessed had its appointed place. Every minute of her day its scheduled use. In the Shangoyapalalas four-roomed house, she established herself early as a person who was to be neither crossed nor denied. In order to reach the school in plenty of time to be seated at her desk by seven o'clock in the morning, when the roll call started, Batjibilibili had to leave her home at six-thirty. In order to leave the home at six-thirty sufficiently well turned out to meet her own strict standards of personal appearance, she had to get up at five-thirty. In order to get up at five-thirty, she had to be asleep by nine o'clock the night before. The atmosphere of the whole household would be rendered unpleasant for an entire week or more, if her father and aunt, entertaining friends in the living room a bit later than usual, prevented Batjibilibili from falling asleep promptly at nine or her father should be accidentally in the bathroom at five-thirty in the morning when she came to the door. She would be surly for days afterwards. Most of the time, she did not bother to explain to her aunt or her father how they had offended her. They had to guess. In order to avoid friction, they found it simpler to adjust their lives to hers.

By the time she reached puberty, Batjibilibili had left her imprint on almost every inch of the Shangoyapalala household. In the bathroom she had her toothbrushes, her soap, her comb, her hairbrush, all laid out with almost geometric precision on the window sill over the tub. The left side of the towel rack was reserved for her. Once, after her father took a bath, he hung his towel on the left end of the rack without thinking and pushed Batjibilibili's towel over to the right. She did not talk to him for three days, until he found what was wrong. In the kitchen she had her own tumbler set in a wire cage over the sink. Nobody was permitted to use it, and she refused to drink from any other glass. The Shangoyapalala dishes did not come in sets. They had been accumulated over a period of years, odd pieces in different sizes and colors and patterns, picked up in various shops as resources permitted. Batjibilibili soon established her preference for a certain plate, a certain cup and saucer, certain spoons and forks. She refused to eat unless her food was served on, in, and with them.

She was very precise about the amount of work she would do in the house. On Sundays, from eleven in the morning to one in the afternoon, she helped her aunt clean the house and cook lunch. If her father or her aunt slept later than one o'clock on Sunday, Batjibilibili would do no cleaning that week. On weekdays, she limited her housework to her own bedroom, which she kept spotless. Her wardrobe was free from fripperies as a soldier's knap-sack. Her closet was almost forbiddingly neat. Her drawers, with their piles of handkerchiefs, underwear, stockings, looked like carefully laid-out designs in white and pink file. Her taste was good, and she had an instinct for styles that would last. She was seldom taken in by the endlessly swirling fashion trends. She bought for years rather than for the eye. As a result, her choices were all simple in design, and simplicity suited her beauty.

She bought little, but she tried to buy good things, and she made them last by the sort of care that a fanatical fisherman might lavish on his tackle. The one thing that Batjibilibli was even more fussy about than her personal appearance or the arrangement of her toothbrushes, was money. The purchase of something a little expensive; a dress, a coat, a hat, was a matter of mental contemplation and negotiations that went on for weeks. Once, when her aunt presented her with an exotic large bottle of lotion as a Christmas present, she refused it coldly on the ground that it would accustom her to an extravagance she could not afford. She had better uses of her money, she said. When her father or aunt, annoyed by some act of unnecessary thriftiness, complained about this unwavering predilection to parsimony and wondered loudly why she was so desperate about saving money, Batjibilibili would smile wisely and say, with a casual shrug, that she had learned only one thing of importance during her childhood in Naledi village: the person with money in the bank was the person who slept well. Even though she smiled with assurance when she said it, there was in her voice a small hint of tenseness, a sort of faint terror, as though she was convinced that what she was doing was right, but she was afraid there wouldn't be enough time in which to do it.

Batjibilibili's treatment of the young men who were obviously mad about her, was at first a source of amusement, then puzzlement, and finally worries to her aunt, Chandiwana, and her father, John. At first they enjoyed the highhanded manner in which she dismissed the young men of the village, devoting herself to tasks they deemed important for her future like schooling and sports while other girls concentrated their time and energy in trivial pursuits, damaging their young bodies and future, things like unprotected sex, taking drugs and marrying men old enough to be their fathers. After a while, it began to puzzle and even disturb them. During her term of study at the University of Cape Town, in South Africa, she had accumulated a bank balance that was her own secret as to size. At graduation, she was almost twenty-three, she was still unmarried, and she was still treating the young men of the neighborhood, as her aunt put it, like so much dirt under her feet. Her parents, including her mother who had lately reinterred her life, became definitely worried. It dawned upon them that there were many nooks and crannies on the girl's mind that they had not fathomed and probably would never explore. But she came from the same world they had come from. She was subjected to the same unwritten rules. To her, as well as to her father's parents and their neighbors and their countrymen, marriage was the most important event in a girl's life. Why was Batjibilibili so careless with the many opportunities that were tossed in her path? Batjibilibili told them, in the icily polite tones that always came as a shock from her sweet innocent face, to mind their own business. Her parents were insulted. But they had been insulted many times before by Batjibilibili. Their feelings were soon smoothed down, but their worry about Batjibilibili's unmarried state mounted. For her part, Batjibilibili continued her way of doing things with a sense of caution verging on the point of punctiliousness. In the end, everybody would come to deeply regret this unhappy state of affairs. But, who could have foretold the future that fate had designed for their remarkable daughter?

"How is your job? You don't look happy. Is your life all right?"

"I'm tired, that's all. Things are hectic here. No time for respite, not even the slightest moment."

"Augh, modern women. Why don't they call you a celebrity? That may make you happy, I should think?"

"Mum, I'm not a celebrity. I'm a teacher."

"But everybody calls that loudmouth, what's her name now? Your old friend who works for Radio Botswana a celebrity, and she's not even a graduate!

"She's good at what she does, Mum. Also, we move in different circles. Her lifestyle is different from mine."

"I think you underestimate yourself. That little bitch is a school dropout. Some of the students you taught are already celebrities. They are rich, and very happy, I should think."

"I don't know about that. The word celebrity really means nothing. I have my own way of doing things. I look at the world, and life, in a different way. From the look of things, I don't even think those people are rich. I don't even think they are happy. But again I might be wrong. A few years from now, will they still be celebrities?"

"I don't know; you are the teacher, you should know."

"I know nothing about their lives. Now let's talk about you, Mum. What is this I hear about you running for a council seat?"

"Well, I just want to sit on it."

"Really, Mum? Shame on you."

"I'm dead serious. What do you think councillors do?"

"I don't ever think about it. It's none of my business."

"Well, then let me enlighten you. They just sit on their seats and nest like birds. It's quiet a lucrative business without any fuss at all."

"Is that what it's all about? Food and nesting? Is that it?"

"Well, I just think women should make themselves more visible in society, and going into politics is one way of doing it. I mean it's an easier way of getting to the top and making a better contribution to public life."

"And how do you intend on doing that? It's a men's world out there. Have you thought about that?"

"I'll campaign like everybody else, take my chances, and see what happens. If I don't make it, too bad. If I win, happy Christmas!"

"The men won't allow you to win, though they will not mind much if you eat dust."

"Oh, let them do what they like, the party has set a quota for women's political participation, and that's what matters. They'll support us."

"Words and empty talk. Why can't you see an illusion when it starts drifting your way?"

"Because it's an illusion . . . ha . . . ha . . . haaaa!"

"Very funny. Now listen to me. Men have far too many ways of dominating women. They are also greedy and shameless cheaters. I still have to see a man who believes in fair play, and I have been around for God knows how long. I know that you socialize, dine, party, work and consult with all these men in all sorts of ways, and they know you in and out: all your secrets are public knowledge. Men are worse gossipers than women. They even have resource centers for peddling lies, falsehoods, and malicious gossip about other people, their little clubs, and of courses, pubs, stag parties and institutional boardrooms. These people are setting you up for a big fall, and of course, public humiliation and embarrassment. Do you want your little secrets and weaknesses to be known to the whole world? Are you prepared for public denigration, denunciation, and degradation? First, they will bankrupt you. A community librarian does not make much money. Then, they will take you to the cleaners, wash your dirty linen in public, unmask you, and undress you in public. Then, they'll steal the vote from you in broad daylight. Finally, they'll laugh at you, behind your back, of course. When you're down and out, they'll dangle another little carrot, an even better quota for women's participation in politics—catch another gullible woman still intent on making silly mistakes, humiliate her, get a good laugh and so on. Women never learn."

"Well, I agree my generation made lots of mistakes, conceding a playground for all things in the world to men. But one would think a time for corrections has now arrived, with more young women well educated like you but . . ."

"Mother, don't be such a dupe. Men are well educated, too. They know what's good for *them*."

"Ahaaa! That's exactly what we used to think, that our men were decent, considerate, fair and compassionate. That they knew what was good for *them*, including their women and children. Look at me now. Look at you! Where is your father?"

"Oh, I see. Now we are back to Father. Mum, when'll you get it into your head that he was always depressed?"

"Depressed, eh? There is a meaningless word if ever there was one. Celebrity sounds much better. I hate this language of convenience. Uneducated people don't get depressed, Bafi. The word does not even exist in our language. There is no room for it in our culture. Our people do get poor, become grumpy and disgruntled; that much I grant. They don't get depressed! That's simply a convenient way of doing nothing about their troubles. Now, take your father, for example . . ."

"Can we talk about something else? I didn't mean to bring up this matter . . ."

"No! No way. Hear me out. Don't fear the truth like your father. The man left me for a woman half your age. We struggled for a good thirty years to establish that small business. Now look at me. I live alone. He has got the love of his life, friendships and companionship. Well, *depression* did him a great deal of good, didn't it?"

"Mum, this is not the place for . . . I mean, really. Let's talk about other things. I can understand your disappointment. But, really, men are changing. Even you can't deny that."

"I hope so. I really do. What happened to that nice lawyer you used to date? I hear he's defending that terrible murderer for free. He must be a rich man, now. Didn't he say he was leaving his wife?"

"Mother, I don't want to pick an argument with you. The relationship didn't work. These things happen."

"He is still with her, then?"

"There's a still trouble in their marriage. Not long ago, she tried to kill herself."

"For him? For that good-for-nothing . . . God gives us strength. What a world?"

"Maybe, she was just unhappy, you know, *depressed*."

"Don't you think the world would be a better place without that word?"

"It's not a word, Mum. It's a disease, a clinical condition, a really terrible disease, Mum."

"A disease, eh? I think it should be eradicated. We can all do without it. The UN must do something about it. I wouldn't be surprised if it wasn't this disease that's driving us all into politics and certain ruin. What happened to courage and realism? Even distinguished soldiers coming from war claim to have terrible mental disorders, an excuse to spit on people, insult them, rape, loot and murder for fun. Look what's happening in Zimbabwe! Every war veteran is depressed and a mad hatter, and there are millions of them. Robert Mugabe is so depressed he kills at will and claims political madness just to circumvent retribution, and everybody calls him a hero. Father of the nation. Really, what next?"

"Mum, I've got a headache. I think I'll sleep for a while."

"Just like your father, you hate ugly facts don't you? You can't face the truth even when it's staring you square in your eyes."

"Leave Father out of this. That woman is giving him a hard time. She's . . . oh . . . why bother?"

"Good for him, the rotten bastard."

"Would you take him back if he wanted to come home?"

"No. I learned my lesson. I don't want his beer farts between my clean sheets anymore. Not at my age, thank you."

"Mother! That's so gross."

"Ja. I earned it. Call it freedom, not grossness. It's as good as a graduate certificate."

"You really hate him, don't you?"

"No. I want him to suffer. That'll make him a better person."

"He's has suffered enough. She treats him like dirt. The sad thing is he knows it and can't do anything about it. He's too honourable to break the law. He fears the shamelessness of it."

"Well, still, he's not welcome in my house. He's free to join me in the grave when I die. Then we won't have to lie to each other or trouble each other. In death we are all truly equal and answerable to a higher power. No nonsense about depression and all those meaningless words they teach in school today."

"Maybe you should talk to him. Hear his side of the story."

"No way. It's none of my business what happens to him. It's he who discarded our way of dealing with troubles. He and I belong to a different world, you know. When we were growing up, secrets were not treasured like you people do today. If a husband was not strong enough to do a certain job he told his wife. She would brew beer or just cook food so that her husband could raise a work team to do the job. If he had problems in bed he talked to his father or the uncles who recommended appropriate treatment or a good and trusted healer to help him. If he was not happy with his wife, he could sleep with her sister with the consent of all parties, including the parents. He did not just abandon his wife and children. There were even men who wanted to sleep with other men even though they were married. That too could be arranged. There were even "aunts" who never married even though they were terribly beautiful and often stronger than most men in society but lived with each other for life raising village orphans. Everybody knew why they behaved this way but left them alone. I can tell you those women were always together, thick as thieves, and enjoying the knowledge of life like everybody else in the village. They had access to property, markets, public office and all the ordinary neighborhood relationships and social connections. In other words, there were no cases of absolute entry and departures in married life. That's how our culture worked. It was accommodating, sympathetic, and compassionate. Your father chose to be a modern man, to do things his own way, the modern way. I am not surprised he is now trying to use empty words like depression to solve his personal troubles. He's a hollow man, a husk, all the grain is gone, and you want me to take him back? What a joke. Do you think I'm a fool?"

"But, Mother . . ."

"Child, just concern yourself with your life. Think about the future. If you need help talk to me. Mollycoddling social losers and worrying about all that rubbish will not take you anywhere. I want you to live real life, in a real world, to dance to the rhythms of life in your own terms but still mindful of tomorrow and the many more days to come. If you want to go into politics, do it out of conviction, not because the time seems convenient to do so. Don't be unprincipled and reckless like your father. Think before you act. Don't rush into things you don't understand. Don't do things because other people expect them of you. Do things because you care and you are truly committed. Only that way will you find happiness in life."

"What about you? Are you happy, Mother?"

"What a question, child. I'm too old to worry about happiness. I'm not a fool, and that's happiness enough."

This conversation took place between Bafi and her mother three years after she and Batjibilibili had moved into a small flat in Maruapula. Her baby had been born dead. Batjibilibili, already budding into a restless social butterfly in higher Gaborone social circles, could not take part in the conversation; she lay supine in the couch, suffering from a terrible hangover and a brutally broken heart. The weekend orgy had turned out to be a disaster for her. The usual crowd had turned up, all packed into the dance floor. Ndofilani Tapela had reckoned that a good bender would be the best way to start their weekend and was feeling really high when the party got under way. But he had reckoned without Ntungamili's sudden lapses into melancholy whenever Batjibilibili was present. Ntungamili and Batjibilibili had been knocking around together again for some months, on what Batjibilibili liked to call a "none-heavy basis". But it was pretty obvious to anyone with eyes that, while outwards accepting Batjibilibili's stance, Ntungamili had really gone gaga on the fiercely gregarious and outgoing girl with the tight jeans, artificial flowing black hair and, Ndofilani had to admit, not unscrewable body. At parties, she would always be right there in the middle of everything, while Ntungamili, beer can in hand, followed her around, trying to keep pace, eventually ending up sprawled on a chair, pissed, morose and silent. Curiously at the end of the evening, Batjibilibili and Ntungamili would invariably leave together.

Last night's party had been different. Ndofilani had been chatting up one of the girls from the village but getting nowhere, when Batjibilibili asked him to dance. His first reaction had been to say: what about Ntungamili, you bitch? Or do you just want to see him squirm? But tonight was different, Batjibilibili seemed to be inviting and welcoming in her coquettish way. Also, Ntungamili's behavior was detached and strange, rather restrained and, besides, Ndofilani felt really, really horny. He badly wanted to be laid. Soon they were both locked together in the middle of the floor, bumping and grinding to the Congolese music. It was obvious that Batjibilibili had been waiting for this occasion, Ndofilani felt. She was laughing as she pressed closer to him. But at the end of the party she left with a total stranger, a tall high cheek-boned artist working as a part-time teacher at Gaborone Secondary School.

It was the most terrible feeling she had ever had. This wasn't like the times other boys had kissed her in the cars, not even like the time she had kissed boys at the back of the cinema at Capitol House. This was a terrible, fierce drowning, a pressure of their bodies, mouths, hands, of their faces moving frenziedly against each other, and of his muttered, feverish declaration of love, a terrifying madness. They were in a large room, which was lit very dimly from a distant street light shining through the lace curtains. She could just make out his face; his expression was one of complete, ungovernable emotion. He gasped, and her dress was unbuttoned and pushed away from her shoulders, and she felt his mouth, his hands, his face burning into her body, kissing her . . . kissing her hair and neck and breasts. She felt wetness fall on to her shoulders, and she saw that he was crying.

"Beautiful, my sweetheart! Oh! So beautiful!"

And she knew she was beautiful. She freed her arms from her dress and raised them over her head, and she saw in her mind's eye that now she really, really was beautiful, standing there naked in the presence of this frenzied Lothario. She knew her hair was soft by the way he kissed it. She knew her shoulders, and her throat and breasts were smooth and lovely. His lips were very heavy, very warm, and they were trembling. The trembling spread to his hand and then to the rest of his body, and every time he kissed her he murmured, "Love, oh, sweetheart" into her flesh. She found she was capable of things she had not believed she could do—she was able to undress with grace, with a seductive, gently movement that turned her full body into that of a lush, wild creature. She was able to smile at him, without shyness or humility, so that her smile was an enticement, an invitation. She was able to lift her hair away from her shoulders, stretching her arms, arching her body, feeling music and emotion and power flowing from her, capturing and ensnaring him, he who was so much older, stronger, more powerful, more worldly, more experienced and much, much more wild than herself.

Her gracefulness made him, in turn, clumsy and awkward. He fumbled with shaking hands at his shirt. He was reduced to a supplicating passion that was only aware of the need to capture her, to subdue and tame her to his own emotional needs. When his arms locked around her, when his chest met her breast, there was a quick in-drawing of breath—a soft cry at the conflict of flesh between them. He drew her down beside him, and his body was as she had pictured it would be, full and strong and very smooth. Her eyes had grown accustomed to the dim light from the street. Over his trembling shoulders, she could see the fantasy shapes of the room, the heavy furniture, the ugly china and ornaments, the photographs standing on a table besides the huge bed, a photograph that was just close enough for her to see . . . he sensed her sudden withdrawal from him, sensed that she was no longer completely submerged in the desire that had carried both of them this far.

"Batjibilibili?"

She didn't answer, but she was quiet and so still that he knew the moment when he must have loved her had gone.

"Batjibilibili?"

He turned to follow the direction of her gaze. She was looking at the photograph, the big one of his wife, children and himself. She became burningly aware of where she was, of what she was doing. Her gracefulness vanished. With ugly movements she tried to put clothes on and hide her body from him at the same time.

"No! Batjibilibili, no!"

He struck her violently across the face, then encircled her neck with his claw-like hands and pounded her head back and forth on the pillow. She struggled hard, fought fiercely, and uttered the shrillest cry of her life.

"Quiet, Batjibilibili!" he screamed, "Quiet, I say!"

Terror paralyzed her, made her limbs uncontrolled and dead. She tried to think of something, anything she could say that would calm him, but she knew it was too late. He had gone past the point of reclamation. He was immersed in his terrible, mad dream. His fingers pounding her head back and forth and the space between them grew tighter and tighter, smaller and smaller. She thought he was really going to strangle her, but he stopped just as she was about to lose consciousness, and then he began slapping her, poking and jabbing at her body to bring her round again.

"Now you will do this!"

He said obscenely. Weakly, feeble, not understanding anything and no longer able to think rationally, she began to cry.

"Batjibilibili! Do what I say!"

"Leave me alone, Godfrey! Please leave me alone."

She screamed. Hands encircled her throat again, blows and kicks rained on her body. She tried to fight him, to push him over, to hit his face or his groin, but he was possessed—his strength was fanatical and inhuman. One hand foisted into her hair and jerked her head round. "Do this! Do as I say. You must do as I say!"

"Leave me alone!"

"I'll kill you!"

He was clawing at her. The hand not holding her head down was clawing at her body, violating it, hurting, sending shafts of excruciating pain through her.

"I hate you, Batjibilibili! And unless you do as I say, I will kill you!" The pain was unbearable. She felt as though she were being savaged by a mad dog.

"Will you do this?"

"Yes," she sobbed.

She would do anything to make it end. Anything to have it over, have the nightmare finished, the pain stopped, the horror ended. He did everything he asked. She let her body be abused and treated obscenely in his wife's bedroom. She tried not to know what was happening to her. She tried not to know what she was doing. She screamed when he hurt her too badly, and she heard him scream also, but that was a sound born of ecstasy, of mad delight that had satisfied the terrible sick need in him. The point came when the desire and pleasure he experienced could ascend no more. His strength did not abate but he stopped torturing her, and then she felt him striving for the final culmination of his manhood—the ultimate act between loving men and women that should be the seal of unity and instead was nothing more to her than disgusted relief. He screamed one last time, called her name again, and then fell limp over her body. She lay shuddering and sick, knowing that the worst part was over but recalling that for her time would continue to play out the final act of her humiliation.

When she started feeling better, Batjibilibili phoned Satjilombe, one of her many upward mobile and older friends. She just wanted to talk to someone. If she told Bafi about her terrible experience last night, Bafi would rush to the police. That was just how she was, impetuous, stubborn and protective to the point of madness. He invited her to come over in the afternoon.

Batjibilibili could not believe her luck. At last things were turning around for her. For that, she profusely thanked her lucky stars. For a long time she thought she had lost him for ever. They had met some months ago then went their separate ways because of his work commitments. And now they were together again. She turned on her side, careful not to disturb him, and felt pure pleasure mixed with some apprehension, watching the heavy features with their noble nose, the thick greying hair and the massive brow of cabinet Minister Satjilombe Gudogulu, almost as if she hoped to stare right through his skull and into its thoughts. She got up, seeing herself in the mirror and taking her handkerchief and wiping at the sweat on his narrow face, her eyes looking into his eyes as she forced herself to consider what she should do, and what she shouldn't do, and what he was going to do. What did a woman have to do to keep a man who mattered? If only Satjilombe had been just a teacher, or the vice president of a small company, someone the size she could have a handle on, a really tight iron grip. But Jesus—a Cabinet Minister! This was a little god. The shrine to the Bitch Goddess: Success. The Mother Lode. Bond, security and surety combined. She picked up her doll, a childhood present from Aunt Chandiwana.

"Hello, black beauty," she said, affectionately to the rugged and careworn thing, "we've fucked around a great deal you and I. And always messed up things. Here is our last chance in this Goddamned life!" She always said that when she spent a night with a stranger, especially first thing in the morning, because the doll was old, and it was faithful, a really true friend. On a bad day she'd say other things, talk to her like she'd talk to a horse, because there wasn't ever anyone else she could talk to, or there hadn't been for the last many months. Bafi had started drifting away long ago, soon after the kid had died, and Ntungamili had gone out of her life three months later. He had moved to Francistown in search of green pastures at the gold mines not long after she had met him there in a thunderstorm. Ntungamili had always been a kindly person, the only man in the world, the real one, the true one, with his intellectual mien and the lovely way he said of their love, "Killing me softly," just for her, "killing me softly, my lovely B-girl." But it wasn't a happy meeting. If anything, it was a mess. They had drifted far too apart.

Batjibilibili was a loner now and talked to her doll. They said it was the first of a sign that she would end up in a mental asylum, but she didn't care. She had to talk to somebody, or something, or she'd end up in a mental asylum, that was her way she coped. The air was quiet down here, and because of the way her own voice sounded, talking to nobody, it felt very funny. She could hear the wind again, crying softly out there, and had to talk again, shivering just once and unexpectedly in the warm air. Batjibilibili Shangoyapalala, she said to herself in her mind, if you play the cards right this time, play them right just this once in your life, you might hit the jackpot. She sat in the bed a long time with her head resting on her knees, or it seemed like a long time, but it was probably only a couple of minutes.

Far away she could hear the whine of the wind, but down where she was, it was very quiet. She sat listening to how quiet it was. She blew out a breath, laughing. "It's just too much!" she thought. She watched Satjilombe, thinking how alive he looked, even in his sleep, and wondering what it is that attracted her to him. Was it some kind of flame? Or some kind of vibration? Would she lose it just as easy as had been the case with the other men? He was moving his hand, bringing it out of the blanket and covering his eyes, as if there were light in there. He lay like

that for a long time. She sat there with her thoughts drifting through the
ebb and flow of consciousness, and her fears dragged her, time after time,
awake. Often she saw Ntungamili, looking at him as if for the first time
in her life and this time seeing him for what he was. And because she had
never looked at him like this, his own face was strange and she couldn't
recognize it, and she wondered how they could have lived so long together
as companionable strangers. These were the images, drifting through the
coming and going of consciousness, that she could not take, and this was
why she had drawn her hand across her eyes in an unreasoning attempt to
shut out the sight.

Boy, what a break! It suddenly occurred to her that events that matter
most in people's lives are essentially occasioned by circumstance.
Something she never really thought about. It terrified her how the weight
of circumstance bears infinitely more significantly upon our lives than
does the weight of events. She was painfully conscious of the horror of
being trapped by circumstance, a horror as illuminatingly terrifying as, as
claustrophobic as, being trapped by bars; the terror of permanent
inconvenience, the threadbare poverty of elementary reality. She lay
listening to the wind, feeling alone, even with the Minister of the State
right there in the room, feeling more alone than she had ever felt before
in the whole of her life, because she was going into something so new it
had her scared. She thought about the man lying there beside her, about
what she should do right, and what she should not do, and what she was
going to do to keep this one relationship going. The whole thing whirled
in her mind. No clear picture presented itself to her tortured mind. There
were still things she should not know and would have to find out. May be
she had got it wrong.

She imagined he had just been setting her up for a lay, stealing
something from a kid, sort of. Did the whole thing hang on sex? The
whole of the beautiful goddamn scary thing? No answer presented itself,
and she sat there lonely and afraid, and hoping, casting and interrogating
herself, wondering what the hell she was doing here, with a strange man
in the middle of the night with nerves in her stomach, how the hell she got
here, and how it happened. She had not been ready for this. She thought:
sometimes people do things they never believed they could do, and this
time it is her. It was funny because she almost did not care how things
would turn out.

There was a kind of numbness in her mind, as if this thing was so big
that it had sort of blown a fuse to stop her from going raving mad. She
wondered if she was big enough to handle this thing. At school, the girls
called it joining the racket. Large sums of money. Private means.
Substantial income. Wheeler-dealing. Substantial shareholding. Financial
brokerage. Stocks in big companies. Heavy duty. That's what the girls

called dating rich old men. They never called it love. They never called it a relationship. It was business. A transaction. The words tumbled in her mind. And all the time she felt afraid, her heavy lids were drooping in private defeat. Her thoughts returned to the new feeling, a feeling that stood for something, a feeling that stood for everything. Nice manners, politeness, going out in the night and doing things together. This bigness of even things inconsequential was the most exciting thing to happen to her. I have had a lot of chances, she thought, the kind of chances everybody gets as they go along in life, but I've always lost out, never came up with anything bigtime. It's always been too late, or some guy has let me down. But this time . . . this time I cannot lose. And this time it is the jackpot. This time God and the magnificent fates have offered me a certain reprieve, possible acquittal, depending on how much humanity there is in Satjilombe's makeup.

People will talk, say my God is Mammon. So what? They can go on seeing things in me that aren't there. I am out for a good time, while I can get it! Why bother about senseless talk by self-destroyed, morally crippled, spiritually embittered and good-for-nothing rumourmongers? The wind cried past the building, and water gushed along hidden pipes. She wondered how it felt to run a lot of people's lives, to be useful to your fellow citizens, to become a legend in your time, as man of law, a man of justice, a man of the people. She lay on the bed feeling a kind of awe for herself. She was not scared any more like she had been all through the night: the thing she was sharing was gathering speed, and she could feel the power of it, like the first time snuck into her father's car and drove it a few feet and realized the terrific power that was in her, just to be doing this, making this huge thing move along the ground. And she could feel the thing that she had never been able to explain in words, but she could call it surprise, the kind that caught her breath, surprise that when she really made a pitch for something so big that she could not ever dream of getting it, she got it, just like that, because this time, for the first time, she had dared to dream. She had to dream. She had to dream it first, then she went out and got it and it was yours, hard and safe in your goddamn fist where no one could take it away.

Surprise and something else, a kind of rage she could not help feeling when realizing just how big these bastards were, the ones at the top, the men like Satjilombe, a guy she would have to wait in line for a whole day to see, just to get near, if they ever let her get near at all. They were so big that people could not imagine they were made of flesh and blood, but if she knew the way, if she saw the chance, she could bring them down like a demolition squad brought down whole buildings. Play it my way, Mr. Minister, or I will bust you, she thought to herself, smiling. She could easily use her own brand of intuition to turn things her own way. She knew that people like him, venal and opportunists as they were, would do anything to avoid public shame. She felt a kind of rage, not because it was so easy to secure his cooperation and partnership, but because these God Almighty bastards made it look so difficult.

She lay on the big bed with her nerves secretly galvanized by awe, surprise and rage, winding her watch and listening to the sounds in the building. She could still feel the insistent beat of her heart as she pondered these things. She was aware of strangeness, a slow cold feeling that normal life was going on its routine way, while some other kind of life, some other passing of time, was secretly proceeding in a place she had never visited—the place where Satjilombe, at this moment, was taking her. For a long time, she had lived by the odd philosophy that the attitude of the mind towards any event must be appropriate to what it is, not to what it might be. Otherwise she should find herself living through unreasoning hopes and fears instead of calmly coping with life as it comes. Now it was time to abandon this reckless surrender to fate. It was time to move on to better things through sheer will and personal determination.

She felt mean and knew people like him only had contempt for her: they were out of her class, way out, and that was funny, how she had him in her hands, could break him if she wanted, yet she was still outclassed, and there was nothing she could do about it. But that was all right. She did not want to hurt him. She did not want the poor bastard to suffer, that was not her idea. She did not want to hurt either of them, him or that classy-looking lover of his in the mansion at Broadhurst. In the magazine and newspapers, she looked like an ex-model or a showgirl or something but with plenty of style. They were just kind of temporary associates, she and the Minister, doing a thing together, looking after each other, in a trying and turbulent world. There wasn't any need for anybody to get hurt. She learned over the bed and stared at the big ragged looking face of Satjilombe, not hating him, not liking him, and just seeing him as another human being on his way through life. They needed each other.

He felt warmth for her, a kind of gratitude, not because of the sex thing but because he needed her comfort, the young smell of her, the remaining aura of her mother's womb, and the way she was excited by what he was doing, without asking too much about it. Their little association would pour thousands of clams and opportunities right in her lap and for the first time in her life she would be a winner. This association was going to make the difference between spending the rest of her life in squalid misery and setting herself up in a nice little place in the northern suburb and letting the rest of the world go screw itself.

Jesus, no wonder her nerves were shot. Here was the chance of a life time. And it did not bear thinking too much about. The very thought of it was maddening. The only thing was to think about something else. The Minister had asked her if she had any friends, and she could not think of any, and she had never realized it before. It occurred to her she did not know what to say because she was not used to thinking about people the way they really were, the way they got on with living, like they are meant to, able to do things right. She felt a wave of something like self-contempt because Satjilombe was perfectly free to kick her out of here and he knew it. But he could not, could he? He needed her.

For an absurd moment she began wanting to laugh. In fact, a secret laughter began bubbling up inside her, and the whisper came hissing through her teeth, "Oh . . . Jesus," she felt like letting it come out of her chest in long quiet jerks, "Oh, no," she thought desperately, "I think I better start looking around for something ordinary to think about because if I think about the other thing I really do not know what would happen. I have to take it slowly, sort of ease my mind into it so there would not be too much shock. That way lies insanity, pure madness." She shut her eyes tight and started dreaming. Seeing the sky in her mind's eye, feeling perplexed how big it was today, how really enormous, the roof of a whole goddamn world, she had never noticed it before, a blaze of dazzling blue flung from horizon to horizon and all hers, all her own to walk under, the laughter coming out of her in long steady jerks as she walked under the roof of her whole new world and had to shut her eyes because it dazzled her, having to look up again and taking a deep breath as the last of the laughter came out and died away and left her weak and spent with it, her legs slowly stopping till she stood alone in the midst of a wide road and the rising heat of the sun thinking, "Batjibilibili, you've made it. You've made it. You've done it at last, girl."

Satjilombe, a nominated Member of Parliament and Minister of Home Affairs, hung up the phone. The door from the lavatory opened, and Batjibilibili came out. She wore his bathrobe over her blue slip, and she carried his nightgown. She watched Satjilombe replace the receiver on the hook.

"Who were you talking to?"

"I was just . . ."

He stopped and felt his face grow warm. The night before he had learned something that surprised him: he could grow angry with her. Now he knew with certainty something he had really known for three months: he could not lie to her.

"I was talking to your mother."

"Your drunken friend?"

"Batjibilibili! That's not the way to talk about your own mother."

"What does she want?"

"She wanted to know how you feel."

"How I feel? Wonders will never end. How in the world of hell . . ."

"I told her last night you weren't feeling well."

"Why did you tell her that?"

"I had to explain why you didn't want to come and have a drink in her house."

She opened her mouth, and her eyes creased angrily, but she didn't say a word. She threw the nightgown on the unmade bed and picked up a box of face tissues.

"You'll do me a big favor, Satjilombe, if you don't go telling people lies about me. It's okay for you to lie about yourself. It suits your position, comes with the job, so to speak. I don't want to have anything to do with that woman. You either. And I don't want you lying about it."

"She is my friend. She was very nice to me when I came in this neighborhood. I don't see why I should . . .?"

"It isn't necessary for you to see. I see. And I say we are not going to have anything to do with her."

"But why? You don't know anything about her. And she happens to be your mother no matter what you think and feel about her. All the politicians and many bigwigs in this place know her very well and speak well of her."

"Satjilombe, for God's sakes, let's not . . ."

"What's the matter, Batjibilibili? What's happened? Ever since last night you've been . . . I don't know, sort of acting strange."

She straightened up, drew a deep breath, and smiled. It was not a good smile.

"Nothing's the matter," she said calmly. "And nothing's happened. Now you go up to the lounge and wait for me. I want to finish dressing and straighten up the bedroom, and then we'll have some breakfast."

"All right."

"Wait a minute."

He looked back, his hand on the knob of the door.

"What's that?"

"What's what?"

She pointed to his wrist. He took his hand off the door and held it up. "This?"

"Yes. What is it?"

"A wrist watch. Your mother gave it to me last night."

"She did what?"

She came towards him. She stopped in the middle of the room.

66

"What did she give it to you for?"

"My birthday. She said she wouldn't be around when my birthday came next month, so she wanted me to have it now."

"That's very nice of her."

She didn't sound as though she meant it was very nice.

"What did you talk about?"

"With her?"

"Yes."

"Nothing. Just about things."

"What things?"

"I don't know. The watch. My birthday. Things like that. It's not a regular watch. It has all sorts of things in it. Look, over here. It tells you how far you walked. And a stop watch, this thing, here. Tells you how long it takes to do something, like running a hundred meters or so."

"Or make love for a second?" she said sarcastically.

Then she laughed shrilly, stunning him into a profound silence and bewilderment.

"I'm sure it's very nice."

She continued giggling. She was back at the lavatory door, picking a tissue from the slit in the box.

"Go on to the lounge now and wait for me. I won't be long."

The door slammed behind her. Satjilombe felt foolish with his wrist watch dangling in the air. Make love for one second, my God! What could she mean? He felt inadequate and embarrassed. He dropped his arm and went out of the bedroom and walked to the lounge. He wasn't very fond of his young lover at that moment, a feeling that disturbed him. He looked around the lounge. The large room was empty, except for a Zimbabwean housemaid in uniform who was sitting on one of the couches along the wall, playing with the short length of a rope. He walked along the room to one of the windows. There was no sun, and the sky was oily gray. He was still angry because of the argument with Batjibilibili, which didn't seem like an argument at first, and the sight on the dull-gray sky did not make him feel better. It wasn't so much that he didn't know what had got into her, or that overnight, in fact, in one week, she seemed to have changed completely from the girl he had known for three months, or even that he resented the way she was ordering him around. What burned him up was the series of remarks and answers he should have made to her at the time but didn't think of until now. He turned from the window and walked across the lounge to a table of newspapers and magazines.

"They are all old," the housemaid said.

"Last week's *Reporter* and last month's *Guardian*. All of them are old."

67

He looked up at her. She seemed to be Batjibilibili's age, although she could have been a little younger. Sixteen, he figured out, maybe fifteen. She was short and round faced, rather on the plump side. Her voice was husky, sexy and very attractive too. By some artwork wonder, her hair was clipped close and was held so firmly in her scalp that it stood up straight all over her head, like a brand new expensive hairbrush with shining black bristles. Satjilombe didn't like the way she sat slouching back in the middle of the couch, fooling with the ends of the rope.

"Are they?" he said.

"How do you know?"

"I looked at them. All of them are old. I mean the whole lot."

"There may be a few new ones," he said stubbornly.

"You can't . . ."

"All old. I looked."

"It doesn't matter," he said with injured dignity.

"There are a few here I missed."

"Go on, let's see," the maid said cheerily.

Satjilombe gave her a long glance, patting the fine moustache of perspiration on his upper lip, and then nodded.

"That girl in your bedroom. What she told me last night. Is it true?"

"Yes," he said in a slow voice.

"It's true."

The admission she had wanted him to make did not help her. Now she did not know what to say.

"But you told me . . . you said . . ."

"I know what I said."

"I thought you meant what you said. You promised. Now all my friends have moved on to South Africa and England and you want to get rid of me?"

"Well, you want to be paid all the time and . . ."

"We agreed I had to work so that your friends would not get you into trouble. I've stuck to my side of the deal and now this . . ."

"I'm not beholden to you in any way."

He could feel his voice going up. He tried to control it, but he couldn't. She looked straight into his eyes. His voice stopped. He wanted to drop his glance, but he couldn't do that either. He could feel his eyes beginning to close slightly, and he wondered stupidly if it was anger that was narrowing them so badly.

"Satjilombe, do you love me?" she said suddenly.

He stared at her.

"Do I..."

"Yes?"

"You?"

68

"Yes," she said.

"Do you?"

He was thinking about so many things at once that he could follow any of them, but he knew this: he didn't have to think about the answer to that question.

"Sure I do."

"Then will you do me a favor?"

"What?"

"Get rid of her. She will be the ruin of you. Don't ask me any questions. Just do it. Now. Today."

He didn't answer. There was a long pause.

"All right," he said finally, in a whisper.

"Sure."

She left the couch and went to him. They hugged. She let out a small gasp and folded him in her arms and kissed his cheek. He could hear her heart pounding against him, going so hard and fast that it made his chest rustle, but he felt nothing, neither pleasure nor sadness. He didn't even feel her lips when she kissed him again. It was as though for a moment or two he were dead. He had no way of knowing that all at once, in a single moment, he had grown older than all the years of his life that stretched ahead would ever make him. He felt nothing at all. She let go of him, slowly, trembling, and she was experiencing the strange, blinding shock that comes with the first realization that someone you love has betrayed you.

"All right," he said without hearing his own words.

"I will get rid of her."

"I don't believe you," she said.

"I think we should come to some financial arrangement, you and I. South Africa's just around the border, and it's not going anywhere. I wish you luck."

Satjilombe was the Minister of Home Affairs at Government Enclave. That, in itself, was not dangerous. What changed the world beyond all dreams was the fact that he looked like a Minister of Home Affairs. Ntungamili might have taken proper action if the Minister had been the owner of a large, square chin, flashing eyes, flat and flaring nose and broad shoulders. As it was, Satjilombe defied that description and some more. Ntungamili found himself staring over a huge mahogany desk at a mild-mannered individual, whose faded brown eyes looked at him wistfully from either side of a low-bridge button noise, somewhat watery and bespectacled. He distinctly felt he was staring at a man in hiding, an impression further buttressed by a peculiar conservative middle-class costume that adorned the Minister's body. Satjilombe said pleasantly, "And now, what can I do for you, Mr. Madandume?"

A queer idea came into his mind that he should shout: "Please be kind enough to fuck my girlfriend less often."

But he decided to keep that one at the back of his mind. Ntungamili said in a soft voice that went well with the rest of him, "Honorable Minister, I came to you because you're top man in the Civil Service."

Satjilombe smiled.

"Not exactly. Above me is the Big Lion. *Tautona*."

Ntungamili shook his head.

"His Excellency is not interested in Departmental matters. I'm good at administrative work, at working with ordinary members of the public, or so my friend thinks. I've come through her recommendation."

Satjilombe coughed a little bit, smiled again and said, in a chuckling sort of way: "And your friend, Mr. Madandume, would be . . ."

"Ms. Shangoyapalala" said Ntungamili quietly, "I don't suppose there is an irregularity . . ."

"No. No. No. Mr. Madandume. I'm sure there is no question of irregularity," said the Minister soothingly.

He flipped the thin application forms in the folder to which Ntungamili's name had been attached. And while he turned the papers, Ntungamili's voice continued in a soft monotone.

"Honorable Minister, I'm good at what I do as you may have learned from my girlfriend, Batjibilibili. I know government work is a very delicate process. But all it really needs is focus, getting the proper things in view and holding them . . ."

He said much more.

Satjilombe, who thought he had unnecessarily been interrupted, frowned and said.

"Yes, Mr. Madandume. Undoubtedly."

To deny the professional competence of Batjibilibili's feeble boyfriend would be unforgiveable bad manners.

"But you must understand how long-drawn-out even the simplest government business is. Everything we do takes generations to accomplish, things just keep on piling up, including filling up vacancies. And there is a long waiting list for younger graduates and an even longer waiting line for the party cadres who guide us in our use of natural resources."

Madandume stirred unhappily.

"But can nothing be done? For five years . . ."

"A matter of priority, sir. We really must get our priorities right. I'm sorry . . . cigarette?"

Ntungamili started back at the suggestion, eyes suddenly widening as he stared at the pack thrust out towards him. Satjilombe looked surprised, withdrew the pack, made a motion as though to take a cigarette for himself and thought the better of it. Ntungamili drew a sigh of unfeigned relief as the pack was put out of sight. He said, "Is there any way of reviewing matters, putting me as far forward as possible. I don't know how to explain . . ."

Satjilombe smiled.

Some had offered money under similar circumstances which, of course, had gotten them nowhere, either.

He said, "The decisions on priority are computer-processed. I could in no way alter those decisions arbitrarily."

Ntungamili rose stiffly to his feet. He stood five and half feet tall. "Then, good day, sir."

"Good day, Mr. Madandume. And my sincerest regrets."

He offered his hand, and Ntungamili touched it briefly. Ntungamili left, and a touch of the buzzer brought Satjilombe's secretary into the room. He handed her the folder.

"This," he said, "may be disposed of."

Alone again, he smiled.

Another item in his devoted service to the human race, service rendered through negation. At least this fellow had been easy to dispose of. Sometimes threats had to be applied and even physical force. Five minutes later, he had forgotten him. Nor, thinking back on it later, could he remember feeling any premonition of danger.

Satjilombe went to the bedroom and shouted, "Batjibilibili! Come here, you horny bitch."

That is the way in which he speaks to me, she thought wrathfully. No really decent woman would stand it. I should not care to address a lady or even a family dog in such a way. She would give me whining notice of some sort. He went towards her. He was a great hulking fellow who was always in the grin. He had a decanter of brandy in his hand. He filled her glass with the neat spirit.

"Batjibilibili, what do you say to a glassful of brandy, the real thing, my girl?"

"Thank you, Satjilombe. Just a little tot."

"And what would you say to a roll of ganja when the brandy is drunk."

"Ganja? Here?"

The fellow is sharp enough when he likes, she told herself. She saw him look towards the bedroom, and then at her, and then a gleam of intelligence came into her eyes.

"Here's the brandy, drink it up!"

She drank without a word, draining the glass of every drop.

"And here's your *zol*!"

"Is it very strong, Satjilombe?"

"Very strong? What do you mean?"

"It isn't the first time I've seen your tricks, Satjilombe, is it now? And you are not the one to give away valuable stuff for nothing at all. If it kills me, you'll send my body to my mother. She'd like to know that I was dead."

"Send your body to your mother! What a way to put it, you brazen urban rebel. Sit down and smoke."

They entered the bedroom.

Satjilombe sat down just at the edge of bed. He rolled the *zol*, and handed it, with a lighted match, to her. She declined the match. He handed the *zol* very gingerly, turning it over and over, eyeing it with all his eyes. She sat beside him and snatched it, a little bit unceremoniously, she thought.

He smiled.

"Thank you, Satjilombe. I'll light up myself if it's the same to you. I carry matches of my own. It's a beautiful *zol*, entirely. I never see the likes of it for craftsmanship. If only you guys were as good at matters of state and public service."

He laughed uproariously and heartily.

"We do our best," he said.

"Come, we don't want to sit here all day. Smoke."

"I'd like another drop of liquor if it's the same with you."

"Another drop! Why, you've had a glassful already. You don't want the bloody thing to knock you off. It will kill you before you hit forty."

"And isn't it better to die a natural death?"

Satjilombe emptied the second glass of brandy as though it were water. She believed he would empty a barrel full without turning a hair. Then he gave another look at the *zol*. Then, taking a match from his jacket pocket, he drew a long breath, as though he were resigning himself to fate. Striking the match, while shading it by his hand, the flame was gathering strength, he looked at her. She distinctly saw him wink his eye. During this process of lightning the *zol*, they sat together. They sat and watched the alcoholic haze engulf them as though they were witnessing an action which would leave its mark upon the age. Someone walked past the door, and she gave a start. Satjilombe was calm. He rubbed his palms together with a chuckle. She took the *zol* from between his lips and then thought otherwise. Her head was spinning.

"Batjibilibili, honey, put that *zol* back into your mouth, and smoke it for your life! It cost me a fortune."

"So what? I am smoking it, aren't I? But it's too strong for me. Positively poisonous. Here, take the bloody thing. I'm not going to throw my life away for any amount of money."

Satjilombe, whose temper was not at any time one of the best, was seized with a spasm of rage.

"As I live, my girl, if you try to cheat me by taking that *zol* from between your lips until I tell you to, you leave this room this instant, never again to be a friend of mine."

She knew from bitter experience when her lover meant what he said, and when he did not. The deliberate reference to "their friendship" and not the true relationship that it was supposed to be, also cut her to the quick. She continued stolidly to puff away. At some point she must have started dithering, laughing foolishly and grasping for breathe intermittently, and she had lost control of her senses. Satjilombe caught her by the arm; he, too, was puffing away and acting funny. At last, whether in obedience to his command or whether because the drug was already beginning to take effect, she made no movement to withdraw the *zol* from her mouth. She watched its brightly and frightening butt burning, spitting red-grayish stars before her drowsy eyes which were coming closer and closer towards her nose with an expression of such intense horror that she must have passed out several times.

For a moment she remained motionless. All senses dead. She was quitting her nerves with the reflection that what she was experiencing was a sort of nightmare. At one point, she was seized with what seemed to be a fit of convulsive shuddering, yet there was an element of joy and happiness in it, a strange sort of momentary lucidity. But she seemed to be in agony at the same time. She trembled so violently that she expected to see herself lose control and fall to the floor. She really had no inkling, no idea at all, of what might happen. She was wholly unprepared. All of a sudden, and to her utter horror, she saw a dreadful human-looking creature coming closer and closer towards her eyes, and her pupils dilated to twice their usual size. She hoped for pity's sake that unconsciousness would supervene, through a stronger action of the drug, but before she passed out through sheer fright, her senses left her. Waking up again, mechanically she puffed steadily on. Then just as suddenly as it began, the shuddering, and the purple haze ceased. There was an instance of quiescence. Then she began to crawl along the bed towards Satjilombe. She moved with a sense of deliberate abandonment, completely entranced, the merest fraction of an inch at a time. But still she moved. Their blurry eyes were riveted on each other with a fascinating and insidious anticipation that was nauseous. For years afterwards, she felt unpleasantly affected whenever this horrendous scene stirred the broth of her memory. Not even her worst dreams of the other nights had been anything like this. Slowly and slowly they shuffled nearer and nearer to each other's red-bloodied eyes. They were both, for the most part, speechless. She was momentarily hoping that the drug would take complete effect on him. But either his constitution enabled him to offer a strong resistance to narcotics or else the large quantity of neat spirit which he had drunk acted as he had malevolently intended that it should as an antidote. It became clear to her that he could never succumb to the charm of intoxication. It was a battle of wills under the most unsightly and cruel circumstances. She would have given the world to scream, to have been able to utter a sound. But she was spellbound. She could do nothing else but watch the nightmarish scene play itself out. She could only watch and wait for the inevitable; for the grand finale to which she would be the abject sacrifice for the propitiation of his wanton desires.

In the morning they were silent. There lay Satjilombe. Close beside him lay, right in the bed, the bottle of brandy, half full. Satjilombe was the first speak.

"I think a little brandy won't be amiss."

Emptying the remainder of the brandy into a glass, he swallowed it at a draught.

"Now, for a closer examination of our friendship since that unpleasant business with your boyfriend at the office," he said languidly.

She politely and firmly rejected his amorous overtures.

"I rather fancy that this is a case for discretion," he said.

She said nothing.

There was subdued but tremendous noise in her head. It sounded like the echoing tick, tick, and tick of some great beetle, like the sort of noise that a death-watch makes. She lay in bed in that curious condition which is between sleep and waking. When, at last, she knew that she was awake, she asked herself what it was that had happened to her. She got out of bed. It was ridiculous to think of sleep during the continuation of that uncanny shrieking of hellish sounds in her fevered mind. She waited with a certain sense of anxiety. She waited in vain. When she thought that she perceived that nothing seemed likely to happen, that her head would not bust open, she silently returned to sleep. On a morning like this, one does not care to be disturbed from one's sound slumber in the small hours of the morning. But that gargantuan noise in her mind was maddening. She needed an explanation of the events of the night before, but Satjilombe was such an untruthful man that he was in a chronic state of suspicion about the truthfulness of others.

It soon dawned on her it was useless to think of sleep while that disgusting mental orchestra was going on in her head. She sat up in bed once more. She somehow managed to summon enough will power to sleep for a while. To her surprise once she was between the sheets she was seized with an irresistible drowsiness, a drowsiness which so mastered her that she imagined it must have lasted till long after the day had dawned. When she woke up she had a sort of consciousness that her waking had been caused by something strange. What it was she cold not surmise. Her own impression was that she had been awakened by the touch of a person's hand. But that impression must have been wrong because as she could easily see by looking round the room there was no one in the room to touch her. She wondered if it had been the Hand of God. But she had no patience for speculation. What instantly came to her mind instead was the horrifying dream she had just awakened from. Outside it was broad daylight. She looked at her watch. It was nearly eleven o'clock. She was a pretty late sleeper as a rule, but she did not usually sleep as late that. That scoundrel, Satjilombe, would have let her sleep all day without thinking it necessary to wake her. She was just about to spring out of bed with the intention of giving him a piece of her mind for allowing her to sleep so late and to confront the bastard with the abominable actions of the night, the coarseness of his behavior and attitude to her, a guest in his house, when she heard footsteps approaching from the door way. The words had scarcely escaped from her trembling lips when the door burst open. At the sight of her in his T-shirt, Satjilombe began to shake his head.

"What hours, Batjibilibili, what hours! Why, my dear girl, I've breakfasted, read the papers and my letters, and you're not up!"

"There is something I want to discuss with you," she said.

He eyed her doubtfully.

Then advancing, he laid upon her shoulder a slightly shaking hand. "Satjilombe you wouldn't play tricks, I mean really dirty tricks on an unsuspecting young woman, would you?"

"You are right, Batjibilibili, I wouldn't, though I believe there had been occasions on which many a women have had doubts upon the subject ... he ... he ... heee ..."

"Meaning?"

"Nothing. By the way, Batjibilibili, I believe that I'm the oldest friend you have."

"Maybe. Except my father, I can't think of anyone else."

"You wouldn't compare my friendship to the friendship of such a man as your father ..."

"No. No. No, not at all. My father is a noble and honorable man. He's by all accounts a gentleman."

"And me?"

"You are one of the so-called modern men in the social chessboard. Men who think honor a negotiable article. How could I know you for who you really are?"

"Think of the tastes we have in common, you and me."

"I value character, courage, honor, respectability and truth in other people more."

"Am I to understand that I'm deficient in that respect?"

"It depends on what transpired here last night. I told you I'm not on the pill and . . ."

"Batjibilibili, I don't think you need to take that tone with me. It isn't friendly."

"I see. Now you are threatening me. What a fool I was to trust you. I knew I couldn't trust you. Men are all the same aren't you? Always looking for one thing. Can't keep your penis in your trousers. Oh, no! You've got to flash your manhood to every hapless woman. Don't think I'm a fool. The purple haze is over. I know exactly what I'm going to do if anything happens to me. Mark my words."

As she said this, Satjilombe's face was as quiet as a picture. His eyes were glistening behind his spectacles. He gasped for breath. She could see he trembled. He actually took out his handkerchief to wipe his brow. "What do you want from me, girl?" he said hoarsely.

"One thing only. I want you to know that should there be adverse consequences for last night's actions, I'll make my interests yours, and you'll make your interests mine. Isn't that fair, Honorable Minister?"

"Let us understand each other, okay?"

"I don't think it necessary that the terms of our little understanding should be expressly embodied in black and white. You are a representative of law and order. I'm an ordinary citizen. We understand each other well enough. In your world you plunder friend and foe alike. We'll meet on the day of reckoning. Now I'm out of here. If you'll leave the room I shall be able to dress. It's no good talking to you, not the least. You're dead to all the promptings of conscience."

"May I enquire, Batjibilibili, what it is you propose to do?"

"I propose to do nothing, except summon the representatives of law and order. I know very well the company you keep, the attitudes and lifestyles you cultivate and nurture, all the broken hearts and broken honor. Believe it or not, it's this moral darkness that gives me courage. It's strange isn't it, that instincts which we do not understand form the motive-power of most of our life's actions, and yet we refuse to admit them as evidence of any external truth. I suppose it is because we must act somehow, rightly or wrongly; and there are great things which we need not believe unless we choose. I mean, provided that they are distant enough, how little, after all, do we think of the results of our actions. There are few men in this country that would deliberately instil into a child a love of drink or wilfully deprive her of her reason, and yet a man with drunkenness or madness in his blood thinks nothing of bringing children into the world tainted as deeply with the curse as if he had inoculated them with it directly. Well," she said, smiling, "let us console ourselves with the thought that we are not all lunatics and drunkards."

"Damn it all, Batjibilibili!" he said with a savage passion.

"I will be master in my house. Can't you be quiet?"

There was a long drawn unutterable anguish in his tone and his voice. He stood trembling in every limb, incapable of speech or action, and she faced him, as silently and motionlessly as a statue. He looked sad and worried and the thought suddenly struck her that his extravagant spirits the night before, and even his careful cheerfulness of the morning, had been but artificial moods at best. He turned, and finding her eyes fixed on him, at once walked out of the room. A few seconds later he was at the cursed door again, screaming at her in the most demented way possible.

"Don't tell me that you didn't want to experience what happened here last night, that you didn't want it and you didn't desire it or that you didn't enjoy it! I merely fulfilled your ultimate expectations of the virile male host. Don't play innocent or be righteous with me because I'm not capable of any wrong-doing, at least not in the eyes of the law and the all too muted traditions of your society. When you play with fire you must be ready to endure the burn, be able to put out the flame. We are in this thing together. Don't you ever forget it!"

Then, he marched out.

In the sitting room, she found no one except the maid. She was still in a temper and was maliciously hoping that other night had been as much disturbed as her own. To her surprise, however, she found that she had been the only sufferer. The housemaid, radiant, and resplendent in a sickeningly white-starched attire, was so satisfied with the quite in which her night had been passed that she boldly expressed shock at her appearance and declared her intention to set everything to rights, beginning with breakfast, of all the things. Evil, murderous thoughts floated in her mind as the still living memories of dead horror inflamed her brain. There is nothing more annoying when you feel yourself aggrieved by fate than to be reminded of your incongruous appearance in a brilliantly shining morning by a housemaid, especially one who is intimately familiar with what may have happened to you during the night. So she dropped the subject. Her heart was heavy and aching, and she tried with true feminine docility to follow the lead that she had set: one wounded woman drawing on the courage and experience of the other. It was not a very attractive option. She felt disgusted, humiliated and nauseous.

"Horrid people," the maid said quietly.

She was full of apology for the trouble she was giving her.

"I don't think people, married or unmarried, must be treated like dead wood," she declared wrathfully.

Batjibilibili said nothing, hiding behind that moral fortification in which every well-bred Motswana takes refuge in the presence of their accursed Zimbabwean brothers and sisters. Her eyes and attention seemed everywhere at once: one moment she was addressing inane remarks at Batjibilibili, and the next breaking an embarrassing silence in the monologue by some rapid sally of nonsense addressed to no one, to the wind. Her riotous energy and excitement finely dismantled Batjibilibili's defense system, and she burst into tears.

"I don't expect men to be saints," she wailed, "but could they not have something of vigorous completeness, something of the intensity of feeling and belief? Could they not have courage, respect and honor to do things the right way like us?"

"Oh, I don't know. The MP is very considerate, and at times when people are troubled one ought to be nice to them," said the maid carelessly.

"You don't mean that, do you? You surely can't encourage such behavior, can you?"

"Of course not, but what choice do I have? What choice do you have, my sister?"

She stopped, her voice quivering; and then after a pause went on again more calmly, "Throughout the world it is the same. Men everywhere will not admit of compromise or limitation where we are concerned. They are at war with our strongest passions and our best intentions. I am a Zimbabwean. I should know better. Their law is infinite, universal, eternal; there is no escape, no repose. Resist, strive, endure, that is our lot; that is existence."

"And peace, and respect?" exclaimed Batjibilibili appealingly. "Where is there room for peace of mind and physical security, if that be true?"

"Peace seems a long way off," whispered the maid. "It surely is for me," she said gently, almost calmly, "not necessarily for you."

"Oh, but I am worse and weaker than you," said Batjibilibili. "If life is to be all warfare, I must be beaten. I cannot always be fighting."

"Can you not?" said the maid.

"We must strive, for the promise is to him that overcomes. You must fight. You have citizenship in this country, personal identity and resources. You are your own person's guardian and your soul's warden. There is nothing you really need fear, at least, I suppose, nothing worse than death."

"Why should I fear death?" asked Batjibilibili with sudden violence. "What is life after all but one long death? Our pleasures, our hopes, our youth are all dying; ambition dies, and even desire at last; our passions and tastes will die or will live only to moan their dead opportunity. The happiness of love dies with the loss of the loved, and, worst of all, love itself grows old in our hearts and dies. Why should we shrink only from the one death which can free us from all the others?"

"It's not true, Batjibilibili!" cried the Zimbabwean hotly. "What you say is not true. There are many things even here in your country which are living and shall live; and if it were otherwise, in everything, life that ends in death is better than no life at all."

"My own soul's warden," Batjibilibili reflected bitterly.

That abominated man's action had dragged its slime over her soul. Shall I allow the memories of his despicable conduct to poison my life with a fouler corruption still, she wondered silently? To live life, however, tainted by dishonor and scandal surely is not a fate to fear? But these were just thoughts, simple words dancing in her head. What did they mean for her, to creep back now to bed by his side and to begin living again tomorrow the life that she lived today? She had come to him to ask for help. Now her heart and pride were dead together. He had stung them to an aching, shameful death. Now what could she do? God, if you are stronger than evil, fight for me, she prayed silently. I have endured enough. Evil has governed my life, and evil is stronger than I am. If the devil continues to be triumphant, then the devil is my friend, and the friend of the world. God is not a God of love. He cannot wish such a man to live. He made him, but the devil spoilt him; and let the devil have his handiwork back again. Then something strange happened. With a low, shuddering sob, Batjibilibili threw herself down upon the rug at the feet of the frightened maid and lay there for some minutes, her limbs trembling and her heart shrinking within her. A mist of evil, fearful and loathsome, had descended upon her, she thought sadly, blighting her girlhood's life, sullying its ignorant innocence, saddening its brightness, as she felt, for ever. At last, she spoke.

"You have known of it all, I suppose, of this curse that is in the world—sin and suffering—and what such words mean?"

"Yes," said the other, looking at her with wondering pity, "I am afraid so."

"And yet men who know this, who have seen it, laugh, talk, are happy, amaze themselves . . . how can they . . . how can they? Why is it so? I cannot understand it."

"When you have found an answer to that question, Batjibilibili, come and tell me and mankind at large; it will be news to us all," she said quietly. "We cannot go outside the limits of our own nature," she continued, "our knowledge is shallow and our spiritual insight dark, and God in His mercy has made our hearts shallow too and our imagination dull. If, knowing and trusting only as men do, we were to feel as angels feel, earth would be hell indeed."

It was cold comfort, but at that moment, anything warmer or brighter would have been unreal and utterly repellent to Batjibilibili. She hardly took in the meaning of her words, but it was as if a hand had been stretched out to her, struggling in the deep mire, by one who herself had traversed her inner being just in order to survive, just to exist, and not truly live. Where she stood, Batjibilibili also might someday stand. We all have our own sorrows to bear, she realized, the suffering that is near to us to grapple with. She could no longer dwell on the foul, coarse, shamelessness of Satjilombe's language and behavior, on his contemptuous incredulity, and the social damnation that loomed ahead of her. She now looked at the tormented young Zimbabwean woman with respect, her courage and indifference to discomfort and the brutal realism of a world made only for calloused man, helped Batjibilibili to carry the day.

Chapter 3

Trouble In Paradise . . .

December, 2000

Bafi had announced to her husband that she could not go on living in the same house with him. All members of her small circle of friends were painfully conscious of this unfolding state of affairs. Every family friend and relative felt that there was no sense in their living together. Mapopota felt mentally oppressed by the hopelessness of his marriage situation, and worst of all, his own fault in the matter. Yes, she won't forgive me he said to himself a thousand times a day. And the most awful thing he thought was that it was his entire fault. He could not deal with the expressions of horror, despair and indignation on the part of his young wife. In spite of the unpleasantness of the whole business—alienation, mutual recriminations, suspicions, intrigues, the avalanche of tears, hurtful and cruel words—he refused to defend his actions, he refused to be hurt, remaining completely and unutterably indifferent. He contended that she must be happy in her children and live in the needs of the daily life like everybody else. Who was she to ask for complete happiness, for a dreamland? In a country where everyone is content with the needs of the day, asking for happiness was an unnecessary indulgence. All must aspire for the dream of daily life, live for the moment, seize the day and leave everything else to chance and luck.

To rebuild their marriage was impossible. She was already worn-out and no longer attractive. He was too messed up and too old to inspire love. To set right their relations simply meant settling for a false position with more deceit, lying, bewilderment, humiliations, contempt, appearances, suffering and loathsomeness. Of course, he was unutterably sorry for her.

She too saw in him sympathy for her but not love. Respectful familiarity and modest consciousness had now replaced true love, intimacy, friendship and companionship. There was no word for it. They were utterly ruined. She felt a fearful tragedy in her marriage. All the charm, all the beauty of life had gone out of it. The whole thing was now simply too great a mental and spiritual strain. She only wished for a moment to wound her husband, to wound him cruelly, to tell him she didn't love him. She profoundly hated him! To tell him to go away. To set her free. To start again.

But that would be a lie, a terrible lie. She felt nothing of these things. She loved her husband. She loved her family. She loved herself. She wanted order and happiness. She believed in her own ideal of true married happiness to actively dislike and disown her husband. She was too terrified to arrange her own life for herself. To abandon marriage meant exposing herself to vulnerability, doubts, insecurity, loneliness, even ridicule: heel and cad, one night stands, unpredictable crimes of passion, even venereal damage. Then there were the children . . . the whole business was horrible and positively loathsome. She felt hurt, pierced to the heart, abused and abandoned. But she would not go away. To abandon a marriage, in her mind's eye, was a bad thing. Marriage was wearisome but it was still better than most things. To just resign herself to a life of doubtful conventional sympathy, living alone, sad and even lonelier, was plain madness. Her youth and beauty were gone, taken by him and his children. Her own home and husband were the only things that gave substance and meaning to life in a society of extreme insecurities and vulnerabilities. Besides, her husband was not really unfaithful. His crime was a divine one, simple infidelity of the heart. I can surely forgive that she thought. Yes, I can, I can. But if one forgives, it must be completely. No half measures.

To her horror and mortification, Bafi found she really could not forgive him completely, not in this way. Her resolve was too weak, her faith too wanting. There simply was no possibility of explanation and reconciliation in the matter. Her husband's actions had plunged her in a mysterious world that was not open to her. The whole world seemed lost in the fog of her soul's chamber. Her life was a moment of despair and horror. She felt crushed. She felt alone in a crowed city; she who had been so successful in society. Now she was a leper; damaged; invisible and there was something terrible and cruel, uncanny and devilish in her social milieu. At times she admonished herself.

There is something in me that is hateful, repulsive, she thought. I am myself to blame. Who am I and what am I? A nobody, not wanted by anyone, nor of use to anybody. Everything in the world is base and loathsome. Everyone turns away from me with horror. And disgust. Why should I live? What do I live for? What is the meaning of my life? People despise me. Is this ugly existence worth struggling for? Why bother about this suffering and cruel existence? An existence beneath even the house floor! There is no need for such extreme self-flagellation. I better die.

She felt that her association with a doomed relationship was just an anchor to save her from self-contempt. She even felt that holding on to such a marriage itself was just giving way to a low passion. The whole thing was a sham, a sort of confusion of social ideas, a pseudonym for shame and self-dissatisfaction, a delicious social escapism and nothing more; something foreign to confident temper and perfection, not the chief affair of life on which all happiness revolves. Once a paradise of complacent satisfaction, health, daydreams, happiness and a clear conscience, her marriage was now an ugly monstrosity in which she could do nothing, a mere heart with cobwebs and no blood, skeletons and no life.

She particularly felt disgusted when her husband turned to his usual homilies of family disintegration:

"It's all my fault. Everything is clear and you really are good in your heart. You will find someone deserving of your kind love in no time. Remember all the things you have done for me and the children. I shall never forget. I love you and shall always love you as my *best friend*. I know you will leave off hating me. To tell you the truth this is all for the best. We can't live in a worried mood like this. It's all for the best. God knows you are a good woman. Your life will go on in the old way, all nice as usual. I have been the cause of torture to you instead of pleasure. I am truly, truly sorry. It is all my damned fault. I am not worth your love. It is better for all concerned that this whole thing should come to nothing."

Her husband aroused in her a feeling of absolute disappointment. She had imagined him better than he was in reality. In her shattered private world, he now resembled wanton sorrow and evil. Sometimes she told herself it was all the same before and wondered why she had not noticed it. The man was evil. Right from the start he had been nothing but trouble, she would wail in her broken heart. He was the source of causeless shame right from the beginning. Always resolute and irreproachable, he was always the devil incarnate. Why did she not notice all this before? Why did she attach importance to what was so useless and ephemeral for so long? What was wrong with her! The man was nothing but a trivial incident of social life. Why try to exonerate such a fool from blame, she would start wondering again! Maybe there is no reason to speak of it? The man is a scoundrel through and through!

What do I see in him? What did I see in him? Oh God, grant me wisdom! I was born a Christian, and a Christian I shall die. But what do I do now? I am lost. To try reconciliation is to invite humiliation; to turn a worthy effort into a farce. For is divorce not an ignominyious social farce? It is. Undoubtedly. I am ashamed. I must get over my shame. But what to do? Break up family habits? Oh! Why aren't there laws against such base and dishonorable people as my husband? He has deceived me so horribly! He has treated me with contempt. To think I have been in love with given my entire life even to a man who did not care a straw for me! What a shame! An abomination! To care for a man who does not love me? Ignominy of the worst order. A social scandal of gargantuan proportions. And to think he is such an insufferably repulsive creature, a good lawyer? Oh merciful God, help me. Everything has become hateful, loathsome and coarse to me. Who can imagine what loathsome thought I have about everything? Just what did I see in him in the first place? Why did I marry the bastard? For love? Can one talk of love these days? Did I marry for convenience? No. Prudence? Sex? Love? Procreation? However I look at it I made a mistake, a terrible mistake. Why did I marry this man who is still a stranger to me after so many years? Does he have an understanding of what is honorable? Any sense of commitment? Obligation? Duty? Does he have any conception of human friendship, companionship and fellow- ship? Does he belong to the real world of so many minds, so many hearts, and so many kinds of love? Does he see only a chance of despair and wretchedness in life? Doesn't he have an understanding of what is honorable! Does he have any heart, any real bleeding human heart at all?

Bafi was standing face to face with the brutal reality of life, with the grim possibility of spousal abandonment, and this seemed to her very irrational and incomprehensible because it was life itself, relentlessly breathing into her consciousness, her soul, her inner being, her somnam- bulant universe, her dreamland, her internal somnolent reality, the true meaning of life. For the first time she pictured poignantly to herself her personal life, her ideas, her desires, her ambitions, and her idea that she could and should have a separate life of her own, and this seemed to her so horrifying that she made haste to dispel it. On the other hand she felt herself clad in an impenetrable armor of falsehood, and she was not one of those women who submit to uneasiness and worry, and in her fevered dreams, when she had no control over her thoughts, her precious position presented itself to her in all its hideous nakedness; ferreting in her frac- tured soul, harrowing her bleeding heart, and blasting her tortured mind. She felt that at such moments she could not put into words the sense of being betrayed, of humiliation, of shame, and of horror, and did not want to speak of it, to confront it, to embrace it. The very thought of rejection tortured her with shame, mortification and despondency. She felt ashamed of these feelings, told herself that she was in no way to blame, but the unpleasantness of her situation; its contemptuous indignity, its unten- ability, its vulgarity, its loathsomeness, appalled her.

What was he thinking of, of his happiness and her unhappiness? Am I not the wife of my husband? What will people think? What is their business in this matter? Are there a few unpleasant things, little humiliations, we can conceal from the gazing eyes of an indifferent world? What will happen to me? What will I become? A public laughing stock? A whore? A beggar? An outsider? A vacuous social butterfly? A nothing in the social chessboard? A . . . a...divorcee . . . what a loathsome word! I know all the baseness, all the horror of my position! Have I, in reality, been all along a whore and a beggar? What is a wife, in real terms? Oh, the horror! Did he know what the result of our marriage would be beforehand? Did he deliberately choose to disgrace my name? How will I relate to the select crowd of the upper world? The gossip! The publicity! The scandal!

She was trembling as though in fever. Her eyes flaming, full of fire. Being a woman of a very warm heart, she was seldom angry; but when she was angry, then she was dangerous. Her breath came in short, sharp gasps. Her husband was making a fearful, unpardonable mistake, and he knew that something awful would happen to her, to both of them. It was his fault! Shameful, unpardonable! She felt utterly wretched. For the first time in her life she knew the bitterest of misfortune beyond remedy caused by the wretchedness of love and the pursuit of happiness. He was so urbane, so sophisticated, so subtle and astute in public life. Did he not realize the sensibleness of such attitudes to his own wife, their absolute necessity to the entire family? He did not want to see and did not see that many people in society cast dubious glances on his wife. He did not want to understand and did not understand that his wife was wretched and suffering. He did not want to know and did not know that his children were suffering. It was too awful, too unnatural. The callous indifference. The public abandonment. The emotional rejection. The renting betrayal. The impropriety of odious self-conduct. The indecorous public humiliation. The exposition to malicious tongues, ridicule and solitariness.

I can't bear it. I hate him. I hate him with the solid rigidity of the dead. My God, how I hate him. I don't want to see his face.

It seemed to her that his big, terrible eyes, had always expressed a feeling of hatred and contempt and not genuine love and respect. Oh, how unpleasant! This bastard will worry me out of my life with his immoral ways. What is there in him? What is it gives him the power to look down on everything? How could he make me so unhappy? He has no heart. Oh, the shame of it! Isn't it humiliating to think that a man has disdained your love, which he has not cared for it? The shame, the humiliation of it! To provide home, children, comfort, love, companionship, friendship and care in thousands of ways with spiritual passion for nothing? Doesn't he understand that in all human sorrows nothing gives comfort except love and faith? What does he want in life? What does he expect of me? What have I left undone? How have I failed him? Why should I now be alone in the world, without friends, with only a melancholy disappointment in the past? His painful attempt to seem hearty and lively in her presence revolted her. It serves me right, she thought, because it was always a sham; because it was all done on purpose, and not from the heart. What business had I to marry him? To seem better to people, to myself, to God; to deceive everyone? To deceive myself in supposing I could be what I wanted to be? That I could create my own universe, my own life? Well, let me be what I am. I shall never marry, again. Never, ever. My shame is as big as Mother Earth. It is hard for me to believe men any more. I will never marry. There is no hope in earth, and God seems to have forgotten me. Didn't He ordain and sanctify the bloody marriage institution? Damn Him! Damn God to Hell and damnation! I am now on the side of the devil. My heart has turned into stone. I hate myself. I hate life. I hate God. I have lost faith in everything. My experience is a valuable antidote to the corrupt influence of external reality. Now I have to do without affection, to survive mired in condescension and moral pollution. I may end wallowing in sexual contamination and dread disease, bereft of human fellowship. To whose society shall I belong? A woman savaged by venereal damage is soon disabused of all claims to male companionship. That is the lot of many women in our society. I know it for a fact. I used to despise these women. Now, I too am beyond the pale. Even my best friends will send me to Coventry without the slightest hesitation. Isn't that what we all did to poor Gadzanani? She ended up a careless drunk, a woman without method, a vicious gossip and liar. Once a woman with her heart in the right place, her life ended filled with appalling contradictions and dominated by little pleasures of the moment that destroyed her body, her reputation and her mind. She died a corrupt woman with no honor, no heart, and no sense of propriety, no moral scruples and no religion: a con-temptible woman with a poisoned existence with no disposition to common decency and social decorum. Shall I now be the object of similar horrid irrational ridicule and decay? Will I, too, die in the gutter? No, I shan't! He should get due punishment for his crime. I long for him to suffer for having destroyed my peace of mind, and my honor; and for what? For a deathlike rigid external status quo that has no positive reality? What could be more important on earth than to love another person? Love, true love, is the only real and most profoundly rewarding emotion on earth. It is sweeter and more comforting than all human emotions combined. What right has he to repudiate love, true and pure love, freely given and cherished? Oh, the indolent beast! How am I to get out of this insufferable position? He struts around the national stage with a calm sense of being prepared for everything. What about the fearful calamity that has burst upon us at home? What a vile, base creature! He doesn't know how he has crushed my life, crushed everything that was living in me. He has no thought that I'm a live woman who must have the love of her husband. He doesn't care how at every turn he hurts and humiliates me. Haven't I striven, striven with all my strength, to find something to give meaning to my life? Haven't I struggled to love him, to love my children, to love my home, to love my neighbors, to love my country? What more can a woman do within the range of limited possibilities available in our prejudicially wretched society? Hasn't God made me so that I must love and live? What wrong have I done? He is a man, a man with powerful friends, and strong connections. No doubt he'll keep himself in the right, while me, in my ruin, he'll drive still lower to the most infamous, the basest of women's sordid little worlds and through my unrelenting wretchedness will amplify his virtues, no matter how sordid, or artificial. But what can I decide upon alone? What am I to do with all the uncertainty, the indecision? What kind of concealment can I contrive, if only to breathe, to still love a little, to live, to be human?

Bafi spent endless days thinking about all these things, lamenting her husband's impervious attitude to the religion of things. But her husband looked at these things quite differently. Mapopota was a truthful man in his relations with his conscience. He was incapable of deceiving himself and persuading himself that he repented of his conduct. He could not repent of the fact that he was in love with Batjibilibili. All he repented of was that he had not succeeded better in hiding it from his wife. Possibly he might have managed to conceal his affair better from his wife had he anticipated that the knowledge of it would have had such an effect on her, and, more significantly of late, on his career. In their last unhappy confrontation, Bafi had not hesitated to emphasize a more definite and explicit assertion of her rights. She had had, no doubt, means of keeping watch upon his movements, and steadfastly refused to relinquish all hope of him abandoning her.

The unfortunate woman tried to bargain for some proof of his affection, some proof of his commitment to their marriage, but he refused her terms. He had never clearly thought out the subject, but he had vaguely conceived that his wife must long ago have suspected him of being unfaithful to her and shut her eyes to the fact. Most unpleasant was the day when on coming home happy and good-humoured from Notwane club with a present for his wife, he had found her in their spacious bedroom sniffing the clothing he had worn the week before, and her teeth unpleasantly barred, the nose violently upturned to the point of tenderly, and violently caressing her temple, she yelled: "Have you been in bed with another man?" she said, assessing the damage in the war zone; shirts, ties and trousers strewn everywhere: "the weapons of mass destruction," he thought, with melancholy dissatisfaction.

"It's the smell of the clothes" she asserted violently, dangling his favorite jacket in one hand and a dirty shirt on the other.

"I swear to God, this smell is oriental," she declared.

"Beyond any shadow of doubt there is an odour in these clothes that has not been there in all our lives together. I swear to God this is not the scent of flowers! It is an odour peculiar to human nature. It's not perfume, male or female, or any artificial essence. It's body odour. It's human smell. But it smells like a He Goat. It must be another man. Now tell me the truth. I can't conceive of any human odour that can contaminate clothes so fondly and so densely. Have you been cheating on me? To me these clothes reveal everything. If you are going to lie or argue, remember I have physical proof."

"The legal expression is material proof."

"Whatever!" she screamed, indignantly, throwing the offending articles to his aghast face.

"I'm not a fool, you know. I have connections, and I can get fingerprints from these clothes. There must be, God knows what here. Semen, urine, tears, blood, hair, sweat, saliva! What's this?" she asked, picking up a silk white shirt and pointing tremulously at an embarrassingly huge dark stain.

"What kind of semen smells like caca? Or is it your rotten sperm?" she said, looking at him with an expression of horror, despair, and indignation.

"Maybe . . . I think . . . well . . . they died," he said idiotically.

"The sperm died?" she asked incredulously.

"Well, maybe just rot . . ."

"You are a murderer!"

"What!"

"You heard me. A killer. That sperm could have been somebody's child . . . Ooohhhh . . . what am I talking about. I'm so mixed up! Oh! How dare you! To think . . . no I don't think you are the man I married."

She turned away from him in an effort to collect her wits. It was then that he made the greatest mistake of his life. He had always thought her vulnerable, beautiful and sexy when she was angry. Without thinking he took her into his arms and kissed her . . . his mouth working slowly on hers, urging her soft lips to open and yield the sweetness within. It was the sort of lazy sensuous kiss that he imagined would banish every thought and sensation save passion.

"You've missed this, haven't you?"

His strong hands moulded her buttocks, drawing her closer. Bafi struggled mightily.

"Loosen me, you molester of women! Brute!"

One of her flailing hands flew out to catch him across the side of his jaw.

"Animal!" Bafi railed.

She could not believe this was happening, this boar cupping her buttocks and pulling her hard against his shameless masculinity . . . at a moment like this . . . it was madness. Wildly, she struck out, but Mapopota ducked, as any good lawyer would do under the circumstances, laughing foolishly, and caught one recalcitrant hand. No sooner had he pinned it to the small of her back than Bafi's other fist struck him in the nose with surprising force.

"Bitch!"

"Bastard!" she hissed in return.

"I have completely misjudged you; you're a typical man! A stupid pig!"

"Don't be a sore loser!"

"I hate you! This other woman . . ."

"There's nothing in it . . ."

"Oh, shit! You really are a degenerate son of a bitch!"

There was no point in denying or defending himself or prevaricating, caught as he was in something so disagreeably disgraceful. Catching sight of his idiot smile and horrified further by his idiotic admission, his wife abruptly cut short her flood of cruel words and rushed out of the room. Since then she had refused to see her husband. After her abrupt, violent departure from the bedroom, he had sat on the matrimonial bed, contemplating the complexity of life, its terrible ironies and little absurdities. The week before he had given the buck-toothed barmaid at one of his watering hole's a lift home at night, and they had had sex at her place. He remembered particularly her confusion when in response to her question he had told her his real name was Phallus.

"What's that supposed to mean?" she had asked drunkenly.

And he had answered: "Phallus, the ancient male god of fertility, who was also a philosopher."

"A prophet? I didn't know you go to church. Please pray for me."

"Yes, I will," he had said happily, and mounted her most vigorously for most part of the night. The whole thing was a misunderstanding, a philosophical miscalculation, a confiscation of innocence; and it turned to be the death knell of his marriage. What Bafi did not know and would never know was the deep nervous torment that had always been part of his life. At each time, as he paused, Mapopota had a morbid sensation of fear, of which he was ashamed and which caused him to frown and blink intermittently. At first, Bafi thought this shy blinking very romantic. In fact when he laughed there were times he blinked so fast that his eyes disappeared for a spell into the eye socket. There had been a time when he wanted to confide to her his terror at these irrational torments, but Bafi was so happy he found it hard to tell her anything.

Recently he had been in a constant tense, irritable state of mind that verged upon hypochondria. So absorbed in himself had he grown, so isolated from everyone else that he was actually afraid of meeting anyone at all. Outside the heat was terrible, with humidity to make it worse. The unbearable stench of car fumes in the street below, and from the Chibuku depots, of which there were inordinately too many in their street, and the unshaven, dirt, and shabbily attired drunks hopelessly loitering around, reeling under the weight of poverty, and sordid wantonness, completed the sad and loathsome coloring of the scene as God must have seen it when he looked down.

Mapopota lived in a mess. It was a depressingly dreary world in which he lived. Every second or so as he surveyed this numbing wretchedness, often only in his mind's eye, the eyes tightly shut, an emotion of the most profound repugnance overwhelmed him to the point of faint dizziness which might more correctly have been described as kind of somnolent oblivion. Every human being, he reflected morosely, must have a friend. Of course, he had Bafi but . . . this life of concentrated depression, of banishment from other people, as though one had literally been swept out of human society with a broom . . . this life of the most intensely eloquent alienation from all things human was a sin. It was an insult to manhood, and an offence in the eyes of God. Man was not created to lead a reptilian existence devoid of all meaning and substance. His major fear was that his self-contempt would soon simply degenerate into sterile resignation; transforming what was supposed to be human into a concrete mummified monument; a truly living monument, but ossified, breathless, mute, and unfeeling. The shadow of a man. A zombie, master less, lost, and without any singular place where any human being may take him.

How would it feel, he wondered, to live in a society that has declared compassion evil? It was a terrifying thought, but a real one enough. A kind of thought akin to madness. To live in a blackguard society where the only occupation is constant looking for human feeling and compassion. To live a life without purpose and honor, and be pungently conscious of your absolute insignificance and worthlessness. To live in a society of one individual with only his sorrow and tears for company. Wouldn't it be blasphemous to still regard such a person human, he wondered? But then if such existence is blasphemous, what about the fate of the mass of the entire society who actually lives within the belly of the Beast?

Suddenly he was ceased by a sort of whimpering anger, a sudden silent emotional frenzy that lacerated his soul and split his heart apart. Yes, he could feel his heart bleeding! For a second he shuddered and trembled like a leaf. Does death feel like this, he wondered? Is it possible to be dead and alive at the same time? What a world! What a cruel fate.

When Mapopota was a kid his parents had definite ideas about how to bring up a child. There were certain rules and standards to which he had to conform. He had to be obedient, docile, well-behaved, seen and not heard, and made to fit in with certain social requirements and moral standards. Conformity was the name of the game in his parents' home. The idea was to lick him into shape, and promote good behavior, as his mother and father constantly reminded him. They also tried to provide love and security in the home but within certain strict limits. Restraint and self-control were encouraged and smacking on the behind not uncommon (this latter, the unquestionable prerogative of his father when he came home from work). He was made to eat up all he had in his plate. It's good for you, his mother would say. His parents wanted him to be a clever, good, moral man of service to his fellow human beings and to the community.

At school he listened intently, absorbed what was taught him, retained it in his memory, and trotted it out most accurately in examinations, so that he won a scholarship to college and ultimately became a lawyer. As a young man he joined the ruling party and developed a strong sense of camaraderie, obedience and dependence on its leaders. His best kept secret as a child was masturbation. In public he loved acting, public speaking, painting, writing, and being a good storyteller. He focused his ambition at gaining a position of prestige. His desire for admiration and desire for approval was intense and unashamedly pronounced. He wanted to count, to be recognized as somebody, to be noticed for something.

His major private torment was constant constipation which inadvertently often made him fart in public; a minor inconvenience that his more enduring friends learnt to ignore. However, he grew increasingly morbid, even though he also felt loved and capable of doing great things in life. He enjoyed the privileges that his society provided and never failed to remind himself and others that laws are made so that all should enjoy freedom. For many years he had lived and worked in Francistown, and almost from the moment he moved there from Mapoka, he suffered totally inexplicable fits of anxiety, physical illness, and the kind of bottomless despair that at times even led him to flirt with the idea of suicide. It was his solitary discovery that in certain parts of the year, the air in the city became sick, and it appeared to be depleted of the vitality that is essential to the creation and health of all life. Neither doctors nor psychiatrists could explain why he felt tired or irritable or just generally below par in a city that many considered a paradise of sorts.

In cars, buses and most high-rise office buildings and apartments he experienced inexplicable anxieties, tension, weariness, and unnatural bursts of hyperactivity. Postcolonial economic liquidity had transformed Francistown into a sprawling city almost overnight. Inevitably, there grew up a lively, sophisticated, and cosmopolitan community of which he became a part. His job was challenging and exciting; the parties almost constant, if one accepted all the invitations.

His hedonistic life was marred by only one thing—he caught a cold and could not get rid of it. It hung over him like a small black cloud for some months until the constant headaches and other common cold symptoms began to get him down. In fact, he experienced a physical and then mental decline so serious that after some time he began to lose his moral sense of well-being. The cold was followed by a bad stomach. After eating all but the plainest food he would feel nauseous. He began to avoid the social circuit and at times even found that he was beginning to lose his sexual drive. Nothing he did would restore his old sense of vigor and well-being. A gastroenterologist diagnosed a malfunctioning gall bladder and ordered it to be removed. This, she said, would limit his gustatory pleasures and remove the unpleasantness that plagued his life in the city. She thought his stomach would start to behave itself and he would feel energetic and positive once again. But the symptoms of bad stomach and fatigue continued to dog him.

After the operation he remained apathetic, and his stomach again rejected everything but bland food. A specialist concluded that his thyroid was underactive. The doctor prescribed thyroid stimulant drugs, and within days he began to feel better. Even so, on occasions he still had to take tranquillizers to steady the nerves during periods of feverish anxiety and sometimes stimulants to shake him out of fits of lassitude. At times he still needed sleeping pills to cope with insomnia. It is important to point out here that these problems were not apparent to other people, either friends or business associates. He became a secret pill taker in much the same way that some people are secret drinkers. He felt a wreck, but made quite sure no one else suspected it.

For much of the time he felt fit, full of life and energy. But for no apparent reason there would be days on which he would be so tense and anxious that he would almost lose his ability to function. He would be beset by nameless fears and doubts that were all the more devastating because there was no explanation for them. Typically, such feelings would be accompanied by insomnia, and were often punctuated with periods of either frantic hyperactivity or total lassitude, of exhaustion and the sort of despair that was almost paralyzing. He would, for instance, find it too much trouble to make a simple phone call, or to cook a meal for himself or even put the garbage out. And at such times tranquilizers, sleeping pills, and stimulants were of no help; by then his body had grown so used to them that they were not very effective. He even tried booze, but drinking did not help him either, though the temptation to seek oblivion by any means led him to have a fresh sympathy for those who have become alcoholics.

In all this there was one besetting paradox. Whenever he left Francistown on business trips, he felt fine. After a few days out of town he could eat more or less what he wanted. He slept well. He had no trouble reaching conclusions and making decisions. He began to look forward to such trips, assuming that the stimulus of travel offset what he had now came to describe as his condition. But in the end he went back to the doctor again, and this time he recommended a psychiatrist on the grounds that if the problem was not physical it simply had to be psychosomatic. So for the next five years he spent four hours a week on an analyst's couch examining his life for hidden fears, conflicts, and guilt that had waited until his midlife to emerge from the subconscious to haunt him. Even so, after five years of analysis he felt no better. He would still lie awake worrying about little things something idiotically trivial at the office, or about the future. And he worried about the fact that he was worrying.

Life and work were, for the most part, rewarding and challenging. He was not a physical or emotional cripple, nor was he going out of his mind. But at times he found himself just not being himself. He would swear at the children, find fault with his wife, eat too much and get fatter and fatter, and be so depressed and quarrelsome that even he could not stand himself. One day he would be optimistic and enthusiastic, and on another day depressed and unhappy. This happened regardless of whether the sun was shining or the rain was falling. There just was never any sane reason for these turbulent mood swings. The worst part was the frequent feeling of fear, which varied in intensity during the day, and his mind was preoccupied with pessimistic and frequently angry outbursts. He had minor discomforts—a chronic pain in the neck area and mild stomach upsets. The happiest part of the day was the time when, with the help of sleeping medicine, he was asleep. The real surprising thing though is that his life was happy, and there was no rational explanation for his fears, angers and anxieties. Also, whenever he was away on trips or in the country for the holidays, his mind ceased to be constantly active, to nag away at minor and largely irrelevant problems and things. Also, when he began to voice his believe about the city air being unhealthy, a close friend astonishingly agreed with him, and to his utter amazement, confessed to him that he suspected a Witches' Wind was responsible for his troubles. The proof, she asserted, was evident in widespread fights at homes, suicides, murders, traffic accidents, divorce, sexual impotency, xenophobia, even plane crashes! He was astonished but politely reserved his judgment. After all, they were both experiencing trying times, and Francistown was a violent city.

Then something completely amazing happened. Train whistles. As he lay awake, one windy day, reading, he could explicitly, but faintly, hear the sound of trains. This in itself was usual, since the tracks were miles to the south of his apartment. He decided to drive into the city just to while away the time. For some reason he noticed that many drivers were behaving like madmen. When he asked his friend for a possible explanation of these things she whispered to him ominously: "wind sickness." In the garden, even in the house, he began to notice, or imagine, that animals were restive and insects, inexplicably, suddenly erupted with an explosion of energy and became a plague instead of just a nuisance. To him nothing could reasonably account for this state of euphoria, of tingling excitement, interspersed with murders and suicides and violence. No one could explain why the wind was evil; why it brought misfortune and unhappiness. What was it? The climate? The food? The minerals content of the water? Industrial pollution? The thousands of tons of dust and sand that the wind picks as it crosses the arid, trackless Kalahari Desert? Celestial constellations like the moon, for instance? Rats, insects and plants? No reasonable explanation presented itself to his tortured mind.

To make matters worse, it was at this moment of greatest perplexity that some rascal decided to murder Batjibilibili, the celebrated columnist and writer, bringing to his life a thunderstorm he never dreamed of encountering in his otherwise sedate, if only boring, existence. It was at this time that his friend Satjilombe advised him to close his small office in Francistown and move to the capital city of Gaborone where business was booming for lawyers, as the economy was being routed by the global recession and white collar crime was skyrocketing. He agreed to do so. After all his wife had lived all the time in their home in Gaborone, spending only a bits of time in Francistown whenever it suited her purpose to do so.

One thing that really bothered him was his relationship with Bafi. Try as he might he simply could never understand the woman. There was a look in the eyes of Bafi as if she was expecting something unknown, about which she was eager. She had that air of readiness for what would come to her, a kind of surety, expectancy, the look of an achiever, conqueror and possessor, all rolled in one. She was fresh, vibrant, and alive to the instinctive reality of her world. Listening to her speak was a revelation constrained only by an aversion to give utterance to the external reality of the world beyond her reach. She recoiled with terror from the spoken world beyond her reach. Her fancy always turned to the heat of the blood, to blood intimacy, to complacent sensual domesticity. The world of politics, government, public goods, action and personal sacrifice terrified her beyond measure.

Her only world was her married life, a magic land where secrets were made known and desires fulfilled. Dominant and creative life—its compromises, deals, half-measures and bargains—she shut out from consciousness, banished to the unfathomable darkness beyond. She strained to listen to the horrible sound in the distance but refrained from the battles waged on the edge of the unknown. She was native to the earth, eschewed outwardness and any range of emotion. Inert, complacent, palpitate, and drowsy, Bafi had yet a quickness and range of being that made her husband dull, dry and parochial. She knew her husband, all right. She thought she had power over her husband, a power guaranteed by knowledge, a power inviolable and sacrosanct. They both had money, education and experience: the all mighty common denominators in modern society.

They had children, his children, she didn't think of herself as a mother—she was a homeowner, a partner, a married woman, and her blood flowed heavy with the accumulation from the living day. The children, like her husband, were parts of her heart. Her life was the epic that inspired their lives. Her duty was to protect them from the more vivid, vital circle of life that in her belief was the ruin of many a happy and prosperous home. Freedom, whoever suffered from lack of freedom when they were rich? Wealth made their lives finer, bigger, free, happier, not action, the power of thought and comprehension. People of action, thinkers and idealists were inclined to hate. Bafi loved her self-contained world with fearsome pleasure. She was a big, pretty, dark woman with a humorous puckering at the eyes, a sort of fat laugh, very quiet and full, rather querulous in her manner, but intrinsically separate and indifferent, a being to herself, she loved people who could convey enlightenment to her through feeling. She was more sensually developed, more refined in instinct than her husband (who adhered with all his tenacity to his work and to his professional position, making many friends, and becoming fairly well-off.) He pursued distinction stubbornly, with anguish, crushing the bowels within him, adhering to his commitments whatever it should cost. He roused himself to determination, with a passion for outwards refinement in social milieu, got mad when anything clumsy or gross occurred.

Their marriage had not been unpleasant; they had enjoyed the companionship of their youth or had thought they enjoyed it. The time had passed very quickly (in endless activity for him, and languid contentment for her). She considered herself the conscience-keeper of the family, a belief strengthened by her innate desire to find in a man the embodiment of all her inarticulate, powerful impulses, strong impulses derived from religion and love and morality. She made a strong, instinctive fight to retain her native cheerfulness unimpaired, with a balanced, easy-flying voice: at times scowling with mortification at the things her husband said, his companions, friends comates and associates (of whom were many), she treated with courteous contempt, specially their fine-textured, subtle-mannered dispositions and idiosyncrasies.

She desperately, painfully, fought for the world to submit to the well-known circle of her own life, the enclosure of her reality, passionately and intensely resenting to be burdened with the unreality of established conventionalities. It was to her a profound satisfaction to confront actualities that she could handle, so that she retained completeness and perfection and an inviolable power. Anything that tended to destruction of this complacent reality filled her heart with a bursting passion of rage and incompetence. She deeply resented such vague collapses, and she must defend herself against it, for it was destruction, a symbol that she was incomplete, fragmentary, impotent, essentially contemptible, and an unutterably bad wife. She wanted to give her husband all her love, all her passion, all her essential energy, all her life, all her companionship. She wanted to be his center of living, his center of truth, his center of knowledge, to be vitally connected to him and him alone. She hated it when human life was used for cold, unloving purposes. She secretly despised him for unreasoned commitment to technical functionality, a resentment generously assuaged by the material utility accruing from active public life.

For the most part she was happy to be quiet, secure, unnoticed, unnoticing, sitting safe and easy and unadventurous. She was too much the center of her own universe, too content to be aware of anything outside. She deeply hated ugliness or intrusion or arrogance, however. She had plenty of acquaintances, but few friends. Very few people whom she met were significant to her; they seemed part of a herd, undistinguished, uncouth, and amorphous and a threat to her individuality. She would stay at home and avoid the rest of the world, leaving it illusory. Life had to have a certain freedom and largeness, within limits. She assiduously cultivated tolerant dignity in her family but cared not for what other people thought, or said about it.

The people she met outside seemed to begrudge her very existence. She was exceedingly reluctant to go amongst them. At the bottom of her heart, she despised the other people. She instinctively felt they had disproportionate power over her. Her capacity for living her own life without attention from her neighbors made them respect her. She existed beyond their petty considerations inside her own world, from which the other people were outsiders. She lived a life of strange, profound ecstasies and incommunicable satisfactions, of which the rest of the world knew nothing, a life of utter surety, confidence and strange satisfaction, even triumphant power over all things and people around her. She did not want things from outside to be dragged into consciousness.

She had a strong dark bond with her husband, a potent intimacy that existed inarticulate and wild, following its own course, savage if interrupted, uncovered. She hated to hear things expressed, put into words. The only man she knew was her husband, and as he was something large, looming, a kind of Godhead, he embraced all manhood for her, and other men were just incidental.

They lived their life vividly, swiftly and intensely. In her world, there was this one tense, vivid body of a man, and then many other shadowy men, all unreal. In him, she touched the center of reality. And they were together, he and she, at the heart of a mystic secret. His body was the center of all life. Out of the rock of his form the very fountain of life flowed. Inside the home was a great steadiness, a core of living eternity. Only far outside at the rim, went on the noise and the destruction. Here at the center the great wheel was motionless, centered upon itself. Inside, in the softness and stillness of the house, was the naked kernel that palpitated in silent activity, absorbed in reality. Here was a poised, unflawed stillness that was beyond time, because it remained the same, inexhaustible, unchanging, unexhausted, and complete and beyond the touch of time or change: a silence absorbed in praise and joy and gladness.

It was her business to keep steering the splendid ship of their dual life. She assiduously asserted her position as captain of the ship. As peace reigned there was a great trembling of wonder and anticipation for better things to come, through her soul. It was great to master a domestic craft that made up the great fleet of society, to accomplish emotional and philosophical unity within the vitality of her domestic craft, to fulfil the hidden passion of her spirit, without being actively part of the greater society, to remain distinct, separate, different even recklessly indifferent to the wholesomeness of all things outside, yet remain part of the whole through explicit social identity and recognition, to be at the bosom of the most beautiful moments in life, to be fulfilled and separate and sufficient in her little part of the world, to be complete in herself, to be free, separate and independent out of the vastness of humanity. She felt that the whole of human society was exterior and extraneous to her own real life with Mapopota. The great mass of activity in which mankind was engaged meant nothing to her. By nature, she had no part in it. She was an absolute being, an absolute being of Eternity, outside of Time. The world outside, the fabricated world, was nothing. Why should she be part of it? It was too artificial, strange and encumbered with unknown realities: unfulfillment, alienation, disillusion, ennui, illusions, umpteen incalculable outrages, and unconscious darkness. She was happy to have made something beautifully enchanting out of the nothingness and indifferent mass of the outside world. Who wanted a world of crowded people, duties, and reports? Bafi was the direct opposite of Batjibilibili, with whom Mapopota thought they shared a similar view of life, even though she too was just so much of an enigma to him. In many ways she frightened him, and most of the time he was just content to listen to her talk. He particularly enjoyed her public spurts with Satjilombe, which he unashamedly encouraged whenever he could and never felt bad about eavesdropping. Take the conversation they had over dinner at Notwane Club the other day, for example. It sounded so innocuous at first that even he felt like chipping in a word till it dawned upon his mind that it was punctuated by subtexts and agendas that were beyond his comprehension.

"Doesn't it bother you, Satjilombe," asked Batjibilibili indignantly, "that we live in a time of fear, that the world makes no sense, that too many people are fragile, insecure, vulnerable . . . I mean don't you worry about the fate of our age? Doesn't today's world worry you? Look around and think about fear, the wanting feeling of security, human goodness and people's dreams of happiness. Look at the daily lives of people in our huge sprawling cities, the wretched lot in rural areas, pollution, and political corruption: do you think human creativity and ingenuity can win the battle against these fears and terrors? Look at what AIDS is doing to our people. Malaria, cholera, tuberculosis and cancer. Look at the rapid disappearance of religious feelings, taboos, ethics, morals, idealism and human fellowship and love in our society. Look at all these things and tell me there still is hope for better things to come for us. How are we going to manage our daily lives? Look at all these things and tell me the truth. Do you have answers for our non-existence? I mean . . . we live in the age of destruction, mass deaths, mass misery and great suffering. The politics of grief has taken center stage in public life and popular imagination. Aren't you afraid that you'll go to sleep tonight and that'll be it? No tomorrow. That's what happens to people who die in bed, you know. It doesn't matter what kills you: disease, a terrorist, a fire accident, your lover, the witch living next door, a thief, a ritual murderer, your child, your wife, your husband, your political foe, torrential rain, the food you eat, your own heart, your President, Tony Blair and George Bush. Anything can kill you these days. Social ties, too, are disappearing every minute, every second. There are too many rifts within communities, within neighborhoods, within families, rifts of every kind; from the irritatingly persistent but benign to the cruel, the ridiculous and the absurd and they all bring untold pain, anguish and suffering to millions of people. The law is already a dead institution. Crime walks abroad. Do you think there is hidden hope somewhere? Enlighten me . . . a little secret in the office of the President?"

"Well, vision 2016 is our solution to these demented problems. I now know what people mean when they say women have active imaginations. What makes you think up all this stuff? This can't be good for your mind, not to mention your health."

"You're evading the issues. You're always happy enough when I blab and think with my vagina. Then you behave like the true scavenger that you are. Now, answer my questions. You are not seriously suggesting that vision 2016 will inaugurate a Millennium Utopia are you? The prophesied one thousand years of human happiness?"

"Well, I don't know what you are talking about, but it's a step in the right direction."

"Oh, so there's hope after all? Boys, boys, boys. When are you going to share this great revelation with the wretched of the earth?"

"Very funny."

"Am I to it take it that the scandalous imperfection of the modern world doesn't concern you at all?"

"Simply amusing. These things happened before and the human race survived."

"Really? When? To my knowledge, the earth has ever experienced mass extinction. A few other species, maybe. Human beings? Nope. We just have no past experiences to learn from. We really should worry about our lives today."

"You speak as if you belong to some imagined community no one knows about. Get real. We are doing just fine. Tomorrow and tomorrow, and tomorrow we'll still be here making money, fucking, talking and laughing our lungs till kingdom come. Disappointment is part of the human experience, an integral part of our history. Are you disappointed at still being alive? Want to meet the Maker soon?"

"Don't be silly. I worry about other people too. You probably don't see them. Politicians aren't supposed to care. As an ordinary human being, I worry about the problems of everybody existence."

"Honorable, very honorable. Most women just think about bread and butter. Don't turn into a prophet of doom. People will laugh at you."

"I'm a realist. A humanist. I think about things. Is that a crime? Is that funny?"

"It seems to me you believe too much in nothingness. Why do you fear things that do not exist? Don't hate the world too much. Learn to love your condition. Be calm. Take a walk in the forest. Enjoy life."

"You don't get it, do you?"

"What?"

"No wonder you are such a monstrous criminal! For criminals like you, life is one fabulous party, a ritual extravaganza. Wait till death pays you a visit. I hope you'll remember my word before the penultimate blink."

"Batjibilibili, all I'm saying is that you should deal with the void of your maladjustment to reality in a better way."

"I don't think I can make a good thief. My conscience is in perpetual turmoil and revolt."

"No need to be rude."

"I'm not rude. I think you don't know what constitutes a normal human being. Given an opportunity, you'd probably refuse you are mortal. It's amazing what little power can do to people. A simple temporal thing: people get it and immediately forget they are part of the human story. They start orchestrating and living parallel delusional human narratives. People like you conceal from themselves the risks that threaten their very existence, that threaten their future, or, at least the future of their children and generations to come. I think it's a terrible thing to be a one dimensional being in a world that has already succumbed to complexification. Tell me about reality! Mad men like you are creatures of unreality. If you aren't careful, you'll not even live long enough to witness the consequences of your complacent indifference to reality. Everything, including human inertia, is always wasted away by time. Serve your time, tomorrow is another day. All things age. The ungraspable reality of today will be unmasked and exposed, naked, to your weary eyes tomorrow, and you'll not be in a position to do anything about the tragic encounter because of reckless unpreparedness. Think of what happened to Louis Nchindo, no less dramatic, really, than the decapitation of Louis XIV of France after the busting of the Bastille."

"It's good to see that you have a well-developed sense of humor. I think your brain, too, is equipped to cope with a certain historical unfolding. But you're too judgmental, and too hard on yourself and those of us who love you so much. We live for between fifty and a hundred years. Who cares to be trapped in endless and meaningless philosophical disquisitions about life?"

"But that's exactly my point, that far too many people are trapped in a time warp of unconsciousness and oblivion, and that is even more dangerous for our well-being, and the generations to come. Don't you think we should strive for more ardent, more visible, palpable, more imaginative, conscientious, and meaningful lives; to strive for life that is introspective, more somber, and dynamic at the same time?"

"Don't worry about time. There's a time for everything. The world's time. The soul's time. Old time. Dead time. Rising time. Time to love. Time of war. Time to live. Time to die. We have hundreds and thousands of invented time dimensions. Time will always take care of itself. Right now we're all very happy as it is. It's time for happiness. Unwind; enjoy yourself, tomorrow is another day. I hate this attitude of there is no time to lose. Think about tomorrow. Why? What for? Tomorrow will take care of itself. Always remember that God is outside time. Our Lord and Savior is free from this tyranny of arbitrary little time frames of our life. Time may diminish human possibilities, exhaust itself, even disappear. In the end your fate is dependent on God's will to replenish human possibilities and choices, and our creative genius to grasp and use evolving opportunities for better and healthier life."

"You're a thorough-going optimist, aren't you?"

"No, not really. I'm a politician, and I believe in human happiness."

"What a contradiction of terms! Do you know where the human race is headed?"

"No, and I quite frankly I don't care much. As I said, we're doing just fine at the present moment. The very concept of time annoys me; human time treats us with disdain. I hate it. It's better to subscribe to absolute, supreme, divine time. That way, we can all have a good time and leave everything to God. All we have to do is pray and retain our divine right to rise up to God. All this can be done without us forfeiting life, the real life. I rest my case. How about a little sexual chitchat for dessert, honey? Let's leave this place."

"Go to hell! You really are full of shit. I've never met any person more conceited, selfish, self-righteous and ignorant than you. You can't even define the period we live in. You seem to think that institutional innovation will ever change human nature. What an illusion. You fail to grasp that human greed is the ruination of us all. You exalt in nothingness. You don't even know what you don't know. Why on Mother Earth's name should I have sex with such a ferocious moron? Give me some credit, damn it! Why are you looking at me like that? I could easily gouge out those pathetic bleary eyes and save you the trouble to worry about the wretched reality around us. Why don't you ask God to do something about your brain time?"

"What a tirade? I still have to meet a better champion of spleen and anguish. No one loves wretchedness the way you do. I think you need to grow up."

"Ha . . . ha . . . ha . . . look at what growing up has done to you! You're a perfect human ruin. A fossilized relic of a past long gone and you tell me your life is meaningful, has a future. How pathetic can things be?"

"At least I don't have reasons only to despair."

"No you do not, you're blind, lost, at sea, and you don't even know it."

"I'm not having this conversation with you; you are an incorrigibly arrogant nutcase."

"It's really good to hear that from the veritable Apostle of the Immediate. The outrageous gambler. But then you're a swindler through and through; the beauty of life and the world means nothing to you."

"I think you've lost your mind; soon you'll go mad. Still, there is a certain beauty in that terrible moral anguish of yours, what you need is great sex."

"I think you're a very, very sick man."

"I don't believe this. I've tolerated your senseless ranting and raving for a stupefying unimaginable length of time, and still, you refuse to have sex with me. What a humiliation!"

"For a scoundrel like you, I should do more."

"This is pathetic. I think you use your arrogance as a way of escaping from the world, a way of avoiding reality, avoiding living real life, with real people. You seek oblivion in an imagined dreamland. There is no other way of explaining this wayward behavior. I advise you to break out of this mind-set, to be more human, to take full possession of your senses, to get your brain talking to your ass, to regain your wandering femininity. You're European, the way you see things, do things; your entire conception of human reality is foreign to me, and probably to you as well. To me the past is no more than a second, at most a day, away. I live in the present and afterlife with my community and our ancestors. History is a seamless river flowing throughout our intermingled lives, uninterrupted, unceasing, and relentless. The night is the time of love and happiness, daylight anguish, toil and work. At night, life has a pleasant rhythm and from time immemorial, it was always a time of drumbeats, singing, dancing, divine invocations, copulation, and more significant coupling between the living and the dead. Our people's conception of time and reality is deeply rooted in the night. A walk around the African village at night was always a journey as long as thousands of miles match around the world. Children played until midnight. Elders sat chatting, drinking, dancing, and even quarrelling around fire till sleep claimed its sovereignty over their old bones. The greatest hunters preyed on weary creatures well before dawn. But the greatest delight of night life was always the mysterious enchanting dance between lovers: young and old, married and unmarried, visitor and host, even friends and foe. Outside marriage, of course, sex was expressly license and not greatly celebrated. The moment animal blankets started emitting seminal odour and fresh animal fat, parents knew the children were actively experimenting with sex, thigh sex or the real thing. Same sex activity was very common, even bestiality, in fact, old men often talked of virile young warriors of past ages who had courage and strength enough to mount lionesses."

"Well, you can go and mount lionesses for all I care!"

That's Batjibilibili for you, a woman of many seasons and a brave heart, a woman with a mind of her own. Bafi is something unfathomable altogether.

How Batjibilibili had first met Satjilombe is something that Mapopota would have killed to know. Yet there really wasn't much mystery about it. Her aunt, Chandiwana could have told him the whole story for a song.

"He's a friend," said Batjibilibili, companionably, "just a casual friend. There is nothing in it. Really. Nothing at all."

Chandiwana twisted her hands nervously together. She was exploring troubled waters, and she knew it. Crossing personal boundaries could easily ruin their friendship.

"But you've been so funny lately. Sort of . . . occupied . . . your father has noticed it. And I wondered . . . well I thought it might be something to do with him....Of course, it's not my place . . . ."

"Well it isn't," Batjibilibili snapped, and then when she saw the hurt on her aunt's face she felt guilty, relented a bit, and grimaced a sheepish smile. But how could she explain to her aunt about the excitement, the fear, the delight, and violence of her meetings with Satjilombe Gudogulu, nominated Member of Parliament, and the Minister of Home Affairs. Every week they quarrelled, every week they shouted at each other about the accursed questions of life and death; about sex and happiness, love and hate, disease and travel, duty and honor, or whether it was right that so and so was entitled to this and that, or, more frequently, whether the coming elections had any real bearing on the larger issues of freedom, justice and public equity. And every week Satjilombe would fire her with excitement, would lift her out of herself, making her feel that she was living in a world where things were happening, where anything was possible. And every week he would surprise her with his sudden changes from vehemence to tenderness and joyous delight. Once in the middle of a heated debate, he had turned towards her, grasped her soft face between his hands and, impulsively and violently, ravished her with kisses and the tenderest and caressing words. Often he would snatch her hand and hold it against his face. Always the right hand. Sometimes the tide of emotion between them would grow so intense he would just keep saying, "Honey, Ohhhh...honey."

Batjibilibili thought that was stupid, Hollywoodish gibberish designed to gently reel her in, and she vigorously swathed away the temptation. She was glad they met in public places where even he had to control himself. She was quite sure that if ever they were alone together, alone and private and unseen, their passionate intensity would flare into something violent and uncontrollable.

"You like him, don't you?" said Chandiwana doggedly.

"Of course not..."

Batjibilibili began, and then quailed under her aunt's passionate gaze. And then to her horror, the temptation to confide in someone, just a little, grew too much and she burst out, "Oh, Aunt! He is so interesting. He's got all kinds of ideas, some of them are stupid, but they are different. And, once, when he had time, he took me to an orchestra concert in Johannesburg. It was lovely. I never heard music like that before. Not in my whole life. It made me . . ."

She flung her thin arms out in the air, trying to describe in movement the way she had felt.

"He makes me feel . . . oh . . . I don't know . . . The world is so big! He makes me feel the world is so big."

"Is that all? The world is so big? Is that it?"

Chandiwana sighed her disappointment with dramatic flourish.

Aunt Chandiwana felt nervous. She was really worried about Batjibilibili.

"Why don't you take him home? If he's that special, you ought to take him to the village to meet your father and the family."

Batjibilibili burst out laughing. She laughed till real copious tears coursed down her cheeks. Taking Satjilombe to the village? What madness!

"I can't."

"Why can't you?"

"I just can't."

Another peel of laughter seized her violently.

Batjibilibili loved her father. Army life had impressed upon him the value of orderliness over impending chaos, but she doubted if he would really understand a man like Satjilombe. She admired his sternness in the face of little insurrections, the subject of endless quarrelling when she was a little girl, and his believe in polishing, spitting, and polishing again, against all the combined forces of darkness. He was an honest, industrious and caring man. A true soldier, through and through. He didn't question things deeply, and most things he understood, but she instinctively knew that he would see through Satjilombe, and deeply dislike all the things that she turned a blind eye to, the strange things that frightened her and drew her to him at the same time. Satjilombe was callous, ruthless and dishonest to an alarming degree. He claimed these things came with the job. He could convince her of anything, but in her heart she knew these things were wrong. No decent job required competence in violence and flagrant disregard of conventional morality. Not even politics. She knew that in the village his wild words and violent actions would shock and frighten people, even provoke the wrath of others. She couldn't bear to think about it; to have her father and her aunt and all the good people attacked and violated by his uncouth ways and foul aspersions on all things good and orderly.

"But what's going to happen?" said Chandiwana.

"I don't know."

"And what about him? What about the Honorable Minister? Such a big man, really, Batjibilibili, this thing can't be kept a secret. What does he say about it all? What does he think?"

Batjibilibili giggled.

"Auntie, politicians don't make decisions. They lie, prevaricate and dither around issues. They operate in a muddled world. You can't trust a politician to clearly and unequivocally decide a real issue. They always swim with the tide and hope for the best."

"Don't give me that horseshit. You spend so much time talking about things. What does he say?"

"Nothing, really. Well, I don't know what to say. We don't talk about it. That's all. It's really best that way."

"I don't believe a word of it. A whole Minister of the State and an intelligent and beautiful young woman spend thousands of hours arguing and arranging problems of the world, but they never talk about things like going home to meet their families? That's strange, really strange. Someone must pump sense into your head, girl. Your brain must be completely depleted of energy and good old common sense."

Batjibilibili turned her face away and fiddled with her flowing hair. It was true that at times she sensed that there were areas of background and family in his life that she must not explore—things he would not talk about and did not wish to share with her. Now she stared into Aunt Chandiwana's face—good, honest, simple—and said again, "I can't take him home, Auntie. It's no good. He and father just would not like each other."

"Oh, Batjibilibili!"

The distress she felt registered in her voice and her face. She looked so doleful that Batjibilibili began to laugh again. After the conversation with Aunt Chandiwana, Batjibilibili's relationship with Satjilombe changed. She could no longer pretend that he was just a friend. The arguments, the fights, the ideas, the time, the pleasures, the fun they had together; these were important; but now she had to admit that more important were the swift kisses, the rare stolen passions in the dark, the way he smiled at her and grasped her shoulders, the way her stomach knotted inside every time she saw him waiting for her at the bus rank.

She couldn't take him home but she wanted to. She wanted on these occasions to be free in her choices and desires. To love, and be loved, to do everything the right way, at the right time, and in the right place, and to have her feelings for him blessed by the approval of family and friends. After talking to Chandiwana, the unspoken but keenly felt attraction between them became more intense—so intense it was sometimes unbearable. It was as though Satjilombe, instantly recognizing the change in her, responded quickly to her lack of restraint. At the end of April he took her to another concert, only the second she had attended in her whole life and this time, with her emotions towards him no longer controlled, she found the soaring introspection of the music more than she could bear. It was big, painfully delightful music during which she became hurtfully aware that he was beside her, that his arm was touching hers, that if she turned her head she would see his rich, curved features and intense face enraptured. She blissfully surrendered to the beauty and emotional authority of the Soweto Orchestra Ensemble.

Batjibilibili was not to know it, the way, that is, Satjilombe entered the world of politics and how he operated as a politician of note. The election campaign sensitized her to a few unsavory parts of his character, a few unsettling things apparently common in campaign trails. He called them weapons of war. Batjibilibili was new to the game of politics, but she was not a simpleton. She hated Satjilombe's politics and said so. They agreed to separate the loathsome world of politics from the pleasures of their private life. But from the margins of party activity, she saw him at work, and felt nothing but terror and admiration. Satjilombe bargained, bribed, blackmailed, fought, blustered, used violence, burned and fumed like nitric acid just to get his way with everybody and everything. He spoke to workers, vendors, students and boisterously noisy crowds in the slums and outskirts of the city. He asked names, gossiped, talked about their families, working conditions, ambitions, hopes and fears. He explored, smelled and felt. After exhausting hours he returned to his campaign headquarters. He glanced through his campaign manager's notes, absorbed them, closed his eyes and stood still and silent in the middle of the office like a man straining to hear a distant whisper. The following day, the campaign team reassembled and marched out of the office into the wilderness again. People grabbed their chance to take photos and touch the great man. He asked names, introduced and amused. The team returned to the office. Again the great man looked at the confounded notes, closed his eyes and stood still and silent in the middle of the office. Time too stood still. Nothing ever happened. March in, March out. Batjibilibili was disappointed.

"We should do something," muttered someone.

"What the hell is the matter with him anyway?"

One of the assembled men inquired.

"Who knows?"

Another exclaimed in exasperation.

"He screams. He curses. He fires. He appoints. He sulks. He travels. But nothing happens. Don't ask me why. It's something buried in his past."

More silence. Time still stood still.

"Haven't you asked him?"

"How can I? It's like an epileptic fit. He never knows it happened."

"Take him to a psychoanalyst."

"Out of the question."

"Why?"

"He is not our friend. I think he needs a friend. People talk to their friends."

"We're his friends."

"No, we are not. We're hired hands."

"Has he talked to you?"

"No."

"And, you?"

"No."

"A woman, I think. A special kind of woman. That's what he needs."

"Damn it, man! It doesn't make sense. He's got the whole country at his feet. Under his thumb, whatever the bloody idiom. And he needs a woman? I don't think so. We'll have to hire him a friend. We're rich enough to afford it. From now on we cut the program to one campaign a week. Someone must break the news to him. We need a decision maker here."

"Who?"

"You."

"No. I'm not his friend."

Shocked and bewildered, Batjibilibili fled the city.

A few days after marrying Ludo Shango, the Vice-President's alcoholic daughter, Satjilombe could make decisions; he could make friends. His voice was still high but soft. He was a powerful man in his own right. He moved with the athlete's lazy poise that is almost feminine. He charmed you without knowing how he did it, or even wanting to do it. He charmed Ludo, but Ludo also charmed him. They became friends. They moved into a huge suburban mansion and bribed their way back into political office. They golfed, tennised, and went to cinemas and expensive restaurants. Satjilombe Gudogulu was appointed Chief Minister in the Office of the President. Ludo soon realized that he was known everywhere. A bewigged call girl told her in the little ladies room, in the purple haze of cocaine snorting, bluntly: "They know him the worst way."

"By name? The Decider? It's a beautiful masculine name,"

She said confidently.

"By nickname. Wasteland, they call him."

"Wasteland? What a terrible name!"

"Well, I don't know about that, the terrible part I mean. The girls call him Mr. Devastation."

"That's just terrible. But, why?"

"That's his name. It's what he does. You don't know this?"

"I don't know what?"

"They say he runs through women like a prairie fire."

Ludo shook her head.

"There is a terrifying quality to the possessed way that your husband runs through women. They know him in every city from Cape to Cairo. And they know him the worst way. It's like he's working against time. He's hard to please. Some of the girls, I'd call them sensational. But he doesn't pay any mind to them. Others, dogs practically . . ."

"Enough!" Ludo was stunned, but took the insult quietly.

She was in love with him. It was big romantic stuff. God damn it, they were married! They were friends! But the call girl was not finished. "You ever hear the expression 'one girl in a million'?"

"Who hasn't?" Ludo smiled sadly.

"You are one lucky girl, Mrs. Ludo ShangoGudogulu," said the stoned whore as she stood in the doorway quietly drifting into the purple haze. Ludo didn't know whether to laugh or cry.

"It's going to be one long night," said the whore enigmatically and vanished, leaving her astounded.

That afternoon she had been reading Fitzgerald's *Tender is the Night* and laughing off her head silly. What a terrible coincidence she told herself as she turned to the huge mirrored wall and screamed. She remembered the saying the moment a great man finds his girl, he heals himself. He stops being great, and turns into a nobody, a man in love . . . just a man in love. Why should he care about greatness anymore? He only wants to be happy. Everybody wants to be happy. He is not different from other men. Thought. Rationality. Doubt. Wonder. Fear. And terror, assailed her the whole while. I want him to be happy. Every man could be happy if only we we'd lend a helping hand. She'd look the same. Act the same. Pretend everything was the same. Play the game of life. Let things drift on. Damn that whore!

And thank God for small mercies. Her husband was a political celebrity with a tremendous animal magnetism. And a lot richer than most man his age. Why shouldn't a few beautiful women throw themselves at him? Why bother about his past? We only remember the past, and think little to nothing about the future, don't we? But time goes on, and farewells should be for ever. What about the past? What did it matter? The past, she reckoned, is another country. A different world. A different reality. Things change. People change. Why can't we understand and forgive people who do wrong? People aren't always in conscious control of their actions; very often the unconscious takes over. There are times, she told herself when all the good sense in a man shouts a warning that what he is about to do will only create grief, but he goes ahead and does it anyway. All this is in the nature of human beings.

"Hasn't that happened to you?" she wondered aloud.

A voice answered behind her. "Never, my dear."

She started and turned around. She hadn't realized her soliloquy was in full blast. That she had actually been talking to herself like a lunatic. That she had been addressing the woman on the other side of the mirror. That another woman was standing behind her, watching and listening. And she had completely failed to register the presence of both. It was a terrifying experience. The woman behind her was smiling. She decided to be good spot and let the conversation continue. "Well, can you see it happening to other people?"

"Not intelligent people. No."

The woman was resolute.

"Intelligence has nothing to do with it. We are talking here about the brutal reality of an everyday human experience. Can't you concede that a nice guy who only wants to do right can be compelled by the beast within to do wrong?"

"No," said Batjibilibili smiling.

A stubborn bitch, Ludo thought ruefully. But the impasse generated a more congenial conversation about the rawness of life and its impact on the human heart and both women acquitted themselves with a compassionate brilliance. Ludo did not know it at the time, but she had found a great friend in the little ladies' room.

Satjilombe looked with displeasure at a thin film of dust on some of the furniture, at the wall pictures awry, at the unwashed plates in the kitchen and cigarette ash, and the cork tip floating in a brackenish water filled glass. He bore his shortcomings from a dislike of change, a deep disapproval of self-improvement; not that he was really conscious of this perverse inclination.

Nothing was strange here. He was a creature of habit. He decided to go to bed early. He had eaten at his club, which he used a great deal, and if not exactly a very popular man, he was well known in his club, and prized by other members as an eccentric. He would have been startled to know this. He thought himself quite a senior member with the distinction only of eminence. As he undressed and climbed into his crimson-curtained French bed, still rumpled and unmade, his heart was as steady as a rock, everything he had eaten and drunk having been perfectly assimilated. He mused on the strangeness of the human mind, which could allow fear and apprehension to grow so large that all else was blocked out, yet a few hours later, the fear, having been adjudged groundless, was so far shrunken as to be hard to reimagine. One couldn't quite believe it was correctly remembered. Was I so upset? Did I believe those pains were an early coronary? Am I not now recalling it as worse than it truly was? He fell into a pleasant reverie and allowed past memories and future ambitions to lacerate his heart.

At midnight he suddenly woke, feeling terribly alone. The sound of distant traffic had almost stopped, and he lay between the cool sheets with a curious sense of desolation as if he would never again have communication with the outside world. It was as if the loneliness were so intense that it became claustrophobic. One fought for movement and air. One was buried alive in loneliness, tied down by the silence, struggling to have someone to speak to, to confide in, and to care. At times like this one did lack companionship, the confidante, the friend. The soliloquy went on, turned into a dream, a sort of dream that was also half-nightmare. Drive through the a half-silent city, check in at the soulless, sleep-walking, dehydrated, hygienic social club, wait in the bar, eat something to kill time, mingle with the idiotic crowd, elbow someone aside to get the best seat by the door, jog through the night, half yawning, half afraid. He woke up with a start again, drenched in perspiration. He fought his way out of bed, and started looking forward to another day.

At the office he fell in with the crowd, a motley crew he thought, with cheap clothes, shabby hand luggage, the ineffable air of appallingly ordinary people, people without real quality of any kind, except perhaps the quality of feigned respectability. He felt nausea mounting fast . . . he despised them all. One of the most maddening things about politics, Satjilombe always felt, was that people could talk at will to you, and worse, expect the impossible from you. This breeds a degree of frustration that makes the blood pressure mount all the time, and one always has to laugh at the complication of it all.

A buzz of conversation now broke out, partly humorous, partly nervous, and he found himself caught up in the common impulse and communicating his feeling to the honorable member beside him. He felt annoyance at him calmly. A total lack of imagination; docile, commonplace, ignorant, one of the crowd; cannon fodder, just slightly but deceptively different because of his youthful looks. An inveterate opportunist. Millions of such bred and lived and died unnoticed all over the world, as they rightly deserved to. Lucky bugger! To think that this insignificant oaf . . . there was an ugly bruise on his neck, an ugly, raw dirt mark, something resembling the mad scratch of an angry whore. For a brief and inappropriate moment the annoyance he felt for his neighbour changed to compassion as he thought...then it dawned on him . . . a fear of sudden extinction jolted him tremulously, a purely primitive reaction just as an old tree will try to flower when its roots are endangered. Then the unpleasant sensation passed, leaving only normal terror again, a little reprieve after a perfectly sickening lurch. Life, he reflected, peels off the layers of fluff with which we are born and eventually leaves us stark. Then from nowhere, another honorable member, a physically strong, brave, but small bald, cruel man with blandly innocent twinkling eyes and a candid smile spoke.

"Do you always have to vote this way?" he said petulantly.

"Always the old way, the safe way, so simple and safe," he countered maliciously.

The game was over. Honorable members filed from the House.

Chapter 4

A Peculiar Mess . . .

New Kalahari Village, 1997

"That's the way things are like here. It's our own way of doing things, the Botswana Way," said a heated Jadibolole Mongwato.

He had worked himself into a perfect frenzy over a remark made by Howard Johnson, an African-American photographer currently resident in New Kalahari Village. The quiet Canadian, Bill Bell, watched the animated exchange with a subdued indifference. Bill had an intense distaste for human passion. The memory of the ruckus between Indians and Quebeques still rankled. His interest lay in diamond exploration, something he considered a professional virtue, not that he had anything to show for seven years of trampling the desert sands and dunes, always under the worst heat possible.

The British Labour Party parliamentarians, comfortably sitting at the other end of the bar counter pretended not to be aware of the impassioned conversation. They had been in New Kalahari Village for three days at the invitation of the Botswana government. Their mission was to see for themselves how well Basarwa lived and report back to the international community. In exchange for this valuable humanitarian service, they had agreed to spend some three weeks enjoying a stupendous, and free, Safari Holiday. Ketilepele Lefatshe tried to interject but Jadibolole cut him short with a thunderous howl.

"We hate you," the District Commissioner exclaimed indignantly.

"The air in the whole country hates you. You are tarnishing the beautiful image of our country. This very land you are standing on hates you. The diamonds you are always moaning and crying about hate you. The water that you so much thirst for hates you. The entire Kalahari

Desert hates you! There's no purpose in your staying on this land. Our grandparents vanquished and conquered you, and everything you own. Now you belong to us. This land belongs to us . . ."

He abruptly stopped as if he had been struck by an epileptic seizure. Everybody in the bar held their breath. Ketilepele fervently hoped the fool would lurch forward and die. He watched his adversary with an unconcealed fascination. The two grimy and profusely sweating civil servants sharing rounds with their boss sniggered, irreverently nudging each other, and struggling very hard to contain their laughter. Bill's eyes popped like a kid gawping at a huge wrapped Christmas present. The African-American photographer stared, open-mouthed. Suddenly, Jadibolole swayed, seemed to take some furtive steps forward, threw back his unkempt head, belched indecorously and sneezed non-stop for several minutes. Laughter rocked the entire bar. Ketilepele sighed his disappointment, and ordered another beer.

"We do not care to direct to ourselves the anger of the damned," enunciated Jadibolole with contemptuous menace.

"Botswana for true Batswana, I say, the real owners of the nation. Basarwa out! I'm Dimo the Impaler," and he roared with laughter, wiping his running nose, and ignoring the tears of drunken joy coursing down his plump cheeks.

"We'll hang them directly by their foul bushman tongue!" he added maliciously.

"Why should any Mosarwa own land? The Central Kalahari Game Reserve is a sanctuary for animals, a gift of nature, and one of our finest tourist attractions. You can ask these white gentlemen here. It is an engine of economic growth. Basarwa will never understand these things. Whatever the world says, we will strike fear in the heart of the bushman, the real enemy of peace, tranquillity and prosperity in our beautiful country. We're masters of this universe, this beautiful land, this globally revered democratic utopia. Rights, rights, rights, what rights do you mean? Aren't you free? I mean we even allow you to go about naked . . . he . . . he . . . he! Isn't that da . . . da ultimate freedom? A nation is no . . . not an artefact of human imagination, it is a Manifest Will of a people. Ever heard of Manifest Destiny? Do these people have any conception of nationhood? No, they don't. They are born wanderers, idlers, swindlers, beggars, thieves, and not nation builders. Our fathers built this country through hard work, sweat, toil, really donkeywork. I'm talking grind, slog and slaving, and not this sloth that Basarwa and some of our misguided youths call working today. Go out now and see Basarwa loitering about, dirty, poor . . . I mean they own nothing, nothing at all! How can such people have a nation? How can they have culture? Even their language is disappearing . . . vanishing into thin air! Here are people who go around

114

wailing for freedom when they are not interested in anything, they can't accumulate anything, and they are completely loath to keep anything. I mean what do they know about freedom? How will they safeguard, defend and preserve it? Any people stupid enough to abandon their language are not worth much in life. In any case these people are deep stuck in the past, they are just one whole ossified lump of human carcass drifting along, refusing to live normal lives, a veritable mass of paralysed human fossil. A historian friend of mine at the University, a really nice drinking buddy, tells me they haven't changed a bit for a thousand . . . a million years."

This jarring harangue was delivered in part-vernacular and part English as Batswana are wont to do when they are extremely excited to a largely listening and indifferent inebriated audience. Throughout this diatribe Ketilepele maintained an inscrutable countenance, quietly sipping his beer, his eyes vacant like a mask. Deep down in his aggrieved and suffering heart he forlornly hoped Jadibolole could have a violent and fatal heart seizure and spare his people all the maddening Tswana frothing and physical botheration. At last he turned to Howard, deliberately ignoring his vociferous foe and delivered his own rejoinder.

"People like my friend here never cease to amaze me," he said.

"They have ransacked all we ever owned, broken our hearts, shattered our dreams, fragmented our society, ruined our lives, done just about everything terrible and ghastly to us for God knows how long, and they still treat us like things. Every time a Motswana looks at a Mosarwa he sees a thing, not a human being . . . just nothing, and it makes them feel good. They have humiliated us by making billions of money from our soil and toil. We're naked, exposed, unsheathed, brutalized and miserable simply because God, in one of those determinations that makes one worry for His sanity, decided long ago that Batswana should be our neighbours. I don't think there have ever been such tiresome, deadly and poisonous neighbours in human history. We're just unlucky, truly, truly, unlucky. It's these sort of unending and timeless humiliations that in reality damns an otherwise good and decent community like us. These people are implacably toxic, dangerous, and untrustworthy and congenitally mad. Have you ever had a madman for a neighbour? You give him a few cents for bread out of pity, and he cries for your house like a spoiled child. You know the sort of thing I'm talking about? There are Batswana for you! They take everything from us. Entire Tswana villages, towns and cities have sprung up in this way, literally from under our feet. We are afraid to speak. They beat us. They molest and torture our children. They kill our people. And there is nothing we can do. This thing has been going on for so long it's now a sporting pleasure for them. We have nothing. Everything we earn is spent just to stay alive, to see another day. Just to catch sight of another day—have you ever worried about such things?"

Howard was embarrassed. For no apparent reason at all Bill tried to gulp down his whisky, choked, spattered and swore violently. One of the rugged civil servants, convinced Ketilepele was simply making a pitch for a free drink, roguishly offered to buy him a drink. This exasperated Ketilepele so much that he quietly put down his half full can of beer and walked out. Feeling snubbed, and quite clearly shocked by this unexpected turn of events, the civil servant ran after him, staggered and half fell, somehow got his bearing, and stood in the middle of the bar room, shouting and gesturing drunkenly, "Come back! Come here you good for nothing sonofabitch . . . don't you want to own something? Hey, Mosarwa . . ." he turned suddenly as his boss, Jadibolole, fell with a crushing thud to the floor.

Bumblebee Pip, one of the British MPs exclaimed, "No wonder, this poor chap is dead drunk!"

"Oh, man, what a load of bullshit? Talk about the Freudian slip. The man is a social monster," said Howard with undisguised exasperation.

"Careful Howie," said Bill, "We're guests in these parts."

"Kiss my ass," said Howard carelessly.

"Are things always so tense here?" inquired Bumblebee politely. Everybody ignored him, except Howard who roared with laughter. To Bumblebee's extreme discomfiture the still seething civil servant, momentarily recovering from the exertions of attending to his boss, chose this moment to directly inform the MP about the multiple faults of Basarwa.

"They are no good. Basarwa are nothing but trouble. They are always dirty, threadbare, and many have this rotten habit of eating snakes, insects, and roots. That's why our government says they are a danger to conservation efforts. They even eat and sleep with dogs, Your Honour! Our intention is to crush this unpleasant mind-set, to catapult them into the modern age. The old ways, the bushman mentality, base excrescence of the past, sir, the Basarwa way of doing things, is just outdated, passé, and antediluvian. The President hates it.

Right now nothing of substance is known about them. We have Batswana lawyers, doctors, and professors, did you know we have our own real professors? I mean you can't measure those fellows for calibre, you really can't. And they agree with us that Basarwa are an embarrassment, a non-achieving society in this time and age. Batswana tycoons, richer than some countries, oversee multibillion dollar financial empires in our cities. And they don't need outside consultants to do that. That is now a thing of the past. Never mind what you read about us. The thing is why should we retain Basarwa way of life? Why bother with their archaic cultures and social insularity? They can listen to rock-and-roll. Everybody loves rock-and-roll.

These people have no manners, spending sleepless nights howling unintelligible songs and dancing on top of billions of carats of hard beautiful diamonds? What will our models wear? And think about the film stars in Hollywood. How will they manage to collect their Oscars without diamond jewellery? And the Queen's Jewels! How can we deny the world such luxury and comfort just to please a bunch of losers who are noisy, pushy and spit everywhere? Basarwa should leave this land. What surprises me is that they really don't care about politics and money. They are totally out of the system. They are apathetic, fatalistic and droopy most of the time. They have no sense of pride, ownership, and identity. Only one thing unites them: the vow of perpetual poverty. Have you ever seen such a thing, sir? Can you imagine the absurdity of it all? See, sir, we Batswana have a virile commercial libido. We are patriots. We love our country. Only the rich can afford to build our nation. If we allow paupers like them to have their way, we'll probably die as a nation. Basarwa have an inveterate contempt for business.

No wonder they are the object of so much raillery, ragging, burlesque, contempt and disrespect in the film world and in polite society. They are an embarrassment to the nation, especially to our politicians and statesmen; did you know we now have our own international statesmen, sir? Perfect roses, untainted, virtuous, uncontaminated, real aces. You should visit them in Gaborone, see things for yourself. And, of course, never mind what the other people write about them in the papers. While we are still talking about the lighter side of things, let me tell you something. Basarwa women are different. If only we could deal with them only, I mean their menfolk maybe vile, slanderous and traitorous but the women pass muster.

Basarwa women are beautiful, lascivious and very, very fond of us Batswana men because we are handsome, successful and great lovers. We are affectionate and imbued with ardent bodies. The real Mosarwa male is not now, or can ever be, anything but a despicable clown. Their women are much, much better people, real patriots. Just imagine it, every hour a Motswana businessman makes five to seven hundred pula, more than the average Mosarwa male earns in a life time, if he ever chooses to do anything at all. Is that patriotic, sir? These fellows' idea of business amounts usually to selling razor blades, matches, peddling mirrors, beads, handmade sandals, cheap clothes, watches, sweets, and draw out cigarettes.

We've long moved into import-export, finance, banking, mining, transportation and a little bit of manufacturing. That's what real Batswana men do these days. But Basarwa . . . they are still behind. They are stubborn, disobliging, truculent . . . perverse . . . I mean they won't even obey the President, sir. Can you imagine living with such obstreperous and insolent people? They are behind in eeeeeeeverthing!

If I had my way with them I would sjambok the whole cussed lot of them. And I mean it. But it's not so easy now. They have started to fight back. We just don't know where they get the courage and impudence . . . I mean . . . can you really think of more ingratitude? We have done everything for them all these years while they were monkeying around, playing games in the desert, and refusing to settle down and live like everybody else. What makes them tick . . . what gives them the nerve . . . one thing that confounds us all is this thing . . . ehhee . . . mention diamonds, sir and the whole tribe goes batty, real mad, I mean, really, really, really bonkers . . . it drives them nuts. Do you think they are somehow allergic to them, sir? We really don't understand these fellows. Why can't they be company directors, managers and government administrators? Oh, what a curse to our nation!

All this patriotic denial? It's maddening, really galling. It's the sort of thing that makes somebody's blood boil. I mean they take positive delight and satisfaction in denying us the chance to make money. They hate us inside out. They are also consumed with self-hate. Surely some of this revenue could trickle down to them in time. But no, they won't hear of it. They just don't want to improve their wretched condition . . . convalesce a little bit . . . get stronger. They are just content to wallow in this drunken like stupor . . . this languid blankness . . . oh, what a terrible slur to black consciousness! What shall we do? Right now the President is in America talking about this diamond hot potato . . . hee . . . heee . . . hh . . . ooo . . . even American kids now hate us too. They are convinced we mistreat Basarwa.

Can you imagine our President, the Big Lion himself, sir, arguing with foreign kids about such matters? Our own children understand us. They don't bother the President about it at all. They know Basarwa are useless. So why should they care? One impertinent white professor, a confused old man real, tried to pump some rubbish into their empty heads and we kicked him out. Children have plasticized minds, sir, they need protection. Those American parents have a lot to answer for. We don't mind them buying kids diamond jewellery . . . but to let their kids bamboozle our revered leader . . . our Big Lion . . . whenever he returns from there he is always very, very subdued, really flummoxed. What do you think those kids do to him, sir?

Do you think the Americans can really stop exporting their movies and other things to us? Is that possible? I mean, what would we do without movies? Can they really stop beaming TV soapies in our homes, sir? It's terrifying to think . . . anyway these barbarians are now taking us to court. In the past such a thing was simply unthinkable. A Mosarwa seeking justice in our own courts? This is a tragedy that calls for really serious philosophical contemplation. Of course they can't win. We are not stupid. No, that's not in the realm of any possibility. But still . . . Basarwa are very, very, tricky, they have lived with wily foxes in the bush for too long. They are really cunning . . . very unpredictable, and dangerous to national unity. They are a threat to national security. They maybe uneducated, slum-dwelling, disease-ridden and grotesquely poor, but they pose a real threat to society.

We just don't know what to do. Maybe you can help us here. It's ruffians like these who destroyed the majestic British Empire. I mean the whole thing came down crumbling like a pack of cards in less than twenty years after what . . . five hundred years of unprecedented imperial hubris. Did you learn any useful lessons? Poor people are dangerous. That's what history has taught even the mightiest Empires. Botswana is just a tiny nation . . . I mean . . . a really teeny miniature nation. If we give these hooligans the teeniest chance to realize their wicked and preposterous ambition, the whole caboodle, the whole enchilada will simply go pop! We need these diamonds . . . I mean the peril is desperate. They will help us manufacture a few millionaires. Can you imagine a country without millionaires, sir? It's bad for the image of the country. Who will welcome our rich white friends like you when they visit the country?

Diamonds will help us to be a little more cosmopolitan. But Basarwa just want to sit on top of them while the whole country suffers international humiliation! Is it a sin to create a few millionaires? I mean we need the gatekeepers, people with suave . . . really, really charming fellows . . . to keep our visitors and guests entertained. And it's hard to talk to Basarwa about such things . . . I mean . . . debonair . . . impeccable . . . bla bla bla . . . these are meaningless words to them. It's not that they are tongue-tied, gauche or anything. They just don't understand our language. We need to make them see things our way, to stop spitting and gobbing everywhere.

Now they have started spluttering and sizzling about things that really do not concern them. What do they know about mining law? Nothing. They are just raging about nothing. This is just one of their offensive expectorations, a meaningless game. They don't know they are playing with fire. All the bigwigs in Gaborone hate what they are doing. I mean sitting like an elephantine anthill on such beautiful gemstones . . . it's really nasty, rude and boorish to the extreme. Many of those great children of Africa there are having fainting fits. It's no longer nice to attend dinner parties. Everyone is very, very distressed about what Basarwa are doing to the image of the country, sir. One lady, a really nice person, in Phakalane, has lost so much weight you can see her bones, sir. It's really sad. See, Basarwa don't understand the importance of a few millionaires even to our beautiful women. Can you imagine what will happen when all the women in Gaborone start shedding their flesh because of Basarwa's intransigence?

First, tourists will stop visiting, in really large numbers. Then, men will have to do all the cooking and looking after children. A bad business all round. You must help us to civilize, assimilate and incorporate these obstinate fools. It's for their own good. They need to gravitate towards business and commerce, to enjoy access to the golden bowl of government contracts and diamond windfall. Who knows one or two of them may become millionaires. What does it matter if the rest remain in the manger? They will survive. The government is behind them.

And Basarwa really must stop telling the whole wide world that our state is deformed and what people think is a democratic culture is actually one amorphous tarantulish ugly beast! I concede our government fuses power and capital to gain popularity, but to call it "a predatory bacterium" as that dissolute reprobate Ketelepele Lefatshe did in London last year is fucking unbelievable. Of course we do have our own privatization wars . . . I mean woes . . . and isolated unsavoury political shenanigans now and then but there really is no need to wash our dirty linen in public, in London of all the places. Do you think the Queen heard that one? She must have seen the bastard grinning on television. That hurt, it really miffed Government Enclave.

An entire nation has never been so mortified . . . oh, the horror of it all. One cabinet minister's daughter fled the UK to be with her chagrined family in Gaborone at that trying time. She is still receiving regular psychological counselling. And of course she flunked the bloody examinations. Three times! After proper rehabilitation the poor father intents to enter the wretched thing into Harvard. I wish her well. Stories like these break my heart. See, Batswana are emotional people, we have really strong feelings. We are a weepy and teary lot, and Basarwa are doing all these things just to see us cry. Unfortunately we can't disappoint them in that regard. They have turned us into a weeping nation. Every time I try to pray to God for the deliverance of these maddening sinners I wind up teary, confused and then I start cursing and crying even more. Oh, to live with Basarwa is a sin in itself. How can they hate money so much? And Basarwa are liars, incorrigible liars, really professional fibbers.

All this talk of pogroms in the Kalahari Desert is damaging to foreign investor confidence. Not that the real money mongers will be deterred. Oh, no, the real money lovers, who happen to be the people who have lots and lots of money, are very much capable of signing mining contracts using the enfeebled body of a dying Mosarwa as a table. All the same these lies are malicious, offensive and ridiculous. I forget the other words lawyers use in such matters. What I know for certain is that it is incorrect to say these deaths are the object of homicidal fury. There may be justifiable anger and hatred on the part of Basarwa at the present moment, but people always die in the desert. We are angry too.

Our millionaires are dying and the few remaining ones are old, dowdy, decrepit and boring. They can no longer welcome our foreign visitors. Or entertain our beautiful women. They are only good at hawking smelly and smeary gob on the unprotected mouths of defenceless babies at their homes. They are really good for nothing. The nation must start manufacturing three or more ardent, fervid, strong, suave, elegant and truly cosmopolitan moneybags too keep the gates."

This was the finest speech the raggedly shabby and scruff civil servant had ever made. It profoundly disenchanted him that the rowdy crowd did not see it fit to show any appreciation at all. But then he had been more or less addressing himself to the Labour MP, and through him, the British public and their Queen, who were really not present to give him a little pat on the back for his trouble. That was little consolation to the dirty civil servant who now stood, mouth hanging open and struggling hard to get his breath. The heat and the humidity in the bar, and outside, were terrifically intolerable. The patriotic civil servant was exceedingly bathed in sweat, and the combination of bodily secretions, dirt, dampness and the merciless perspiration made for a deafening stench, made worse by the reek of alcohol and the pervasive human odour in the bar.

Honourable Bumblebee Pip was also something of a mystery. Throughout the civil servants' exuberant and fecund, if only slightly faltering, peroration, the beleaguered MP kept a frightening din of exclamations and entirely incomprehensible stream of interjections, which at first the extremely excited civil servant mistook for a veritable English conversational tradition. But as he vociferously and pleadingly put forward his case for the pacification of Basarwa the Englishman got correspondingly paler and paler, muttering and uttering nonsensical rubbish like, "Oh, dear! Oh, dear!"

At one point the ashen pallid MP screeched: "Good Heavens!"

And his colleague, O'Brien Law, cried back, "Bleeding hell, it's Londonderry all over!" and noisily shifted on his chair spilling his gin and tonic all over the place.

The wretched civil servant, blinking tremulously, shifted his tortured eyes from one politician to the other in utter bewilderment. Bumblebee was so pale he looked like the World Cup prophetic octopus. He kept on making furtive and incredibly hurried glances to Honourable Law who responded with terrifyingly booming, "Hmmm" like a frightened bull dog.

The Batswana present were no help at all. At one point the now very suspicious and no doubt disturbed civil servant observed the barmaid, Dimakatso, shamelessly and voluptuously scratching her ample buttocks, desperately trying to prise open the cleft between the cheeks, and he inadvertently slurred, quite loudly, "It will take a really sharp instrument and a broom to get there!"

And the usually sweet woman rounded on him menacingly, declaring, "And it will take a bloody war to put common sense in that empty head of yours!"

Dimakatso hated her job and was forever embarrassed that her old mother proudly told anyone who would listen that her daughter was a hotel manager when everybody knew she worked in the bar serving bawdy, vulgar and farting drunkards and loose women who always unashamedly accosted strangers for booze and delighted in being subjected to lewd and course suggestions, insults and violations.

The greatest disappointment was the District Commissioner. Most of the time he kept his eyes fixed on the ceiling, completely unblinking, and feigning stony inebriation. It was as if the fellow was catatonic. But the civil servant knew better. The whole thing was a game. Civil servant Number Two kept on scratching his balls, belching and winking by way of apology and half felt commiseration. The civil servant noticed that every time he alluded to the *Great Anxiety* afflicting Gaborone, the District Commissioner actually winced, only with his shoulders. It's no wonder at the end of this fraught deliberation the poor mangy dog fairly sprinted out of the bar. But before his brusque and undignified exit he noticed something really, really strange.

Bumblebee, drenched to the bone, breathless, and in evident shock and shuddering turned to Mr. Law and said in earnest, "Another rumpus at our door step, Law. What will Downing Street No. 10 make of this ruckus?"

Law had locked his blurry eyes on the unhappy Bumblebee and bawled in the strangest, and the most musical brogue, "I don't give a shit about London! Certainly not that soapy sentimentalism about English sensibility and all that sickening rot! Just tell me what brought us here? It was your idea. You have always been a good one for bright ideas, Pip. Now we are in hot soup. I mean really stinking broiling shit. Talk about egg on a man's face. Wait till the press get this one straight. Oh, it will take time. But sooner or later some fool will stumble on the truth. What then? Just wait till my Mary hears this. I'm a dead man. Now listen to me. This enchilada must be kept in wraps. Total secret. No leaks to the press. And I'm not putting my signature to any bloody report! Get that straight, Pip. I'll not betray my long suffering Irish blood so that a bunch of black-arsed daylight robbers and murderers can manufacture three millionaires.

No way. I won't do it and you can't force me. This whole business is too weird for me. I mean these people have a Trinity Complex. It's like some mystical religion, this worship of money and the quest for three millionaires. What the hell is it all about? Alright, Christians have their God the Father, God the Son and God the Holy Ghost, Three Persons in One God. Then there is the Hindu triad: Brahma, Shiva and Vishnu. All these have divine functions, supposedly. But what's in these bloody three millionaires business? The Devil takes it! This is bloody nonsense. For all I care they can mail-order the Three Stooges from Hollywood! I'm not going to upset my Mary, or worse lose her over this nonsense. I mean why in the world of hell do they need these damned *manufactured* millionaires for?"

"Well, old chap, even in the worst predator states acts of corruption have to have a foil, a person, or persons, on the side of angels. That's just one part these rich zombies may play. They are also used to create an illusion of grand opportunities in the country and great individual success stories. This way, even failed states are often able to give a fallacious and fantastic illusion of substance to the notion of economic and political freedom. In effect, they camouflage the usual rot of commonplace personal horrors of absolute abjection, alcoholic stupor, reckless self-abnegation and nervous exhaustion within the state and society."

"I don't understand you."

"They are necessary for the overall concealment of widespread mongrelisation and suffering in society. Politicians are always able to point at these zombies and say to the whole world, 'Just look how our really hard working sons and daughters are doing.' Go to any rotten banana republic and you'll find poor sods like that, manipulating government tendering processes and contracts, dispensing state largesse through local commercial banks and numbered accounts in Switzerland, greasing the ruling party machine, entertaining ladies of the court, marrying numerous wives and having numerous love affairs across political divisions to create a semblance of order . . . oh . . . they are really busy fellows . . . conduits for all for sorts of things, the really channels and watercourses of the state machinery and when people complain about corruption, ruling party elites are able to point at these little gods and goddesses and proclaim loudly: 'What's all this rubbish about incompetence and corruption in our country? We are doing just fine . . .' The irony is that the moment they get out of line, these worshipped gods are publicly eaten by their worshippers, they are maligned and crucified through farcical court trials and humiliations, tortured and murdered in such ridiculously grotesque ways that every citizen is able to feast one way or the other on their carcasses . . . it's the worst public demonstration of 'theophany', worshippers eating their god or goddess."

"Bloody damnit, boyo! You knew all this . . ."

"Look here, old man, these fellows have a record . . . till . . . now . . . oh, hell why bother! Who really knows what's happening here! Everything in this continent is a bloody façade, a farce!"

"Still, you haven't answered my question . . ."

"Damn it, O'Brien! Is this Twenty Questions or bloody Trivial Pursuit? How the hell was I supposed to know!"

The protagonists stared at each other, and for a frightening split second something terrible passed between them, something vividly unpleasant, primeval, and unconcealed; a manifest mutual hatred of vast proportions, an unbridgeable chasm of distrust, hate, spite and mutual contempt. It was a disgusting sight to see and the now thoroughly befuddled civil servant did not know what to make of the whole thing.

Chapter 5

The Concentration Camp . . .

Molapo, 1998

At Molapo village, a group of terrified, sweaty, apathetic, resigned and long-suffering Basarwa sat beside dirty black refuse collection plastic bags and tattered hand-me-down suit-cases with their even more horrified wives and nervously bewildered children, some of them sleeping in their petrified parent's scrawny arms. Government had decreed that all the villagers be forcibly removed to the new Kalahari settlement. A similar fate had befallen other neighbouring Basarwa communities and the message was not to be ignored. Rumours were rife that the dread army and wildlife personnel were on the way to deal with any troublemakers. Everybody was in a frenzied state of apprehension. They were all clearing out in a hurry to avert the impending bureaucratic menace. It was an old game, a ritual so common it was communicated to even infants at birth. Every Mosarwa child grew up with the knowledge that life was a haphazard occupation, a hide and seek game between state and citizen.

Government officials and politicians invariably treated Basarwa as scallywags and a peril to their political agenda in the desert, a monstrously ambitious plan to roll the Kalahari Desert back through ruthless social and economic penetration. They were determined that no rapscallions, rogues, ne'er-do-wells and good-for-nothing scoundrels (the definitive official designation for Basarwa disapproval and hostility to unbridled and callous state penetration into their lives) could stand in their way. Now the Mother of all Battles was looming and these communities were once again at loggerheads with government. Diamonds had been discovered in the area, and it was time for Basarwa to move. Everyone was in a rush to catch the first truck to the new settlement, any lift to relatives in Gantsi, Gaborone, even Namibia. Others had jumped the border to join fellow tribesmen in South Africa over the preceding few days. It was a moment of turmoil and unrelieved trepidation. Basarwa elders had approached Jadibolole, suggesting that the mining company designate part of the Central Kalahari Game Reserve a human settlement and employ their children instead of trucking everyone hundreds of kilometres away. Jadibolole laughed at their ignorance and kindly explained that the mining company was still outside the country.

"You mean they were given our land in *absentia*?" asked a puzzled old man.

"Well, their lawyers worked out all the details with our government. Everything is above board, square and proper," said the District Commissioner amicably.

"Maybe they have an office here somewhere."

"Not, really. See, *Rra*, all these things are done through paperwork and lawyers. The agreements can be signed anywhere."

"But we can't talk to papers!" said the now visibly agitated old man.

"Well, you can talk to me. I'm here to represent government and protect its interests. And I say to you this is the new way of doing things here. It's all there in the mining law."

"Can we see it? This mining law..."

"No, no, no. You are not experts. What do you know about the law?"

"Maybe we can get a lawyer . . ."

"What . . . you grizzled . . . stop grumbling . . . I don't want any trouble. These things are done in Gaborone. Lawyers cost money, old man. Why don't you be reasonable? We have arranged to compensate you. We know many of you have nothing and the land belongs to all of you. So we'll compensate you for the land. In the end some of you will get as much as ten thousand pula. That is a lot of money."

"How long will it last us? When it's finished what will we do? And the children, what are they going to do? What will happen to them?"

"Ten thousand pula is a lot of money in the desert. This is not a city, you know. We are giving you a few donkeys and food parcels as well. That should see the lot of you through life."

"I don't see how. Things are too expensive in the shops. There's nothing to hunt in the new settlement. Our women will not be able to work. There won't be any jobs for us, I mean for all of us; father, mother and child in every family. I don't think this thing is going to work for us. There must be a better arrangement. Maybe government will talk to us . . ."

"I'm the government!" the clammy and distressed District Commissioner roared. The old man laughed politely.

"I was thinking the area MP, Mr. John van Nierkirk . . ."

"He knows nothing about government business . . . I mean mining law. You better accept my explanation."

"You haven't explained anything."

"Look you raucous and disorderly old fool! I have a job to do here. And I do it well. Remember that. I'm a professional. I know these things. Take my word for it. If you chose to bypass this office you are doomed. Now, let's be serious a bit. Stop playing stupid games and do the right thing. I don't understand why you just can't do as you are told. That would save us all a great deal of time and energy. So, here is the deal. We have found a nice piece of land to settle your people, on a permanent basis. No more roaming about the desert frightening poor animals and begging from tourists. Such actions undermine government business. No more indiscriminate trampling on endangered plants and insects, killing protected animals and inconveniencing big game hunters, who are our guests and international friends. Did you know that the President is painfully aware of your nefarious habits, and that all your daily actions are a direct and present danger to the economy? These are matters of grave concern to us. I mean we could prosecute, convict and sentence to jail every Mosarwa in this area for all these bad things . . ."

"But we've lived that way for hundreds and thousands of years."

"Ah, that was before we came on the scene. Now we do things differently. We do things our own way. It's a better way of doing things. We call it international best practice."

"That's all good I suppose," said the old man, "but this is our land. Does international best practice not recognize that? I think our way of doing things is good too. It has endured the test of time. For thousands of years man and beast amicably roamed these desert plains together and we are both still here, living side by side. We do very little harm to each other. If my memory—I'm an old man but I'm not a fool—if my memory serves me, well, there was a time when our neighbours here were only white people, the ancestors of John van Nierkirk and others like *Rre* van Past . . ."

"I think you mean van der Post."

"No, van Past. He used to come visit and go just like that. But he was good to us, and I know he was a friend of the British Queen's little boy."

"Ah, that's certainly Laurence van der Post, the naturalist and philosopher."

"I say van Past, and van Past it is. Now his friends used to hunt here with us. There was no problem at all. Wild animals are our friends. We don't just kill them. I for one have reared many orphaned young animals and birds and returned them to the bush. Even animals eat each other but rarely do we hear of mutual extermination to the point of extinction. Like us they simply kill to satisfy hunger. I think the trouble here is this company that refuses to talk to us and uses foreign rules to take our land . . . don't protect them. Tell us the truth."

"Really, I don't know how to put this. We're nation-builders, not philosophers. I think to understand our actions you have to look at the big picture. That company is simply coming here to dig out diamonds and then sell them . . ."

"Couldn't we do it ourselves? If government gives us machines and educated Batswana to help us we can do it and still keep our land."

"I don't know, old man. We have never tried that before. I doubt it would work. Our people know almost nothing about diamonds."

"But we have been mining them for so many years. Surely Batswana at the other mining towns can help us?"

"It's just not the way things are done," said Jadibolole brusquely and irritably. "There will be Batswana employed in the company administration to work as the eyes for our government just as I am the eyes of the government out here. That's how things are done."

"This is so disappointing. There has to be a better way."

"It's the best possible way."

"If that's the only way then we are dead. We must do something. We can't just die smiling like sheep."

"Do something like what, old man?" said the panicky government official wiping perspiration with a solid white handkerchief.

"We're going to get a lawyer," said the old man ominously, feebly banging the mahogany oval table with his gnarled arthritic fingers for emphasis, his completely grey head trembling violently.

"That's a stupid thing to do. A wrong decision all round. Lawyers don't take clients from the desert. Can you imagine a lawyer visiting this dreadful place to talk about wild animals, insects and plants? Are you real? Don't embarrass yourselves. Listen to me and everything will be alright."

"We want to talk about diamonds. We have no fight with animals and plants. We need someone who can talk to this company in a language it understands, someone who can tell it to fuck off, to leave us alone."

"That's a terrible mistake. Don't provoke us. Government won't like this even a little bit, not at all. Think about the consequences before you embark on your foolhardy purpose. Even I'm already wondering at your motives . . ."

"Don't worry yourself *Rre* Mongwato. We're going to see Ketilepele Lefatshe. He worked with Nelson Mandela and others against people like you and your company in South Africa for quite some time. He'll tell us what to do. We're going to fight this thing like the ANC. We'll be like freedom fighters."

"Old man, you are looking for trouble, but then, you people have always been nothing but trouble. I tell you that you will regret this decision. Now listen to me. That Ketilepele is an unreliable fellow. I've no doubt he'll mislead you . . ."

"It doesn't matter if he does, he has one of our own," retorted the old man with furious contempt. "You people have always treated us like children. I don't understand how it has taken us so long to fight back. I just think this time you have gone too far. Enough is enough."

"Old man, that is a declaration of war. I welcomed you in my office with open arms and human kindness. Now you are abusing my hospitality and kindness, threatening me and my government with war. If you follow through your mad threat and approach law courts to intercede in this deeply and terribly sensitive official matter, I'll wash my hands of you. I'll deny I ever received you in this August office to discuss it, and you better start remembering right now that I never mentioned anything about diamonds to you or anyone. I've just been talking to you in a very friendly Setswana way about our government's new Conservation Act. And I've a copy of it in my desk to prove it. The issue of compensation for your *voluntary abandonment* of some ecological fragile parts of the Central Kalahari Game Reserve cropped unavoidably up because you and your people are eager to move to the new settlement in Kalahari Village and need money and food to settle in with the least possible inconvenience . . ."

"But . . ." stammered the old man, clearly confused and shocked beyond comprehension at this extremely unexpected turn of events, "we did talk about diamonds . . . mining law . . . *international best practice* and all the other things."

"No we didn't. Maybe you misheard a few things. You are an old man."

"There are three of us."

"And all of you are old, uneducated and unqualified to discuss serious government business. This was just an informal meeting between friends, people I've worked with for a long time, and my message to you is that I'll be addressing a *kgotla* meeting in your area next week Wednesday morning at 8:00am. Please be kind enough to send word to all Basarwa in your area."

Jadibolole had metamorphosed into a completely different person, his face inscrutable and the eyes unblinking, cruel and fiery red. The heat in the room, already terrible at the beginning of this encounter was now unbearably hot, intense and agonising so that everybody was literally dripping with sweat.

"Surely even in this country of mad and greedy rulers the word of three honest old men should count against the raging frothing of an incompetent and corrupt bureaucrat," said the old man firmly and resolutely.

To his further amazement the District Commissioner suddenly threw back his unusually huge head and issued a terrifyingly hoary and beastly gurgling laughter. All the old men watched this spectacle with a mixture of horror and concealed amusement, as Jadibolole reached for a secret table drawer and brought out a huge bottle of Teachers' whisky and proceeded to drink straight from the bottle, still laughing his lungs out. As they filed out with uncertain dignity they heard him screaming something to the effect that he was the District Commissioner and his word was the law in the entire Kalahari Desert.

Now the time of reckoning and terror had descended on all Basarwa, father, mother and child, like a nuclear holocaust. Almost all of them had never left their native area throughout their lives. It was as if the devil himself had paid them a social visit and the chasm of hell was now preparing to gorge itself with their bony and emaciated bodies. Jadibolole had not bothered to talk to them, choosing to use force and intimation instead. For days, Basarwa had lived in the open waiting for government trucks to arrive and relocate them. Those who had tried to resist evacuation had been thoroughly beaten up and driven by brutal force to cramped open air concentration camps. They were perpetually soaked and miserable because that most unreliably desert visitor, rain, had chosen this ill-timed moment to make a social call. The nights were long and icy cold, the mornings wintry and frosty, and this glacial atmosphere was compounded by broken hearts and gloomy brooding all around.

The unfriendliness and aloofness of the police guards exacerbated an already appallingly heartrending and dreadfully grim situation. For many of these ill-fated people, desert conditions, aided by the hand of man, had never been more calamitous and devastating in their callous and hubristic indifferent to their presence. Their lives were poorer and sorrier now than they had ever been, but they endured their agony with dignity and an almost maddeningly terrifying philosophical dismalness, completely unwilling to give their tormentors the satisfaction of seeing them weeping, complaining, begging and pleading.

One woman sat stony silent, lullabying in her lacerated heart the dead infant in her arms, a dirge of such catastrophic proportions that it naturally radiated and reverberated through the bodies of all the people around her creating a most surreal atmosphere, and still no one cried. Everyone felt lost, strange and abandoned as the long hours of catatonic numbness mercilessly dragged on with a horridly throbbing silence. Not one of them knew exactly who to curse for their anguished situation. So they waited for the longest night in their lives to take its course.

By sheer bureaucratic fiat, the government had provided the world with Africa's answer to Belsen and Aswitch. In a way the whole catastrophic saga was more than mere historical rendering of man's cruelty to man, the whole phenomenon was a concatenation of the loose, fantastical, even ethereal, nature of man working vigorously in tandem with the beastly part and the entire kaleidoscopic mirage of common suffering playing itself out against a background of dark humour and human folly. The foregathered Basarwa accepted even the looming tragedy with stoic foreboding. Rumours circulated fast and thick that soldiers were on their way to the beleaguered villagers. Every one lived in morbid fear of the soldiers. Previous experience was a constant reminder of what they were capable of doing. They would burst in and sweep up in a madness of destruction and hatred, drunk, drugged and demanding blood and submission. It was a well-known old story, a story now imminently about to be retold in human blood, not just through word of mouth. Nothing could be done to hold back that martial madness. They would be screaming obscenities, terrifying children, beating women, insulting, furiously sjamboking and clubbing hapless men. The most boisterous ones would rape, murder and wallow in bloodbath with sadistic pleasure.

Major Mponang Morwakgosi was in a foul mood when he descended on Molapo concentration camp. His divorce had gone terribly bad, so bad that he harboured a horribly dark grudge against mankind as a whole. He blamed his job for the breakup of his marriage. And the humiliating fact that he had lost her to a junior officer was so horrifying that he had taken a secret pledge to crush, throttle, squash, thrash, hang even, any person, male or female, should they cross his path unsheathed and ungirded. When this assignment came up, the cuckolded Major tirelessly pulled strings, including making a discreet appeal to officers working in government offices, of which there were now inordinately too many. In the end he managed to get the assignment, and he was determined to treat it as a holiday, and people on vacation general are free to indulge their passions as they see fit.

After a most adventurous drive to this desolate place, including the shooting of wild animals trespassing in the major highways and the terrific clobbering of a drunken driver, Major Morwakgosi now felt truly at home in Molapo. It was a strange sensation for the usually dashing and debonair officer but then that sordid affair was now almost behind him. Here was a chance to once again reassert his manliness in the eyes of his colleagues and their loathsome friends. He surveyed the Basarwa gathered before him with malicious glee. He opened his mouth to speak and was terribly appalled when his voice failed him. He noisily and rowdily cleared his clogged throat, revised his military posture a little, opened the bloody mouth to speak again only to be rewarded with clattering jaws and rattling teeth. He abruptly turned to Jadibolole and whispered, "How long have these people been corralled in this damn thing?"

"The encampment was initiated three weeks ago, Major," said Jadibolole primly.

"And what is the temperature this morning?"

"It was minus two degrees Celsius at sunrise. I should think it's around three to four degrees right now take or add or subtract one either way, sir."

"Jesus Christ! Any casualties?"

"None reported so far."

"Can something be done to relieve this suffering?"

"We can start trucking those who are willing to go now."

"Ahaaa, so there are rebels among them."

"Only a few. I'm sure you can persuade them to cooperate, sir."

"You mean we are free to shoot the bastards!"

"No, we cannot do that, sir."

"Why not?"

"They have lawyer."

"What? Basarwa have hired a lawyer? What's this country coming to? I was ruined by a legal . . . oh forget about it. Something must be done for the women and the children. Whose idea was it to treat these poor people this way?" said the Major irritably, and he was surprised to hear his voice rising. "It's abominable," he said quietly as if he was speaking about a personal injury. When he turned to survey the somnolent mass of humanity before him again he found to his intense horror that his courage was failing him and the only thing he really wanted to do was to go to bed and sleep immediately. It was a terribly unmanning experience but a horrible drowsiness was enveloping him, numbing the senses and taking possession of his very life. Jadibolole looked at the delirious Major with revulsion and disgust. How, he wondered, did this viral worm end up in the army? The defeated Major was escorted to the temporary barracks set up a little distance from the concentration camp, leaving Jadibolole to take command of the battlefield.

"We hear some of you want to fight us," the District Commissioner whined petulantly.

"All I can say is that we are ready for you. We have the capacity to fight you. And we'll bring all of you to your senses in no time. This time we'll teach you a lesson. We'll kill you. The Major is too upset to talk to you. That should be a bad enough sign of what awaits you. We'll kill you like flies. We have the means to do so. We're too strong for you. No ant can defeat an elephant. Small ants can get into an elephants trunk and manage to irritate, infuriate, and annoy it for some time. Insects can lodge, embed, graft and entrench themselves in various parts of its gargantuan body and comfortably enjoy their obnoxious games, pleasures, thrills and all the fun for a long time. But once the elephant gets really and truly aggravated, it simply resorts to just a few weapons to obliterate all these impudent little things in no time.

It can plunge itself in a huge pool of water, wade across a deep flowing river, scratch its colossal bulky and hulking body against strong giant tree trunks, wiping out all the nasty little ants and insects in matters of seconds and completely cleansing itself. We too are going to scrub, purge, disinfect, sanitize, decontaminate, refine and thoroughly clean, dust, vacuum, mop and polish our body politic which you have insensibly and irresponsibly soiled, muddied, stained and fouled with your petty and selfish concerns. Yes, we are here to do a lot of laundering, sweeping, wiping, brushing, sprinkling, dry-cleaning, and furbishing. You call us names and we know you are itching and hankering for a war. Well, here we are you marijuana-and-orgy addicted rascals! Give us a good show! Defend your barren, unfruitful, bare, bleak and windswept empty land. Stand up for your loose, fun-loving, decadent, dissolute and debauched women and ways of life. Come on you degenerate and licentious little brutes, give us a good show! The battlefield is level, dead even, well balanced, neck and neck; a whole bellicose, belligerent, loud-mouthed, argumentative and warmongering tribe spoiling for a fight against a well-trained and tenacious small army commando under our very able patriotic Major Mponang Morwakgosi. As I said, the Major is right now so angry he can't even talk to you. But we are ready for you. Even I can take you on, right now. And don't think you can run away from this thing. In fact the worst offence you can do to yourself is to run away. Take our mighty machine on, you sick puppies! Look at you. Just look at you, sitting there playing at being miserable and outraged. Remember it's you who started this thing. We are only joining your game. I have always said you people are provocative, aggravating and maddening beyond measure. So far we have treated you with hand cloves. Now is the hour of reckoning. It's payback time. You call our leaders and peace-loving people outright thieves, crooks, vandals, trespassers, colonists and criminals? Well, we're going to show the whole wide world that you, my dear friends, are law-breakers, troublemakers, malefactors, rebels, scoundrels and miscreants to boot. We'll make you shallow your words and your pride, with human blood. That's what you have been pining for isn't it? A bloodbath. Well, we are here to grant your wish, to give you satisfaction. We will teach you that we are your rulers, your masters and that without us you are nothing.

We'll raise your famous survivalist pain ethic to a dizzying level of suffering. We'll show you the real unabridged, unexpurgated and unedited meaning of human ugliness and political terror. The thing is we really don't have time for your stupid games and we certainly have no time for weaklings and traitors in our quest to found Africa's greatest and most prosperous nation and civilization. We are prepared to sweep everything aside, remove all the obstacles with whatever means, to achieve this noble ambition. We already are Africa's shining democracy thanks to the groundwork laid by our forefathers. Now we just have to rise to another level and we need a few millionaires to achieve that objective. If you want to fight we'll give you the most memorable war ever. And if by any chance, or the through the monumental grace of God Almighty, you survive this ruckus please, please; I really, really beg you, learn to make money. Our aim is that through the diamond industry we should have a nation of millionaires only by 2016, the Fiftieth Anniversary of our painful liberation from oppressive and pernicious British colonial rule. That is what Vision 2016 is all about. All Basarwa must be part of this vision. You must learn to make money, speak Setswana and English, and live in big mansions and to love all Batswana. It is very important to make Batswana friends if you are to move on with the rest of the nation. Stop living in solitary confinement in the most inhospitable parts of the desert as if you are animals, and not good citizens of democratic Botswana, the world's finest democracy. It is very, very critical and vital that you immediately, unequivocally and unconditionally disavow, recant and repudiate ethnic politics. If you don't we'll rip apart your miserable bodies, smash your faces to a pulp, shot your women and children at point-blank range, and feed the cadavers to vultures and wild animals. Is that understood, you greedy, miserly, mean and tight-fisted Basarwa locusts! If you don't listen we'll swoop in your desert country like hungry vultures to carry off all your little possessions and natural resources, all your women as well. What'll you do all day and all those long and terribly lonely desert nights without sex? We have already banned beer drinking in this country. Only visitors who stay in hotels, lodges and Parliamentary Flats can drink. Government revoked all your hunting licences by Presidential decree last week. How will you pass the time? If you don't do as we say we'll introduce more strictures, dispossess you of everything, every joy, every occupation, every little comfort and every form of entertainment. We'll ruin you and go our own way. What'll you do about it? Nothing, absolutely nothing. The whole world knows we are building a nation and they are hundred per cent behind us. That's why white people encourage their companies to come and help us dig our diamonds out of the ground. They know we need the diamonds to complete our national project. We need to work together but if you keep on dragging your feet and pulling in the wrong direction we'll lean on you brothers and sisters. We'll be forced in the end to round up all of you and send you all to the next world, to the world of sinners, reprobates and evildoers. Our country will finally be free of too many people with strange sounding names mingling and interfering in its internal affairs. We cannot afford all these splitting, divisive, disconnecting and detaching attitudes. We know you want to take apart our nation, to split up, to break up everything and to become estranged from the national vision and purpose. And we can't allow that sort of thing to happen. We'll burn your tongues! We'll turn you all into squealing pigs. We'll not rest until Operation No living Thing Among the Basarwa is a complete success. And there will be no more leeches, parasites, bloodsucking and noisy mosquitoes after Operation No Living Thing. We'll then become one happy and prosperous nation. Real Batswana, the true nation-builders will then live in peace. Yes, the wind of destruction shall prevail! And what a fascinating carnival romp we are going to experience? Just look at all these soldiers, these full-blooded, sturdy, robust, strapping and muscular true Batswana patriots. They are ready to die for their country. Isn't that wonderful? What a great honour to this country to have such young men, such healthy, strong, energetic, vigorous, enthusiastic and solid men of character and durability lay down their lives so that the whole nation can realize its dream. I can see that most of you look feeble, spindly, rickety, puny, fragile and in poor health. But things are not always what they seem. A friend of mine was telling me the other day that the mighty British Empire was brought down by paupers. Just imagine that. A squalid bunch of dirty, naked, filthy, smelly, foul, grimy, uneducated, coarse and un-couth screaming, yelping, howling, yapping, baying, yowling and growling Indians, Asians and Africans wearing tattered and thread-bare tribal costumes, and singing horridly unintelligible songs, many hiding behind frightening grotesque masks and blindingly shining icons, demolished the biggest Empire in the world in the shortest time ever recorded for the absolute ruin of any great civilization. Yes, the mighty British Empire, covering no less than three quarters of the planet earth, was brought to its knees by this monstrous and barbarous din. Can you believe it? We don't want that ridiculous puppet show to re-enact itself here. I just can't imagine how the British still feel about this most unceremonious smashing and extinguishment of their pretty little applecart, I mean the whole kit and caboodle was wiped out by miserable creatures like you. You may also remember that just before this existential catastrophe befell the poor Brits, a most unruly mob of callow, arrogant, conceited, egotistical, narcissistic, and yet very emaciated, pallid, skinny and very, very naïve German youths, led by a completely madman, a raving, unrestrained, limpid lunatic, dark and obscure as the Baltic winter midnight-many of them shoeless, penniless, unemployed, starving, ragged, blindly enraged, fuming and thoroughly riled by a vengeful, hostile, and uncharitable world-tried to subjugate the entire mass of earthly humanity by means of terror and blood and came very, very close to accomplishing their mission. Just because you are scruffy, unkempt, tatty, dirty, indigent, unhealthy, diseased, sickly and completely out of shape and feeble to the point of being insubstantial, even virtual nothingness, does not mean you are not harmful to society. So we are going to fight you shivering, quaking, wobbling and dying lot square and proper. You have your bows and arrows, we have our guns. That's democracy for you; fair play and no *manga manga*. We'll have a good time killing, maiming, defacing, disfiguring, hurting and wounding each other. It's going to be a jolly good show, with only birds and animals for an audience. Don't forget the nearest hospitals are hundreds of kilometres away, and we don't take prisoners. After we have vanquished and firmly incorporated all the survivors all these dirty desert wagon ruts and your dirty little children will become things of the past, fascinating only to dull historians and thoroughly bored and stupid tourists. This country will remain essentially Tswana. Everybody will speak only Setswana, attend Setswana schools, study the glorious history of Batswana and maintain Setswana customs, traditions and culture at all times. As technology keeps on making more and more remarkable breakthroughs we should even be able to detect those who are unable to dream in Setswana and deal with them accordingly. Nothing alien in character, disposition, temperament and personality will be admitted in *Tswanadom*. We'll teach mathematics, science and history in our mother tongue. Tswana dress and deportment will apply to all the true owners of the nation. No outsider mentality will stand in the way of our great vision. Oh, you can keep on hating us in your hearts and minds for all you care but the whole world loves us. They perfectly understand why we are doing these things. You know, there was a time when decent folks were ashamed to write their sins and crimes across the heavens. Now things have changed. Traitors and monsters like you can do anything they like. So you bad mouth us all over the world. We'll delete you! We'll disappear you! Why do you hate us so much? Why this senseless envy, anger, defiance, rudeness and indiscipline? Our beloved Vice President is so incensed with your wayward behaviour he was admitted to hospital three days ago. I really . . . really can't understand how you people can do these things to us . . . it's so painful . . . I...I...I . . . . the Vice President . . . I . . ." stammered Jadibolole incoherently before he succumbed to the ocean of his terribly anguished emotions and disintegrated into uncontrollable crying.

A deafening silence fell among the gathered crowd and only the plaintive moaning of Jadibolole punctured it; the pathetic throaty wail of a shepherd who had lost his sheep, as he was being politely and elaborately carried away by a cheekily grinning, extremely drunk and rattily attired civil servant, who kept on slurring, "What a rotten job. It's a bad business. Cheer up boss."

To the horror of stupefied government officials, still recovering from this dramatic spectacle, a disgustingly ill, weepy, desiccated and shrivelled Mosarwa old man miraculously managed to drag his moribund corpse of a body to an amazingly distinguished posture and shrilly and stridently demanded to be heard.

Jadibolole's rambling speech had been disturbingly and unpleasantly characterized by heart breaking coughing spells, and occasional spitting of blood, which he hysterically wiped on a huge white handkerchief that kept on getting red and redder till it was crimson red and dripping with blood. His colleagues were also concerned with his rapid and inexplicable loss of weight. Now this decrepit desert creature, clearly on his last legs was threatening to subject them to another risqué, vulgar, boorish and obviously discourteous rabble-rousing show.

But what the old man did next was more macabre and loathsome than even their worst expectations. He made sure that he got everyone's attention and then calmly and purposefully walked to a supine and exhausted young woman who was silently weeping and kindly fondling her baby. With utmost kindness and nimble fingers the old man took the sleeping baby and walked to the gathered government officials, stopping just very short of taking up the podium.

In a steady, almost triumphant, voice, he said, "Fellow countrymen, we welcome you in our home. My name is Kaboyamodimo Lefatshe. We thank the government for keeping us together in this place at this trying time even if it's not our real home. We have tried to keep each other warm and alive as best we can under the circumstances but some of us have not been lucky. This child in my hands right now is dead. She died several hours ago but cold weather has preserved her tiny body. Her body is like a solid lump of ice. We have not been able to bury her for fear of violating camp regulations. May her soul rest in peace. She has undoubtedly escaped the trials and tribulations that await all Basarwa children in this country. I think she is safer and happier dead than she could ever have expected in real life. Several other people in this camp, including more children, are dead, and we still have to bury them. So when you speak please don't forget that you are addressing the dead. Now, my fellow countrymen and women, you all heard what the District Commissioner said. What I don't understand is why we can't allow nation to speak unto nation in this country. We call ourselves democrats but operate in a spirit very contrary to democratic virtue. I dare say even human virtue. There can be no doubt that we Basarwa resent the dominant Batswana's power to seduce. Why, we wonder all the time, should you be allowed to control the images of the whole country? Culture, politics, economics, education, everything. What is at stake here is the cultural identity and ecological sovereignty of our people, the right of each nation to its own destiny. Why should everything that define us dwindle into insignificance? We should all learn to live together. We are not cultural freaks. We are human beings with a long history, and a profound human experience. We belong to deep time. And future time is ours too. Every human identity; Sesarwa, English, Irish, Afrikaner, Tswana, Tutsi, Jewish has its own character, its own story, its own meaning, its own significances and its own sacred gleams. All these must be respected by other human beings. We don't like this dreariness, this drabness and insalubrity surrounding us. It's nothing of our doing. Why blame us for our present condition? We did not invite Batswana here. They came of their own volition. And now they are more trouble living with than the Taliban. What is happening here right now as I speak is not our fault. Blame it on history. Maybe part of it is our own doing. We have been too kind and recklessly generous to intruders from distant lands all through our recorded history. We should have been more discriminating. Certainly we should never ever have accommodated Batswana. So I suppose our present condition can be blamed on human folly as well. We are just beginning to learn, in the most painful way possible, that passivity and hospitality are not always rewarding human virtues. Throughout history we have been so reckless with our resources and tranches of humanity that we now spend all our time and energy desperately trying to correct mistakes of the past. We have pawned, mortgaged, prostituted and bastardized our heritage and sovereignty with reckless prodigality. Perhaps there is no better time done now to remedy these past acts of criminal negligence on our part. If your leaders agree to tame their passions and interests, as well, a way forward will in good time present itself to both parties. Death, destruction and humiliations of people are things best left to God. Much of this suffering is the result of a terrible misunderstanding. We have never claimed to be pristine and separate, only that we are different in the way we do certain things and that that difference must be respected. We are very much conscious that we live in a larger society, with a community of equal nations. What we have always said is that our political hope lies in a democracy with constitutional constraints tailored to our local realities. Unrestrained markets, for example, are painfully hurting our local economy. Bureaucratic brutality is hurting our political traditions. Our culture and way of life are under siege from all sorts of extraneous circumstances. Why should we suffer so much violence and desecration? Throughout the Kalahari heartlands public administrators tolerate such violations in exchange for petty bribes, kickbacks and small favours from developers, speculators, explorers, contractors, farmers and unscrupulous politicians. In our communities child labour is conducted under indentured slave conditions. Government actors charged with policing workplace and safety laws also corruptly benefit from these violations. The ruling elite rejects our own vision of life, yet wherever I go I see your shopping malls, posh restaurants, fancy hotels and lavish weddings, full of Batswana who are allowed to do things their own way. In fact I no longer know if there is really any difference between your own way of doing things and that of white people. But that is not a matter for our concern . . ."

At this point, the drunken civil servant who had so far maintained an unobtrusively long running show of sniggering, snorting, sneering and the most foolish drunken tittering and guffawing to the delight and horror of many of his colleagues on the podium, brusquely interrupted the old man, as a consequence of being constantly nagged and badgered by an uncommonly corpulent white woman, Daisy Teresa, the government's international consultant on diamonds for development (reputed to be pocketing a cool million pula a month, which translated to US$200,000 per month at the time). The events of the day had taken the podgy and oleaginous consultant by surprise, and the old man's tiresome blabbering was just the sort of thing that could ruin everything. So that chunky lady was eager to stymie this querulous and disgusting wiry Spiderman.

"I . . . caaan . . . appreciate your . . . hmmm . . . anxiety over this whole business," interrupted civil servant Number Two uncertainly before getting the knack of things and launching forth with that rare lucidity that God in His equally rare moments of madness impart to drunken souls.

". . . but we cannot allow your insularity and indifference to undermine the national project."

"Is that really the reason why you daily unleash man-eating dogs on our women and children?" asked the old man, unperturbed by this unseemly charge of blinkeredness.

"We want you to make significant . . . I mean meaningful contribution to the larger society . . . all these measly, paltry things . . . you know . . . eating roots and feasting on Eland seven days a week . . . When will you come to the national table brother? Don't you want to be part of the *demos*? There is room for everyone there. It's a very huge table and food and snacks aplenty for everybody"

"You can give my seat to that very nice-looking white female friend of yours for all I care," said the old man insolently.

"We are free people. Basarwa are born free. And we die free. That is the way of our world. We don't want to end up living behind barbed wire fences, walking about with personal bodyguards and breeding man-eating dogs. You want us to live in fear and insecurity? Is that it? Well, I've a few words for you. We want to be free. To live free and sustainable lives.

To remain who we are, to be our true selves and not some poor gossamer caricatures of foreign cultures and ideals. We want to remain human, truly human. Your national project is misguided and infuriating. We hate your philanthropy and your other ways of dealing with us. We want to do things our own way, to do things the right way. We want to be free from greed, pillaging, rape, brazen officialdom, cultural humiliation and majoritarian indifference. Give us access to our resources and let us be. Why do you hold so tight to our resources and heritage if we are so terrible? Why? Why? Why?"

"Ehemmm . . . I really cannot answer for conditions created by history and the infallible will of God Almighty . . ."

"Ahaaa, so now you blame God for your misdeeds? I think if you are really men—I see that pudgy white woman has a lot of influence on you, let God bless her—if you are really men you should concede to the fact that your national project is not morally defensible and politically viable, that it is a source of political violence and madness. I really don't think you all want to commit moral death . . ."

"Old man, please don't insult our guests. Human respect is a fundamental cornerstone of our culture and tradition. Ms. Teresa is here to help us polish the image of our country abroad. We need humanitarians like her to walk this long and tortuous journey of nation building. If she didn't love us so much, she could be at home playing with her grandchildren and watching Hollywood films. She volunteered to come here and make sure that the whole world buys our diamonds. So let's be polite to her. Now, old man, you know that our laws protect you from discrimination and prejudice . . ."

"And they don't protect us from unscrupulous mining companies, Safari operators, police brutality and soldiers . . . just look around you . . . see what is happening to us . . ."

"This is exasperating beyond measure. Old man, how many times should we remind you that it's a contradiction of terms for Basarwa to claim rights of a special character over other citizens?"

"Don't you think Mr. Civil Servant that those other citizens have very good reasons of their own for abandoning, surrendering, eliding, abrogating, negating and abjuring their rights, values, virtues, sensibilities, morals, significances, mores, civilizations, religions, ethics, cultures and identities?"

"They need money! Why else would they do it?"

"Really? Surely they should have . . . anyway, that's none of our concern. But they certainly do have many good reasons for doing so."

"Money, money, money," insisted the now visibly excited civil servant. The old man ignored him. Daisy Teresa frowned and said nothing.

". . . I mean they can be no doubt they are paying a very high price for this luxurious commitment to fun, song and dance. All the same they are exercising their democratic choices. In the same vein we have the right to claim, assert, defend, protect and vindicate our own rights, cultures and identities. Where lies the contradiction? We demand a permanent political and cultural identity! We want a thorough review of the constitution to redress these iniquities. We demand education in our mother tongue. We demand protection from callous and indifferent settlers and resource developers and users. We want to dictate, direct and prescribe the conditions for our integration into the larger society. We refuse to obey, yield, follow and submit to authority like little children. Any common legal and political identity emerging in the end must bear the imprimatur of voluntary and visible Basarwa signature. It must be a true ethnic mosaic, a historical fresco and portraiture of all citizens equally agreed and just. We want to remain an intact and rooted community, not a disparate ensemble of haphazardly dispersed, mixed and assimilated groups with no identity. What we really want is a differentiated citizenship that promotes a value of equality that accommodates difference."

"Why in the damned world of God should we entertain such a gratuitous claim against other members of the Republic . . . ehmmm . . . I mean against the larger society?"

"Precisely because we are a republic! By the way who are the larger society?"

"Ehemmm . . . Us. All Batswana, I mean . . ."

"Aha, you mean Setswana speakers?"

"No, no, no. Us. All of us . . . ."

"Does that include us? Does that include our dead and unburied brothers and sisters here? Does that include this dead child in my hands?"

"I . . . I . . . guess . . . if we bury them here . . . the Republic . . ."

"Mr. Civil Servant, don't you really think the historical claims of *Tswanadom* erroneous, fatuous, fatigable and dangerous? I mean what's wrong with people asking for recognition and peaceful coexistence in a democratic order? Many of us simply hate and refuse to accept the destabilizing consequences of the harmful decisions of the larger society. And that too is our democratic right. We cannot allow the larger society to deprive us of the conditions necessary for even the most minimal survival safety-nets. No people want to be dispossessed and deracinated. That's why Africans fought wars of liberation against colonial terror and hubris. They were defending the same existential principles. We are doing the same thing. We must halt, block, break and end these depauperating claims on our society, on our bodies, on our lives and on our individual beings. It's the right thing to do."

141

"Should I take it, old man, you want special rights regarding land, natural resources, language, representation . . . eheee . . . a set of community rights that protect your interests?"

"Yes. Absolutely. As it is right now, rights are unequally distributed between groups in this country."

"I find your argument dangerously close to treason. Do you want to secede?"

"What? No! Only equal rights and freedom. This sort of thing is happening all over the world. What we are demanding is being done throughout the whole wide world. Why should we be the exception? This is how true democrats, humanists, statesmen and civilized societies are responding to such claims all over the world. Why are you so stubborn? What are you afraid of? You must be hiding something from the world. There must be an explanation for this rotten political staidness. I think it's your actions that are treasonable. I mean, how can you demand that the cause of liberty find, and take root, in the autonomy of significant Others? This is a most unreasonable proposition. This anthropological Othering must stop. You are exploiting us, pure and simple. We demand a free society for free men and women, a society predicated on robust and viable precepts of human fellowship and modern juridical conceptions of justice, peace and human security. We are a people with a historic life, a most tortuous and remarkably beautiful life that is the subject of legends and myths, a historical life terrifyingly embedded in the finest lineaments and bloody contours of our consciousness, and a people whose life is the story of human tradition itself. Our life, our culture, our philosophy and our needs are quite different from yours. Your way of life curtails rather than expand our rights and freedoms. We don't want to live our fate to an adjacent Mother Community that is perpetually indifferent to our plight and ever dwindling opportunities. Our children have already lost their compact, self-conscious and culture-maintaining entities; their whole world of religious things, their entire world of existences and animations has cruelly been reduced to nothingness. There is a real and present danger in allowing their nonbeing and somnolent condition to remain at the mercy of callous bureaucratic indifference. These mining companies are coming here to finish off were your people left, to eat us up alive, to ravish our souls, to harrow and lacerate our already broken and bleeding hearts, to entrance, bewitch and kill our children with alien, unforgiving and unmitigated influences."

"That's madness. We are all here to *civilize* you. And you are calling us names. How can you insult your only benefactors in this way? Come what may, we'll slog, haul, draggle and graft you and your miserable people into the twenty first century. You can come along reasonably and sensibly or we'll have to drag and yank the whole lot of you screaming, bleeding and crying to our ultimate purpose. The British civilized us. Just look at us now. We have cars, big houses and we mine our own minerals. We're civilized. Mother . . . ehem . . . Ms. Teresa is here to see that we too civilize you the right way. Don't worry about anything. White people have experience about these things. They have been civilizing other people for ages. There is no need to worry at all. These things will work themselves out beautifully in the end. In the course of time we shall all be rich people. Right now you are demanding illegitimate and divisive benefits, and that is not a good thing. You even saw Ms. Teresa shaking her head. It hurts her to see how you people are behind in everything. We shouldn't be greedy. That's against our Setswana way of doing things. It would appear you are agitating for ethnic repudiation of integration. That is scandalous and improper. There are better ways of doing these things. Just trust us to do the right thing. In any case these are not really genuine and realistic fears. Everybody in this country is doing just fine."

"That's not true. Don't lie to me. How can you lie in the presence of all these people, the dead and the living? They are all witnesses to your pack of lies. I may be old but I'm not a fool. My mind is sharp as a razor blade. If there is anything that's good for the mind, it's pain and suffering. We'll always be wiser and more honourable than you. We have intuitive and philosophical perception of our human condition. You really cannot teach us anything. The oppressor chastises, brutalizes, and abandons himself to the most wanton passions, but he never really learns anything. Anyway, you care too much for your stomach to worry about real life, about the real burden of human life on earth. We know better. We live close to nature. We are human."

"Old man, please save that drivel for Sunday school. We have no intention of rewriting our history. We don't give a fig about the past. The past is always a treacherous minefield. Who really knows what happened in the past? No one, not a single soul! The past lies out there ravaged and atrophied by the merciless match of raw time, wordless and voiceless. Why care about that unspeaking and speechless cadaverous wasteland?"

"What ignorance! Sir Seretse Khama, one of the founding fathers of the . . ."

"Seretse Khama is dead . . . all his wishes and sayings are buried with him. The living must carry on . . . we have our own wishes and our own sayings . . ."

"Really, young man . . . such ingratitude . . . is there no room for appreciation in this brave new world of yours? Where really is the harm in acknowledging certain things and truths as sacred principles? Sometimes I wonder . . . are you people still human? Even your forefathers, those rascally wicked, dishonest and completely

143

untrustworthy bride beggars were a much, much better lot to live with than the present generation."

"Now you are insulting our brave and venerable ancestors . . . bride beggars . . ."

"I'm telling the truth. What would you know about it? What do you know about the truth? Not long ago thousands and thousands of rampaging Ndebele warriors cut a terrible swathe across this land, obliterating everything on their evil path, much as you are doing to us today, leaving a trail of blood and tears in their wake and an ocean of grief, bereavement and anguish. A polygamous and aristocratic martial society, the Ndebele kidnapped children, who they turned into slaves, and thousands of Batswana young women, who were indiscriminately distributed to warriors, chieftains and generals. Many among the abducted women were royals thoughtlessly and hastily abandoned by your cowardly fleeing rulers, their councillors and fighting men. Overnight these cowards swamped our desert heartland, frantically seeking refuge from us. We knew the desert well and we helped them even though they were our historical foes. They had left food, children, wives and thousands of unmarried young girls at the mercy of this brutal promiscuous horde. We called them bride beggars because they had no women to marry. We gave them our daughters to marry and restore their almost extinguished blood lineages. That was kindness. You may not know it but you probably have our blood in your veins. The past is always a pregnant treasure full of wonder and knowledge but you don't care about it, do you?"

"I don't know what you are driving at . . . revealing such secrets . . . I mean . . . washing our dirty linen in public . . . how do you know . . ."

"How many Tswana princes and princesses survived the depredations of the Ndebele? Why don't we have true, strong, vibrant and visible Kingdoms in this country? How many royals married our women and outsiders after these wars? My friend, you are good at rubbishing history but you really don't know anything about it. Just listen and learn. True knowledge may yet humanize you and your friends at Government Enclave . . ."

"I really don't know what you are driving . . . our forefathers let Mzilikazi and other Zulu marauders pass . . . peacefully gave them the right of passage . . . we love peace . . ."

"That's most unlike the bridebeggars I knew . . ."

"Really, old man . . . we have visiting friends here . . . international guests . . . please don't upset Mother . . . Ms. Teresa . . . all this talk is now dangerously drifting towards historical slander . . . there is what we call retroactive justice you know . . . and stop these uncouth references to our democratic leaders, I mean if you don't cease and desist . . . there lies the evil seed of . . . eheee . . . subversive element and intent. Please let's

144

forget this turgid tale of cowards and bridebegging, it's so much unbecoming of a civilized people . . . this historical slur . . . I mean if we listen to you next you'll be demanding exemption from laws and regulations that are simply inconvenient to your people, and to what end? This whole argument is simply outrageous, impertinent, insignificant, and irrelevant to the point of meaninglessness . . . Ms. Teresa this . . . the note you just handed me is incomplete . . . ohooo . . . what a rotten job . . ."

The old man honked with uncontrollable laughter.

"Don't you think you should listen to your own people, Mr. Civil Servant?" asked the old man before surrendering to yet another bout of roaring laughter.

The entire crowd, from both sides of the terrible divide, between the suffering and dead on the one hand and the merry-go-round mass of virile, healthy and thunderously boisterous youths on the other, was now enraptured. It was *kgotla* democracy at its best. Even Daisy Teresa had abandoned her English primness and prissiness, and the fat lady was actually singing! Her wobbling laughter, although confined to tremendous sniggering, snorting and sniffing, was punctuated by clear physical evidence of mirthless surrender to the inevitable. A mysterious softness, almost languid and gentle in its vivid quietness, was maliciously and pitilessly racking her corpulent body and this extremely exasperated Civil Servant Number Two, who now suspected the consultant of secretly sympathizing with the enemy.

"This . . . is just," slurred the profoundly sweating and dithering bureaucrat, ". . . this is just one more example of the enduring quality of political demagoguery in a thriving democracy. No one really takes you seriously."

"No one else feels our pain and humiliation. We who suffer take ourselves seriously. I can't believe you have the nerve to extol the virtues of a system capable of reducing a human society into an anthill. Do you see how we live? Ants are better off in their dung heaps, spiders wealthy by comparison in their catacombs, ruins and grottos. And we are part of your much vaunted democratic culture. How can the world be so blind?"

"There is nothing wrong with our democracy. I'm paid to support it and you are free to get a job and do the same. Ms. Teresa and our many friends in the international community see nothing wrong at all in what we are doing."

"And you really don't think we should have a wide freedom of choice in terms of how we live with others and how we lead our lives?"

"There lies the road . . ."

". . . to Damascus," piped the old man amid much laughing, cursing and tears. ". . . no . . . eheee . . . this word Ms. Tree . . .," and more wild hilarity, joshing, twitting, nose blowing and flowing tears of both joy and sorrow. ". . . ahaaa . . . the road to outlawry, freebootery, anarchy, wickedness, revolt and rebellion . . . a little drink please. I'm dying of . . . ohooo . . . what a rotten business."

"Really, son. I don't think these borrowed plumes are doing you any good . . ."

"That's a good one coming from you idle, nasty and uneducated desert rat!"

"That's no way to speak to an old man."

"You are not an ordinary old man. You are a revolutionist. Obviously we are wasting our time here. Revolutionists are never real. They are intellectually obtuse . . ."

"Any of you, sir, are obdurate, hard, unfeeling, insensible and maddening . . ."

"Wow, wow! Cut it! I see your game now. People like you have no respect for authority and order . . ."

"Oh, you sentimental fool. Do you ever think before you start frothing . . .?"

"Next you will tell us that minority rights are consistent with individual freedom. I'm not going to argue with a charlatan libertarian. I'm a constitutionalist."

"Surely freedom is nothing without culture? Culture, art and philosophy are the basis of freedom in our society," said the old man with dignity.

"Life becomes meaningless to us if you take away these under-pinning foundations of our community. We have our own view of the world, our own way of life, our own way of doing things. Under normal circumstances, cultural attachments and commitments are more important in our life than political action. To us freedom is contingent upon the sustaining viability and strong presence of a social culture . . ."

"Why, I wonder, should your people be free to choose their own plan of life? The government has a good plan of life for all Batswana. What will happen when you start making imprudent decisions, decisions that in the long run are harmful to you and the national interest as you are doing now? Remember we are the guardians of public goods, the national interest and the general will of the people. It is our duty to prevent citizens from making mistakes with adverse consequences for the public interest. It is our duty to force you, if need be, to lead the truly good life. Experience teaches us that Basarwa's lives go better by being led from the outside. That's why we have to civilize you, to heave the whole lot of you screaming into the modern world. Governments do that sort of thing all the time."

"I don't believe this! Maybe I misheard? You are behaving exactly like colonial rulers. Only a usurper and tyrant would completely take over

146

peoples' lives that way. If we allowed your government to have its way in everything, in every part of our lives, in every part of our social fabric and constitution, in the very brick and mortar that is our physical being, in our entire beingness, what will remain of our humanity as a people? It would appear to me your democracy is a matter of splurges, binges and overindulgences, a matter of veritable and out-and-out orgiastic madness."

"That's an exaggeration not worthy of even a desert rapscallion like you, sir. What is really important is that we strongly believe in what we are doing. As long as we are doing things well, all Batswana are happy with us. That is democratic enough. We are part of the modern world. We cannot allow you to continue living your wretched lives from inside of old, redundant, obsolete and unfashionable social and cultural lineaments. Why, really, should you as reasonable people, stick to these out of commission structures and constraints?"

"Because they have served us well for hundreds and thousands of years, that's why."

"But what will people think of us?"

"That you are sensible rulers?"

"I don't mean that you unruly desert fox! I'm talking about modern civilization."

"We are doing fine without it. It really doesn't seem to have done much good for you."

"Sir, I have a university degree and a car. I'm a civilized man."

"And I have my land, my life, my freedom, my honour, my integrity, my dignity, my community and common sense. I'm a civilized man."

"That's rubbish. You cannot live a meaningful life without modern conveniences. People tell us we are neglecting you, that we are leaving you behind, that we don't care about your welfare. And these things hurt us. So we have invited foreign companies to come here and modernize you, spruce things up a bit, teach you how to use condoms, to tidy up your scruffy, shambolic, seedy, frazzled and sloven lives."

"Ahhhhh, the way you put it, it's as if you are talking about a bunch of children. But then you have always treated us like children. I often wonder if your own lives are really that well-ordered, dapper, easy going, smooth sailing and invigorating to the soul and mind as good life should be at all times. But that is not a matter for our concern."

"No offence intended, my good old friend. But you really can't call these muddled higgledy-piggledy loose social arrangements life. It's an antiquated chaotic mess, a terribly cluttered existence. A tangled web and a mystery. I'm giving you the facts of life. Hard facts, to be sure. Governments all over the world treat people like children. And it's all for the public good. If everybody was allowed to live their own lives as they

147

wished, without the slightest consideration about its worth, hundreds of thousands of human souls would be ruined. That's why governments are caretakers of human life and national destiny. Left to your own devices, you would all end up at sea, completely lost, and quite frankly, dead. It's our job to judge what's valuable for the good life and to provide the necessary means for better ways of life. What's so special about Basarwa, I wonder?"

"I don't care what Batswana think. What I know is that we have suffered unmitigated structural debasement and decay for centuries at the hands of foreign rulers including Batswana marauders, white settlers, missionaries and other busybodies like you. At one point there were so many anthropologists in this desert we were afraid they too would create their own government over us. I won't be surprised if we are governed by tourists next. It's time to protect ourselves from further humiliations and the ever present danger of dying out as a nation and a people. Every community has its own soul, and our soul is dying. We should do something. The government wants us to disintegrate, to become extinct. As you rightly say your job is to help us find another culture . . ."

"I didn't say that!"

"Well to be part of better cultures . . . Scandinavian, English, Afrikaner . . ."

"No, no, no, sir. You misheard. I said . . ."

"Young man, you must have a terribly forked-tongue to deny . . . anyway, why shouldn't we have a say in these matters? I have known the van Nierkirks for ages, and I can tell you I don't like the way they do things. I don't like the way they treat us. I don't want to behave like them. I've seen government officials rounding up our children, many of them babies, and corralling them behind barbed wires, and I don't like that a bit. No child should be barricaded behind barbed wires and refused the community of parents, relatives and friends for months on end. What will become of these children? Why are you doing these terrible things to them? These mining companies are just going to do more terrible things to their already disturbed minds. I don't understand why we shouldn't have a voice in these things. These are matters of life and death. Why should we put our trust on indifferent caretakers like you and your administration?"

"I'll answer your questions . . . eeehhh . . . a few more words please, Ms. Teresa . . . The truth is that we are entirely convinced your people are not really attached to their own culture in any deep way. We really, really believe a freewheeling cosmopolitan life is good for all Batswana regardless of what they think. We know what is good for you. As a matter of fact, I can't think of any Batswana who are still rooted in any particular way to their culture and other old ways of doing things. You all pretend cultural consciousness out of a misplaced sense of nostalgia; you can't deal with modernity, and you are looking for scapegoats. We'll give you a proper sense of direction with the help of our Western friends. And we'll all move forward as a nation, one gloriously sizzling melting pot matching with determination to the future. Isn't that great? Just think about it. Someone once said we Batswana are scrambled eggs, greasy, slippery dough; the proper combination of cock semen and chicken sperm wallowing in boiling oil. Just great, isn't it? We're completely inseparable. I think it's Festus Mogae who said that and you know what? They gave him the Ibrahim Mo award for that shrewd observation: pots and pots of millions of US dollars . . ."

"Are you saying they gave him money for calling Batswana chicken shit?" said the old man incredulously and the whole crowd roared with laughter. "How can they give a man millions of US dollars for suggesting people be fried like chicken egg? Some of us are already in the frying pan and I can frankly tell you it's a terrible experience. I would never wish it on any fellow human being. Not even your glorious nation builders."

"Once again you misheard, my dear old man. We have no intention of boiling people in cooking oil. We just want to make you better people by example and the most delicate political persuasion. In the end you will come to like, and I believe, very much enjoy modern life. There'll be movies, television and all that enchanting Hollywood iconoclastic stuff for public enjoyment throughout the Kalahari desert...and chewing gum."

"Just what I thought," said the old man with disgust and unconcealed contempt, "your democracy is nothing but a fancy spectacle; a subversive and insidious exhibition of manifest evil. You want to turn decent lives into a pageant, into a display of wonderment, terror and anguish. I don't suppose you have the brains to see where you are really headed. We have seen these things before, and we are painfully conscious of what they can do to people, communities and decent public life. We don't wish these things upon our children; we don't wish them upon future generations."

"I really don't see why you are so worked up about nothing. We have given you our language, a new identity, a whole new way of life: food, clothing and shelter. Good roads, schools and modern entertainment are all at your disposal. What more do you want? Don't you want to be part of our courageous and fearless historical tradition?"

"No, no way. We just want to be ourselves. Just leave us alone. We have enough valiant and gallant history as it is."

"Old man, we . . . I really don't know what to say now . . . Ms. Teresa . . . but we really cannot allow you to keep this vow of perpetual poverty. We're not that irresponsible. Rulers must govern. We have a job to do. Our democracy aims to fulfil all your reasonable expectations."

"What about our legitimate expectations?"

149

"Null and void. As I said, we're scrambled eggs. No process of filtration can separate us. You are part and parcel of the whole nation. We know you are troublemakers and rabble rousers. For all we care you can howl to the mountains till the chicken come to roost, but sooner or later you'll heel."

"These people are really colonists, aren't they?" wondered the old man loudly and sadly.

"No, sir, we are realists . . ."

"Don't take us too lightly, Mr. Civil Servant. We are men well known to have hard balls . . . we'll not take this thing lying down . . . mark my words," said the old man indignantly.

"We'll get our own Ibrahim Mo award for teaching you manners and the true meaning of courage."

"Not in this country. We lay down the law . . ."

"In Mandela's country they do these things differently . . ."

"Here we do things our own way."

"But the whole world is moving towards better understanding of people like us . . ."

"We are the exception. We do not accommodate differences. One frying pan for all. One melting pot. Scrambled eggs. And we are ready to burn to ashes, kick to dust and vaporize all those who stand on our way. Keep up this funny game and we'll make sure that you all quietly fade away. The whole world will watch you wither and waste away. Building a nation is not a children's game. We can't allow everybody to choose and pick what they want. A lot of sacrifices will have to be made. Give us these diamonds and we'll give you a new civilization. I think in the end you'll all thank us for what we are doing to you now. You'll build statues commemorating our unwavering courage . . ."

"Courage? Courage? This is savagery, the worst possible human savagery. I doubt anyone amongst us will ever remember your implacable cruelty except in their worst possible nightmares. Even if there were few traitors amongst us determined to remember you well in their hearts, they wouldn't live to express their gratitude. You are killing all of us. I've never heard of the dead paying homage to the living. I know you are capable of the strangest things..."

"You speak of us as if we . . . were . . . some weird creatures . . ."

"You are a Vampire State, that's what you are and everybody knows it . . . your politics is about the belly, senseless gorging, freeloading, sponging, begging, borrowing, stealing, looting, killing and raiding. What more do you want us to say? We know you for who you really are. There is just too much bloodletting and bloodsucking in this country. There is too much bad blood amongst citizens. There's too much of everything that's bad, negative and evil. We see these things daily, happening in broad daylight and they worry us. You on the other hand are obsessed with politics of the guts, greedy guts; glutton, gormandizing, guzzling and you seem not really to have any courage and strength of character to rid yourselves of all this moral death . . ."

"Now you . . . aaaa . . . exaggerating. I concede only a little bit of suffocation . . . I mean too much liveliness . . . eheee . . . here and there . . . nothing serious . . ."

"What about the mass bingeing . . . the uncontrollable mania of consumerism that's decimating communities, households and individuals . . . the spiralling domestic debt . . . the daily repossessions and liquidations . . . our children tell us your companies are busting like balloons every minute. Modernity is cutting a terrible swathe through your lives, and you don't even see it. You really are a pathetic lot."

"Now I'm completely at a loss. I've no idea what you are talking about. We only kill when it's in the national interest to do so. We know the science of risk taking behaviour. I can tell you now that there's worthwhile reward in life that comes your way without pain and suffering . . ."

"But why should we suffer for decisions made by others?"

"Because you are citizens, damn it! You have no ability to make . . . eheee . . . holistic decisions . . . those are made by us . . . your rulers. We're the deciders. We're the elect . . ."

"I don't remember electing Ms. Daisy Teresa . . ."

"Ohhhh, damn it! Forget about . . . Ohhhh . . . I'm so sorry Moth . . . Ms. Teresa . . . I'm now confused . . . We too suffer you know . . . drink . . . I'm dying . . . It's painful to make political decisions . . . ohooo . . . diamonds . . . somebody . . . zeee gut toooo make them . . . more wine please."

The crowd had to wait while Civil Servant Number two treated himself to his constitutional for a silent three minutes. Then the old man cleared his throat and said, very politely, "Couldn't you just let us make our own decisions?"

"No!"

"Why?"

"Because we already know what you think and we disagree with you!"

"What happened to the give and take spirit of democratic politics?"

"It's easily abused. Good faith negotiations are alien to radical revolutionists like you."

"I thought it was the other way round. That it's people who are drunk with power like you who subvert democratic institutions and culture."

"We only do what we can. We always try to avoid unpleasantness. But cynics like you make our lives difficult. It's this sort of thing . . . this

151

insolent self-righteousness that'll be the ruin of us all. We need more empathy than adversarial insolence."

"We're the people who need more sympathy and empathy, not the other way round. What we resent most is this magnificent starchiness and imperial aloofness of your messed up rulers and the rigid bureaucratic indifference of their puppies like you. If truth be known you really are not interested in our plight. If anything you're intent on visiting more blight, more diseases, more scars, more damage and more ruin upon us. Your only object is to drive personal, private and partisan agendas that have nothing to do with genuine state craftsmanship . . ."

"Are you accusing us of corruption . . .?"

"What a stale . . . flat word . . . in this morass of moral contamination, filth . . . this truly authentic house of the dead . . . I mean what should I say to this dead child now thawing in my sweating gnarled old arms . . . her flesh rotting . . . that there is corruption in this country? What a meaningless word . . . what an insignificant utterance. Where do you people get this endless passion for destruction . . . This utter contempt for human life and all things beautiful and precious?"

"Ahaaa, doesn't your interminable capacity for national fragmentation bother you? Always remember you're the ones who want out, not us."

"Maybe, you are right. No one has really tried to gauge our motives . . . to listen to us . . . All you want is to dominate and dictate . . . to rule by decree and prescription. I've news for you, young man. We spurn, reject and repudiate this beastly marriage. We completely and categorically turn away from it, shrink from its terrifying stranglehold . . . we recoil from its cacophonous warring roar and balk at its arrogant sense of pride and vanity. We refuse to be part of a silent system. We are not prisoners. We are free citizens. We demand to be heard, to be seen, to be respected . . ."

"Good God, I'm out of here! This is the worst assault on constitutional patriotism I've ever heard . . ." wailed Civil Servant Number Two already on his way to the back of the podium where rowdy and bawdy soldiers, policemen and government officials were thoroughly revelling in copious alcohol to the blasting music of Bob Marley and the Wailers, smoking marijuana and singing songs of freedom.

Selibe-Phikwe, an exceedingly and permanently sulphur contaminated toxic dump and industrially polluted mining town, is a theatre of the most dramatic, traumatic and hilarious economic projects in Botswana. It is a clear portrait of the peculiar mess of urban life in the whole country. It's only that the victims, the majority of them desolate, desponded, bewildered, fragile and hopeless young women cut in the prime of their lives by poverty, disease, unemployment, and preventable deaths, find nothing amusing in these dramas. The narratives behind these failed projects, however, teach us a great deal about the attitudes and behaviour of the elite involved in them.

Selibe-Phikwe was founded as a mining town in the post-colonial period after joint government and foreign capital investment on the exploitation of copper-nickel deposits in a cattle post landscape offshoot Serowe, home to the seemingly emerging Khama political dynasty. This mining project was plagued by persistently intractable technical and capitalization problems right from the beginning and, unlike the diamond mines that are mushrooming all over the country, the cattle posts there simply refused to surrender to the demands of market forces and it soon became clear that it would take more than ordinary efforts to turn them into money spinners like the diamond mining towns. What to do? Extensive, and very expensive, infrastructure had already been laid out and millions of money poured into the mine in rescue operations. Diamond global markets favoured Botswana and De Beers for a long time because of De Beers' cartelization of diamond mining since the turn of the nineteenth century and its monopolization of the diamond industry.

Copper and Nickel presented a much more complex way of articulation with global markets, especially because of incessant fluctuations in the global prices of base metals in the 1970s to the late eighties. So the Botswana government had to respond more rationally to the forces of globalization. Unlike Zambia, whose copper industry eventually collapsed for lack of extended government subsidization, Botswana opted for a while to divert revenue accumulated from diamond windfalls to the ill-fated cattle post project at Selibe-Phikwe. It eventually dawned to the ruling elite that Selibe-Phikwe was one hell of a mess and, with international partners withdrawing support, it was decided that the town and region should be opened to international capital other than mining.

The problem now was that Batswana businesspeople were not willing to relocate businesses to Selibe-Phikwe. The problem? Too much pollution, and of course a laid back mining town like Selibe-Phikwe, surrounded by cattle posts, simply could not compete with the cattle industry and property markets that turned some local entrepreneurs into millionaires overnight through political patronage and cronyism. So the government threw caution to the wind and put into preparation a regional development strategy that would turn this ghost town into an economic zone. The Selibe-Phikwe Regional Development Project started with a seed World Bank loan of 7.6 million US dollars, and the government pledged a further P3.7 million pula capital injection. What followed is a classic illustration of Murphy's Law: if something can go wrong, it will.

The major actors in this drama were the Anglo American Corporation of South Africa, American Metal Climax of the United States, the World Bank and the government of Botswana, all of them major international players in their own institutional right. Problems came to the surface right from the beginning. Besides managerial and technical teething problems, that would unfortunately eventually refuse to go away, cost overrun amounted to 140%, interest costs ballooned to hundreds of millions of US dollars, and the project generated substantial pollution and failed to meet the physical tests for completing the project that lenders had imposed. Some of the companies involved sought to recover lost revenues in courts, and the whole thing degenerated into a costly circus. Government financial restructuring exercises, including deferment of royalties and meeting some of the debt service obligations to the creditors dismally failed. The government realized that it would not be easy to attract more local and foreign investors to Selibe-Phikwe. In the meantime, the town had become a jam-packed unkempt ghetto of swarming humanity, teeming with desperate job-seekers, dissolute traders, vendors, prostitutes, ruined investors and opportunistic cattlemen, all plying their innumerable trades, searching for the very heart of the promised Eldorado, and refusing to simply give up hope and move away.

And so the inevitable happened: this congested, dishevelled and bedraggled monstrosity metamorphosed into a political constituency with an idiosyncratic character of its own, and it commanded clout. This transmutation suited the disgruntled mass of unemployed, low paid, discriminated, indigent, starving and diseased throng of humanity just fine, and Selibe-Phikwe soon achieved fame as the place where the first miner's strike took place in Botswana. It was put down with such brutal callous zeal that no mining workers have ever challenged the government or foreign capital in similar fashion. So this peculiar mess, that pretended to be a town, now had a history and identity strongly ingrained in the national consciousness and political imagination.

To overcome investor anxieties about this mess, a Special Incentive Package (SIP) was put up to lure investors to the town. The SIP provided a capital grant towards the establishment of a firm (a maximum of 65% of the capital invested, or P1,000 per citizen job), a step-down reimbursement of unskilled labour costs over five years, starting with 80% in the first two years, a training grant in the first five years covering 50% of the costs, a sales argumentation grant, a company income tax of 15% and exception from withholding tax. These financial incentives were extremely generous for a developing country, especially given the fact that the primary and only target group were foreign, and not local, investors. In addition to these liberal provisions, reserved industrial plots, factory shells, housing development and free training of local officials were also thrown into the package. The only slight irritant was, perhaps, the stipulation of a less generous oversight element under the eligibility criteria, namely, the demand for compliance with the said selectivity criteria *in toto*; the delivery of 400 jobs to locals within two years by each company; obligatory investment of 25% of the project's fixed and working capital, and proven existence of the investor as a well-established global company for at least the previous ten years before coming to Botswana.

Analytically, these oversight measures provided an important deterrent against open abuse of the prior mentioned liberal incentives for market entry and should not only have been left in place and closely monitored over time but also strengthened in the long term to avoid or at least stem the tide of capital flight, real or imagined. But, alas, that was not to be. For some inscrutable reasons politicians and cabinet ministers caved in to the demands of behind the doors international capital lobby campaigners, and to the dismay of local critics and workers, the government quietly chose to disregard its own selectivity and control mechanism, opening the doors widespread to exploitative abuses of workers, trust and the entire Selibe-Phikwe Development Project itself.

The result? Not a single company survived a decade in Selibe-Phikwe. None made any profit. Overnight capital flight and subsequent firm closures became a norm rather than an exception. Almost all these firms were engaged in the manufacture of textiles, sportswear, travel bags and suitcases and thousands of their workers were young women who were desperate to take any jobs available and hoping to acquire important life skills through the training programmes that were supposed to be provided by their new employers and paid for by the government under the contractual arrangements agreed to under the provisions of SIP. But nothing of the sort happened. Funds earmarked for training firm workers simply disappeared into thin air, and when female employees, who unlike the estimated five thousand male workers at the financially haemorr-haging copper nickel mines in the same township were not allowed to unionise (the availability of recourse to constitutional provisions and rights notwithstanding), complained about poor working conditions, low wages and lack of training, firm managers, all of whom were foreigners accused them of laziness, stupidity, and ignorance.

In a famously reported story, one firm manager said all the 250 female employees in his company were too unstable and therefore untrainable, and loudly made it known that he had not come into the country to run a mental institution. Other managers told local newspapers that Batswana women were too stupid to be trained in any worthwhile skills, publicly stating that these females were incapable of learning. The government agreed and went out of its way to placate the distraught managers. When curious observers visited Selibe-Phikwe to research these apparent abuses, both government and foreign employers languidly told them that their major problem was controlling the girls. Yet, many of these companies were folding and collapsing one after the other.

Thousands of women reporting for work, especially on scheduled pay days would be confronted with locked factory gates and elaborately embossed closure notices, the worst thing that a company can do to a highly vulnerable and already battered wage earner in a highly imperfect labour market. Politicians and public regulators ignored appeals, petitions and the most desperate public outcries in the private media by parents and relatives. The government's position was that it did not have the experience in running any business other than issuing loans to foreign investors. Meanwhile, all the companies that had invested in Selibe-Phikwe collapsed, leaving thousands of unpaid, traumatised, wailing and bewildered female employees clutching at locked but brilliantly sparkling new gates, just another case of disorderly, anarchic, unregulated, rapacious, and "footloose" capitalism in postcolonial Africa, and all this with the connivance of government, partly through indifference and mainly through corruption and inefficiency.

Thousands of vulnerable, poor, unskilled young women and mothers were all sent away. Botswana elites can, and do, look after their own interests well, but a vulnerable young woman with little education cannot do anything to protect her interests from systematic exploitation and daylight robbery by footloose or fly-by night companies like Beach Club Clothing, Seemac and Sportsline International in laid back downtown Selibe-Phikwe. Democratic cultures simply do not condone such blatantly self-serving, discriminatory and truncated practices principally because they violate political morality, liberal political principles and political communities. Not a single person or organisation did anything to help these women.

Batjibilibili was just one of thousands such unlucky victims. She too ended up back in the boondocks an irate, livid, disenchanted and disheartened young woman. Molapo village welcomed her with open hands. She was visiting her old uncle, Kaboyamodimo Lefatshe who was always in poor health and never out of trouble of one kind or another; in other words a man of many seasons. What she didn't know was that another, even more deathly, peculiar mess was on the horizon. Batjibilibili listened quietly as the her grandfather narrated how the experiences that are so close to our own age, like the knowledge of culture and politics, are more than thousands of years old.

She thought it exciting, enlivening, and provocatively awakening that questions that dog political and public domains today about politicians, power and politics were, for example, already common in the world of her ancestors. The Old Man was telling her that as an individual her happiness was the key, and the only goal of her society, and that if social institutions hampered her flowering and happiness, then those institutions should be reduced or abolished. He argued that government, with its laws and regulations that were more numerous than the hairs of an ox, was a vicious oppressor of the individual, and more to be feared than fierce tigers. He pointed out that the more laws and regulations are given prominence, the more thieves and robbers there will be.

Her amazement was that his concerns were as modern as any can be: especially the point about strategies best suitable to direct social change towards liberty, freedom and happiness. It amazed her that for centuries this concern had remained unresolved both for human beings and human society in many parts of the world. She started wondering, for instance, what was the best way to confront the problem of power? Do we have to convert a large majority, a narrow one, or merely a critical mass of an articulate and dedicated minority? What was the best way to pursue social change? She suspected that most of the time politicians knew the answers to these matters but kept them to themselves. Did tyranny, in spite of how coercive or despotic, rest in the long run on the consent of the majority of the people? If tyranny is kept in power by popular consent, what was the best way to get rid of that power?

The Old Man was saying it was the duty of the poor, the wretched, and the stupid followers, blind to their own good, deprived of their properties and homes, to cast off their chains by refusing to supply the tyrants any further with the instruments of their own oppression. The tyrant he pointed out had nothing more than the power you confer upon him to destroy. Where has he acquired enough eyes to spy on you, if you do not provide them yourselves? How can he have so many arms to beat you with, if he does not borrow them from you? The feet that trample on your cities: where does he get them if they are not your own? How does he have any power over you except through you? Why do the masses customarily give consent to tyranny, and thereby support their own misery and destruction?

The Old Man talked about the mystery of civil obedience and Batjibilibili dreamed on about the mysteries of ancient knowledge that some people called ignorance. Was the Old Man telling the truth? Was he hallucinating? Why hadn't education prepared her for these things? Why do people, in all times and places, obey the commands of a small minority of society that constitute the government? Why are people steeped in the habit of consenting to their own subjection? Is there an insidious power of habit, which accustoms and inures the public to any institution, including its own enslavement? What would happen if all the public sunk into submission? Would all ruled people eventually disappear from the face of the earth? What if liberty and freedom entirely perished from the earth? Would still a few men and women of vitality and spirited-mindedness invent them?

The Old Man's relentless rendering of apathetic history intermingled with her thoughts: the devil of violence, the devil of greed, and the devil of hot desire were brought into sharp relief, stinging her complacent conscience. The mental picture of inappropriate, undesirable, inefficient and structurally violent modernising interventions in her village started to take shape. Its flabby, pretending, and weak eyed devilish bureaucratic sensibility predicated on violence, greed, unrestrained desire and lust assaulted her moral sensibility. The hollow men contracted by the devil to turn her village into a wasteland were unmasked and exposed in the eye of her mind. The inefficient extension workers, disaffected councillors and local leaders, envious subordinates and defensive superiors perched in Gantsi started to assume a new meaning to her. She started to understand why the government, although purporting to be a paragon of democratic excellence, continued to give identities to unwilling minorities like her own people, establishing purposes for their living, and assigning destines by presidential decrees and bureaucratic fiat. She started to understand why ministerial statements depicted her people as lost and uncivilised human creatures caught in the wilderness of the innermost deep end of the country, human creatures that need the civilising agency and benevolence of the state. She started to understand why the government dismally failed to civilise the behaviour of its own employees, why it refused to reign in the traumatising course of untrammelled market fundamentalism on her people and their resources. She began to understand the terrible historical incongruity between value and fact, between the system of meanings and functions that the state invented for unwilling victims like her brothers and sisters. She began to see how a disorderly capitalism in Botswana constituted systematic assault to the weaker and more vulnerable sections of society, especially her own people who lived in the margins of the emerging modern social order. She began to see why land reform and management were driven by petty bureaucrats, and why most of them were not only poorly trained but also underpaid, resentful of working in the countryside, and therefore lacking both motivation and drive to carry out even the minimal tasks expected of term. The devil's insidious hand was working everywhere to promote this criminality of inefficiency. She began to wonder why her people should readily accept the fostering care of ruling elites' benevolent enterprise when most of it was so terribly destructive to their way of life.

The imposition of national parks, game reserves, tourist safaris, mining towns, heritage centres and endless human settlements: all these things began to worry her, to dominate her thinking, to plant seeds of doubt and suspicion in her mind, to take different and terrifying meanings. All these things involved a great deal of forced removals and resettlements in the name of development. But she was beginning to see how it was actually the richer and more enterprising outsiders who benefited from them. Her own people received only the most spiritually, ideologically and structurally deformed version of enlightenment idealism. In pushing their modernisation drive in her village, the political elites seemed not only to see bankruptcy in her community but also actually exhibited a high degree of the desire to see such alleged cultural and political bankruptcy become a fact of history. Why, she wondered, should her people succumb to a modernizing logic that not only sought to elide them as a social category but also failed them as a governing principle that would sustain their identity and obtain the natural justice and natural conscience behind the activities of mainstream society?

The fact of the matter was that the logic of absolute control of diversity in Botswana, the logic of benign and liberal order, masked hideous biases within a context of heterogeneous bodies and public policies. She wondered why these biases remained unconfronted, unacknowledged and unnegotiated in reality. She felt terrified, disgusted and appalled by the grim emptiness of these elite agendas and the vanity of political powers' claim to civilization.

As far as tenure democratisation is concerned, Botswana still had a long way to go. The Old Man was saying that government needs to acknowledge the resilience of her people's ethnography and environmental management. Their ideology and institutions had not dissipated in centuries of unprovoked aggression from first colonial, and then, capitalist forces. There was still a close relationship between Basarwa social organisation and the environment, and any process of ecological transformation must take cognisance of this fact; the conservation, development and enlightenment ideals advanced notwithstanding. Land expropriation and wage labour practices that drastically changed Basarwa structures of social organisation could not be in their interest. The rationalist interpretations of ecology in the form of land conservation and husbandry should not be abstracted from realities on the ground. The same goes for the deployment of science and technology to manipulate nature, and the expansion of the emerging capitalist economy, and the bureaucratic apparatuses designed to

159

transform social actions in the countryside into rationally organised action and the elaboration of formal legal systems for economic and political actions in national life. The postcolonial elites, she now realised, were bent on yoking nature to economic gain, and their actions were driven by the profit motive, greed and selfishness. Conservation discourse was being manipulated to serve economic interests. Mineral explorers, ranchers, government officials and public policy scorned Basarwa's social reaction against this utilitarianism in general. The story of her people was a classic example of how far the excesses of utilitarian resource exploitation propel themselves.

A deliberate, intensive, and guided effort was needed to reverse this process. Dialogue was necessary to prepare people involved for changes in their way of life, to convince them of the need for these changes, and all changes would require administrative discipline to ensure that personal gain was not allowed to overshadow the long term national interest.

Batjibilibili had always been aware that, in modern society, the agency view of the state enjoyed deep articulation, particularly in the contractual theories of justice. The idea of citizenship, with its constituent spheres, namely, the civil, the political and the socio-economic, is central to any discussion of human welfare. Briefly, the civil element of citizenship consists of the rights essential for the basic liberties, especially the fundamental right to justice. In a democratic society it finds legal expression in the organic structure called civil society. The political element consists of the right of a person to participate in the exercise of power, as a member of a body invested with political authority or as an elector of such a member, and by the socioeconomic element was meant a range that encompasses the right to a certain share of resources; the right to share to the full in the social heritage, and live the life of a civilised being commensurate with the standards prevailing in the society in question.

Historically, Botswana had had all these elements of citizenship embodied in the institution of the *Kgotla,* traditionally the omnipotent assembly of council to which all aspired for welfare and deliverance. The principle underlying both the social organisation and political function of the *Kgotla* was, and still is, consultation. The problem with *Kgotla* democracy is the failure by both its advocates and practitioners to appreciate the inadequacies of this system of governance in the traditional past. In all historical Tswana societies the chief rarely consulted his subjects on matters of national importance. He merely consulted his assorted body of immediate councillors and elders for political advice before acting in the "public interest". It was purely up to the idiosyncrasies of the chief, and the occasional need, that the advice of the chief's cabal would be supplemented—but never effectively contradicted—by a communal gathering's deliberations. Even then, women were forbidden to attend, and those held under various forms of subservience and vassalage like Basarwa were denied the right to public speech.

The postcolonial state sought to pre-empt meaningful political dialogue about critical policies by using the idiom of a democratic past that never existed in order to prevent people from embracing modern contractual theories of justice. This was facilitated by the fact that, albeit protected by Parliament, courts and local government, civil society in the country was weak and therefore its aspirations were highly susceptible to perversion by powerful groups which eventually gained control of the bureaucratic apparatus.

As a result, when the government started its consultation exercise on any matter, it always resolved to carry it through regardless of any opposition from both within the state apparatus itself and without, arguing that this was the established way of doing things. Any form of consultation was always done in such a way that it simply gave a semblance of democratic participation in the execution of the policy. In other words, political participation was not used to mean involvement in decision making by all social strata so that decisions taken do not favour only those groups that already have privileged access to resources and that the people also take an active part in implementing decisions arrived at rather than leaving this to an outside agency.

This bastardized form of democracy failed to allow a large number of people to take active and direct participation in government or the formulation of public policy. Politicians argued that every citizen was allowed to participate and influence the political process but in reality there was, more often than not, an unequal degree of political participation and influence. In the end a situation emerged in which participation without power was more characteristic of the poor and working classes while power with or without participation was characteristic of the rich and upper classes. It failed to make people feel more responsible for their well-being. This made people, especially the poor, less critical of public policy and more likely to blame themselves if things went wrong.

Batjibilibili was feeling distinctly nervous. She was sitting almost on the edge of a chair in a small room in the offices of Desert Companions, a charity organization which was part of the New Kalahari Village people's project of which until recently, she had never heard. She had seen the advertisement for a job there while recovering from an abortive suicidal bid—the result of maniacal despair and deep depression. Her psychiatrist claimed she had not really wanted to commit suicide, only to call attention to her predicament. She was inclined to agree with her. Her life was a mess.

She had been jobless since the peculiar experience in public life at Selibe-Phikwe. She worried incessantly that wanton deskilling would ruin her chances of ever working again. Even now she worried if she really could hold on to the job if she got it. It would have been better if God had taken her for good so that that fat psychiatrist would not have had the satisfaction of accusing her of extravagant passion and emotionalism. Altogether she blamed herself for bungling the job.

As an adult she ought to have known how to cut her thin wrists efficiently. But then not many adults try to operate with nail scissors when they are three parts dead drunk. And to think that she screamed for help the very moment she sighted her beautiful crimson blood spouting out, spewing in every direction as though pontificating on the mystery of life and death and was sending forth a message to the whole bloody village: here goes the bitch, I've had it! What an embarrassment, what horrible humiliation! She shuddered violently and tried to turn her tortured mind to the business at hand. The job advert was interesting. It said simply: is your IQ high? Are you in good health? Have you one or more special skills? If you are bored to death with your life, have no burdensome family ties or romantic connections, call. Maybe we can make life interesting. She had called the number given. A foreign sounding female voice, later confirmed to be Swedish, questioned her, checked all the relevant particulars, recorded her personal details and directed her to attend an interview. After the interview, she had been given an intensive physical examination. It was only then that she learned the names of the researchers that had run the ad. She was still not much wiser. The title of the mission statement of Desert Companions seemed meaningless, too academic to be of help to the local people whom they sought to help.

As she waited for that decision that would redefine her fate she felt a ghost pain in her left thigh. What her grandfather would call bad omen. She knew it was not real; but it felt bloody real. Real enough to make her surreptitiously swallow a pain killer tablet courtesy of the failed departure to heaven and the kindness of village clinic nurse Antoda. Real enough to scare the daylights out of her mind when she started to assimilate, and then read and reread about the Swedish researchers from the opposite wall poster. There was too much emphasis on human rights that reminded her of government's war of words with the indefatigable Survival Inter-national. For a fleeting intense moment she was struck with total horror. What would that bastard government lackey Jadibolole think? And the people at the district headquarters, many of whom were close friends, if only in deference to her relationship with their boss? What would the mob at Government Enclave think? She felt the sweat break out of her forehead. The terrifying intense sweat of absolute fear, made even worse by the thermal heat and humidity of the desert. But to turn a job down? The only road to personal freedom? That would be madness. She would be taking part a very small part-in the Basarwa Survey Project.

Her people were having to be catapulted quickly into the twenty first century because of government's voracious appetite for energy and minerals; especially diamonds. She would be working with her former lover who had already been appointed Project Manager-in an isolated part of the Central Kalahari Game Reserve. Their job? To monitor and assist an Environmental Impact Assessment company from Gaborone and establish the validity of forcibly removing local Basarwa communities from the area on ecological, conservation and health grounds. When she was told she had got the job, Batjibilibili wept with joy and dismay now waking up to the reality that she would be working with a man she treated in a most shabby manner not so long ago. But work was work, and they both wanted to help their people as best they could. Under the circumstances, they had nothing to lose by trying to accommodate each other for the common weal.

Out in the bush one solemn night, wildlife officers, cops and drunken soldiers struck without notice. They called themselves patriots, and other highfalutin names. Incoherently blabbering and yammering about nonsensical rubbish like community redemption, ecological justice and national consciousness, the highly inebriated but well organised promiscuous horde ran amuck: They left the Gaborone outfit well alone concentrating their ferocious patriotism on Batjibilibili and her former lover, both of them Basarwa. They made the bloodied and terrified Project Manager watch while they raped her repeatedly, rattling on about phallic justice and going on and on about the need to compel their community into submission. She was raped by thirty or more attackers. After the first three or four rapists had had their sensual fill and were giggling and patting each other on their backs for a job well done she had stopped counting.

To demonstrate that they were beyond reproach and possessed the power of life and death, this bunch of subhuman sadists gouged out the eyes of her colleague after they had satisfied their brutal needs and quietly disappeared into the night. Throughout the silent night she could still hear the way she had screamed though she kept slipping in and out of consciousness. The eyeless Project Manager finding courage only in rage, as all oppressed people are wont to, made her chew a bitter strong stick to try and deaden all feeling and managed to call for help using his cell phone. The attackers had bound her tightly with leather thongs round her thighs and cut off her clitoris. They laughed and joked, drivelling about the educated Mosarwa woman who would now no longer be desirable to any man. Then they threw the severed clitoris to a pack of hyenas, laughing hilariously as the mongrel scavengers fought viciously over that tiniest and most precious of human parts. Mercifully their Swedish co-workers came in before she could die of infection, trauma and the recurring agony of unrelieved pain and mental anguish.

Sparing neither effort nor money, Desert Companions flew her to a South African hospital, refusing to put any trust on local ones, and kept her there for a whole three months at their own expense. Though she got that beautiful country's finest physical and mental treatment, Batjibilibili never did feel like a complete woman again. Her experience may not have been too bad if the jilted lover who did so much to save her life had survived. At least they could have shared their misfortune and perhaps have tried to make a living together. Such things sometimes happen. But the Project Manager had been unable to bear what he had seen and endured. He had retreated into insanity.

Finally, he had managed to briefly elude his nurses and had hurled himself through a seventh storey window. In the meantime a mining company had been given an operating license and more Basarwa relocated to New Kalahari Village. For a long time, Batjibilibili's tormentors would not leave her alone. She was instructed not to talk or write about her ordeal. To escape further torment she quietly abandoned all efforts to work and moved in with the Old Man, her only surviving relation in the whole region apart from her troublesome cousin, Ketilepele. She knew, of course, that even if she applied for a job, any kind of job, she would be turned down. Word had already quietly gone out from Government Enclave that she was an undesirable element. The democratic government would not allow her to further prostitute her body and her life to ruin its good intentions to serve the public. She tried to approach Jadibolole seeking only justice and he scorned her. Who in their right mind would give a job to a failed suicide, to a woman not averse to making a public nuisance of herself? Every sensible Motswana already knew she was unstable and therefore not be trusted. Turning to the Old Man, she fatalistically anticipated an incongruously stifling life. No matter. Next time the do-it-yourself surgery would be more efficient, she thought sombrely. But she was again to be disappointed.

"May I offer you a drink . . . a cigarette?" said the Old Man.

"A drink, yes. A cigarette, no"

"Very sensible, I should think. I'm afraid I only have the hard stuff."

He didn't mention that he got it in the black market. Government had pushed alcohol prices by more than forty per cent, opening a wide door for a parallel economy.

"Gin and tonic, please."

"The same for me, then," said the Old Man, speaking like a real gentleman. He went out, emptied one of the drawers in the kitchen, took out a bottle and glasses, and poured the drinks.

"Still a demonic chess player? I never won a game even when you were a little girl," he said sitting down, making sure he retained a clear vision of his sister's lovely daughter.

"Actually," she said softly, "it's the other way round. You always found a way of exposing the Queen. I have always wondered if that had something to do with my mother. Or was it simply that your manly ego would not permit you to humiliate a little girl?"

"Well . . . you are becoming your real self, aren't you? A good drink shouldn't do much damage."

"No, I suppose not."

She enjoyed her drink and the usual singsong chitchat with the Old Man. Later she would terribly regret the booze on top of the strong pain killers that she indulged secretly like an alcoholic. In the meantime, she seemed to enjoy the calming effect of pain killers mixing with one of the people's most cherished poison.

"You know, uncle. I think you and I are wasting your time and mine. Honestly. What good is a woman in my condition? Or should I say predicament?"

He didn't answer her at once. He studied her objectively. She seemed almost frail, quite unsure of herself. When she had first lifted her glass her hand had been shaking. But he knew from her past experiences that she was physically tough, and had a high organic intelligence and that she had achieved much with little help; as a young girl she was not afraid of the whole world, but now she was afraid of the night and this terribly pained the Old Man. Her recent trials and tribulations would have been sufficient to totally destroy any ordinary woman. Batjibilibili had come very, very close to destruction, but the important thing was that she had somehow survived . . . the way thousands and thousands of her people had survived thousands and thousands of indifferent terrors of the world and the malevolent depredations of fellow human beings . . . and that was the vital factor . . . she had lived up to the deep time immortalized courage of one of the most brutalized nations on earth.

He felt sorry for her; but he knew he must not allow it to show. That was the important thing. If he did, she would swallow the pity like she guzzled the gin and tonic. And then she would feel even sorrier for herself. Someday, perhaps, he would be able to allow himself the luxury of telling her that she was one hell of a woman. But not now. Now the only thing to be determined was whether she was going to pull through this latest brutal assault. So the Old Man checked an impulse to smile too broadly, an impulse to touch her, an impulse to reassure her. Returning to the earlier paternal irrelevance he said a little bit sharply than necessary: "Excuse my lack of sympathy, young lady, but I just may be able to use a woman of intelligence for a wee game of really interesting chess, a mind teaser to tweak my codger's rotting brain cells. I don't care much for your ragger psychobabble. One day you'll choke on it. Now drink this poisonous thing as good as you can and then we play chess, girlie."

To his surprise she smiled sheepishly and then sighed coquettishly.

"If it's your pleasure, and if it will brighten a dull afternoon, let's play to your heart's content. No more of that past molly-coddling, I'm a big girl now."

"It is my pleasure, and it will certainly brighten a dull afternoon for both of us. This much I promise."

Recklessly Batjibilibili accepted more gin.

"Let's play it on, as the old song says."

"Please, child, drop this negative attitude. Don't dwell too much into the past. If we are going to get anyway at all with your recovery, we have to help each other. I'm a scrapheap material as you can see. You are my eyes and my future. I didn't have it anywhere near as rough as you did, but still we are both on the junk heap, it's the lot of all our people. And that is what matters, the tragic commonality of historical experience. It's all that really counts. Forget about abstractions like justice, freedom, rights, democracy and all the pompous bullshit. They always cost a great deal and more often than not lead only to more trouble. Are you listening? Do you hear?"

"Keep talking, uncle," she said, "I have nothing to lose now, not the teeniest thing. I've nothing to my name, nothing to my personhood, and nothing to anything . . ."

"Oh, but you have something to win . . . the real world to conquer . . . the future is a closed but fascinating book. We shall yet prevail. The game is not completely lost. The whole wide world is watching. There's something aloft, something in the air . . . high up . . . I can feel it in my bones."

Batjibilibili shrugged.

The Old Man showed signs of irritation, a meaningless gesture; she had never ever felt intimidated by him, it was just an old game, a profound show of filial attachment. Somehow it always brought them closer together, building more and more bridges between them, breaking barriers, driving them both into moral and mental maturation as if they were lovers. It was his silent way of acknowledging the magnitude of her personal trauma, an act of intense and philosophical moral compassion.

"Batjibilibili, it's not a good thing for a young woman your age to nurse a death wish. Our people have been known to survive the most dismal experiences. Think of . . ."

166

"They came out sane?"

"They came out sane."

"How did they do it?"

"Now, shut up and listen. Not too great, maybe . . . people like me and you . . . does it really matter to anyone whether we live or not in this damned country? I've lived long enough to know the dangers of putting a premium on hope in this wasteland. It just doesn't pay to even think of human empathy. You are still alive, and that's better than nothing. Not long ago they used to hunt us for sport and hang us from trees like dogs. Your boyfriend walked through a high window. Who cares, who really cares, but us? If you or I do the same we shall not be missed, either. Think about that. Don't give them the satisfaction of turning you into some sordid Botswana Television news item. That would kill me too. This is one thing we must avoid: letting them choreograph our deaths for sensual pleasure. Let's die with dignity. Let's die fighting."

Batjibilibili was beginning to feel angry. It was true what the Old Man said. But it was the way he said it that hurt. It made her feel like a piece of human garbage, it made her feel like a worm slumbering in a huge rotten cabbage, and not a young woman living in a democratic society. This offended her pride; a slumbering worm having forty winks and completely dead to the world knowing even in its loathsome catnapping that it was already stillborn. She was even amazed to discover that she still had any pride left; that she still possessed any thread of human consciousness, even if it was only that horrific dare devil; human pride. It was still something that defined her as a person in a country where any moral definition of her personhood was taboo. And for the Old Man to condemn her to the fraternity of the damned, that hurt, too. Dreadfully. Terribly. Yet it was in many ways so true.

"I'll be damned if I allowed myself to join the dreaded community of the walking dead," she asserted defiantly, a daring that sounded more like an echo, for deep down, try as she might, the shame and horror of her experience was still too much of a reality to be ignored. Silkily, white-hot tears streaked and speckled her fragile face in a most disorderly fashion and she brazenly allowed them to roam free. The Old Man lifted himself to his feet. He looked at her and grinned good-naturedly.

"Always remember one thing, girlie," he said softly. "Unlike that beastly lot at Government Enclave, you have committed no crime against society. Your luck ran out with a bunch of brutes who are really devils in the eyes of God; evil incarnation personified. It's not for us to judge them. Like many people the brutes out there will always have a weakness for violent politics. It's up to us to stand up to them as best we can. I know it's not an easy thing. But someone's got to do something. We're still part of the global society. Someone out there will help us, but only if we first do something about our situation. I've lived with bullies all my life. I know their types well. You really have nothing to be ashamed of. The pity is they always get away with horrible things like this because for the most part we are powerless to do anything about their atrocious actions. But things are changing. Be strong, my girlie. You simply happen to have been born in the wrong place at the wrong time. What happened to you could have happened to any one of us. It's a terrible thing to be a victim of chance and fate when you are still so young. But don't judge the world. They haven't taken your life . . . at least not yet. Right now you are weak, you need energy, and you need food and rest. I really wish I could know how you really feel . . ."

"Oh, defeated. What's a woman supposed to think and feel in moments like these? I just follow my impulse casually . . . go through the motions of living. I am really not at peace as I had hoped. An immense confusion bewilders me. Do you ever really feel at home in this terrible world?"

"Well, I find the world quite good for me . . . it's the bride-beggars I can't stand," he said.

"I have nothing, and curiously enough, I even feel I don't deserve nothing. Everything round here seems to me altogether meaningless. A woman should not have so many problems . . . so many living problems. I keep recreating the scenes of those horrible experiences in my imagination . . . my mind is still a little bit numb . . . corroded I suppose. Everything is so blurred, so unreal. How am I supposed to move on? Everything evades me: work, love, hope, life . . . I mean just ordinary dreary existence . . . not much really."

"It's a hard thing to try to recapture the intensity of any horrible experience. However the numbness will pass, only the confusion and fear will linger around for some time. In my experience even the greatest human suffering has been known to give way to light . . . to some revelation . . . a reasonably good life even. But I don't want to raise your hopes. We live in trying times. I just want you to know all is not gloom and doom. We must hope, otherwise what else do we have? Nothing."

"How can I really hope . . . I'm speechless. To me all words are dead. Every word I think of lives untouched . . . is powerless to affect the intensity of all these loathsome horrors. I'm ashamed of my life . . . I feel like a leper . . . a fetid cadaver. What really can I do? Their brutal actions continue unabated reminding me every day, every hour, every minute and every second that I'm nothing . . . insignificant and completely at their mercy."

"The important thing, my girlie, is to rein in your emotions and not give in to despair, which is what they want. That's how a totalitarian system operates, by obliterating your inner vitality. It's not easy . . . I know it's not an easy life. But try, girlie. There can be no hope for restoration of any sense of order to your personal life if you don't try hard. It may seem there is no hope. But deep down you know the truth. Start from deep there and work your way out of the oubliette . . . time and patience are your only really useful doctors. Everything else is in the hands of God . . ."

"But that's just the thing. I really don't believe any good will come of this horrid nightmare."

"My girlie, you still have a lot to learn . . . a long way to go. Believe me. I've been where you are right now, seen it all, and still, here I am . . . a little bit dead but still alive and kicking. And that's all that matters."

"I think life for me is at the end . . ."

"Urg, so does everybody . . . even the healthiest and luckiest of people can never completely escape that terrible feeling once in a while. You cannot spend your entire God-given live concentrating on the disaster that blighted your life . . ."

"But everybody lives with reference to past experience . . ."

"Not if you love life, my girlie. All human tragedy . . . personal tragedy is conquered by time and will, not our conscious actions. There can be no timetable for recovery from such savagery. Always remember the significance of human resolve and initiative, if you don't like your life . . . if you don't like what is happening to it . . . you can change it any time. The important thing is to live life itself . . . not skirting the ugliness and horrors that embody it . . . to live it as best you can right out to its inevitable end. However terrible this life is ours and existence is necessary to it. As a writer and well educated woman yourself, and the daughter of the one of the finest women to ever have been born in these parts, you damn well know that human life is not an aesthetic experience. There's hardly any way you can give logic and order to it. We read every day about the finest psychiatrists being locked up in sanatoriums having miserably failed to apply their art to their mental health at the most critical moments in their lives. I don't even want go into the appalling cases of marriage counsellors who live in hell and adorn our divorce courts almost every second. And the bloody crooked lawyers and legislators who are always such an embarrassment to family and friends leading as they do such public lives. As for us, things couldn't be worse. All laws fail us daily. Justice for us is just a cultural myth. Parliament is a cabal . . . an artifice of malice. Even life itself is at best banal, thanks to external intrusions. My girlie, you must help yourself. Sure you live in a cruel world, but your life is still worth living . . . remember it's a gift of God. It must mean something, if not to you at least to Him. Don't fall to the rock bottom of self-contempt, to a level where even ordinary things and madmen negate your life. I'm not saying you should succumb to the fact of raw naked existence. Only that you should be a fighter like all of us . . ."

"I'm useless, and I know it."

"Good. So you feel you have nothing . . . that you are nothing. I can tell you it is only from this nothingness that you can give a lot to yourself and others. For from where you are you can only go to the top. There's nothing beneath nothingness . . . I know strange things do happen in this country. Of that, I'm sure, girlie. There's always a way of living that is not futile and self-defeating. Human life is a journal of undiminished actions and deeds. All this horrible business is not your fault. Always remember that . . ."

"I wish I could believe all you are saying, I really do. I know it's up to you to express sympathy . . . but I really don't understand why there shouldn't be any moral disapproval to this sort of thing . . . to their barbarous actions. Why can't they be brought before justice? I really don't understand these things. I just can't be indifferent to my feelings under the circumstances, can I?

"No you can't. Sometimes it's better to leave things in the hands of God, to just endure. It's easier that way. But you can't just fold your arms and do nothing. Weeping, protesting and showing how overwhelmed you are with this horrible thing is all to the good, no doubt. Still, at the end of the day you have got to pick up the pieces and move on. That's the essence of life . . . the refusal to give up . . . the refusal to die . . . to leave a meaningless life behind . . . like that poor flamboyant fellow . . . what's-his-name now . . . never mind, the poor sod is dead. Sooner or letter all such fellows die, and they die the most ordinary deaths of all; unceremonious deaths."

"Surely those who committed this heinous crime . . . this vile deed . . . should show some interest in what they have done. Isn't that the only human thing to do?"

"The bride-beggars operate in mysterious ways . . . they have a moral code of their own. It's hard to vouchsafe their humanity, they are quite a species. Just forget anything of the sort. They will already have engaged a consultant to tell them what to do. They never think for themselves, only do what they are told to do all the time. I've always found it easier to do business with the Afrikaner. He's not the best of neighbours, but he is honest and straightforward. He does what he likes, says exactly what he thinks of you and—once aware he is wrong—easily struck by contrition and remorse. It must be the religious mania in his soul. The bride-beggar is a human monster, completely unintelligible through and through. Such people are dangerous. But they are also cowards . . . poltroons through and through. They always have a weak point, an Achilles heel."

"This is fucking unbelievable. How am I expected to lay my harrowed heart to this benign indifference of the universe after such a horrendous personal tragedy?"

"It's not an easy thing to do, not at all. I said it before, and I will say it again, my girlie: time and patience are your only weapons of possible release from all this mental anguish and the suffocating burden of unreality. To be sure yours is a very heavy grime of unreality. We can only hope you emerge from it a stronger and better person. You have always been a happy girl, and I bet you will be happy again in good time. Basarwa have lived with betrayal, death and terror from time immemorial. But even today we are still free . . . much free and alive in own way. Freedom my girl is not enshrined in political constitutions and moral tracts, these things can only act as blueprints for real human freedom which is unattainable in a written document. Freedom is the intensity of the human will to find its expression and life in the human being . . . in the moral being in whom it is vested by God and historical experience; in other words like culture, freedom is a way of life, not a political dissertation—it is the maniacal struggle by all human beings to live vital and meaningful lives under any given circumstances. That stinking document our bride-beggars call our republican constitution can never generate and guarantee you real human freedom. If anything, it is simply a catalogue of proscriptions and prohibitions of certain forms of human conduct mutually agreed upon, in fact a mere improvement on the Decalogue . . . .on divine law. That rotten document means little to nothing for people like us whose forms of political action have as yet to find expression in public discourse. It is to all intents and purposes a dead document. It cannot speak the truth to power; it cannot speak to our humiliations, oppression and the moral contamination that has gripped society by the throat in the past few years unless we breathe some life into it . . . unless we compute the reality of our situation into its mechanical system . . . it needs a vibrant software of moral conscience and activism. As it is, it stipulates, quite inadequately, human freedoms, but dismally fail to give them real life and real significant meaning. A Bible in a bookshelf in the van Nierkieks house does not necessarily mean the property owners are Christians and that they live by divine law and moral code. Our task is to conquer and domesticate the republican constitution. We cannot afford to be complacent about our political life like other people in this country. We need to be more active, stronger, noisier—I mean really boisterous, ear-splitting, cater-wailing—than other people if that document is really to mean anything to us and to our lives. There is no better time for that initiative than now. All we need is courage, moral strength and a deep sense of purpose. Sometimes a man with a serious wound in his genitals . . . I mean really painful scrotal damage . . . must

171

consummate sexual union with his woman to set her on the right her way and conquer her love . . . we must fuck that document . . . something that really ought to have been done when it was first adopted . . . married to our public life. If you don't consummate sexual union with your bride, she is bound to mess your life out of spite, hate and humiliation. The struggle must begin . . . there is romance in the air . . . I'm really excited. Brutalized and bruised as we are, let's deal with our fate. It's God's mandate and test of . . . a real test of the strength and durability of our faith and character; I am not saying we are the Israelites, but what other group of people have ever suffered such long and endless historical trials and tribulations? I can't think of any, but then I'm just an ignorant old man. We have our own Emperor and his smug courtiers at Government Enclave and Jadibolole is the little Pontius Pilate . . . the little governor loading it over on us day in and day out. It has always been my fervent belief that God has work for all of us. Isn't that what the good old *dominee* always says? It now dawns I haven't been to church for a long time. It's time I paid that old rascal a visit, this coming Sunday as a matter of fact. Come along too, it will do you a great deal of good. These tyrants can destroy us but they will never defeat us. Under the circumstances our only resource is courage, and our courage should never be doubtful. That way lays disaster: courage must always be pregnant with hope, ready to deliver. And we are very good at that sort of thing. We are desert people and our first principle of survival is tenacity, irresolution is a foreign concept to us, an aberration. We never give up. They have been trying to wipe us off the surface of earth for thousands of years and for the same number of years we have steadfastly refused to die as a nation and a people. Now they are going for the long haul and if we submit and surrender God only knows what will happen to us and everything that we hold dear, sacred and sacrosanct. I shudder to contemplate . . . the unthinkable."

"God, God, God . . . how disgusting? Why does He look with so much aloof indifference upon our suffering? What terrible crime have we committed to merit this timeless punishment? The Israelites broke their covenant with Him and rightly got what they deserved. What about us? We haven't contravened any God's contract . . ."

"Haven't we, girlie? Haven't we? Read your Bible carefully . . ."

"Don't tell me we are one of the lost tribes of Israel?"

"No, we are not, but like everybody else, we are born sinners."

"That's it?"

"Now, now, let's not get bogged down on irrelevant issues. The way I see it we are the injured party in this matter, and we definitely have nothing to lose by taking the war drums to their offices. In the end it's the bride-beggars who will lose everything. Stop worrying about God. It has always been his habit to make His children suffer without understanding. No doubt, He's a most difficult and hard Father. But that, girlie, is not for us to judge. The Man is mighty powerful. Let's direct our spleen and displeasure to the relatively weak and miserable bride-beggars. Life, real human life is invested in us and not those spineless, faint-hearted and delusional little devils that cannot even stand the roar of a mating lion. How can we fear people who are afraid of their own shadows? All these actions and ideas of theirs are valueless because they themselves do not understand them. They are always told by foreigners to do these things and they go along without even thinking about the consequences of their actions and complacent inertia. Before they know it, an exasperated international community will be lugging them to Geneva to answer for their crimes and the owners of these mining companies will be laughing at them. All such fools end up in Geneva or dead before their time."

"Do you think those bastards at Enclave are playing God? Can simple greed turn human beings into such brutes?"

"Adam and Eve were Angels in their own right and they committed the most unforgivable sin. Greed is a deadly sin. Those brutes are capable of the most unimaginable crimes so long as they get money from their actions at the end of the day. What they call government business in nothing short of a flourishing vending service for peddling and hawking their blighted souls. Poor things. And they think they are smart. What a fantastical misapprehension. It's a terrible thing that power can breed such wayward illusions. As far as they are concerned they are beyond reproach, masters of their own destiny. But that's what Nero, Hitler and Idi Amin thought. Look what happened to them? And that poor sod Saddam Hussein, they hung him to international acclaim just before breakfast, and he used to be such a tiresome bantam cock. See, girlie, the real problem with this miserable lot is that a rotten little village boy, all green behind the ears, with dust on his feet, dirt all over the body and plenty of caked mud on his buttocks somehow finds himself in public office, thanks to the fickleness of African politics, and his personal inadequacies, and a general state of unpreparedness immediately fuel wanton passions and desires quite inappropriate to his exulted position. Now well installed, by chance and luck, those greatest of history's slave drivers, in a world of the highest and most exciting thoughts and actions about human being's place in the universe, what does this vacillating, uncertain, faithless and frivolous lout do? He sinks to the lowest levels of human caprice, malice, nastiness and wickedness; the most easily adaptable covers for human cowardice, fear, anxiety and nervous discomfort; and the worst breeding ground for the seven sins: pride, greed, envy, slothfulness . . . look at all these politicians, people whose lives are driven by insubstantial events and actions; bingeing, parties, promiscuous sex, crimes and prosecutions . . . all forms of bungling, muddling and ham-handedness imaginable . . . and they call themselves the cream of society-a bunch of inept, most inelegant, ungainly and gauche bumbling misfits. Is it any wonder that they are so ferocious to their unsuspecting and gullible fellow citizens who put them in office, that they deliberately make choices that harm fellow citizens and that their callow, graceless all-fingers-and-thumbs conduct is the bane of our very existential catastrophe? The most surprising thing is the rapidity with which such ham-fisted, dangerous and callous creatures rises to the top in society. That I should think has got a great deal to say about us, about human nature, about our conception of morality, and about the very spirit of national consciousness. Have you noticed how inconsistent these fellows are? They change their minds constantly, forget things easily, live in the moment, seldom exert will power and when they turn to vice and malice they completely let go . . . going all the way so that nothing . . . absolutely nothing can be done to redeem, reform or change them-nothing can be done to civilize and tame the course of their virulent passions. Why do we call such people leaders? Why are we always happy to keep them in power? I think we should stand up to them. It's really up to us to rid ourselves of this peculiar mess. We must be strong and refuse to be slaves to even the most seemingly untenable circumstances."

"Still, I do feel there is something nauseating, something ugly, anti-life and terribly all round unpleasant about my ordeal, something beyond words and human expression about the present circumstances of our people in this country . . ."

"No doubt . . . no doubt at all. It always feels like this for all people who fail to claim their freedom . . . it sickens the soul, unsettles the stomach . . . I think it's the sense of failure that does that . . . the purposelessness of existence . . . its dreary emptiness echoing hollowly like an abandoned war drum in a windy desert. In your case, of course, the feelings and experience of human horror compounds an already terrible situation. It must be the worst possible nightmare. I really, really feel for you, girlie . . . don't you ever feel you are alone in this traumatic moment . . . our hearts bleed for you. We have to work together to prevent this thing happening soon again to one of our own as it is bound to if left unchecked. We all know how a beast behaves after the first taste of blood. Repeat performance breeds repeat performance till someone breaks the circle of violence and terror by . . ."

"Surely if God had foreseen characters like your bride-beggars He would not have created the world . . ."

"I really can't say, girlie. It's certainly a strange world that we live in . . . very, very strange. But it's also a very wonderful place. You know the good things in life, girlie, don't you? Many of them may be hard to grasp and keep, but the fact is they are there. It's pointless to blame everything on God. It's we human beings who have a lot to answer for. The victims of human terror are to blame for their inaction and irresolution in the face of mounting adversity just as the perpetrators are to blame for their ignoble actions and lack of humanity. Real justice and fair play lie between these diametrically opposed extremes and it is for us all to work our way towards that direction. For me right now the air tastes of expectations; not necessarily good tidings. What is important is that our people are stirring up. We are no longer idle singers of an empty day. We no longer believe the world was not created to satisfy our expectations. The sense of stoical resignation and fatalism is evaporating into the air as I speak. You are troubled and frustrated today . . . tomorrow is another day . . . a soft mellow light beckons at the end of the tunnel and the spirit is willing . . . farewell to horrid nightmares, welcome sunlight and spring. We need to stand for truth, not just imagination, and truth is born of human action; not brains riddled through and through with raging thoughts. It's no longer necessary, even relevant to ask: 'What shall we do with our lives?' Our tormentors thought they had removed the last element of usefulness in us . . . they called us useless people. Well, we'll show them a thing or two about human struggle and determination in the quest for justice, liberty and freedom. Yes, they have devitalized some among us through their ceaseless bouts of pleasure and subjection to the tyranny of sensuality . . . but there is one stubborn irreducible fact they still have to contend with, and that is our unconquerable courageous will to be active and alive to every situation, however dismal, as a people. It is this instinct for survival that has been outraged by this whole diamonds business. A seismic . . . a truly cataclysmic mental shift has been provoked by this bad business. Our entire moral and political outlook is completely focused on this one thing. Our ancestors were right to say you don't confront the real truth and freedom till you come face to face with death. Now is the moment of reckoning. This mental earthquake is our only way to complete freedom. It's a do or die moment for us. What the bride-beggars are doing is contrary to every moral and ethical in our lives and believe systems. How can they throw us into ghettoes and concentration camps? There has emerged in this country a creature of nightmare that is completely inhuman . . . a monster that rejects and repels all moral decency and human fellowship. This thing is more worrisome than an outright declaration of war. We don't even know where we stand with regard to this terrible outrage. It is sneaky, nasty, evil and devilish to the extreme. One thing is certain: on the horizon is war, deaths and mass murders, and far beyond the terror, just behind the ghastly brow of it all lies the breath of human freedom. And I will tell you another thing; this monstrosity transcends all forms of moral conscience. It loves nothing and everything, and does nothing and everything; a terrifying Machiavellian beast is upon us: we are confronted with the real heart of darkness-amoral, deceitful, unscrupulous and base to the core. The Apocalypse is now, girlie. Everywhere we hear ghost stories and smell the palpable breath of scandal . . . tales and actions of murder and suicides; all things sinister and violent. There is no longer peace, order and repose for the soul and the heart in this wasteland. The terrible thing is that this unmitigated darkness is overflowing into our homes, our neighbourhoods and our very bodies; piercing and tearing apart the souls of individuals, communities and nations. Our life is now a sort of insanity, our community a slaughter-house and our homes prison cells. Our lives are blighted, our consciences sore and our minds dins of cacophonous carburettors. This cannot be good for anyone. We are a people used to love, adoration, beauty and wisdom. We need to rise above this brutish and pettish viciousness . . . to bravely ride out this dirty-mindedness. But we cannot escape terror simply by refusing to look at it. If we refuse to face this evil through action we'll gain nothing and loss a great deal more than just our miserable lives. We will die as a people. It's time to stop looking at ourselves as little springy islands. The really irony is that this thing strikes just at a time when we are beginning to suffer the terrible misery of refusing to communicate to each other as human beings. There is no excuse for all this apathy and disunity that is sucking at our vitality . . . this obsession with inanities and banality. Real human life is like a river and its greatest attraction is that it never stops flowing. Why should there be room for failure and defeat at this particular point in time? I always tell people, girlie, that human beings are not like characters in a novel or one of our rock paintings. We are creatures of terrible agonies and ecstasies, spiritual dynamos, always creative and proactive. Without courageous action today, there will be no monuments tomorrow. We can all do without these shackles of surrender and suffering. For too long we have been unhappy, drifting, bored and almost morally dead. And all this suffering and despair is narrowing our world, making it shoddier and rottener, and harrowing our souls, making them simple and base. It's time to abandon and forsake this unmanning sense of discouragement, blame and pity. There is more to human life than weariness and nothingness. The gallery of human life is a rich one my girlie. Unless we act now, we are going past this plague straight to universal death. Just look round you and tell me what you see. All I see are skeletons dressed like priests, politicians, lawyers, beggars, merchants, farmers, lovers, workers and death, in its implacable zeal, is carrying all away one by one, minute by minute, second by second. Is that life? We are forced to send our children to school, what for? There is intellectual sloth, mental indolence and spiritual sluggishness every-where. What will become of these children whose manners and attitudes take after the ways of languid and spiritual syphilitic bride-beggars?

Nothing is as lucid, intelligible and crystalline unambiguous as things were when I was a little boy. The world has grown weary, the minds turgid as polluted rivers, even the eyes are getting cloudy, misty and opaque for there is so much horror in our lives that they recoil at all and sundry. Priests are corrupt and contaminated, politicians rotten as ever, and all this emotional anaemia is killing us; the everyday existence of triviality interspersed with uncontrollable bouts of random violence is not the kind of life I ever dreamed of as a child. Things are getting worse for your generation. We have to find a better way of living and doing things by going out to look for it. What we call life today has taken too much of the awful, unpleasant, distasteful and objectionable quality of a permanent nightmare. A spiteful, obnoxious and odious culture of brutal official impunity is ruining our lives and gobbling away the future of an entire nation. Do you know what that limpid gossamer sonofabitch John van Nierkirk told us at the *kgotla* the other day? I couldn't believe my ears . . . I just couldn't take that shit in . . . it was just too painfully disgusting; something like the terrible concatenation of indigestion, stomach-ache and heartburn that assails a drunkard after bingeing for a whole week on an empty pouch belly. He told us that things will *improve* after 2016, and what's so magic about that bloody year? Government officials, still bored and nursing their grievous millenarian disappointments after the prophesied turn of the century revolution had failed to pass, woke up one sunny morning and decided everybody in this country will only be happy, wealthy, educated, healthy, compassionate, human and start living a full and meaningful life in 2016; the fiftieth anniversary of British voluntary and scandalous abandonment of Botswana as a dependent territory which for some mysterious reasons those illiterate bastards still call the year of *liberation*. *Liberation* from what? This bloody place was a Protectorate. The bride-beggars voluntarily went to London to ask for protection and as soon as they could leave the British did so even though the beggars still wanted them to stay. Now they want us to wait for a golden celebration of a liberation story that never was before we can live meaningful lives, what for? The truth of the matter is that those fools at Government Enclave are desperately trying to legitimate a political order born out of contempt and humiliation. They are painfully aware that their nation was born out of the worst parsimonious British neglect and indifference in recorded history. All this pomp and public ceremonialism is simply meant to give some teeth to a new political order through political myth and senseless symbolic expressions. It's also a good chance to cultivate and sell an image of success and respectability, something different from the usual and real portrait of commonplace personal horrors of absolute abjection, alcoholic stupor, reckless self-abnegation and nervous exhausttion, the portrait of death, disease, and unbelievable human suffering living side by side with disgusting opulence and unimaginable resource waste, the portrait of how the brutality used to resolve human conflicts easily blurs the path between reason and passion, turning even the most remarkable human beings into beasts, and the mass of the people they lead into quiescent victims, the portrait of places and neighbourhoods where personal insecurity, sudden ruin and the possibility of torture and violent death are taken for granted as the moon rises after sunset. Let me give you the facts, girlie as I know them. Their British *protectors*, not *colonialists*; *minders* really, still hurting from the horrors of a world war and the damage inflicted by its disobedient colonies; it's real rich children, the really, really plump plums, India, Kenya, South Africa and Zimbabwe, were so fed up with this crying baby they did not give a damn about it. Botswana was in many ways the most terrible reminder of Her Majesty's imperial misadventure. A mockery of Britain's overseas compassionate political nobility and charity, she was forever sickly, weak, miserable and begging for just about everything under the sun. No wonder the Brits wanted to rid themselves of this little urchin. The bloody thing was just too expensive to keep and too much of a political embarrassment, a festering sore in the conscience of the British public, the poorest *dependent territory* on earth. To make matters worse it's *BaroneCadetto*, the Anointed One, the Great Peasant, the One Awaiting to Ascend the Throne after the British departed, the high-spirited and ill-disciplined Seretse Khama had succumbed to envy and temptation and tasted the forbidden fruit by marrying an English white girl, rousing the ire and wrath of the all-time ill-tempered oldest and richest colonial child, South Africa. Is it any wonder Britain abandoned this burdensome country? It's an open secret that the mandarins at the Colonial and Foreign Offices used to refer to Botswana as "our poor desert rat, such a troublesome child." Now we are told to compound this whole sorry affair by staging a huge golden jubilee show in 2016 to celebrate this terrible business, what a circus! In the meantime we should all sink into a malodorous, soporific state of putrid contemplative inertia. How many of us will be alive in 2016? I know these things, these terrifying little troubles, *this gigantic existential angst*. Did I live a lie, a *Big Lie*, in the past or am I living it now? Maybe, girl, maybe. But now I see things differently. The terrors of those people's ways have taught me a great deal about life. I even often wonder if I am I dead or still living. Is the *Great Sorrow* over, or is it beginning? I just can never tell. But if I can't live for myself, who will live for me? If I am not for myself, who will be for me? And freedom, what do they mean by it? Life, what really is it? Turn to God, does he really exist? A Zimbabwean musician tells me, it's okay to die because death has no membership, really? Government solemnly tells me the answer to these trifling little things lies in its *Vision 2016*, and fulfilment of the *UN Millennium Development* goals, really? And the *Great Ideals*, Liberty, Freedom, Democracy, Justice, the *Greatest Happiness* for the *Greatest Number*, bla . . . bla . . . bla? What a load of rubbish! Thirty years ago, these unanswerable questions, were very, very interesting things, good for an evening of philosophical disquisition with a lover, a proper treat for post-coital languor. No longer so, today they are as real as my DNA signature. I think the whole world wants to know how we really live, and die in Botswana. We have a lot of stories to tell and little time to do so. Am I bitter? No, not at all, this *Great Despair* makes for a great deal of entertainment. Many Basarwa I know, and I suspect many people elsewhere living in condition like ours, die laughing, just wondering at the complexity of it all! Cleaver little guys write about such things every day, get their degrees and graduate with much elation and fanfare. We muse about them, and die. And life goes on. I often wonder how many people really ever think about these things. A government is supposed to look after people of the day, defer responsibility for unborn citizens to future governments save for ensuring the foundation and heritage of the country stays solid. Now I am told my happiness has been *deferred* to 2016, my health, my prosperity . . . my comfort, my whole fucking God-given life has been *postponed* to 2016 by a bunch of lousy, drunken civil servants who treat us all like chicken shit. It would be nice if they could also suspend, stall and put off our deaths; a suggestion I kindly put to that pongy translucent great-grandson of a Capetonian whore. And do you know what the son of a bitch did? He laughed, yes he giggled uncontrollably and burst into a fit of the most amazing laughter. And that is what our lives are to these people, a funny joke. They think we are spring chickens. Human life is too full of possibilities to be spent this way. I am an old man and I want to live now. So do you, girlie; and thousands and thousands of struggling individuals and families in this beautiful desert. I can't speak for the bride-beggars they have always had a funny way of doing things. I would not be surprised if hundreds of thousands of them have already gleefully agreed to this untimely and ridiculous *adjournment* of their lives and gone on a permanent state of somnolence. It's just the sort of thing they would do; stranger beings never walked this earth. Our people too should move away from the politics of grief and chart a new way forward. Yes, these brutes have cheated, beaten, killed and ruined our people for centuries, but isn't it time we moved on? New global ideas and agreements of moral contractual justice are emerging every day and we must take advantage of this new wave of activist liberalism. We have always been a people strongly in love with life. Even the word suicide does not exist in our vocabulary but I hear now our children are taking their lives. I feel very strongly for what happened to you, girlie, but taking your life won't achieve anything. If we work together this problem cannot fail of some solution. Like all people in the end we'll be defeated by one thing: death, but let's not be defeated by life. Let's do anything we can to live, to live all we can and live life abundantly. God gave us life . . . a desert life with prodigious vitality, though we have not always been a desert people. Let's celebrate it both in times of peace and during the querulous and tumultuous moments of chaos and crisis. That's how all God's children have always lived. Let's not be remembered as the people whom time and disillusion heaped up to be set on fire. Let's not die like animals, let's die like human beings. For thousands and thousands of years we have survived the violence and cruelty of the desert and its perilous contempt for human flesh, and emerged stronger, healthier and altogether a better moral people. Let's not be remembered as the ignorant, the deceived, and the superficial, the uninformed, the oblivious, unenlightened and sort of unconscious anthropological mass; for that we certainly are not and never shall be so long as our memories serve us and we steadfastly refuse to be lied to by others. It must always be remembered that we are a people of deep time; people with a strong heritage and a vibrant lively historical experience and record. We are strong enough to withstand and quite strongly rebuff this reign of terror and political madness; we can't just be content with snivelling, scolding, boohooing and wringing our hands in endless shame and consternation. As human beings we already have moral freedom and right on our side and they have might and arrogance on their side; what we need is physical freedom. Let's not forget that pain, humiliation and suffering have been invaluable in determining our moral freedom in the past and it is still pain, humiliation and suffering that will procure us physical freedom as well. We have never shied away from the cruel extremes of enduring these things. Let's once again endure terror with disembodied unconscious flesh and in the full knowledge that this contemptuous attitude will serve our purpose well. Supreme will is all we need, and not willing negation. Let those monsters deprive us of food, water and sleep; years of controlled moral endurance and defiance have taught us contempt of use, a profound lesson for all mankind. We will always find compensation in the blazing energy of our motive. There is no way back, the way lies on ever further into more human struggle and freedom. My experience is that willpower is immense when backed by a strong moral purpose. Our enemy is well defined, let the will of the people operate, and our purpose is justified and clear. That's what Nelson Mandela did in South Africa. Driven by a clear moral purpose, he refused to give up the struggle against hate and terror. Look how happy South's Africans are; they are the envy of the entire world, thanks, in part, to the moral courage of one man. We cannot lose because our struggle is one in which humanity squares naked existence . . . it's an aspiration to life versus sudden and brutal death. It's a struggle in which no half-measures will serve instead of a clear answer. Nothing we possess can defend us from that fate. We have come face to face with the moment of revelation. A horrific truth stares us in the eye. Evil, my girlie, is universal and must be faced. It is something we can answer to with complete assent, confront and defeat as a people. It is easy to face terror in the edge of nothingness. That is what the history of colonial rule taught Africans. What do we have to lose? The bride-beggars do evil because they attach importance to wrong things. Of course, their actions are as base as anything in criminal history, ruthless and brutal like Nazi thugs. We know everything about their extraordinary and perverted patriotism . . ."

"You call those brutes great criminals? That's a terrible misnomer. They are just mindless gorillas . . . a bunch of the most beastly Freudian neurotics ever lived. They are drunk with political power and ill-gotten wealth and such creatures are always extremely dangerous. Nothing, I mean nothing at all can ever explain this concentrated essence of horror on innocent people like us except human greed and the lust for blood. They are not criminal sensualists; they are animals, pure and simple. Why don't you make me a cup of coffee," said Batjibilibili in an attempt to change the subject and save the Old Man unnecessary anguish, "by God, I really need it."

"That's the spirit, my girlie. You are too good to die."

"Thanks, uncle. You may as yet save my life . . . what remains of it."

"The only secret to life is enlightened self-interest. Just think about yourself and look to the future and in time things will fall into place. You'll become part of the community again. However, poorly, vulnerable and nauseating life is it still is what it will always be: life. There are no singular parts to human life. It's organic and self-sufficient. Right now, even at your weakest point in life you are the finest human being in the eyes of those who know and love you. You are my child, the only one I've got. It's a real shame that others should see you as socially expendable. It would help a great deal, if you didn't find it necessary to alienate the many people out there who really love you."

The Old Man was angry now; mostly with himself. He felt confused, not knowing if he was saying the right things at the right time. Experience had taught him that anger—like love and hate—was a dangerous emotion. It clouded a man's judgment. Experience had taught him that the best way to deal with troubles and frustration was work.

"Work shall free you", he muttered and headed straight for the kitchen. Batjibilibili smiled at him.

She knew how bad he was at dealing with trouble, especially what he called "woman trouble."

Even late in life the Old Man had not the slightest inkling of dealing with women, except aunt Gorata, his wandering lover of more than fifty years. Batjibilibili did not really blame him. Her auntie was a strange lover, a terribly strong willed woman and a renowned herbalist. She came and went as she liked. Lived with different wandering Basarwa bands, quarrelling with many and whenever her broken heart needed mending she would walk hundreds of miles, rain or sunshine, back home to the Old Man. It saddened her though to immediately realise it was the first time she had smiled at him in this way and even to think about his own troubles.

It's time I quit the permanent convalescent society, she thought painfully, and pulled myself together. He needs me as much as I need him. As for my tormentors . . . well . . . in the final analysis, what really are human beings? We are all social trash one way or the other. So it really doesn't matter whether we live or die. What matters is what we do with our foetid lives. What matters is that we should keep trying hard not to die; trying hard to live, for that is what God purposed. The meaning of life has nothing to do with us. How we live it, is all that matters. The passion for life, she reflected grimly, ought to always square its challenges. She opened her eyes and adjusted to world that was illusory; a flash of lurid colours in the oddest of places.

"Shit and damnation," she screamed, "some bastard has stolen my booze!"

The Old Man tried to calm her, but the atom bombs were ticking thunderously in her swimming head, garish bright colours competing feebly to illuminate her cluttered mind. If I live . . . she thought . . . and passed out into a deep sleep. The Old Man gazed at her crumpled figure; thousands of emotions surging through him—relief, hate, gratitude, disgust, animosity, spite, love . . . and maddening anger at himself . . . at the world . . . at humanity . . . and above all that negligent but compassionate Master, God. He wasn't strong enough to cope with a calamity of this magnitude. He just stood over his niece, confused and exhausted—wishing, at the same time, that he could kiss her and shake her till her teeth rattled. He opened his mouth to bellow at her . . . at the cruel world . . . but the sound would not come. He took a couple of deep breaths and then let out a great sigh. When she came to, Batjibilibili had a thunderous headache. It was only a few minutes after 7pm and the Old Man was out. She badly needed another drink but there was nothing in the house. She went out and that's when another tragedy struck. The attackers emerged from the gathering darkness, unleashed their terror on the poor woman and immediately returned to the frightening shadow of the night. It was by all accounts a professional job. A clear warning, the final stamp of absolute silence and submission. They obviously had been trailing her for some time, waiting for the right moment to strike. Now the message had been delivered. Once again at a time when she was at a disadvantage, this time drunk and alone in the night.

At Gantsi Primary Hospital where she had been taken by the Old Man and friends after the discovery of her senseless supine body on a quite road by a passer-by alerted by her heartrending moaning and groaning, a Zimbabwean doctor bent over the unconscious body on the intensive care bed in the Emergency Room, and gently massaged, working on key areas according to a long memorized procedure, now almost a reflex action. It was critical that the radiant heat of the electric machine should go where it was most needed. Simultaneously he carefully and conscientiously monitored the minute changes of body temperature, the weak bit gathering heartbeat, the slow climb in blood pressure. Gentle, rhythmic pressure on the chest had triggered a breathing cycle, and the Old Man watched with undiminished fascination and a terrible mixture of dread and revulsion.

The unconscious woman gave a faint, involuntary groan, something disgustingly akin to a sexual orgasm, and the Old Man frowned. To his withering dismay, the Zimbabwean doctor grinned broadly and nodded with approval. A toe twitched, and then a finger and a rapturous joy clutched the Old Man's heart. What had been almost dead was fighting back its way to life. Batjibilibili groaned once more. Her heartbeat strengthened. Her eyelids fluttered, and she struggled to cough a little. The doctor removed his gloves and placed a mask on her nose and mouth. In less than a minute, Batjibilibili was back in the world of the living. She fully opened her eyes and cried out in anguish. The doctor knew why she cried out. The vision analysis centres of the brain were receiving conflicting signals. A moment later Batjibilibili gave a sigh and relaxed. She focused her eyes on the Zimbabwean, staring at him fixedly. The doctor took away the mask. Breathing was almost normal.

"Batjibilibili," said the doctor, "do you hear me clearly?"

"I hear you clearly."

"Do you experience any pains?"

"No, but I feel tired."

"Are you in a condition to talk to the police?"

Batjibilibili smiled faintly.

"I am in a position to talk to anybody except the police. What happened to me? I can't remember a thing."

"Someone tried to kill you tonight. Do you understand me?"

"I understand you, as yet, I don't fully remember. How long will it take before I get out of here? I feel bloody cold."

"I'm sorry I really am not at liberty to say. Some people would like to talk to you. But right now you should feel comfortable."

"What the hell is this business about someone trying to kill me? And the bloody police, do they now have the powers to detain patients? I just want to know what happened to me and then I'm out of here faster than a dart."

"I can't really tell. I wasn't there. Some people brought you here a while ago."

"Am I involved in anything harmful to others, or likely to cause the death of another human being?"

"No, not really, not at all . . . from all appearances it would appear it's your own life that's in danger. Not the other way around."

"Well, good, nothing new in that. You just saved the life of a zombie, doctor," Batjibilibili sighed. "What a life? What a bloody anguished existence! Have you any gin and tonic?"

"Noooooo!" said the doctor scandalized.

"That seems reasonable," smiled Batjibilibili, giggling a little.

"Batjibilibili . . ." reasoned the alarmed doctor, "you almost died tonight and to think . . ." his voice trailed off. Here was a clear case of madness.

"Miss, we have a psychiatrist nurse here . . ."

"Get me a large brandy, doctor . . . anything and shut up. I'm patched. My mouth is so dry . . . I could really die now . . ."

"It is not advisable at this stage ma'am . . ."

Batjibilibili gave up.

She sat up. It hurt her considerably but she made it.

"Get me something to drink, damn you. And do it quick. Do you know who I am? I've connections, right up to the top. Now if you know what's good for you . . ."

Batjibilibili let out a great cry.

"You experience pain, ma'am?"

"No doctor. I'm beginning to remember. Now get me the hell out of here. I'm not staying another minute. Get rid of the policemen somehow. For the love of God, please help me. This old man is very resourceful. He'll know what to do. Just get me out, fast."

Outside the hospital Batjibilibili was confronted by Mualebe Dikwaere, the local stringer for *Tautona/The Big Lion Times*, who looked ridiculous with his stupid camera slung across the shoulder. He was also dirty and sleepy, the result of quite a long vigil, waiting for a little scoop. The whole spectacle irritated Batjibilibili considerably. The Old Man was very sheepish about the whole business and it seemed to her he had wanted very much to give a little interview but abruptly changed his mind when she fixed him hard with her one good eye—the one that miraculously escaped the vicious assault. The moment of awkwardness passed momentarily and she stared ahead impassively, focusing on no one, on nothing. The reporter said something that caught her attention for a while but thought the better of it, focussing his attention on a whispered conversation with the Old Man whose agitation puzzled them both. Batjibilibili ignored them as if it was really not her intention at all to talk to anyone, not ever. It was as if she was only interested in observing, seeing and saying nothing. She seemed not particularly interested in words, in human communication. Like every other person, Batjibilibili had often wondered what it was like to die. Now she was beginning to understand. Because the things happening to her were in a way forms of dying. She was beginning to surrender to her fate. If you were going to die, what was the point of asking for playback? She had dared to live a normal life in a country where her life counted for nothing and the gamble had not succeeded. If you are going to get the chop, Batjibilibili thought, there is no point . . . and hell, you couldn't challenge on the grounds that fate had been a trifle unkind. Who had been the person, or persons, who had tried to exercise charity?

"Batjibilibili, are you okay?" said the correspondent affably.

Silence.

"How do you feel?"

Silence.

"What really happened to you?"

Silence.

The questions came thick and fast. She was unfazed. She was an old hand at the business.

"I do not know how I feel. I do not want to know. The most important thing is that I'm properly dressed and going home," she sighed.

"Does this thing have anything to do with the registration of the First People of the Kalahari Party?"

"The what? I don't know what you are talking about?"

"But you are . . ."

"Enough . . ." said the Old Man belligerently. "Please leave her alone. This is not the time . . . you will do me a big favour by leaving things that way."

"Batjibilibili, after this nasty incident, would you consent to being nominated for political . . . ."

The Old Man lost his patience.

"I said to leave her alone, damn it!"

"Wait a minute. What's all this talk about politics?" said Batjibilibili.

"Quiet, girlie. You are tired. You need to relax. Will you let us pass, please?"

"Batjibilibili, is it true that you have a feud with the District Commissioner, and that . . . ."

"Excuse me; I don't know what you are talking about."

185

The reporter, now ravenous like a dog with a bone, would not be dissuaded because she was today's news. And the bubble of questions came thick and fast. A few government reporters had now also arrived and a little horde of scruffy cameramen had formed an apparently impenetrable barrier. The Old Man was having a hard time fending them off. Batjibilibili, walking very unsteadily on crutches, raised her arm.

"I intend to leave this place and I do not wish any of you to follow me. Is that clear?"

"Batjibilibili, one final question. It has been rumoured that a woman was the cause of your hostility to District Commissioner Jadibilole Mongwato. Will you confirm that?"

"Is it true you are running against your father's friend, Mr. John de Kock?"

Batjilibilibili gasped, quite audibly.

The Old Man shrugged his shoulders and murmured, "I'll explain, girlie."

She was seized by a feeling of disgust and repulsion. John de Kock had been in the army with her father for a while before resigning his commission to run the family business after his father's death. He was married to the daughter of the area MP, John van Nierkirk, and had held the local council seat unthreatened for many years till Kaboyamodimo Lefatshe started challenging him in the previous council election. Her father's friend had never like her, never acknowledged her, and he had used her father dreadfully from all accounts. She had never liked him, too. Her father's friend was a disgusting scoundrel—first, last and always. He hated her politics. He may have been waiting just for such an opportunity to destroy her completely. Not that it mattered. Batjibilibili had wilfully offended de Kock and refused all efforts at working on some kind of relationship, even when it might have been in her best interest to do so. But the de Kocks were hard people, strong-willed and brutal if need be. She was not afraid of him, until now. That was what counted. The rest was catastrophe and the Old Man had a great deal to do with it. A new political party? Why didn't he consult her first? Acting out of pure anger and hate, Batjibilibili raised her right hand crutch and chopped viciously. A man went down gurgling. Some of the media hounds went to help him. A couple of brave ones still accosted her and she turned on them with the same undiminished fury.

"There is a report that you are psychiatrically unstable. Would you care to comment?"

Batjibilibili struck again.

The last man to bar her path said insolently: "This interview is going out live, Batjibilibili. I hope you are aware of that."

A black rage gripped Batjibilibili.

186

"I'm aware, my friend, that you are a vulture, and as such, somewhat obscene. Stand aside."

The man did not budge.

"Do you really want to alienate . . ."

Batjibilibili kicked at his beer belly then, as the men fell, she smashed the edge of the crutch on the back of his neck. There were gasps and cries. Every one drew back.

"I'm very glad you have finally got the message, gentlemen," said Batjibilibili calmly. Bleakly she realized that this little performance had destroyed her reputation in certain quarters for good. She had publicly proved herself to be psychiatrically unstable. But she also knew that she had scored some points with the local population, the people who mattered to her most. Basarwa love a plucky and courageous woman. And the van Nierkirks were well known to be a spirited lot. What would her father make of this spectacle? There was a brief silence. The media men made a pathway for her, and deliberately assuming a regal posture, she marched forward. She had just crossed the Rubicon. The Old Man smiled and guided her like a princess.

"I'll see you are broken for this!" snarled someone from a safe distance. Batjibilibili did not bother to look who it was. She gave a grim smile.

"There is nothing you can do to me."

She walked resolutely away from them all.

Chapter 6

The Holiest Love Affair . . .

Gaborone, March, 2003

The picture that comes to me now, when I remember that time before anything changed, is of the garden, three acres of trees and grass. It is a small garden, private, enclosed, over-looked by the back windows of the tall houses around it, and always filled with the noise of the traffic roaring, day and night, beyond them on all four sides. Walking in the garden was not always an easy thing because its sight was really not beautiful. The gray shadowed depths of its surroundings seemed to hint at some phantasmal break in the time sequence and the blatant cacophony of the ruthless traffic, the tall unkempt trees, the indifferent flamboyance and smell of the small cosmopolitan crowd that walked in it too, the somber facades of the abutting tall buildings, and the impor-tuning of shameless pimps and peddlers were always a terrible burden to my soul and peace of mind. It was in the garden that each afternoon, when the amber sunshine filtered through the browns and yellows of the trees I used to walk along quiet gravel paths and over rotting October grass scattered with putrid fallen leaves, unintelligible words and images swirling in my empty head like some commercial jingle as if I had lost the love of my life in a nightmare. In some places the eternal rattling and belching of the traffic muted to a low roar, like that of an approaching wind. Walking under the trees, over the grass, one might think he was in a village. I remember the near silence, half-solitude of those autumn afternoons. The freshness and clear light. The erratic and terrible rainfalls.

Imagining that time, the time of my slow, numbed walks in the autumn garden, dazed even by the circling, racing, leaf-chasing dog, always

aching the dull ache of an old wound, the healed bone, I see, suddenly the
picture of Ludo Satjilombe's long garden with its trees, the rustling
seesaw, the spade abandoned in the patch grass, and of Ludo, framed in
the window of her upstairs sitting room, on her knees, very still, in prayer,
quite visible through the long windows. There she kneeled, in profile from
above the waist, and starring blindly towards the right hand wall. To the
left of her I could see part of the old sofa. On it was a pair of dolls and
one of the mistreated but beautiful, rich, needlepoint cushions—
Aphrodite rising from the sea was one I remembered, and Salome,
presenting the head of John the Baptist—all embellished in rich reds,
blues and greens, the loving creation of some old aunt or spinster cousin.
Behind Ludo was, I knew, the cluttered kitchen where the wall-cabinet
doors usually stood ajar and the counters sat laden with many unsorted
domestic objects. The sun was beginning to get lower as that small cool
wind began to blow. Ludo knelt there without moving. Her head, topped
with its bouncy, fizzy, light brown artificial hair, which always gave her
face the soft look of a post card brown beauty, leaned slightly back as if
the object she looked at were a little above her. I knew the statue to, or at,
which she prayed. It stood alone on a high white-painted bookshelf
against the wall. Below was a shelf of lopsided pieces of pottery, made at
evening class by Ludo. There was a large jug, a bowl, a couple of mugs
and a calabash painted black and red. The statuette, alone on its shelf, was
about a foot high, ivory-coloured, showing the Virgin Mary, eyes closed,
head bowed, and hands, below long trailing sleeves, placed together in
prayer.

At first I felt concerned. What, I asked myself, could be so badly the
matter that someone, a neighbour, a friend, should be praying, out of
church, on a weekday in the middle of the afternoon? Was her husband
ill? Was Ludo's grandmother, who now lived alone in a huge village
homestead, and still terrorized her scattered grandchildren by the fact of
her existence and her uncannily timed long-distance calls, suddenly
dying? Had Satjilombe actually left, instead of staying on with his young
wife, and ostensibly pining after his voluptuous hot head, Batjibilibili?
Ah, it is not so, I thought. Ludo was not the sort to turn to God in a crisis.
No, she would not ply her God, or Goddess, with requests on her own
behalf and would be sparing in her requests for others. It would be for
love, more faith, more compassion that she appealed. That banal little
statuette on the shelf was just a focus for her outpouring of faith, love and
energy, a way of connecting with a more abstract object, the font and
source of goodness, warmth and light.

Such love, I thought, standing in my parched, self-regarding state on
the rocky bed of a dried up river. Such love. Such strength. If, I thought
morosely, as a dried leaf drifted gently down and settled on the shoulder

190

of my jacket, if I had a God in whom I believed, I should ask for what I really wanted. Continually.

But Ludo, humble, proud, perverted, blasphemous, absolutist Ludo, would not. It had grown much colder and darker. The light was fading fast. The numbness, the distancing of my surroundings which were a permanent condition with me, came down like a fog. Sighing for my friend I started off, back across the grass. Did Satjilombe, I wondered, know that his wife prayed in the afternoon? With any luck he would never come home unexpectedly and catch her at it. Ludo's religion was one of the things Satjilombe seemed most to dislike about his wife. In the past I had spent more than one bad half-hour at their dinner table, as he attacked her for her religiosity, superstition, subservience and for loving God instead of focusing her attention and concern on the people around her. Naturally I could not say this was true or not. Probably his attack on her faith was shorthand for whatever else it was he objected to. Sexual frigidity perhaps, or her alleged drinking congresses, or the peculiar blind stare which would come down from time to time, seemingly arbitrarily, over her eyes like a fog. Or was it her housekeeping, or her flea prone bitch, Lady, or her righteousness, or just the fact that she was his wife? In the past she had been the light-stepping prefect running on the playfields of a boarding school. Now, the old days were past. Now she hated life, did Ludo.

Oh, how she hated it! Well, it was a hard life, the sort of life that offers you nothing. Absolutely nothing. It was a hard life, in spite of the housemaid, and the washing machine. For where the wife of a building worker might spend an hour with a mop, bucket, screaming toddlers and a heavy period, washing all the floors in the house, and then straighten up groaning for a cup of tea, Ludo, in solitude, would spend the same time doing absolutely nothing. The highest dramas in her life centered round the needs of her husband and her father, inseparable friends—in her mind she thought of them as insuperable and insufferable fiends—and colleagues. Thus her life revolved round events in which she was not a participant. Unannounced and unexpected, they would descend on her little fiefdom accompanied by dubious business associates and the ruling party sycophants. She particularly hated the brass and coarse manners of these invaders, specifically Lebanese and Indian men who treated her like a child in her own home. She also hated the exclusion from the chat, cheer, and flatter that dominated these events. She was treated, not as one of the wonderful women of the world, as she thought of herself, but as one who was not civilized, and, like a common whore, compelled to give herself cell by cell, corpuscle by corpuscle, to the lives of indifferent strangers.

No wonder she hated me, too, in her own Christian way, of course. Nothing crude, no malicious intent. What would polite society say? I had

191

to allow that, as a moral being, Ludo had a perfect right to legitimate moral objections about my behavior. But in my position I had become used to being at the end of plenty of moral legitimate objections, and I knew what the real ones felt like. Ludo, for example, really disapproved of me, but she regretted, rather than condemned, grieved, rather than reproached. She wanted to help me. I suspected that more than one candle, every drop of wax an anxious wish, had, lit by Ludo, gone up in incense-laden darkness on my behalf. No, it was not moral objections, I reflected sometimes, but hatred I aroused in Ludo. The whole thing was too complicated to explain. But things are not always what they appear to be. Sometimes, only a few times, I felt that she feared me in case my weaknesses were contagious, in case I contaminated her with my desuetude, lust, sloth, and acidy. Or in case I infected society likewise. And she envied me—why? Well, because I was wretched, ruined, done in, washed up, finished by my own vices, my uncontrollable appetites, my total failure to think ahead, and, having enjoyed the splendors and miseries of my evil acts, here I was—free. Free for bugger-all as it happened, but there is nothing to equal the aching green of the grass when you see it from behind bars.

It was round this time of agonized solitude that I agreed to accompany Satjilombe to church. He never failed to attend. In fact all his friends were fervent goers. It was a political thing, the right thing to do, to polish their celebrity images. I, too, wretched and self-loathing to an appalling degree, decided to drag my cadaver along. The service was good, in fact, quite bright, and the sermon perhaps a little commonplace, but sensible, as it seemed to me, in matter, and adequate in style. I refused to be mentally drawn into matters of substance; that is no domain for a good Christian, I thought, only faith in the written word matters.

The peaceful hymns that followed the short solemn pauses for prayers soothed and refreshed my spirit. A hasty glance at Satjilombe's face as he stood waiting for me in the porch assured me that the same influence had touched him too. Haggard and sad he still looked, it is true, but his features were composed, and the expression of actual pain had left his haunted eyes. It's hard to put into words my impressions of his young wife. In church she sat beside me in the pew, very quietly, her eyes fixed on the golden figure of Christ, hanging on the golden cross of the altar. Light streamed through the windows of the church, shining on the cream of the walls and all the glitter. Above, Jesus hung on his cross. I looked sideways at Ludo, whose lips moved in prayer, her breathing, I distinctly heard, came steadier, slower and shallower at every breath. She sat a little higher in her seat, enraptured. Following her eyes, I saw nothing. There was the altar, covered with its gilded embroidered cloth and the golden cross, hanging Jesus. Ludo was intensely staring into the space behind the altar rails, the red-carpeted chancel—that platform, so to speak—without an actor, lying in front of the altar. I turned my head to look closely at her. Her face was intense and eager, yet she wore a certain air of consideration, of critical intelligence, as if a loved and trusted friend had just brought her good news, but good news that had to be thought over and evaluated. I glanced along the pew, to see if Ludo was observed. At the end, on the aisle, sat Mrs. Antoda Zwandiwana, the vicar's wife. She looked straight past Ludo's rapt profile and smiled me the wan smile of Christian hope, charity, forgiveness and total incomprehension of who and how I was. Her face was drawn tight as a tom-tom drum skin. I smiled back, and saw nothing in her eyes but fear. I wished Ludo would stop staring at that empty space behind the altar rails as if she had just fallen in love.

Outside the church, crisp bright sunshine fell on the street, the trees, over the roofs of the church and the houses around. Silent as we had come we started homeward, but this silence was of a very different nature from the other, and after a minute or two, I did not hesitate to break it.

"It was a good sermon . . ." I observed interrogatively.

"Yes," he assented. "I suppose you could call it so, but I confess that I found the text more impressive without its exposition. Don't you often find it so?" he said calmly, "that priests, for instance, in today's sermon, unnecessarily infuse themselves with something of the written word watering the strength from the text in their efforts to explain them. Never in that wretched priest's holy life can he ever match St. Paul's spirit."

"That's rather a large demand to make upon them, isn't it?"

"I don't ask them to be inspired saints. I don't expect St. Paul's breadth and depth of thought. But could they not have something of his vigorous completeness, something of the intensity of his feelings and belief?"

I was staggered by his vehemence.

"Peace seems a long way off," I said intransigently.

"It is for me," he said gently, "not necessarily for you."

"Oh, but I'm worse and weaker than you are. If life is to be all warfare, I must be beaten. I cannot always be fighting."

"Mapopota, always remember that you are your own soul's warden. Strength is power, and mark my words, you shall prevail. Not exactly my words, but wise words of another person. She didn't know I was listening; they didn't think I was still in the house. What wisdom, all wasted on dissolute little brutes."

I think my face must have shown my bewilderment. Our conversation had become jumbled. He dropped it without much trouble, and trooped on with an impatient sigh.

"How are you?" Ludo asked me as we walked along.

"As well as can be expected," I said, sorry for myself and guilty that I was sorry for myself.

"And you?"

"The same," she said.

I was confounded. If not seeing visions, Ludo had certainly been receiving some revelation not open to the rest of us.

"You seemed to be in a trance, there, in the church," I challenged mischievously.

"I was," she told me.

"Father John Zwandiwana is very worried about me."

"Why is that?"

I have," she said, "visions. Experiences, they are so real. Sexual fantasies. Sometimes explosive orgasms. He suggests I ought to have a job, or more sex, or a holiday-I bet he knows a lot about my holidays. Can you believe that?"

She spoke quite naturally but with an effort. She glanced at me sidelong to gouge my reaction.

"He won't accept the validity of these experiences?" I asked.

"The church will not encourage married women to have such fantasies," she said sadly.

"Not that they are very keen on them in nuns, homosexuals, or anyone, for that matter," she added bitterly.

"What's it like?" I asked neutrally, for of course I did not accept for a moment the idea that Ludo was in touch with God.

"I don't see anything," she said.

"It's just a feeling of closeness, of being near a source of goodness, and intense intimacy. A moment of crystal lucidity. There is something there greater and better than me. Father Zwandiwana's thinking of calling the Bishop to me."

"Have you tried to explain things to him, talk to him a little bit, I mean at the human level, a level he could understand and appreciate?"

"It's hard to explain such things in plain terms. There are experiences in life that cannot really be put into words or easily given human speech, things that are unimaginable and indescribable."

"Is it something Dantesque?"

"No, it's divine, really. See, it's like this, the very moment I set my eyes on that crucifix, and people start singing and all those melodious sounds fill the church, I become transported to another world. I don't really know if I should say I experience sexual desire, pleasure or some form of sensual delight, or even happiness."

"A certain erotic pleasure, perhaps? A sense of being at peace, content, a sort of plenitude, I mean a sense of completeness?"

"I suppose it's partly that and more, much, much more. It's some sort of erectile violation, you know, tactile penetration through mind, perception, body and soul, something painful and nice, a poetico-magical satisfaction that is unique, mysterious and sensual; a rupture of all my bio-psychic energy. Yes, it's something like that, an enchantment of the soul so violent that I immediately lose control the moment my spasmodic muscles threaten to implode my body. It's a sort of orgiastic mystery really, a form of madness . . ."

"No, I don't think so. Not in church . . ."

"I don't think you understand. I look at him on the cross and do you know what I see, what I really feel? You must understand that what I see is what I feel as well. Do you believe sexual love is an irrational force, a form of madness?"

"I don't know, really."

"Well, let me tell you. I look at him on the cross and directly I want to possess him, to taste him, to devour him, to know him, to belong to him, to be possessed by him, to be devoured by him. All my body parts tremble with violent desire so much I sometimes fear I should die of madness."

"Is it an erotic desire?"

"How should I know?"

"Is it an amorous desire?"

"It's really hard to tell."

"Do you feel any bodily pleasure?"

"Sometimes, but a great deal of pain, suffering and unhappiness too. Think of that poor soul, a holy man, on the cross, nailed to a wooden cross, suffering horribly, a crown of thorns concentrating the terrible pain on his head. Think of his penis covered with a simple calico. Think of the humiliation of his nudity. Think of the blood sprouting from all parts of his body. Think of his unanswerable scream and tears of abandonment. Think of him urinating, farting and defecating. Think of him totally grip-ped by fear and excruciating physical suffering. Think of all these things. And then think of the fantastic extenuation of his personal ordeal, the ecstasy in suffering emanating from this divine madness, the redemptive implosion of salvatory violence that is the salvation of a weak and vul-nerable species like the human race. Think of the ultimate civilization of death, the grand prize of human immortality arising from this binge of unmitigated suffering, think of all these things coming from a man who walked this blasted earth like you and me, experienced personal horrors, wretchedness, criticism, disappointment like you and me, a man that suf-fered hunger and thirst like you and me, a man who attended funerals, suf-fered exile, enjoyed festivals, drunk wine, and participated in many won-ders and sorrows of the world like so many people, a man who contended with great misery and unpleasantness like you and me. Think of all these things and tell me why I shouldn't have all these feelings for him? Of course, he is the Son of God, and yes, He is also God, but there can be no denying he's a man as well, and what a marvellous man! It's so fantastic to be so much in love with that much abused, poor little blighter, isn't it? A humble and unpretentious little man who accomplished the impossible: ensuring that existence on earth, such a miserable affair for so many souls, did not constitute all life, that even the most diseased, ignorant and wretched human being could enjoy immortality after the travails of life on planet earth. Isn't that just wonderful? He's my hero, my star. I just love him so."

I was scandalized by this revelation, and the compelling logic of its conclusion, coming as it did from someone who exalted so much in suffering, festivity and drunkenness. For a moment, I thought she was dead drunk. But the lovely secureness and rigor of her intellect and the sober eloquence of her delivery soon disabused me of that crazy notion. The woman was dead serious.

"I don't intend to be rude, Ludo, but how do you cope with this . . . eeehmn . . . salvatory flux . . . I mean salvatory violence?"

"Why, I wear diapers, of course. What a silly question! I've never had such a lively time."

"Do you mean to say . . .?"

"Yes, I'm wearing them right now and new tights as well, all the time. I just love Sundays."

I went home, dry-mouthed and tired, unable to think, and silently cursing my Makokoba ancestors for allowing my life to traverse our cruel world in this agonizing fashion. What cruel fate, I thought miserably, that I should handle the legal matters of a man so mysterious and unknowable. I tried to reflect somberly about this whole matter. Did Satjilombe know he was competing with Jesus Christ, the Son of Man, in the matrimonial bed, for the sexual favors and appetite of his young wife? Can the dwindling sexual libido of the aging Chief Minister win the competition against a salvatory coitus so portent and immeasurable, I wondered? Diapers! For the first time I felt a terrible pity for my friend and many other men who seemed to know so little about the sexual peccadilloes of their wives. I even began to doubt the work of salvation itself, a secret I vowed to keep to myself, but deep down I feared an utter desolation; an almost delirious madness, was beginning to assail me. That secret fear, too, I kept to myself. Life was a-changing, as the colloquial saying goes. And that terrified me as well, a terror that constructed its own delirium. Going to church, I said to myself, can be a nasty business. The only consolation I could find was in the knowledge that Ludo was also known to be a poet, and all poets are by temperament mad as hatters. It was only

196

that forlorn thought that made my day. I have since parted ways with God and church. Once in a while I read poetry though . . . just in case.

Chapter 7

Loose Social Arrangements

December, 2000

I, to clear things up straight, am Ntungamili Madandume. I am completely lacking that drive to succeed that seems to have everybody in thrall these days. Batjibilibili, for instance, lives on it.

She tells me that people like me who, motivated by their character, waver between gentle excess and an equal gentle deficiency come to be defeated by life in the end. I beg to differ. I am a married man. In our home all the things that really matter get done by paid servants, cheap immigrant homeless Zimbabweans. All I have to do is to make decisions. This game is pretty simple, really, because these decisions also come from the servants. All things considered, a husband in a house like ours can never do wrong. It's a safe job all around.

In any case, I detest the idea of being a protagonist. I'm too old, too tired. I'll leave that role to Batjibilibili, or rather the mutation of herself that she creates in her books. I'll be useful enough in my role as reflector. Ours is a two-game intrigue where, when you think about it, I actually am the hero. Now who the hell is this fellow Ndofilani? Damn these names anyway. Not one comes to mind. Who is this bloody Ndofilani? Maybe I don't know him, but she says she had already met him a couple of times, so possibly I've seen him too, might even know him from the past. The name sounds familiar enough. It boggles the mind, all these men who take her to bed. Even more is the quantity of lies she tells.

At lunch they weren't alone. A girlfriend of Ndofilani's was there unexpectedly. A tall white dame. Deep blue eyes, this friend of Ndofilani's; she talked on and on.

"You haven't said a thing to me."

"It's not as if I've had the chance."

"You do now."

"What about?"

Ndofilani touched Batjibilibili's hand under the table.

"What we were talking about before," said the now petulant white dame.

Then he takes hold of her hand under the table. Lovely, these forbidden things. She grazes his jacket with her elbow. Daring.

"Ah, yes."

Batjibilibili finished her steak and placed her knife on the plate. She took Ndofilani's hand and squeezed it under the table.

"Perhaps it wouldn't be such a bad idea to talk about it for a while."

"About the matter?"

"Perhaps after lunch, if you have time"

"Certainly I've got time. Shall we have coffee somewhere?"

"The usual place. I hope they'll accept a check, no?" said the white woman with a heavy foreign accent.

"They usually fuss about that. I'll call the Chinaman and pave the way. It usually works that way."

Batjibilibili, listening silently, concluded they were talking about drugs. She shrugged her disapproval and thought of going straight on to the photographer's studio. Instead they went to Ndofilani's place, where they had trouble getting up to his room. But Ndofilani passed her off as his half-sister who'd arrived after losing her luggage in transit.

"No luggage?" the landlady asked for the third time.

Not surprising.

Batjibilibili looked the perfect picture of a married and wealthy woman. This struck terror into the heart of the landlady who was illegally renting out a third portion of the Botswana Housing Corporation, a house that she had been occupying illegally for seven good years. Ndofilani obviously was expert at manoeuvring these things, something so few men do properly, organizing love. Making love to Ndofilani, and lovemaking with Ndofilani, never ceased to amaze her. In fact, screwing Ndofilani was getting addictive, and, perhaps, toxic. She didn't know what to make of it. Meanwhile, they'd already began calling each other by their nicknames. Just the way it was when they were students.

"How lovely it is to make love to you."

"The idiotic thing you say. What are you thinking of?"

"Nothing."

The windows were closed and all the lights on: it was like being inside a gymnasium. Batjibilibili, a sexually athletic person, was thrilled by the décor, the ambience, the striking imagery. It was just like the atmosphere she tried to portray in her novels. It now occurred to her she had much too hurried with her characters, she hadn't given them time to gel. But right now she did give a damn about them. Her method of writing was most unorthodox. The first book was a best seller, among her social circle and coterie of admirers, and a bloody nuisance. In fact it was sheer hell: the phone ringing incessantly, reports pouring in; she found it impossible to finish anything she started. Ndofialni was twenty-nine, maybe a little older. He had abstract and very mysterious ways of conversing.

"You know what I can't abide? The way other people are always taking your picture."

"Will you please be serious?"

"I am. I'm perfectly serious. Now is my turn to take a picture of you. Look how beautiful you are, all that smooth brown skin."

He had an expensive looking camera. He liked making love, keeping his eyes closed. Nearly everybody makes love alone, it's a projection of oneself that way, a kind of narcissism, he once told her.

"You think so?"

"A clinical fact, I assure you. I must tell you how crazy I am about your face."

She liked Ndofilani's kissing inside her mouth.

"I must tell you how crazy I am about the way you kiss."

"More? Shall we do it all over again?"

Ndofilani's the kind who wouldn't run after any girl. Unusual for him that he took her to bed right off. But after all, she was almost twenty five. After making love with Ndofilani, Batjibilibili took a shower and carefully put on her face. She made up her face. Made up, her face was better, she thought. Put on her face is a vulgar expression. Put on, never; perhaps make up. Put on her makeup. Painted herself, too contrived. Unless I say carefully applied her eyeliner and lipstick. She discoursed these things in her mind as she worked on her face. She was very happy.

"Why are you getting all got up?"

"Certainly not for you"

"I like it anyhow."

"Does it change me much?"

"No, no. But it does look smashing. In fact you look grand."

"I'm having some pictures taken. A famous photographer."

"Are you photogenic?"

"So-so"

"And did you like it?"

"What?"

"The things we did together."

"Of course I did."

They went into another clinch.

"Now let me alone, I'm trying to fix my hair."

201

"All right, I'll let you alone."

"Are you really going to a photographer?"

"Of course I am. You don't think I'd tell you lies?"

"You told your husband so many over the phone."

"My husband likes it that way."

"Who's taking your picture?"

"Osama Bin Laden."

"It seems he's extraordinary."

"Photographers are all alike. The best ones cheat."

"What do you mean?"

"The good ones give you something to do, they talk all the time, and they wind up making pictures of themselves. One of them took about twenty rolls of me: every single frame looked exactly like his wife. Another made me the idea he had in his mind's eye, he said, absolutely pure. I came out looking like a sacred heart boarder."

Ndofilani took her in his arms.

"You really amuse me, you know."

"The world's stage," declared William Shakespeare", said Batjibilibili, "where every man must play a part, and mine a poor one." But through the ages men and women have not been content with this, she thought. They like to create their own stages, and to act, and for that matter, so did William Shakespeare. When Batjibilibili was a little girl her father behaved like mothers. He felt no embarrassment at pushing a pram; he didn't act it. He changed nappies, bathed her, and put her to bed. He enjoyed doing these things. In short, he gave everything a mother can offer except a breast to feed from. He acted like a truly enlightened modern father. He let little Batjibilibili do what she liked, creating outlets for activity in all directions of life. She could tell lies at will, refuse to go to bed and play about with her food instead of eating it.

Batjibilibili was always day-dreaming, frequently spiteful and tried to boss everybody. When Aunt Chandiwana complained about her conduct, her father would counter her protestations by arguing that he wanted his daughter's heart, lungs, liver, skin and brain to always work fully and completely. Nature, he observed, provided each child with a large number of potentialities, capacities, instincts, and intelligence to cope with the problems and difficulties of life and maintain existence. Some of the catch words he used to picture the future of his daughter were completeness, fulfilment, wholeness, goodness: he spewed so many messes that Aunt Chandiwana eventually eschewed further arguments with regard to Batjibilibili's upbringing. Batjibilibili grew up a happy and contented girl, finished her school, and in no time, the grub developed into the chrysalis and then into the butterfly, an entirely different creature. As a girl, Batjibilibili liked being different in clothes, diet, interests, physique and intellectual ability. She was coquettish and constantly desired to attract attention long before the desire for sexual intercourse entered her mind. She was outgoing, extroverted, concentrated on interest in the outside world, and not just on herself. She dreaded to be unpopular, ostracized, isolated, or lonely. So, she always criticized herself.

Her morbid conscience sometimes made her to turn such criticism upon her friends. She enjoyed communal life, the delights of her culture of literature and the arts; school and universities; and especially pubs and cafes where she found remarkable freedom of speech to discuss all aspects of human life. She was full of life, and full of interest in everything in all people, on whom she passed shrewd and often humorous judgments. Now it surprised and angered her that some professionals, especially photographers, could take their profession so lightly and make so much money out of it. But life was never meant to be fair, was it? She wondered silently.

Batjibilibili went out into the rain to hail a cab. Twenty minutes later she paid the cabbie and, still enjoying the remaining languor of lovemaking, rushed to the stairs to the photographer's place. Her vagina was still suitably sore. The receptionist asked her to wait. Pictures everywhere, beautiful, enormous-eyed, enormous-mouthed women. A few minutes later she was ushered into the studio: a cavernous room, reflectors and lights of all sorts, rolls of colored poster paper crammed into the corners, umbrellas covered with tinfoil, machines, automatic shutters, electric and manual fans, cameras, tripods. Batjibilibili inspected herself in a mirror.

"You seem tolerably good-looking," the photographer said, squaring her off.

"Shame, your forehead isn't half an inch higher and your face is so small. Of course, your mouth is a disaster. We'll try to elongate it with the lights. Have to use lenses too. That black lace utterly destroys the tone of your complexion. None too good to start with. Get out of it immediately."

"What do I put on then?"

"Anything, anything, wrap a towel around your bra."

"Good Lord, I'm a writer. I can't have myself photographed like a common cover girl."

"Who says all women writers have to look like hags in their pictures?" Batjibilibili did as she was told.

"What are they paying you to take my pictures?"

"I'm not at liberty to say. But between you and me, it's a total dog's life. Don't let us dwell on it. These are hard times. But you come out of it with valuable experience. Sit still and don't move your mouth. I'll put some glycerine on. Where are those goddamn lights?"

He surrounded her with lights and cameras.

"Your hair's too short. People have told me a few things about you. I, on the other hand am divorced. I've got two kids. I was married at nineteen, can you imagine. Some day you ought to come by my house, it's really swish. What about putting a wig on you, sweetheart?"

"No, then I shouldn't look myself."

"Now dear, let's not waste any more time. Eyes into the camera. I've got twenty or so. You can't work with less. All these parvenu camera bugs who think they know everything."

"It must be a fascinating job?"

"In fact it's a bloody bore. A few more years at it and I've got all the money I'll ever need. Then I'll buy this village a few kilometers north of the city and have it restored. I'll make a fortune off it. All it takes is the construction of a few ghastly bungalows to sell to your typical middle-class rich family."

The photographer smiled devilishly and scratched his head. No laughter. This one was a tough customer. The real bitch.

"Would you mind sitting still? Your mouth is really atrocious. Thoko. The silk brush. What the fuck are you doing, Thoko? Get that other fellow what's-his-name in here. You haven't done a bloody fucking thing all day long. I'm doing all the work myself. I don't pay you for nothing. More glycerine. Take off that towel, let's see some more skin. Now let's put you behind the paper. Move it, slaves, get to work!"

His two assistants wheeled out a roll of black paper from one of the corners and attached it to the ceiling.

"Please sit behind it."

The photographer pulled out a lethal-looking switchblade and began to make slashes in the sheet of paper. First a square that revealed Batjibilibili's face. Then holes that filtered through light from the spots behind him.

"You look like a sculptor."

"Exactly, I'm sculpting the light on your face with knife strokes. Nothing comes through that I don't want. This way I can shape your face and try to improve it."

"But there is nothing wrong with my face."

"What do you know about faces?"

"Well—"

"It's the most beautiful thing in the world."

"What, my face?"

"No. Modeling with light."

Another slash. The light bathed Batjibilibili and the cameras began to chatter.

I must come up with a name for this character, thought Ntungamili. Names are the hardest part of writing novels. If I call him so or so or so, it makes him a culture specific persona. An ethnic portrait. A cultural icon of some culture, ethnic group or nationality. All this invites unnecessary criticisms. The nationality shouldn't be definite nor the setting or time. I must remember to discuss this matter with Batjibilibili tomorrow. She will have to think of a decent name. It ought to be a bit old-fashioned, a name people have already used quite a lot so that it will make the protagonist unique. I know perfectly well what was going on when she rung me up. In any case, she had left the usual note telling she had to have a con-ference lunch with her publisher and won't be home. If not, until late, since afterwards she had this appointment with a photographer. This so-called publisher she is always dragging out as an excuse is perfectly ludicrous. He wouldn't have time to publish one book a year if he did take her out promptly on the half-hour the way she says. Not that I'm that upset or jealous; whenever she is gone, I have a chance to do some work, unless she happens to be in the middle of writing a novel, as now. And then I'm distracted by her notes, which amuse me because I find out everything she's up to. The trouble is she doesn't do a thing but write books. Then there is the diary. She takes no pains to hide it from me. Why should a married woman, a woman her age, keep a diary? The diary form is obsolete and real diaries, i.e. those written for one's benefit, are meant to be thrown away, and not published. But not Batjibilibili. Or no! She must always do things her own way. Once upon the time, I thought if I ever managed to write to any of my friends I might have photocopies made of choice morsels of this monstrosity of Batjibilibili's and send the thing off. The point being that her—forgive the word—"novel" would be exposed prematurely, aborting any chances of future publication.

But I realized I couldn't send these disparate notes off and have them published. If Batjibilibili leaves her notes for this novel lying about, then obviously she intends me to read them. I, of course, pretend never to have set eyes on them. But from time to time I find hairs planted on a page, or a tiny burglar alarm of two pencil marks one atop the other so Batjibilibili can detect whether the paper underneath has been touched. The amusing little games she plays. It seems most of the things she writes about happen to her during the day, but I'm never quite sure. She tends to include confections of her own. As for the so-called novel, the whole thing is one running confession. The lies she tells to throw smoke up around her absences are obtuse and redundant; I'm convinced she tells them that way to make me aware they're true. To call a spade a spade, she does it to torture me. Whenever I check-up I can catch her in lies both to me and the diary. She's simply a pathological liar, that's all. To her the truth does not exist. Still, my relationship with Batjibilibili is theatrical anyway. I have to put up with her, like original sin. But to call her a nymphomaniac or to try to Freudianize her . . . takes away all her mythical substance—the only thing she really is. Like all moral people she verges on the Goddess.

If I were not to search for truth among the jotting she leaves around, and if she didn't know I spied on her, and if I weren't a part of the game, we simply would have no relationship at all. It's not as if this game doesn't keep me entertained. I'm astonished: she actually did go to the photographer's! I never would have believed it. So, she sometimes even tells the truth. Naturally, she would let Ndofilani think I enjoy hearing her lies, but maybe that was only her way of dragging me into the novel. Perhaps Batjibilibili wants to get back at me for something I've done. I know one thing about me that irritates her enormously: that I take my writing seriously. She tells me its sour grapes. Brooding for hours over a single word, writing poems—what makes me do it? None of it brings in any money, not even enough to buy groceries. That's it: she despises me because I earn so little money! I recall, however, that it made her euphoric, my publishing those three poems dedicated to her.

"Though too abstract for me," she said, "somebody is going to read them, and in any case it was sweet of you to dedicate them to me. And they are so full of the cleverest words, none of which I understand, though."

We still make love occasionally. Not that it amuses Batjibilibili. Batjibilibili goes to bed with everybody or nearly everybody—out of insecurity, like all women. Perhaps I'm incapable of entertaining her; I don't give her enough. But I have changed her; before we got married she was worse. This last bit of her is passable. The dialogue is not bad; she has written so much that she's finally got the hang of it. She will spend hours at her desk; then she will tell a couple of lies, make a phone call, and run out. The upshot is that I never see her. Some nights she disappears with her friends and doesn't turn up for a week. I never go along because I can't stand her friends: writers, poets, actors, politicians, artists—or even worse—dancers and theatre people. She makes it a point never to read anything; two or three pages of a book and she knows what's going to happen. Or she skims a review and pretends to have read the book. It's my job to write she says, not to read. How could I find the time? At least she had the good taste not to go to bed with that photographer, or this wretched druggie, Ndofiani, though perhaps the reason she left out the vital details is that it's perfectly obvious who this photographer is. The other day Batjibilibili came to me and told me pointblank that she loved me. God knows what provoked that.

"I wish you'd change a little, honey. You're withdrawing."

She informed me.

206

"Look how you keep yourself occupied—writing those little poems I don't understand. People laugh at you and won't invite us out anymore."

I told her I didn't give a damn if people don't invite us out. It's not that they won't invite me out; they know I won't go away. I told her the truth, that people talk about her all the time and it's because of those little tales she tells in her books.

"They are none too obscure, you know, in fact you go beyond the call of duty making them explicit."

"Well, honey, what are people saying?"

"They gossip."

"Don't tell me you care!"

In other words, we quarrelled, something I rarely do because it makes me very high-strung and I can't sleep. I detest raising my voice. I detest scenes, and since Batjibilibili isn't capable of discussing anything any other way, I retreat to my study and read the papers the minute I see one coming. She upsets my stomach, with all that deafening shouting. Batjibilibili says I'm a coward, and perhaps I am. But I had so many scenes at home when I was little: my father and mother did nothing but fight. It made them happy, they even loved one another. The scene at the photographer's isn't bad. Batjibilibili's quite good at creating a character in a few pages, if she feels like it. What she doesn't make up she simply incorporates intact from real life. One day I will write a book about Batjibilibili, nothing like this though. This is about me and how Batjibilibili views herself. I will describe her realistically. No, that's out of the question. If reality were simply statement of fact, then a kind of cinematographic film would certainly suffice.

After the farce at the photographer's, Batjibilibili did not go home. She rang her husband to say that she couldn't, and then she moved on to spend the weekend at her friend's home in the wealthy northern Phakalane suburb. Possibly the loveliest house she'd ever seen; a bit dark to be sure, but never mind that. Labyrinths of rooms and completely enthralling hallways filled its insides. Her husband had turned down the invitation. Batjibilibili arrived at Satjilombe's place in the late afternoon, his house glowing in the sun and flowers tinted by the sunset. Inside the house there were clouds of narcissus and white orchids; succulent flowers. To her surprise the MP himself answered the door and, immaculately dressed, invited her into the huge sitting room. They hadn't met since the dreadful election drama and his subsequent marriage to Ludo.

"I can't abide places like this," he whined affably.

"Why come here then?"

"I don't often. But if you have got houses, you know, you are obliged to look after them from time to time, to make sure the servants haven't turned them into hotels. Once every two years is often enough."

"It's a shame people who own such beautiful houses don't live in· them. And so many of them?"

"That's right. A bloody shame I always say. What shall you have for a drink?"

"Nothing really. I had a good lunch. I don't drink much. Is your family still at the Parliament Flats or back home? I haven't seen them for ages."

"Well . . . they have so many things to do. Charity work for the wife. All those orphans. School for the kid, we have a little adopted girl, you know. Quite a kid I should say. Everybody is busy."

"Are you spending the weekend alone then?"

"Not really. I'm traveling around. I've to get back soon, as I've been here for some hours. Are you staying long? I thought . . ."

"No. Not really."

"How sad . . ."

"What do you mean, how sad?"

"It upsets me to think that you don't seem to like my company. Up till now I always thought we agreed about everything."

"If we liked all the same things, we wouldn't have a thing to say to one another. I, for example, live on the phone."

"So do I!"

"I adore chocolate."

"I can't abide it."

"How sad?"

"Now you stop saying how sad."

"I love oysters."

"I adore them."

"Power?"

"Me too!"

"You've just let out a well-kept state secret, Mr. Minister. I think I'll see myself out."

"Well, thanks for coming. Pity I can't drive you home. Actually, I'm done in. Fatigue and debility are afflictions that will send us to the graves before our time. All parliamentary business and stuff. You have no idea."

"Good rest and all that. Say 'hi' to the family. Cheerio."

Batjibilibili was relieved to get away. She had had enough sex for the day. She felt exhausted after her encounter with Satjilombe. She rang her friend, Sthembiso, to chat while waiting for a cab. Luckily she got another weekend invitation. Sthembiso is married to a millionaire managing director of a local multi-national company. Nobody can tell how he made all these millions of money from a salary, but they all love his company. His house is superb. A park, waterfalls, marble statues all around. Colonnades, atriums, vestibules. Inside, sublime pictures and autograph furniture. Immediately upon arrival, Sthembiso, who is very busy, escorts her friend to her room for the weekend.

"You must remember to use this staircase always, Batjibilibili. People get lost around here. It's such a huge house. Don't be afraid of the dogs. They make a lot of noise, but they are just letting off steam, showing their high spirits. All bark, as they say. There must be a hundred of them around the house. Mthembeni's always attacking me about the mistakes, you know, the mongrels. He's such a snob. I hope you will be all right here. This is your bath. Then you're sharing a sitting room with Wazha and his wife Tobokani, who haven't arrived yet, as usual. They sleep in the other bedroom and have a bath of their own. I didn't put you in the west wing because last Sunday a canopy fell in on my mother-in-law, you know, the one who hates me, so-so."

They both laugh and Batjibilibili says "How frightful?"

"She took offense and said it was a joke in very bad taste. As if it were the sort of joke I play all the time. It was Mthembeni's idea, not mine. How is your husband? Is he alright? He is magnificent. So nice, and it's all genuine. Top drawer. We never see him anymore. Oh, the Chief Minister in the Office of the President is one of our guests tonight. Hideous to look at, I'll grant you, but exquisite inside. Of course, he's got a finger in every pie in this country. Extremely important. All you have to do is drop a hint, and he can arrange anything. He's gotten together everything from bird sanctuaries to charitable funds. Of course our esteemed solitary female MP is coming. She's a perfect bitch, but so entertaining. I'm positive she will despise you. She's allergic to intellectuals. She says she likes me, not as a friend, but because I'm so loyal and patriotic. One of her more tactful statements. But poor thing, she can't help making other women suffer; and then people who suffer are such bores. But I'll tell you one thing; people who make other people to suffer tend to have bad breath. It's all a question of indigestion, really. Who else? Oh, the University Vice Chancellor, the one who always lends us dreadful books? He's no genius, to be sure, but he's still good looking. Be careful not to criticize anything in front of him; he's chairman of everything and it makes him furious to hear bad things about any of it. Even the newspapers, mind you, so watch out. Of course he is fronting for real business, most of them foreigners and gunning for a cabinet position in the next government. Fat chance. Then there's Taboka and Mandla, who don't count. Taboka's been a friend forever; we insult each other twenty-four hours a day. She's also related to me. Mthembeni despises her, but I love her dearly. Come on, I'll take you out to see the garden."

They descend the grand staircase.

"Look, there is Tobokani. The brat she is talking to, I'm sure you know, is the Minister of Education. A disgrace, if there ever was one, I tell you. He wanders round screwing indiscriminately and dropping illegitimate monsters like him. I bet one of his little whores will turn up soon . . . and ruin my weekend. I refused to sleep with him several times. Now, he takes the most ghoulish delight in torturing me. Well, well, look who's turned up at long last, Honorable Minister Gudogulu. I hope you had a most pleasant journey. This is Batjibilibili. I told you about her so many times. You surely know Batjibilibili, the writer, don't you?"

"We have met."

Batjibilibili was appalled.

She wanted to scream, to vomit.

"How are you?" she said icily to him.

It suddenly occurred to her that he was the ugliest man she'd ever set her eyes on. Fat like an elephant, he looked more like a sea creature than a Minister of the State—an effect enhanced by the fact that all his visible flesh looked like medieval parchment; the palms of his hands had the color of vellum. But he had the fascination of power, so she forgave him his looks. The bastard was also clear. Did he wheedle this invitation? Was this just coincidence? How could he have known she would be here? Did he follow her directly here? The cunning, wily, old fox!

"You write very well," he said.

"Congratulations."

Batjibilibili and her friend excused themselves, or rather Mthembeni elbowed them away in a haste attempt to welcome the boss into his elegant house.

"I'm sure he's never read a book in his life, much less one of yours," said Sthembiso, heading back to the sitting room.

"But he is terrific. He plays everything by the ear. Money for a literary prize or funds for a repertory company, just like that. I imagine how much time it saves him having so many adoring friends, all of the them doing his bidding like well-trained dogs. And it doesn't upset anybody, really. He is a marvelous man. Everybody says he is corrupt, but I don't care. Anyhow, I can't think of a soul who isn't, can you? His wife is magnificent. I'm sure you know her. Not a brain inside that flawless skull, but she is very sweet. She's always curled up in bed, never doing anybody any harm. She sleeps like a corpse. I think Satjilombe fancies you. I saw it in his eyes. I'm expert in these things. If you don't mind, when they're all asleep, I'll come round. What do you say?"

"The aura of power revolts me. I rather prefer the hermitic austerity of my poor poet."

"Well said. Like a lady, you are a pet. Your husband really is top drawer."

Next morning after breakfast, Satjilombe cornered Batjibilibili, and despite his elephantine presence, maneuvered her into a corner of the garden for what he called a little tête-à-tête.

"We need young blood like you, writing."

"It must be marvelous to be able to decide things. I envy you."

"But if you only knew how much work there is. One thing gives rise to a thousand others, not a minute of peace. Phone calls, appointments, parliament sessions, cabinet meetings, round table discussions, people to see. At night I ought to rest, relax, have a good time, but the social life is enervating, incessant."

"There are two things I'd like to ask you, Satjilombe."

"Speak up, speak up. I can do anything. I've got swarms of industrialists and touristy diplomats panting to donate billions to anything. They all want to get in my good graces and, of course, to be helped with taxes and a thousand niggling little things. Also to be invited around. Why not, they've done nothing but work their fingers to the bone all their lives. Beautiful houses, ancient wives, grown-up children: what else is there to go after? Social recognition. Ask, ask for anything you like. I tell you, they hang around clamoring for a chance to give."

"Well, I know a group of very talented young people, a repertory company. Of course, they've no money. And since they tend to do experimental theatre, they don't stand a chance of making any. And individual, but equally talented poets, painters and musicians are also some of my friends who I have in mind. That's the sort of thing I feel is worth patronizing."

"But dear, nothing could be simpler. We'll just get together a couple of big names, a few famous philanthropists, and I guarantee a couple of millions in a few weeks. I'm serious, do tell your young people to go ahead and do anything they like. What's the second thing? If it's something like this, don't give it a second thought; it's no trouble at all."

"Actually, the other thing is my husband, who's a good writer, very serious, very dedicated. He just needs a little recognition. You know the type, hunched over his desk for thousands of years. Writing sweet little nothings. A prize, a political appointment. His sort is also very useful on committees . . ."

"You're married? I had no idea. And you so young? But of course, this is no problem either."

For Satjilombe this was victory, to be accepted in spite of ugliness, and of course his past shenanigans with this pretty and enigmatic little thing was always in the back of his mind. He never let go of such sweet little things. After his surreptitious retreat into the house, Batjibilibili walked to one of the benches in the garden and sat down. 'What have I done?' she asked herself and started crying into her small hands softly.

211

She understood the deal, perfectly, too perfectly to mistake it for any form of charitable concern. At dinner, Sthembiso talked about flowers with Satjilombe who was at her right. He too knew all about flowers. Batjibilibili was seated at Mthembeni's left, facing them. Satjilombe's eyes probed her intermittently. Tonight I'm going to do some divine things to you. I'm dying to. Aren't you? Will you shut up, for the love of God? Read my lips. What for? I'm going to do some divine things to you tonight. Undoubtedly my husband will read about it then, she said to her mind's eyes. After dinner she had no choice but to invite Satjilombe to her room. They both knew they would make love. Satjilombe was a lion in bed. Batjibilibili had never experienced anybody who made love like him. He woke up in the morning and as soon as he'd shaved and showered, he made love to her again, several times, then they left together. At least she had more material for her book. As if one wouldn't know right off who this latest conquest of Batjibilibili's was: everybody will; especially Ntungamili.

Batjibilibili's assignations with Satjilombe, however, turned out to be an instructive lesson in humiliation and humanity. The man dragged her all the way to Kasane for the night, only to vanish into old Kulani's mansion, by the Chobe River. Kulani was a retired Police Commissioner, and perpetual ambassador-designate to Somalia, a terribly bleak prospect given the nature of politics in that country. But still, Kulani's ties to the President remained secure. Nice arrangement, all round. His young daughter, Mary, met them at the gate. The old moron's daughter, and young wife of an indigent and dissipated army lieutenant, was very pretty and nubile. Only a few days before, the lieutenant had arrived at Satjilombe's residence with vague ideas about selling his company. Batjibilibili hadn't been present, at least not officially speaking; she had been behind the curtain, eavesdropping. Satjilombe had done nothing but mouth commonplaces about trends in modern industry.

"These days, it's well-nigh impossible to stand up against South Africa and western competition without enormous capital behind you. You've got to have nerve, my friend, courage, foresight to sell out before it's too late. Courage, yes courage."

That was how he had seduced the poor sod: make a heart-rending speech about bonds of friendship between their fathers. Actually the lieutenant's father and Satjilombe's old man had never really been friends, but the army man wouldn't deny the relationship: just one of those things he hadn't known about his father. Now Satjilombe wanted to meet the retired police chief and clinch the deal. It would take all three minutes to bring him to heel, he told her. However, if he turned out to be a little less primitive, Satjilombe would scramble his brains with lectures on modern technology until it drove him to sign the contract . . .

In the end, a combination of things did the trick: the future of Botswana, the importance of tradition, of personal relationships in business. The old man was dazzled. Mary, the old man's only daughter, recently married to the poor lieutenant, was just leaving on her honey moon but took the time to drop by and pick her father. She was insanely curious to see the famed Satjilombe, obviously. It was the only time they had ever met outside a social environment, but it was enough for Satjilombe's libido to jump boarders; the thought of possessing a virgin bride who was the daughter of a man he'd bought made his mouth water. He engineered the game so competently that no one, not even the bride, could ever have suspected his motives. He brought her a few presents, of course, and flowers. Then he asked her to show him around the old man's house. The whole thing went on so smoothly that, in no time, the retired police chief and Batjibilibili founded themselves ensconced in the huge sitting room dumbstruck and not knowing what really to say each other, as they had no acquaintance of any sort.

Batjibilibili's female intuition, however, told her that he was up to something unpleasant, as usual, and in that she was right. She pictured Mary's luscious warm body; she had seen a lot of it in the magazines and newspapers when Mary got engaged to the unfortunate lieutenant. The bedclothes all rumpled and Satjilombe up to his ears in the sweet warm body . . . Satjilombe was shot with luck, had been since the day he was born, she thought. The overcoat Mary's father was wearing was a gift from the President, he told her with pride, and was a bit well-tailored. That's why he had given it to the old man: everybody was always asking the President for things and he'd got out of the habit of giving anything good. Batjibilibili's eyes lit up at the thought of Mary's body, her heavy lips on his . . . she dreamt on. Meanwhile, the old man, rather ashamed, unexpectedly did the unthinkable: he strode into his daughter's bedroom and found them locked in a mad embrace, both stark naked. The intensity of the Satjilombe's voice startled her.

"Where the hell are you?"

"Over here."

"Who were you talking to?"

"Myself. What have you been up to? I've been waiting for you—in fact, I was just about to give up and leave."

There wasn't a grain of truth to that. Even Satjilombe knew it.

"Listen, friend, we've got to get out of here. The old man's had a stroke. I can't wait round to be caught here in his house. You never know what the papers will make of it."

"The old man's had a stroke? Is he dead?"

"Pretty close to it, I think, at least when I left."

"Why, didn't things go well with Mary? What brought on the stroke?"

213

"Well, one thing and another, business was bad, and then he was getting on, you know."

"Business? But you bought everything he owns and . . ."

"Enough, I don't want to talk about it anymore. Let's go to the hotel, I need something to eat."

At that awkward moment Mary rushed into the sitting room, hair flying wild, bobby pins attaching hairpieces to her very short real hair falling in all directions, face blurred with tears.

"He's dying!" she screamed.

"Who?" said Satjilombe unflustered.

"My father!"

"What happened?"

"Please don't speak. Run and get the doctor. I can't do this alone. What are you doing, standing there gaping at me? Didn't I tell you to make yourself useful?"

"What can I do, darling? Your father's dead and you . . ."

"Dead? How will I on go without him? Oh God, I can't beg forgiveness from you. My sins are too grievous. Will I ever return to a state of grace?"

"Darling, the goodness of our Lord is so great that He embraces all in his immensity. Return to your bedroom, I'll call the lieutenant. He'll look after you, all right?" said Satjilombe.

Mary pressed the wig back in place with one limp hand, and then closed her big, beautiful, black eyes. Satjilombe marched out. Mary's beauty still intimidated him. For years he had kept close watch over her through her infancy, puberty, and adolescence. Now the sight of her wilted person aroused his desire—something he wasn't eager to admit in view of the somber circumstances. He turned his attention to Batjibilibili.

"How do you feel?"

"Not well, in fact, ghastly."

She wanted some proof of his love and devotion: a strange thing to demand, all things considered. In her mind's eye she saw Mary's sinuous body, her full round breasts and buttocks with terrifying clarity. Does he ever have affairs? I mean serious, long-lasting love affairs, real romantic never-ending historical affairs? Thousands of women, and he loves them all. He possesses them all, and then he disappears. Women of every sort, every temperament. Large and well-built, thin and petite. Sensible housewives, sweet young things. Village girls, thirteen-year-old nymphets. Friend's sisters. Rich ones, poor ones, he makes love to them all. Perhaps to have so many, is to have none at all. Who can tell? What can you expect? He's simply made like that. He's a man born free. She fumbled for her small bag, hunting for a handkerchief. After she blew her nose, out came the small mirror. This man had a nerve, humiliating her like that. And she'd suffered so, given up everything. Well, almost everything. Satjilombe must have a pang of conscience; otherwise he wouldn't have fled the room like that. The least he can do is to make some show of pity. Not to whine, but can I really give the best years of my life to such a ghastly beast? I'll soon be wondering around like a madwoman. She waited around for a few minutes and then ran out, humiliated and her mind crowded with the most unpleasant thoughts.

At the hotel, he headed for the bar. A waiter greeted him; some patrons turned to give him long stares. What's he doing in Kasani, do you suppose? Whispers. They say he's in the process of buying. He's old Kulani's daughter's lover. Shhh. Don't be ridiculous, what does he need her for; he's got hundreds of them, shhhh. Strange whispers. Satjiliombe was completely indifferent: good God, how tiresome. Because he was well brought up and because he was tactful by nature, he never showed his annoyance. Impassivity, punctuated with absent-minded smiles, smiles that never registered around his eyes, protected him from the terrors of life.

The bartender watched him move off with a twinge of a loss. The tip, the gratuity, his income, was receding in the person of the stupendous, the Magnificent, the Famous . . . the Loathsome . . . the Coarse, the man who tipped excessively because he hated the motions of paying for things. The bill sir, checking the addition, getting out the wallet—obscene gestures, all of them. The inelegance and embarrassment of touching money was surpassed only by the inelegance and embarrassment of not having it at all. He glided to the back of the lounge. The people in the bar admired the way he walked, his clothes, the elegance of his hands, his remarkably handsome physique.

Some more whispers and shhhs came along with, "Will you please shut up, can't you see it's not Barrack Obama at all?"

Satjilombe casts an eye around the lounge, scrutinizing a girl here and there, trying to find a single good reason to stay in the room. The women were dressed in fake Puccini blouses, fake Gucci bags, fake Schiaparelli scarves, fake Ferragano shoes—as if the real thing were any more chic. Ah, but over there: a good-looking girl. Big eyes, delicious full breasts under a white blouse. What about the legs? Not bad either. She was less frumpy looking than the others, eyes made up properly, and an attractive air of aloofness. The girl avoided his gaze and finally retreated behind her eyelashes. But she kept her eye on him surreptitiously. Finally she worked up enough courage to meet his stare dead on. The corners of her mouth went down in an attempt to keep from smiling, and she covered her head, quietly, almost religiously, submitting to his enchanting bravado, his devilish spirit, and his mania for conquest.

Ntungamili is shocked and dismayed by the latest turn of events. No husband wouldn't be. To begin with, everybody knows the extravagant monstrosity that she calls, surprisingly, and with unconcealed withering contempt, the ideal modern house. She should be more circumspect in these descriptions, really. I ought to take advantage of her being gone with him and try to forge on with my literary enterprise. But there I am throwing away this free time as usual. Nothing's working: I've too many notes and versions and it would take more energy than I have right now to sort them out. The ignominious truth is I would rather work on this book. Batjibilibili was saying that my latest literary piece is perfectly all right in its present state. She is a fine one; she's never so much as read it, just gave it her famous eye glance. As if she was studying a painting, a doodle by a poor sighted child. What would help me would be an editor ringing me up every five minutes to find out how I was coming along, just somebody to care, damn it! But what difference would it make to any of them? My books aren't the sort that coin money the way Batjibilibili's seem to.

Perhaps I was different once. I'm too old now. If I were to describe myself, I'd have to say I'm a man without either ambition or motivation. I'm happy, never seeing anyone. People are hard to take. Once in a while, I think about death and how close I am to it. I'll die soon. If I stay at home all the time like this, I shall certainly die of lack of oxygen. I can see this book already in print; the problem is writing it. It's out of the question to finish this book in less than ten years. Ten years of sheer torture. Ahaaa, there is something here. What the devil! What, really, was this woman thinking? Good God, that explains the Minister's ringing me up. What on earth was Batjibilibili thinking of putting him up to it. Here I've actually gone and accepted the invitation, and I'll have to go by myself, since as usual she's nowhere to be found. A flower of deceit, that man, a corrupt philistine is precisely what he is. Why should I go to his house, be seen with him, pollute myself? And now that I know how the thing came about, it's doubly humiliating. Of course, perhaps some post, some recognition might inspire me to work harder. Some people work by guilt alone.

To celebrate this grand opportunity this afternoon, I rang up some beautiful little thing who gave me her number on the street. She was free, so I told her to come round right away. She wanted twenty Pula in advance. I almost sent her away when I opened the door: she was covered with makeup and reeking of a cheap musky perfume. She brought along two white toy poodles. Nauseating, these women who think tiny dogs are chic. I didn't even offer her a drink; I simply waved the money under her nose and starry eyes and dropped it on the kitchen table. Then I took her to the bedroom. I was nervous and afraid of dozing off. In which case, she certainly would abscond with her twenty pula plus a few trinkets besides.

216

Somehow, they can always pick out the valuable knickknacks. Being in the same room with her annoyed me, the same room I sometimes sleep in with Batjibilibili, pretty and clean in her white pajamas.

Take off your clothes, I told her, and wash that filthy face, too. You'll find some cotton wool and good smelling cream in the bathroom. I never do that, she said. You'll do it now. But without my makeup I'm not pretty. Whatever gave you the idea you're pretty with makeup? I can't stomach lipstick. I suddenly felt violent towards her. I wanted to fuck her and have done with it. I took the cotton wool and smeared the lipstick all over her face to get rid of it and did my best to get that disgusting taste off her mouth, even if I didn't intend to kiss her. But when you make love, sometimes you kiss in spite of yourself. What's your first name? Her name was Mary. Really, how monstrously vulgar. Mary? Mother of Jesus? Holy shit. What's yours? I haven't got a first name, I told her. Don't call me anything. It's better if you don't know my name, it makes things too intimate. But I know your last name, it makes things too intimate. But I know your last name. I couldn't care less, I told her. Here it was, seven o'clock, and I had to be with Satjilombe at eight. Her breasts were big and somewhat floppy, more fun to play with than Batjibilibili's, which are minuscule. Very frustrating, it's almost as if she has no breasts at all. I kissed her, of course, just as I'd foreseen my tongue down her throat. Then I pulled her legs apart roughly. It occurred to me that the poor thing couldn't have been less interested in making love to me; yet partly because it was her job, partly because it was the truth, she told me how handsome I was and how much pleasure I was giving her. And I, like an idiot, asked her if I really did look like an underweight spectator. As if the poor whore knew what that meant. Onward and upward. Three minutes, because I came quickly. Then, instead of sending her away, I set to fondling her all over and several times must have hurt her because she kept saying easy, baby, and easy, that's enough. Then, on top of her again. I'm afraid of getting pregnant. My, my, imagine a professional like you getting pregnant? If you want more money, I'll give it to you. Afterwards, I told her to put her clothes on and kicked her out. But odor was all over the place. Mary, what a name? It's probably a professional name. I took a bath to wash her off and put on a black tie. My tie was all askew since I'm completely incompetent about doing them up neatly. Batjibilibili always takes care of it for me. The idea of Mary disgusted me, her body, having had her on our bed, our house. Batjibilibili would never stoop to that sort of thing.

I went on reading Batjibilibili and almost missed my appointment with Satjilombe. I got there late, as it was. He had on dinner clothes too; he was like an albino slug, doubtless the ugliest creature I've ever seen, a one-man revolution against pulchritude. Also, a thoroughly unpleasant man to be around. In other words, not only was he mentally philistine and corrupt, he was also physically philistine and corrupt. I introduced myself and, since I'm a pig, I was polite and gracious. He told me my wife was divine, which she is not, and that later we would pick up a friend of his (did I by any chance know Mapopota, the brilliant attorney at law, the toast of Gaborone, the beloved of the theatre world?); then we would attend the party where we would be given something to eat, and we'd have a nice tête-à-tête, we'd get acquainted and talk things over. Everything planned out, in other words. Where was Batjibilibili keeping herself these days? His guess was as good as mine, I said.

At the party Sthembiso maintained she hadn't seen my wife for a couple of months. The weekend is part of the fiction, then. But this time, what with Batjibilibili's phone call, I was convinced it was part of the diary. The party was a fiasco. For one thing, there were far too many people. The hostess, hair nearly frizzy, pointy eyes and lips, bitter voice, body and face, but still pretty, especially the fat legs and fat lips, was completely undone by the hundreds of people she had invited. Not to mention the people she had not invited, like me. I asked her to dance because I liked her, and then went back to talk to Satjilombe, who by that time had set himself up on a platform to bask in the full light of his philistine glory. It occurred to me, Batjibilibili evidently envied this old bastard's influence over certain people, the power to take or leave socially. He's just the sort of scum I detest. Miserable philistine swine, snobs, bungling morons! If only I could start a People's War, they'd be the first group whose heads I'd decree superfluous. I didn't know Batjibilibili was married, says Satjilombe most amicably. Now what was that prick after? Is it because in life it's necessary to kiss ass to get ahead, and in the end he had kissed just enough people's asses to gain power over fools like me? What a threesome: Satjilombe, Batjibilibili, me! The turned down corners of his mouth, frightfully thin, leered at me, lines of spite all over his face. Go to bed with Satjilombe? How could anyone manage to get it up over a body liked that? I pigeonholed the idea. I felt like vomiting.

"Do you write too?" he asked, "like Batjibilibili?"

"No, I write differently from Batjibilibili, I imagine you haven't read my books. I am a poet."

"No," he said.

"Do people actually read books these days? I certainly never do, and it would never enter my mind to buy one of yours. Much rather stick to old European novels. The only people who knew how to tell a good story."

"I love them too."

"Why don't you read them then?"

"But I do."

"I mean rather than write new ones. Didn't that ever occur to you? Look, a fascinating man called on me the other day. An educated man, the President sent him round. His references are impeccable. He tells me a man like you would be a boon to any committee. I wrote your wife about it some time ago. Just an idea of mine."

"Which committee?"

"I don't know yet, I'll give it some thought. Do let's discuss it over dinner."

I hated those people at that place, the thought of owing them anything. The very thought of ordinary human beings turned authentic fraud terrified me. I didn't want to become some person's vassal or one of Satjilombe's many moral debtors. Or be forced to accept a weekend invitation from the eminently fuckable hostess who occupied herself slinking along on those fat legs, with that voice. Or to go to Satjilombe's sundowners. The only thing I wanted was to go home. And in fact there I was, at 10:15 P.M. Batjibilibili isn't coming home for several days, she tells me in a phone message. This time she doesn't even palliate the news with an excuse.

Last night, I dreamed I was in a room; in the middle there was a bathtub with Batjibilibili inside, nude. Deafening din: a dozen children crying, women wringing the neck of two hundred chickens. MP's and cabinet ministers were circling the bathtub, champagne glasses in hand, chanting, "To your health, charming Batjibilibili," and pouring the contents of the glasses over her squalid little body. Writers and poets recited their works and sprinkled her body with bits of poems they were writing extempore. The bath water and champagne soon reduced the papers to pulp. The sight of Batjibilibili's body was shocking. Honorable Minister Satjilombe, standing behind me, had on only a white dress shirt and his penis was hanging loose like a broken sword. The guests were murmuring, and this sound mingled with the babies crying and the chickens squawking in their death throes. I had a Rwandese machete in my hand. I moved towards Batjibilibili with a smile on my face, keeping the machete hidden under a towel. Batjibilibili, who in the dream had metamorphosed into a Huge Beast, made as if to rise out of the slime to have herself dried off. I threw myself on her shrivelled body and stabbed her many times. The blood flowed onto the paper mush in pink rivulets. Then Satjilombe came after me, he was completely naked and held a club. I wanted to kill him too. But the phone woke me up. What a shame.

I see Batjibilibili's marked small crosses at the corners of the notebook pages I want to read. I'll have to make sure they match afterwards, exactly as I found them. Ah, what do we have here beneath her abominable notebook? A letter. Probably to another lover. Oh, it's addressed to me. Strange. Very strange, indeed.

Dearest,

I know you always patiently and faithfully wait
for me to come home. I've lost all sense of responsibility
for my actions and behave abominably. We won't see
each other anymore. But I've always loved you, even if I
haven't been the best of wives.

Yours truly,

Batjibilibili.

Well, it's the only honest thing Batjibilibili could have done. I'd rather
she left like this, not after one of her scenes. I don't mind even if the book
doesn't get finished. Anyhow, she's not leaving me for some he-man who
will screw her better or is more successful or powerful than I am. In the
last analysis, without Batjibilibili and her games, I'll be perfectly content.
I won't know how her book ends. That's no great problem; I'll just buy it
when it's published. I guess she will go ahead with the diary. Only she
will have to give up the conjugal lie game. The sweet young thing
abandoned in this populous desert called Life . . . God knows where she'll
go.

I don't want to hear any more about the people she liked. This morning
the paper ran a long article about Satjilombe's shenanigans. It says there
were no grounds for the rumors that he was crooked and had several suits
in court against him; as for the gossip that he went round promising voters
money he never paid out, that was slander.

I'm going to make a new life. I shall work hard, see friends, mine, real
ones, but only when I choose to. Just a few, just to talk. In the long run,
I'm totally self-sufficient, my income isn't much, but all I'm interested in
is having a desk and cot to sleep on. Perhaps I shall even be able to finish
my poem. No more reading about Batjibilibili as she imagines herself or
writing about me as I imagine myself. I shall descend into realism; tell
things from a single point of view in homage to . . . who cares! Better still,
what if I packed my things immediately, put my notes into a trunk, and
ring for a taxi?

"Hello? A single room, please! No bath, a sink would be nice.
Breakfast too. Reserve the room for two weeks, and then let us see. I'll be
over in half an hour, I haven't much luggage."

I'm light with this freedom, the hotel room, and my book. Afterward
I'll write anonymous threats to Satjilombe and company, or appear at their

dinner tables as Batjibilibili's ghost. I'll get my friends together and start a revolution.

The letter hand delivered to Batjibilibili's hotel room at the Gaborone Sun was brusque and to the point: "I shall expect you for dinner this evening. Then we'll be able to settle our differences, and we shall see if your heart is made of stone too." It was delivered in the morning, exactly three days after she had stopped seeing her husband. Satjilombe's wife had no time for formalities. Batjibilibili was unfazed by this attitude. Satjilombe was a powerful, sophisticated, cultured man. He was witty and intelligent—a modern, fascinating creature. He would know how to deal with his piqued wife.

Batjibilibili now had all the perquisites whose lack had been so problematic: free hours, evenings and weekends, more money, and plenty of time to read and write. New contacts brought her out of her isolation. Activities which she had put aside before now became available to her. The theatre. Tennis lessons. A course in ceramics. Parties. Tonight, a rather challenging dinner. She luxuriated in the extravagance of a relationship that opened doors everywhere, every time, and anyhow. Today, after the outrageous invitation, she ate a leisurely late lunch and wound up with plenty of time to take a nap. In the middle of the siesta she awoke with an uneasy feeling. Her dream, still hovering at the edge of consciousness, had been a series of indeterminate shapes—dark, ominous-purple and dusky blue and a vivid blood red. A funereal presence permeated the room, or rather her blurred consciousness. In the dream, the impending dinner had taken place in an empty tomb, a horrorish Shakespeare banquet whose fare consisted of vipers and tarantulas, the wine of vinegar, frost, and ice. And at dessert were a plate of ashes, a chalice of fire, and an hourglass marking the time. She curled into a little ball, one arm clutching her pillow. Slowly, she opened her eyes. Something was in the room. She put her hand out to brace herself on the wall and found, to her surprise, empty space.

At dinner, the conversation was cordial. Ludo was virtue itself.

"It behoves me to tell you that I disapprove of your conduct. I can't believe it is right to make love to everybody the way you do," she scolded Satjilombe humorously.

"What! Would you commend a man for attaching himself to the first female he falls in love with? No, no, constancy is for fools alone!" he countered with the courage, aloofness, aestheticism and personality befitting a Minister in the Office of the President.

The intensity of his words surprised Batjibilibili. But not his wife.

"My dear friend, you are so young," the woman said, taking Batjibilibili's hand. "It shows, just a mere child. Perhaps you don't know who this man is. Or how he will make you suffer. I gave the best years of

221

my life to him, only to be humiliated. Dear friend, now, while you are still innocent, you must get away from this monster, before it's too late."

Batjibilibili soon learnt the truth, or something close to it. Satjilombe wouldn't settle for only one companion—unless he happened to be cultivating a business connection. He monopolized the situation and allowed the other person to participate. He liked to dominate every situation, to be a real Man, raw masculine freshness. The joys of feeling the feeling of being the man, a woman senses this. But Satjilombe often got bored, poor man. Dinner at people's houses, black-tie-get-togethers, and swarms of guests—he despised all of it. Left to his own devices, however, he managed to keep himself entertained. Attractive, rich, he picked and chose, dumped what didn't amuse him. In the meantime, he made the parties concerned his own—never an obstacle being so impressive. Dominating women wasn't much of a challenge: he simply took them all to bed. Except the ugly ones, who irritated him. As for men, he bought the politicians and the businessmen. He rejoiced in stupid people (Mapopota was smart enough to act stupid); probably it was because they relaxed him. But he couldn't abide the conventional types. As for his own family, it was a passion to him. Because he was head of it, of course. His girlfriends numbered somewhere in the thousands; he'd had a different one nearly every night since he took office. Models, actresses, politicians, ambassadors, permanent secretaries, nurses, teachers, beauty queens, secretaries, and all sorts of quasi-celebrities. He devoted himself to them completely for an hour, an afternoon, a day, telling stories, charming them, Mesmerizing them. He revelled in the company, made love to them over and over. Then in the morning, fresh for work, he unceremoniously abandoned them. Of course there had been exceptions. Satjilombe had been rather fond of Sthembiso for a brief spell. Her youngest child was his. He had a hundred children strewn across the country. Sthembiso had tried to do away with herself a few times, after he'd abandoned her at a hotel. For a few months, she chased him like a bloodhound, turning up in the remotest places. Then she married Mthembeni out of spite, but also to remain within the ever widening Satjilombe circle. Was Satjilombe a narcissist? Well, not precisely. When you come right down to it, he was Narissus.

Nearly a week had gone by since Satjilombe had been residing at this house. He loved the sea and never failed to marvel at the enthralling beauty of Table Mountain. Ludo, who had studied at Cape Town University, was much more captivated by the splendor of the mansion. Breath-taking view, tasteful rooms, and efficient staff: she decided to come more often. Hot sun and fresh orange juice on the terrace soon changed his mood.

"Get me a robe."

The order was directed to no one in particular. Ludo came back with a white terrycloth bathrobe draped over one arm. Everywhere, beautiful things, embroidery, ashtrays, lighters were engraved with dates, signatures, and the names of His Excellency's houses. The same lotions were always in the bedroom, the bars always stocked with decanters sporting silver coats-of-arms labelled Vodka: Pernod, Cinzano, Dubonnet, Fernet, J & B, Teachers, Rye, Martell, Courvoisier, and Chartreuse. Satjilombe poured himself a clear glass of vodka.

"Fetch me one too."

Sthembiso's voice came from the terrace. Was it possible he wasn't human, eyes in the back of his head? When one was talking, one had the sensation he was listening to what one was thinking. Ludo heard a loud splash followed by happy gurgling: His Excellency had dived into the swimming pool, not the sea. The sea at this hour must be icy. His arms curling along in a crawl, he shouted something.

Ludo said, from the terrace, "What's that you say?"

"On the next beach . . ."

"What?"

"A good-looking girl. Can you make her out?"

"What do you mean, make her out. She must be half a mile off."

"She's got a bikini on. She seems damn well put together. Send someone over to ask her to lunch."

"She won't come."

"Then you go and ask her."

"Never mind that, I'll send Sthembiso."

The man must have the eyes of a vulture to pick out a beautiful woman at that distance.

"Give her my name, and no doubt, she'll accept. The title itself is an aphrodisiac, don't you think?"

His Excellency rubbed himself dry on the bathrobe and downed his vodka.

"Bravo. You get more useful all the time. You're becoming a decent bartender."

"I feel rotten this morning, so please don't be sarcastic."

"I hand you a compliment, and you go into a pout. What about the girl?"

"What girl?"

"The girl we invited to lunch."

"What about her?"

"Where in hell is she?"

"Be reasonable. The beach is a good way off. Sthembiso has to get there, explain to her, she has to decide whether or not she wants to come, then she has to make herself presentable, and lastly she has to get over here. Give her twenty minutes at least."

"My God, where do people find time to waste?"

Another vodka, which went down the wrong way when Batjibilibili made her entrance. Satjilombe ran his hand through his hair in exasperation.

"My dear Batjibilibili. So good to see you."

"I've been hunting for you for months. Months, do you hear? I write; my letters come back unopened. As for the phone, you've never been near one in your life, or so it would seem. The least you could do is make some show of pity. I really don't mean to whine, but truly the best years . . . I've been wandering around like a madwoman . . ."

"Well here you are, and I asked you to come."

"Only because you didn't recognize me."

"I hardly dared it was you."

"Liar."

The Chief Minister moved for the door, anticipating a row, but a glance from his wife stopped him cold.

"Ludo, please entertain Batjibilibili while I dress."

Batjibilibili drifted in the direction of the bar. She inspected herself in a mirror drawn hastily out of her bag as soon as Satjilombe was gone.

"If you only know how long it's been, Sthembiso. Why did Satjilombe leave me stranded in that ghastly town? Gaborone is a terrible place, you know. Have you any idea? Not so much as a letter or word of explanation . . ."

"These things happen."

"A note . . ."

"He never writes notes or letters."

"He might have phoned . . ."

"He must have had his reason."

"What?"

"Business."

"Business, my foot! People have told me some things . . ."

"My dear Batjibilibili, it's no secret that the Honorable Minister has ways with ladies."

"Spare me the details."

"But you asked me."

"Yes, tell me. Does he ever have affairs? I mean serious, long-lasting love affairs?"

"If I'd written down the names of all the ladies who have thrown themselves at him, truly, truly, my friend, the roster'd take up a hundred volumes. Once, I thought I could make a list just for fun, but their names began to slip my mind. Escapades in the Cape, in Johannesburg, in Cairo, not to mention the mistresses in the Caribbean and various foreign cities, models crawling miles to get to him in New York, prostitutes dreaming he'll come to them in Stockholm, movie stars chasing him across the continents. If there is a lady in the vicinity, it's only a question of minutes. And then . . . you know . . . what he does."

Batjibilibili pulled the curtains apart, revealing a heavy dark sky. The impending descent of rain announced itself in the oppressive quality of the viscous light which framed her body as she turned from the embrasure. Her face, shadowed, seemed almost like a carving: lower lip, chin catching slivers of light, the rest obscure. Sthembiso, uncomfortable, reached for the lamp switch.

"No, don't."

Batjibilibili forestalled her.

"I like it this way. It makes it easier for me to talk."

"Why do you say you are sick when you look so healthy?" asked Sthembiso anxiously.

"I said I feel sick, sort of restless, all the time, and I just can't explain this feeling, but it's making my goddamned life miserable."

Sthembiso's hand slid away from the lamb, as she moved to settle herself more securely in her chair.

Batjibilibili turned to look out the window.

"It seems like a long time since it all began. It's hard to believe it was three years ago . . . less than three years ago. When did I first meet him? When was that first connection made? I know, they sound like such simple questions. I should be able to give simple, concrete answers. But I can't."

Her dark eyes clouded.

"Words like 'beginning' and 'end' don't have much meaning for me anymore."

She shrugged and turned back to face her friend.

"Should I be flippant and say it was my greed for adventure that began it? Or should I be philosophical, or even mystical, and say it began long before that? Perhaps it began when I was a child, forming my view of the world, or when I was born, under some particular configuration of the stars, or back, past that . . ."

Sthembiso moved uneasily.

"Batjibilibili, don't . . . ."

"No, wait. You said you wanted to know about it all from the beginning. Everything. There were lots of things I never told you, you know."

She shook her head as if to free it from unwanted thoughts. When she spoke again, her voice was very soft so that Sthembiso had to lean forward in her chair to catch the words.

225

"If I had to fix a beginning, I could say it began last winter, on my flight back from Johannesburg. The trip was a present I gave myself to celebrate my parting with my husband. I was free at last. Real free, no manga. I treated myself very well there. I was finally one of the people who could afford it. Satjilombe's mistress, you know. What else could a girl ask for in life? Not much these days. I was a real tourist for the first time in years. I went sightseeing, shopping, to nightclubs, and especially to cinemas, museums and the theatre. I could never get enough of the theatre . . . it's vibrancy, its vitality. For the first time, I could afford to buy books that I really liked. I stayed so long in the Exclusive Books shop my last afternoon there that I nearly missed my flight, but luckily everyone, from the hotel people to the cab driver to the airport personnel, helped me along, and I managed to board just in time.

In spite of the rush to get on, I was still incredibly relaxed—tired, in fact—the results, I imagine, of being in that world of books and still feeling that inner glow of warmth you often have for hours after being in a dreamlike atmosphere, you know? Something like losing your virginity to your soul mate. When the stewardess came around for drinks, I ordered gin and tonic and sipped at it, trying to keep my eyes open in order to read an article in a fashion magazine on my lap. "Seven Ways to Look Romantic." Somewhere around this time I began to feel that someone was looking at me. My first thought, with my eyes still focused on the magazine, was that, not knowing who the observer was, I didn't know if I wanted to encourage him by returning his glance. The funny thing, as I remember, is that I was pretty sure that the observer was a man, rather than a woman, even while I was still reading the magazine.

I kept my eyes down, although by this time I was not even focusing on the print. The whole thing was very eerie. The feeling of being observed was becoming more tangible and oppressive. Almost a minute went by; the fabric of the seat was beginning to eat into my legs where my skirt had hiked up, my back was starting to feel stiff, and oddest of all, I was beginning to be afraid to look up and actually see who the observer was. But another part of me was saying, this is ridiculous, it's probably some guy who wants to start a conversation, so I just look and see who it is. I was on an aisle seat. I quickly looked up and glanced around and saw . . . nothing, just other passengers reading or talking or dozing, no leering Lotharios.

I went back to reading my magazine, more awake now, and convinced it had been my imagination. A few moments later, I started to have the uncomfortable feeling again, and now I looked up quickly, determined to catch the gaze of whoever it was. This time, I saw him. But he was not the man I imagined, trying to attract my attention long enough to start a conversation and lead up to asking me out, or in, as the case might be, to his hotel room for a quickie once in Gaborone. Not a traveling salesman on a business convention, sporting a prominent wedding band, or an equally prominent patch where he had removed it in anticipation of an adventure. He was a priest. He stood, awkward, his cropped head bowed, looking down at me from immense black eyes in a face almost equally dark.

'Hello,' I said, relieved.

'Lo' he responded. 'My name is Preston.'

'My name is Batjibilibili,' I said and smiled awkwardly.

'Could I—may I look out your window?' The two seats next to mine were empty.

'Sure,' I said.

'Be my guest. Although I don't think there's much to see.'

'Oh, the clouds are there to see,' he assured me solemnly and, as I swung my legs into the isle, squeezed past and sat on the window seat, straining to look out. I returned to my magazine article, trying to decide whether I really need bother with romance, after all I already had Satjilombe's eyes, or to something worth-while like reading a novel, but in the midst of this internal wrangle, I became aware that Preston's eyes were furtively piercing me.

'I'm going to Gaborone,' he announced. 'To visit my half-brother. Where are you going?'

I told him, and we were soon engaged in serious conversation, mainly as I recall, determined by him, and largely having to do with his experience as a black person living in exile. I thought that he was homesick and tried to console him by describing all the interesting things there were to do and see in Gaborone for a man of his education and worldliness. He was a good listener; not surprising, of course, for a priest. But he looked at me in a way that I can hardly describe. His eyes were so filled with pain, with longing, and with a kind of nameless grief I could hardly bear to return their gaze.

At the same time I was unable to look away. The eyes that looked on mine were not those of a priest—I could have sworn to that. They were the eyes of a man. In their depths was a passion so profound and ageless that I was transfixed by the emotion they conveyed. Time seemed eerily suspended. The eyes were those of a real man solemn, intent, profound, grief-stricken, knowing and old. They were alive with an intelligence and luminosity nothing short of transcendental. The expression I saw in that man's eyes has remained in my mind. It was so bizarre, so out of place, so old—there was no other word for it but old.

I felt drained, exhausted, and chilled. I pulled my sweater around my shoulders and finished my drink in one gulp. My eyes felt very heavy, and I closed them. I didn't wake up until the plane had touched down at

227

Seretse Khama Airport. All around me, people were standing up and grabbing their coats and hand luggage. As the other passengers started filtering into the aisle in preparation for disembarking, I leaned back in my seat, suddenly shaking with a release of tension I had not been aware of. I stood up, and grabbed for my coat, scarf and sweater. As I was frantically stuffing myself into my clothing, I caught a glimpse of Preston standing in the aisle ready to disembark. He turned to look back, and I tried to catch his eyes, but by that time people had begun surging into the aisles in earnest, and my view was completely obscured. I felt the beginning of a bad tension headache, and I started to wonder if I had imagined the intensity of the inter-exchange, misread the expression in the priest's eyes. Maybe I had one stiff drink too many, and it had muddled my head. The people pushing behind me brought my attention back to the immediate task of maneuvering out the plane, to which I abruptly devoted my full attention. The incident began to fade from my mind. But a real if transient friendship had been struck between the priest and me."

Batjibilibili looked at Sthembiso.

"That was the beginning."

End of Volume I

Thank you for reading, "Seasons of Thunder, Volume I," be certain to visit the publisher website (www.donnaink.com) and/or channel retailers for "Seasons of Thunder, Volume II," and "Seasons of Thunder, Volume III."

About the Author

Teedzani Thapelo was born in Jacklas No.1 village in Tati East, Botswana and educated at McConnell College, the University of Botswana, the London School of Economics and the School of Oriental and African Studies, University of London in Bri-tain. He has worked as a teacher, research assistant, research associate, university lecturer, researcher and human rights campaigner. In 2003, he was nominated Fellow of the Institute of International Education at the University of New York and he spent the period 2004-2005 as Africa Guest Researcher  and Visiting Scholar at Nordic Africa Institute at Uppsala, Swe-den. He has lived and travelled in England, France, Sweden, Canada (I was married to a Canadian for ten years), South Africa, Zimbabwe and Botswana, where he is now permanently a resident at Mapoka Village in Tati West, with my eighty-one years old mother and my little boys, Davis, seven and Rabasi, six. Alex, the eldest, now fourteen, is studying in Canada and lives with his mother who teaches at Oshawa in Toronto.

Some of Mr. Thapelo's articles have been published in newspapers, magazines and peer-reviewed journals. *Season of Thunder* is his debut novel.

Newsletter, Mailings, Merchandise

In order to become aware of discounts, events, interviews, signings and promotion activities email: donnaink@gmail.com and put "Mailing List" in the subject line.

Some of Teedzani's publisher sponsored merchandise includes:

Donnalnk Publications, L.L.C.

Publisher
www.donnaink.shop

For bulk orders, special orders, etc.

Special Markets Division
Donnalnk Publications, L.L.C.
17611 Aquasco Road
Annapolis, MD 20613
Email: donnaink@gmail.com

ZENCON ART OF
ZEN CONSULTANCY
PR & Marketing